HAND
FOR A
HAND

Also by T. Frank Muir

Tooth for a Tooth

HAND
FOR A
HAND

T. FRANK MUIR

**SOHO
CRIME**

Soho Press, Inc.
853 Broadway
New York, NY 10003

Library of Congress Cataloging-in-Publication Data

Muir, T. Frank.
Hand for a hand / T. Frank Muir.
p. cm.
HC ISBN 978-1-61695-181-8
PB ISBN 978-1-61695-295-2
eISBN: 978-1-61695-182-5
1. Police—Scotland—Fiction. 2. Murder—Investigation—Fiction.
3. St. Andrews (Scotland)—Fiction. I. Title.
PR6063.U317H36 2012
823'.914—dc23
2012027343

Printed in the United States of America

10 9 8 7 6 5 4 3 2 1

*To all women betrayed by
those they trusted*

Three lawyers' tongues, turn'd inside out,
Wi' lies seamed like a beggar's clout.

—A couplet from Robert Burns' original
manuscript of his epic poem *Tam O'Shanter*,
which he was persuaded to leave out

HAND

FOR A

HAND

Chapter 1

Seventeenth Hole, Old Course
St. Andrews, Scotland

TAM **D**UNN **WATCHED** the golf ball take a hard kick left and slip into the infamous Road Hole Bunker, a sandy-bottomed pothole that fronted the seventeenth green.

Bud Amherst, one of an American four-ball that teed off at 7:00 that morning, first on the ballot, threw his five-iron to the ground. "Goddammit," he shouted, turning to Tam. "Course's nuthin but sand traps. Why didn't you tell me it was there?"

The way Bud played golf it would have made no difference if Tam had first led him by the hand and stood him in the bunker. But Tam the caddy, always hopeful of an American-sized tip, bit his tongue. "My mistake, sir."

Close to the green, the bunker looked more like a hole in the ground, its face a vertical wall of divot bricks that even the pros struggled to overcome.

"Whaddaya think?" Bud asked Tam.

"Sand-iron, sir."

"I know that, goddammit. Which way's it gonna break?"

"About three feet from the left."

"As much as that?"

"At least, sir."

Tam kept tight-lipped as Bud took a few clumsy practice swings. The only way Bud was going to get the ball onto that green, he thought, was to lift it and place it. Bud turned to the bunker, prepared to step down into it, then stumbled backwards.

"Aw God, aw God."

"Sir?"

Bud slumped to his knees. The sand-iron slipped from his grip.

One of the Americans, the tall one called JD, trotted across the green. "Hey, Bud, you okay?"

Bud stretched an arm out and flapped it at the bunker.

Tam stepped to its lip and stared down at the hand, at skin as white as porcelain, bony fingers clawed like talons. Even from where he stood he could tell it was a woman's hand, a fine hand, he thought, except the wrist looked butchered and bloodied, like a cut of meat hacked, not sliced, the bone glistening like a white disc smeared with blood.

And all of Tam's hopes for an American-sized tip evaporated in the cold Scottish air.

Chapter 2

"**Y**OU'D BETTER GET down here, Andy."

"Where's *here*, Nance?"

"Seventeenth green on the Old Course. Next to the Jigger."

Gilchrist drew his Mercedes SLK Roadster to the side of the road and pressed his mobile to his ear. It had been a while since he had heard DS Nancy Wilson as breathless. Not since they had run the length of the West Sands chasing what's-his-name. Blake. That was it. Murray Blake. Rapist, serial shagger, petty thief. How some people thought they could get away with it never failed to amaze him.

"What's got you fired up?" he tried.

"Severed hand in a bunker. Victim's in her early twenties, late teens—"

"*Her* early twenties?"

"Sorry. Yes. It's a woman's hand."

Gilchrist tugged the steering wheel, felt the tail-end throw out as the Merc spun in a tight circle. "Any rings?" he asked. "Moles? Scars?"

"Nothing obvious. Fingernails are short. Not varnished. Skin's a bit rough."

"As in manual labour?"

"As in someone who doesn't use hand lotion."

"Or couldn't afford to."

"Maybe."

"It couldn't have come from the mortuary or been cut from—?"

"Not a chance, Andy. She's been murdered."

"Get on to the University. Find out if any students have gone missing, called in sick, not turned up, whatever."

"Got it."

"Has Mackie seen it yet?"

"Just arrived. Along with the SOCOs."

"Make sure they take fingerprints and run them through the AFR system."

"Got it."

If the victim had no criminal record, the Automatic Fingerprint Registration System would draw a blank. But it was worth a shot. "Estimated time of. . . ." He wanted to say, *death*, then chose, ". . . amputation?"

"Couldn't say."

"How about the other bunkers?"

"We've got a team walking the course. Nothing back from them yet."

"Any thoughts?" he asked.

"Nothing definite. The sand was smooth, which might suggest the hand was placed in the bunker."

"As opposed to thrown in?"

"Odd, don't you think?"

"Maybe." Gilchrist was again struck by the undercurrent of excitement in Nance's voice. He thought back to her statement— *Not a chance. She's been murdered*—and knew from the firmness of her response that there had to be more. "What're you not telling me, Nance?"

"She, I mean . . . the hand was holding a note. Addressed to you."

A frisson of ice touched his neck. He booted the Merc to seventy. "What's it say?"

"Murder."

Murder? "So whoever severed the hand is sending me a message."

"Looks that way."

"How was the note addressed?"

"On the envelope. Your name. DCI Andrew Gilchrist."

Andrew. Not Andy. Was that significant? "Typed? Or hand-printed?"

"Looks like a computer printer. Ink hasn't run. Maybe a laser printer."

Something tugged at his mind. "I thought you said *note*."

"I did."

"*Inside* the envelope?"

"Yes."

"Someone opened the envelope?"

"It wasn't sealed."

Although the envelope was addressed to him, found in the clutches of a severed hand, it niggled him that it had been opened and read. "Why use an envelope to put a note inside?" he asked. "Why not just the note? Why the envelope, *then* the note?"

"To keep the note dry?"

"Maybe."

"Greaves wants to assign you as SIO."

Senior Investigating Officer. Gilchrist laughed. "I would have thought a severed hand clutching a note addressed to me would make it obvious that I should be SIO."

Hearing his own words made something slump to the pit of his stomach. He had always dreaded this moment, the day when he would be targeted by some sick pervert. And the pervert who severed the hand had asked for Gilchrist to be involved. No, more than that, *wanted* Gilchrist to be involved. But why? Was the woman someone he knew? At that thought, a surge of panic jolted his system.

"Describe the hand again, Nance."

"Left hand. Skin's flawless, except for the fingernails. They're cracked."

"Not bitten?"

"No."

Relief powered through him. It was every policeman's fear that their family would be the victim of revenge, their lives threatened by some criminal bent on getting even for some long-forgotten score. The thought that the hand could have been his daughter's had hit him with the force of a kick to the gut. Maureen lived seventy miles away in Glasgow, but bit her nails and picked the skin. Despite the gruesome task ahead he almost smiled.

"Fingernails look as if they've been trimmed," Nance went on. "But the cracks still show."

"Meaning?"

"Not sure. But it might help ID her."

Gilchrist was fast approaching traffic. He eased his foot off the pedal. "I'll be with you in ten minutes," he said, and hung up.

Dear God. Now this. A young woman's hand. What had happened? Had her hand been severed in the course of torture? Was she still alive? No, he thought. She was already dead. But where was the rest of the body?

He floored the pedal, overtook three cars.

And why a hand? Why leave it where it was sure to be found?

Simple. Because the perpetrator of this crime *wanted* the hand to be found.

Hence the note. For him.

But who was this young woman?

Being forty-seven, Gilchrist did not know too many *young* women. His daughter, Maureen, of course. But she had never invited him to meet her flatmates or friends. Not that she hid them from him, but she lived away from home, ever since Gail left him. And then there was Chloe, his son's girlfriend. And that was about it as far as *young* women were concerned.

Still, he needed to put his mind at rest.

He located Maureen's number and felt a flush of irritation as her answering machine cut in. Leaving messages seemed to be his way of communicating with her these days. He kept this one short, ordered her to give him a call, then he called Jack. It was a wild thought. But better to be sure.

"Hello?" Jack's voice sounded tired, heavy.

"Did I wake you up?"

"What time's it?"

"Almost eleven. The day's nearly done."

Jack coughed, a harsh sound that seemed to come from his chest, which made Gilchrist think he had started smoking again. "And to what do I owe this pleasure?"

"Isn't a father allowed to call his son and ask how he is?"

"Come on, Andy. First thing in the morning?"

Gilchrist let out a laugh. Jack was a freelance artist whose creative side seemed to flourish only on the other side of midnight *and* sobriety. Midday could be an early start.

"How's Chloe?" Gilchrist asked.

"Fine why?"

Gilchrist thought Jack's answer was too quick. "I'd like to talk to her," he said.

"Why? What's up?"

Because we've found a severed hand and I'm scared to death it might be Chloe's.

"Might be interested in buying one of her paintings," he said. "Can I talk to her?"

"Sure. I'll get her to call when she gets back."

"Out shopping, is she?"

"Something like that."

Gilchrist pressed the mobile to his ear. Jack had a cavalier attitude about most things, but his voice sounded lifeless. "Everything all right?" he tried.

A sniff, then, "We had a lover's tiff."

"And?"

"And she's stomped off to cool down."

"Sounds serious."

"She'll get over it."

"Good." And Gilchrist meant it. Chloe was the best thing that had happened to Jack. An artist too, she had a calming effect on his wild son, even assuring him that Jack no longer smoked cigarettes or any other substances. He almost hated to say it, but he trusted Chloe more than he did his own son. He held on, expecting Jack to continue, but it seemed as if the topic of Chloe was over.

Gilchrist decided to change tack and felt a flicker of annoyance that he had to bring the subject up. But he needed to know. "How's Mum?" he asked, and grimaced as he waited for the answer.

"Not good, Andy. Not good at all."

"How long?"

"Couple of months. Maybe less."

"Jesus."

"They've got her on morphine."

"Is she still at home?"

"You know Mum."

Gilchrist pulled to a halt behind a traffic jam. Ahead, the grey silhouette of St. Salvator's spire and the Abbey ruins lined the dark skyline. By the University buildings, black rocks fell to a blacker sea. He closed his eyes, dug in his thumb and forefinger.

Gail. Sometimes he felt as if he still loved her. Other times he was not sure if it was being betrayed that had given him the right to wallow in self-pity. He never understood why he still cared for her. Was it hurt over her infidelity? Or her utter rejection of him once she left? Or jealousy at her having found someone else? And now she was dying and—

"Andy?"

Gilchrist looked up. "Sorry, Jack. Stuck in traffic. Is Maureen still helping out?"

"I guess."

"You heard from her?"

"About a week ago."

"I've left umpteen messages on her answering machine."

"That's Mo for you."

"It runs in the family."

"Hey, we're talking. Right?"

Gilchrist chuckled. "If you talk to her, Jack, tell her to check her messages and give me a call." Jack grunted, which he took to mean yes. The Citroën in front lurched forward with a burst of exhaust. Gilchrist followed. "Thanks, Jack. Catch you later."

Gilchrist thought it odd how different his children had become. Maureen and Jack were growing apart, *had* grown apart, professionally, politically, socially and, even though he hated to say it, financially. Where Mo was self-reliant and careful with money, taking part-time jobs for extra cash, Jack could go months without selling a sculpture or painting, and no commissioned work in sight. He often wondered how Jack survived, then ditched that thought for fear of the answer.

But Mo was different. A young woman with definite views on how to run her life, with no sympathy for those who struggled. If Gilchrist struggled with his relationship with his daughter, what chance did Jack have of getting through to her?

He pulled onto the road that led to the Driving Range, then powered towards the Old Course Hotel. He found a parking spot close to the Jigger Inn. Beyond the stone dyke that bounded the course, a white Transit van spilled Scenes of Crime Officers in white hooded coveralls—six in total. The putting green was encircled with yellow tape that trailed to the walls at the side of the road for which the Old Course's Road Hole was infamous.

Nance caught his eye as he cleared the dyke. Behind her, the stooped figure of Bert Mackie, the police pathologist, was slipping into the bunker, his assistant, Dougie Banks, helping him down. Nance signalled to Gilchrist as she walked across the green, away from the bunker and the SOCOs.

Puzzled, he followed her.

When she stopped, he said, "You look worried."

"Ronnie's here."

"Ronnie?" Then the name slotted into the tumblers of his mind with a surge of disbelief. "Ronnie *Watt*?" He eyed the green, settling on the back of a broad-shouldered man in a dark blue suit, felt his legs move as if of their own accord—

Something clamped his arm.

"He's not worth it." Nance tightened her grip. "He's Crime Scene Manager."

"Not on my shift, he's not. Alan can take over."

"No he can't. Greaves has assigned Ronnie."

Gilchrist shook his arm free. "Is Greaves out of his bloody mind?"

"Andy. Don't. It's in the past."

But Gilchrist was already striding away.

Chapter 3

"**G**REAVES SPEAKING."

"It's Andy Gilchrist, Tom."

"Andy. I was wondering when I'd hear from you."

I bet you were, you blundering old maniac. "I've got a complaint."

"Certainly, Andy. Let's have it."

Chief Super Greaves' politeness almost threw him. So, rather than struggle with fake diplomacy, Gilchrist pulled the trigger. "What the hell's Ronnie Watt doing here?"

"He's on temporary assignment from Strathclyde—"

"You do know about Ronnie and me?"

"I do, Andy."

"Well, surely you must appreciate—"

"Watt is back with Fife Constabulary and assigned to the St. Andrews Division of the Crime Management Department, as are you. Part of my remit is to assign officers to solve crimes as I see fit. And with the shortage in manpower I'm bloody grateful for experienced overload relief—"

"As Senior Investigating Officer I assign my own team. And the last—"

"You're not the SIO on this case."

For one confusing second, Gilchrist wondered if he had misunderstood. "They found a note with—"

"Yes, yes, I know all about the note."

"Whoever committed this crime wants me on it. I need to be involved."

"I'll be SIO, Andy. But with all the paperwork I've got at the moment I'm assigning you to take charge. Ronnie will be your assistant."

"I thought he was Crime Scene Manager."

"DC Alan Bowers will take over. Is that clear?"

Crystal. Gilchrist gripped his mobile. He had misjudged the Chief Super. Greaves had no intention of becoming involved. Assigning Gilchrist as a temporary SIO was like fiddling the books. "One final question," he said. "Why put Watt and me together?"

"Because in this Division I don't want anyone to harbour past grievances. We work together as a team. Does that make it any clearer?"

Watt was staring at him, chewing gum like some tough-guy posing. In that instant, Gilchrist made up his mind. "Clear as mud," he said, and clapped his mobile shut.

Watt widened his stance as Gilchrist stepped down the slope on the other side of the green. At six-one, Gilchrist and Watt were identical in height. But where Gilchrist was long-limbed and lean, Watt was stocky and broad. And Gilchrist was a young forty-seven to Watt's ravaged thirty-three. Too many late nights drinking and bullying had aged Watt beyond his years.

Watt thrust out his hand. "Good to see you again, Andy."

Gilchrist eyeballed him. "Don't push it," he snarled. He waited for Watt to lower his hand. "And it's DCI Gilchrist," he added, then turned to Mackie. "What've you got, Bert?"

Watt stepped forward. "This—"

"Is your name Bert?" Gilchrist snapped.

Watt flashed his teeth, worked his gum. ". . . is addressed to you." He held out an envelope, creased where it had been crushed between the dead woman's fingers.

Gilchrist noted his name printed on it. "Tell me it's been dusted," he said to Nance.

"It's been dusted," she said.

"Anything?"

"Nothing." Watt again. "It's been wiped clean."

Gilchrist eyed Watt. "We seem to have a problem here."

"We do?"

"You have a habit of answering questions not addressed to you."

"Oh, yeah?"

"Let's get one thing clear—"

"Oh for goodness sake, stop squabbling and lend me a hand." Mackie clambered from the bunker, his face reddened from the effort, or frustration at having to listen to two grown men bickering. Gilchrist grasped Mackie by his gloved hand and pulled.

Out of the bunker, Mackie gave a stiff stretch, grimacing as he pulled his shoulders back. "Oh to be young again." He peeled back the hood of his coveralls to reveal a bald pate as red as his face. Then he padded up the slope to the green.

Gilchrist struggled to ignore Watt's presence as he trailed Mackie.

On the green, he asked the old man, "What do you think?"

Mackie grimaced. "That it's only a matter of time until the rest of the body turns up."

"So it's murder. Not amputation."

Mackie shook his head. "Impossible to say. But whosever hand that is was dead when it was hacked off." He flapped a hand at Dougie. "Bring it here," he grumped.

Dougie removed a plastic bag from the SOCO Transit van and carried it across the putting green. Although Dougie was a doctor in his own right, in the presence of Mackie he seemed more like a student. Mackie grabbed the bag with a thankless lunge, and it pleased Gilchrist to watch Watt step in beside Dougie as he returned to the Transit van.

Mackie dangled the bag in front of Gilchrist, prodded the fingers with a gloved hand. "See here?" he said. "The tips of the first three fingers are slightly flattened. Base of the thumb, too. And what could be lividity at the heel of the palm. See?"

Gilchrist peered through the clear bag, thankful that it protected him from the smell of decomposing flesh.

"I'd say she was killed first, then placed on her back, probably on something hard, while she was cut up." Mackie held out his left arm, bent his fingers into the shape of a claw. "Imagine this is her arm. If it was by her side, it would rest on the floor like this. See?"

"She died without a struggle?"

Mackie lowered his arm. "There appear to be no signs of distress in the fingernails, or the skin. No self-defence wounds. Nothing that would suggest she put up a struggle. But I'll be more definitive once I've had a closer look in the lab."

"Any idea of age, size, anything that would help us pin her down?"

Mackie puffed out his cheeks, let out a rush of air. "Somewhere between fifteen and thirty. Average height at five-four, five-eight. On the frail side, I'd say. Which could give the impression of being taller than she really was. And from what I can tell, I would say she was a natural blonde, too."

Gilchrist made a mental note. "Occupation?"

Mackie shook his head. "The skin is fine, though a tad rough near the ends, the nails clean, so we can rule out any manual work. If she's not from out of town, I'd be looking at University records. A student, perhaps. But I couldn't say at this point."

"No signs of distress in the fingernails? Nance said they were cracked."

"First guess would be not work-related, but poor maintenance, poor diet, that sort of thing. All in all the hand looks clean, almost delicate."

"Were the fingernails trimmed?"

"They were."

"Before or after death?"

Mackie shook his head. "No clear way of telling. But I'll look into that. If they were trimmed after death, maybe it was to clean them of incriminating evidence."

"Like skin scrapings?"

"Yes. But that would suggest a struggle, and everything about this hand suggests otherwise."

"How soon after death was the hand amputated?"

"Rigor mortis has set in. So, we're somewhere between twenty-four and forty-eight hours. I'd put us smack dab in the middle, say, at thirty-six hours."

Gilchrist stared back along the undulating fairway, seeking out the distant figures of uniformed constables combing the bunkers. From behind the hotel, he caught the dying whine from the helicopter's engine. Groups of people looked out of opened windows. On the walkway below, a straggling line of spectators dotted the boundary wall. He returned to Mackie. "Thirty-six hours places her time of death near midnight the night before last."

"Precisely."

"As good a time as any to kill someone?"

"Then hack them to pieces."

Gilchrist gritted his teeth. How someone could chop another human being into bits was beyond him. What went through their heads as they were doing that? What prompted someone to kill? Most murders were committed by someone who knew the victim. But in this case Gilchrist knew the murderer was someone who knew *him*.

He faced Mackie, struck by how clear the old man's eyes looked against the weathered grain of his face, like jewels set in blemished wood. A narrow line of white stubble ran under his chin where he had missed with the razor.

"Anything else you can tell me, Bert?"

Mackie held the plastic bag level with his eyes. "The middle finger has a nick in the skin," he said, and pointed at it. The bag twisted in his hand.

"A paper cut?"

"No. To the side of the nail. It's almost as if she's pulled the skin back to the cuticle. Not all the way back, mind you. The other fingers are quite tidy."

"Not a nail-biter, then?" Gilchrist worried at his need to seek further reassurance.

"This woman has never bitten her nails. But cuts and cracks and flaking skin and the like are a natural process of everyday life. It looks as if this nick had healed. And maybe reopened."

Gilchrist failed to see the significance of Mackie's comment. "Reopened in a struggle?" he tried.

"No. That's not what I'm saying." Mackie pulled the bag closer. The plastic almost touched his nose. "There's some discoloration in the cut. Here."

"Dried blood?"

"Not blood. No. It looks yellow."

"Like an old bruise?"

"No." Mackie swung the plastic bag towards Gilchrist and pointed at the middle finger. "See here," he said. "It could be paint."

"What kind of paint?"

"Couldn't say at this stage."

Movement to the side caught Gilchrist's eye. Watt was stepping from the SOCO van. "Listen, Bert, I'll leave you to it. As soon as you find out anything else, get back to me." He turned and walked towards Nance.

"Hey."

Gilchrist stopped on the edge of the green.

Watt was walking toward him like a lion with its eyes on a limping springbok. He waved a hand. "We need to talk."

Gilchrist turned, stepped down the slope, and stood at the edge of the bunker. One of the SOCOs was on his hands and knees, brushing samples of sand from an indentation that Gilchrist assumed had been made by the hand. He heard Watt's breathing behind him.

"What's granddad saying?" Watt asked him.

"You'll read his report when he's finished."

"Will he live that long?"

"You had something to say?"

"Been on the phone with Greaves."

"Good for you."

"And I don't like it any more than you do."

Gilchrist barked a laugh. "Don't flatter yourself."

Watt twisted his head, spat out his gum. "Look," he said. "My life's changed. *I've* changed. I'm a different person."

"What're you trying to tell me?"

"I want to put the past behind us."

"Are you asking me to forget what happened?"

Watt seemed stumped by the question.

Gilchrist caught a faint whiff of stale alcohol and knew in that instant that nothing had changed. "For the sake of the investigation," he said, "I'm prepared to do as Greaves wants. But the instant you screw up, you're history." Watt continued to nod, but Gilchrist caught a current of anger ripple across his jaw. "Okay, so far?"

"Gotcha, Andy."

Gilchrist shook his head. "You're not listening."

"Yeah, I got you."

"No you haven't."

Watt frowned. "Oh, yeah, right. DCI Gilchrist. I got it. Yeah."

Gilchrist turned to Nance as she approached him, notebook in hand.

"I need the two of you to talk to everyone who buys, sells, or uses paint," he said. "Ask if they remember seeing a woman, a natural blonde, in the last several days, maybe as far back as a week. Someone slender, tending towards frail. Might be worthwhile starting at the University, students who paint as a hobby, or know someone who does—"

"That's asking a lot."

Gilchrist eyed Watt. "Any other suggestions?"

"Yeah. Put out an appeal on the telly."

"And ask what? Know anyone who's lost a hand? Get real. It's early days for that." Something in Gilchrist softened at that moment. Maybe it was because they now stood at the start of a major investigation. Or maybe it was the thought of the massive task ahead. If he was to solve this crime, find the killer of the young woman, put to rest the grief of her family, he needed all the help he could muster. Maybe Greaves was right. Maybe he was going to have to bite the bullet of the past. "We can try that later," he said to Watt. "When Mackie gives us a better fix on her ID."

Watt nodded, and Gilchrist knew from the tightening of the jaw that his reluctant agreement had been noted. "Any other questions?" he asked.

"Yes." Nance had her notebook open and was scribbling in it. "Why paint?"

Despite Mackie's uncertainty, Gilchrist wanted to sound positive. "Bert thinks he's found some traces of paint."

"What kind of paint?" Nance asked.

"What kind of paint can you get?" Watt said.

"Oil. Watercolour," said Nance, then gave Watt a smile that failed to reach her eyes.

"Maybe even printer ink," Gilchrist added. "But it's too soon to say. We need to start digging while Bert does his stuff in the lab. So get going." He stepped away. "Debriefing's in my office at six."

As he strode towards his car he shoved his hands deep into his pockets, felt his body give an involuntary shiver, and wondered if he was trying to shake off a chill or memories of the past. *For the sake of the investigation*, he heard his mind echo, *I'm prepared to do as Greaves wants*.

Work with Watt? As if the past did not exist? Could he really do that?

As a detective in charge of a murder investigation, perhaps.

But as a father, that was asking for the impossible.

Chapter 4

THE REMAINDER OF the day consisted of meetings and phone calls. After debriefing, which turned up a list of one hundred and twenty-seven students who had an interest in painting, or knew someone who had, Gilchrist found himself stepping into Lafferty's.

"Pint of Eighty, Eddy, and a couple of sausage rolls."

He cocked an eye at the television set in the corner of the bar. The Old Course Hotel in the background swelled as the camera zoomed in on the seventeenth green, closer still until it slipped from view and the Road Hole bunker filled the screen.

"There you go, Andy." Fast Eddy glanced at the television. "That one of yours?"

"Afraid so."

"Was on earlier. That plonker, the one you had the run in with years back, he was on. Chewing gum like some big-shot. Should've heard Marge." Fast Eddy's eyes glistened. "Wetting her knickers for the guy. God knows what the women see—"

"Sausage rolls?"

"On their way." Fast Eddy slipped from the bar and headed to the kitchen.

Gilchrist took a sip of his Eighty-Shilling, removed his mobile from his jacket, and dialled Nance. It barely rang.

"Where are you, Nance?"

"Just leaving the office."

"Care to join me?"

"What for?"

"A pint."

"I meant, for what reason?"

"Come and join me and find out."

A pause, then, "Let me guess. Lafferty's?"

"Sherlock Holmes the second."

"Sherlock was a man. I'm not sure if that was an insult or a compliment."

"I would never insult you, Nance. You know that."

She chuckled in response, said, "Give me ten," then hung up.

By the time Nance arrived, Gilchrist had finished his plate of sausage rolls.

"Well, hello, darling," said Fast Eddy, his eyes lighting up. "My most favourite Detective Sergeant on the entire planet."

"The answer's still no." Nance pulled up a stool beside Gilchrist.

"You're breaking a lonely Irishman's heart, my lovely."

"Give it up, Eddy. My knickers are cuffed to my bra."

Fast Eddy laughed his staccato chuckle. "How do you know I'm not a Houdini in disguise?"

"Houdini got out of tight places," Nance said. "Not into them."

"Ah, but a man can live on dreams for only so long."

Nance rolled her eyes. "Keep this up, and I'll have to charge you with indecent—"

"Exposure?"

She shook her head. "I'll have what Andy's having. And make it two."

"Ah, you've cut me to the core." Fast Eddy pulled the first of two pints, letting one settle as the other swelled. "And I'll never know how you manage to keep that lovely figure so slim drinking all this real ale."

"I get plenty of exercise running away from hard-ons like yours."

Fast Eddy snickered.

"Anyway, I'm far too young."

"Not at all. I think we'd make a grand couple."

"I think they should change your name to Past Eddy."

"And a wit as matchless as her eyes," said Fast Eddy. "How do you stand it, Andy?"

Gilchrist pulled out his wallet, removed a twenty.

"I'm getting these, Andy."

"I owe you, Nance."

"Since when?"

"Since teaming you with Watt."

Her face hardened. "In that case, you owe me more than one."

Gilchrist tried a smile, not sure he pulled it off. He pressed the twenty across the bar. "One for yourself, Eddy."

"Now that's what I call a gentleman." Fast Eddy pushed two pints across the bar, heads settling on a rising creamy base. "There you go," he said. "That's one for the lady, and another for the gentleman."

A woman sidled up to the far end of the bar. Fast Eddy flashed a smile. "With you in a sec, love."

Gilchrist tapped his pint against Nance's. "How'd it go with Watt?"

"One guess."

"Don't tell me he tried it on."

Nance screwed up her face. "Not a chance."

Gilchrist hoped she read the plea in his eyes. *Let me know the instant he does*, he willed her. Like a leopard could not change its spots, Watt could not change his personality. He looked to his pint. "Well, keep me posted."

"You wanted me to join you," Nance said. "Let's have it."

Gilchrist twisted the pint in his hand. "You know how sometimes you get a feeling that something's not right and you can't quite put your finger on it?"

"Every paycheck."

He smiled as Nance took a sip and, as if for the first time, noticed how dark her eyes were, almost black, how little make-up she wore. Maybe Fast Eddy's patter was not just patter, but a genuine attempt to find a date.

"And?" she said.

"I don't know." He shook his head. "It's like a sixth sense."

"I know all about that sixth sense of yours," she said. "It's not to be scoffed at."

He tried a smile, but felt tired—tired of the endless pursuit of criminals, the pointless aim of it all, the charging, the sentencing, the jailing, then the early release so they could go out and do it all over again. The futility seemed overwhelming, like trying to stop the rising tide of a sea filled with the rough-and-ready scum of the earth who would rather rob a ninety-year-old blind pensioner than do an honest hour's work.

"You're a bit of a local hero," Nance said. "Especially after that last case."

"I got lucky."

"Well, get lucky on this one."

He felt a frown crease his brow, felt that familiar weight of failure shift through him. "I think that's why I asked you to join me for a pint. I don't feel lucky on this one. I don't like the feel of it. Not at all."

"Because of Watt?"

"I don't like my name being on an envelope, Nance. I don't like a hand being delivered to me. We're being toyed with."

"You think we'll find the rest of the body?"

Bit by hacked off bit. "I'm sure of it," he said. "We'll be given more clues. Why else write a single word on the note. *Murder.* What the hell's that supposed to tell us? I don't know. What I do know is, that when we finally work it out we're not going to like it."

Nance sipped her beer.

"I think this case is going to be painful, Nance. I think that's what I'm trying to say."

"Painful for you?"

He nodded and surprised himself by placing his hand on her shoulder. He flexed his fingers. "And you watch yourself with Watt. Don't trust him." He removed his hand, turned back to his pint. "Just watch yourself, Nance. Okay?"

But he knew it was not just Nance he was worried about.

It was himself.

ON THE DRIVE home, that night came back at him, swirling dark as the blackest smog, settling and clearing until he saw her face, her eyes, the shock still there, still unmistakable, as if the vile event had not happened eight years ago, but only yesterday. He tried to shift her image, but it impinged on his mind like the thickest of syrups that slowed the action of his memory until it seemed he was watching the scene one frame at a time.

Maureen was naked, sitting upright, her back to him. She turned as he entered the room, her face pale and blank with the rigidity of shock. Then she pushed herself up, her underage buttocks flexing with teenage ease, and he tried to keep from looking at her private parts as she slipped off her partner.

Hey, Andy. What's up?

He remembered looking at Watt's face, puzzling over it, as if looking at someone he had met a long time ago, but could not place when or where. Then the frames sped up.

Get out.

Get out of my house.

He turned to Maureen then, turned to confront his fifteen-year-old daughter, her back pressed to the wall as if she had no place to run. One hand covered her pubis, the other her half-developed breasts. Her cheeks glistened with tears. Then, as if by legerdemain, her clothes were in his hand.

He threw them at her. *Get dressed.*

He turned on Watt, who smiled up at him, mouth chewing, arms folded behind his head, his unprotected erection flat to his belly, still veined and full and glistening with the spoils of his conquest for all to see.

That was the moment Gilchrist snapped.

He remembered stepping forward. He remembered that. He could still see it. And looking down at Watt's smiling face. He remembered that, too. But the next memory he had was of standing upright, chest heaving, lungs burning, wondering why there was so much blood, and why Watt had not tried to fight back.

And now here was Watt again, back in St. Andrews, somehow involved in a murder case clearly earmarked for Gilchrist. Fuck it. He tugged the wheel, accelerated hard past two cars, and had to slam on the brakes as he powered into a sweeping bend. Of all the people for Greaves to assign to the case, he had to pick Watt.

Greaves was no fool. Gilchrist knew that.

So why on earth had he put the two of them back together again?

Chapter 5

GILCHRIST WAKENED WITH a start.

He slid his legs to the floor, stumbled against the wall, flicked on the wall switch.

Light exploded into his brain.

He peered through half-opened eyes. His trousers, socks, shoes, shirt, lay strewn across the floor. His leather jacket dangled from the wicker laundry basket. A surge of nausea threatened to engulf him, then hung in the pit of his stomach.

He reached for his jacket, retrieved his phone, and choked, "Yeah?"

"Christ. You sound rough."

He coughed. "Who's this?"

"DS Watt. Sir."

For a moment, he almost hung up. Then it hit him. "Another body part?"

"Right first time."

Gilchrist slid his hand down his face, felt the rough crunch of stubble on his chin and neck. His nightmare had started. "The other hand?"

"Yes."

"Bagged and sealed?"

"Lying where it was found. In the Principal's Nose."

"The what?"

"Another bunker on the Old Course. Sixteenth fairway."

"Any note?"

"Yes."

"What's it say?"

"Massacre."

Massacre? "Spelled correctly?"

A pause, then, "Yeah."

Well, at least he could write. "Who found the hand?" he asked.

Watt gave out a sigh. "A man by the name of Charlie Blair, while walking his dog," he said. "Would you like the dog's name?"

Cheeky bastard. Gilchrist felt the back of his eyes throb, caught a mental image of Nance leaving Lafferty's after two pints, only ever two, blouse loose, a flash of cleavage as she gave him a quick peck. Then how many after that? Four? Five? More? Bloody hell. No wonder it hurt. He glanced at his watch—6:24—then growled, "Tell me we inspected the Principal's Nose yesterday."

"Every bunker on the Old Course was looked at yesterday. Including half the rough."

"Who was in charge?"

"Constable Tommie Murray."

"Double check it."

"Way ahead of you. Tommie's already confirmed the bunker was clear." A pause, then, "We didn't miss it. The hand was placed there overnight."

"Anyone see anything, report anything?" Gilchrist tried.

"Not a thing."

What had he expected? "Stay there," he ordered. "I'll be with you in fifteen."

Watt hung up before Gilchrist.

Shaved and showered and feeling shakier than a sea-legged sailor on dry land, Gilchrist jabbed the key into the ignition. He drove with the window down, the cold air blustering around his neck and face, blowing away the remnants of last night's beer. Once Nance left, he had sat alone at the end of the bar, reviewing the list of names and addresses Nance and Watt had collected, making notes, scribbling thoughts, and returning home at the back of eleven none the wiser.

He parked his Roadster close to the Jigger Inn again. He removed a set of white coveralls and gloves from the boot and fought off another wave of nausea that threatened to have him heaving over the stone dyke. But it passed, and he carried the protective clothing under his arm and walked along the side of the seventeenth fairway onto the sixteenth.

The Principal's Nose was not one bunker, but a cluster of three on the left side of the sixteenth fairway. In the distance, dragonlights lit the scene like a druid's party. As Gilchrist neared, he noticed the SOCO van on the fairway. A pair of SOCOs shifted through the scene, white figures drifting through spheres of light like ghosts blown in from the sea.

As Gilchrist neared, the scene developed before him.

The stiff figure of Watt stood a short distance from the bunkers, on top of a hillock in the rough, talking into his mobile. His hand flapped, finger stabbing the air, voice lost on the cold sea breeze. Close by, a solitary figure in a yellow anorak and green Wellington boots looked seaward. Something moved by the man's feet, a shape that manifested into a black labrador with doleful eyes that followed Gilchrist's step.

He reached the scene and donned his coveralls and shoe covers, then slipped on his gloves. The Crime Scene Manager, DC Alan Bowers, ordered him to sign in. He scribbled his name then stepped into the lighted area, lifted the yellow tape and slipped under it. He half-expected to catch Mackie shoulder deep in the bunker.

"Has Bert been called?" he shouted to Bowers.

"On his way, sir."

Gilchrist stared into the bunker. The sides were steep, about two feet at the back face, rising to five at the front. The fairway fell towards the cluster of bunkers, a graded catchment for stray drives. Shadows danced around him as a SOCO grabbed one of the dragonlights and shifted it several feet farther away. Gilchrist crouched.

The hand lay in the sand, close to the back face, curled fingers up, a note clutched between thumb and forefinger. For a moment, he wondered how Watt had known what was written on it, until he leaned closer and saw the printing. He cocked his head to the side.

Massacre.

Murder. Now *Massacre.* What was the killer trying to tell him? Was the clue to be found in the words? Or in the location of the body parts? First the Road Hole Bunker, next the Principal's Nose. Was that significant? Or, first the seventeenth, and next the sixteenth? Should they now be focusing on the bunkers on the fifteenth?

Gilchrist stared off across the dunes towards the hidden sea, the wind like ice against his face. It would have been colder when the hand was placed in the bunker. What had the killer worn? Something dark, so he could flit unseen through the night? And why only a note this time? Why no envelope? The ink had bled where the dew had settled on the paper. Had the killer not worried that the printing might become illegible, that his message might be lost? He turned his attention back to the hand at his feet.

White skin was beaded in moisture as fine as condensation. Several hairs stood out, as if bristling with horripilation, or from the shock of being cut off from their source of life. And in that matter, he saw that the hand had been sliced from the forearm in a neat cut this time, several inches above the wrist, as if the killer had chopped it with a sharp blade and not quite hit his mark. The sand appeared undisturbed, as if the hand had been placed in the bunker with care. Gilchrist looked to his feet. Had the killer stood on this same spot?

He moved away from the edge, stepped off to the side, and crouched again. The grass was thin and hard, worn bare from the harsh east winds and winter sun. His own prints were barely noticeable. Was that why the killer chose the bunker closest to the fairway, to avoid leaving evidence in the long grass? He eyed the rough, followed the telltale trail of Watt's advance up the hillock, and that of the man and his dog, and came to see that this killer knew what he was doing, and why he was doing it.

Gilchrist looked across the fairway, at the stone wall and the Eden Course beyond. On the other side of the wall lay a gravel path, all that was left of the abandoned railway line. That was how the killer had come, he thought, walked along the pathway that ran the length of the sixteenth, then leapt over the wall, crossed the fairway and placed the hand in the bunker. He would have returned the same way, maybe walked along the fairway a short distance. Or maybe he had it all wrong.

He turned to the hand again, intrigued by how unreal it looked, as if death had moved in and removed whatever vestige of life remained. But he felt haunted by a vague sense of familiarity. He had seen a hand like that before, the hand of a wax dummy, years ago, as a child in Madame Tussaud's in Blackpool while holidaying with his parents. For one moment he wondered if the dragonlights were playing tricks with his eyes, and he felt annoyed for not having noticed sooner. Perhaps he was wrong. He *had* to be wrong.

He leaned closer.

He was not mistaken.

The fingernails were longer on this hand.

He kneeled on the grass, felt the cold seep through his gloves and coveralls, leaned forward as far as he could. It was the thumbnail that settled it for him. The nail was long. Not too long. And not square, but rounded, flush with the curve of the tip, so that it looked white, a healthy solid white, as if it had been varnished.

But the white tip, the white tip was. . . .

Gilchrist felt his chest drain.

Dear God. Don't tell me.

His mind tried to tell him he was wrong. But he knew he was not.

The underside of the nail was thick with paint.

He now saw traces of paint in the cracks of the cuticles, a tiny spot embedded in the skin by the half-moon. Other marks, a touch of green, a hint of yellow, had him thinking that the killer must have scrubbed the first hand, trimmed the nails to make identification difficult. But now the second hand was on display, as if the killer wanted them to know who the victim was. Or worse, needed Gilchrist to make the identification. Which was why the first note had been addressed to him.

He stood as Watt approached, shoes glistening black as he scuffled through the long grass. Either Watt had removed his coveralls, or he had never put them on. He stopped on the other side of the yellow tape.

"What d'you think?" Watt asked him.

Was it possible to recognise someone by their hands? If his own hands were found lying apart from his body, could Jack or Maureen identify them as his? He thought not. So why did he think he knew who these hands belonged to?

"You look rough," Watt added.

Gilchrist remembered the first time he met her. *You don't wear rings*, he heard his mind say. *I don't like them*, she whispered. *I find them distracting*. He had thought it such an odd thing to say, that he had taken her hands in his and held them, looked down at fingers long and slim, at nails trim and clean, just the tiniest bit ragged from working the paints, scrubbing the canvases. Would he describe them as being cracked?

Dear God, tell me I'm wrong. Not this. Not this.

He stepped away then, pushed under the yellow tape, and stumbled through the long grass, to the peak of the hillock vacated by Watt. He faced the dark sea. His breath rushed in hard gasps, lungs filling and deflating as if seeking the last ounce of oxygen. He removed his mobile and on the sixth ring got Jack's answering machine.

"Damn."

He hung up, tried again.

Six rings, then the answering machine.

He hung up. Tried again.

Come on, come on, I know you're home.

Shit. And again.

On the fifth attempt, Jack picked up, his voice heavy with sleep, or worse. "This had better be good," he slurred.

"Jack, it's me."

"Aw, come on, Andy." A deep breath then out with a tired yawn. "It's not even seven o'clock yet."

"I know, Jack, I'm sorry, but I need to speak to Chloe."

"Chloe?"

"Is she there?"

"What for?"

Gilchrist felt his head slump. This was not good. Not good at all. "If I can't speak to her," he tried, "just tell me she's okay."

"What?"

"Tell me Chloe's okay." Gilchrist tightened his grip on his phone, prayed Jack would simply pass his call to a sleeping Chloe and have her speak to him.

"What the hell is this, Andy?"

"Let me speak to her."

A pause, then a defeated rush, "She's not here."

Gilchrist felt his breath leave him. There. He had it. He was right. He stared at the sea, felt the breeze squeeze tears from his eyes. Then a flicker of hope. Maybe he was wrong. "She's left you," he said. "Hasn't she?"

"What the hell's that got—"

"Jack, listen—"

"No, Andy. You listen. What Chloe and I do with our lives has got eff all to do—"

"That's not why I'm calling."

"Why, then?"

Because I think someone's murdered Chloe and is feeding her to me in chunks. He took a deep breath, tried the soft approach once more. "Jack, please, if you know, just tell me where she is."

"Are you listening to me?"

Sometimes with Jack you had to take the direct approach. "I am, Jack. Now *you* listen to *me*. This is not a personal call. I'm talking to you as Detective Chief Inspector Gilchrist of Fife Constabulary's Crime Management Department. Do you understand what I'm saying?"

Silence.

"I need to talk to Chloe." He heard a hand brush the mouthpiece, caught an image of Jack pulling himself from bed, blonde hair tousled with bed-head.

"You're serious?"

"Deadly."

Jack's breath came hard and deep all of a sudden. "It's that hand thing," he said. "Isn't it? It's been on the news."

"It's too early to say."

"Don't lie to me, Andy."

"I'm not lying, for crying out loud. We don't know."

"Why call then?"

"To rule Chloe out."

"I don't know where she is. We had a row. She stomped off in one of her moods."

"When did you last talk to her?"

"Three days ago. No. Four. Christ. I don't know."

"Settle down," Gilchrist said, struggling to keep his own voice steady.

"Jesus, Andy. What's happened to her?"

"Probably nothing, Jack."

"Why're you calling, then?"

"To rule her out."

"You know it's her."

"For God's sake, Jack, will you just listen?"

"That's why you're asking to talk to her. You know it's her, don't you? The hand. It's hers. You know it is."

Gilchrist felt his lips tighten as he listened to his son cry. He wanted to speak, but found his own voice had deserted him. He heard Jack say something, the words thick and unintelligible. He clung onto the phone, pressed it tight against his ear, and whispered, "Jack," then felt a puzzling sense of relief wash over him when Jack hung up.

He folded his phone. His chest was heaving, his heart racing. He had handled it all wrong. Why could he never get it right with Jack? Why did he always feel as if he was pushing him farther away? He felt the tight sting of tears, the cold flush of ice in his lungs.

Christ. What if the hand was not Chloe's? What if all he had done was upset Jack? Dear God, he would love Jack to call him back and give him a right old reaming. Then Chloe would be safe and alive. He could stand that. In fact, he would welcome that. He stared off across the dunes, felt an odd reluctance to leave that spot, knowing that doing so would mean having to look at the hand again in the knowledge that if he was right, if his worst fears were realised, then the rest of Chloe would be presented to him piece by slaughtered piece.

Now he knew why his name had been on the envelope. What better way to hurt another human being, to *really* hurt them to the core, than to hurt their family?

But why? And why him?

He could think of a million reasons for someone wanting to even the score.

He closed his eyes and prayed to God he was wrong on every one of them.

Chapter 6

GILCHRIST DID THE necessary.

He dialled the number for DCI Peter "Dainty" Small of Strathclyde Police HQ, Pitt Street, Glasgow, and asked him to put out a Lookout Request on a young woman, five-ten, twenty-two years old, a freelance artist by the name of Chloe Fullerton. He gave her last known address as Jack's tenement flat in Glasgow.

Dainty and Gilchrist had joined Fife Constabulary at the same time. But eight years later, Dainty married Margo Cunningham, a young PW, and moved to Glasgow the following year. They had kept in contact over the years, exchanging Christmas cards and information on relevant cases as the need arose. Gilchrist ended the call by saying he hoped he was wrong, hoped Chloe would turn up, then slipped his mobile into his jacket pocket.

From his hillock, the golf course was beginning to show signs of life.

Behind the first tee, the Royal and Ancient Clubhouse stood like a misplaced mansion, alone in its stone splendour. People dotted Grannie Clark's Wynd, the pathway that crossed the first and eighteenth fairways and connected The Links to Bruce Embankment on the shoreline. To the east, the sky glowed crimson with a hint of blue through tattered clouds.

Gilchrist could not rid himself of his fear for Chloe. He searched the dunes for the spot where they had picnicked on the beach in January. It seemed absurd. But it had been Jack's idea. Freezing cold. Wind whipping in off the sea. *At least we'll have the beach to ourselves.* Gilchrist almost smiled. They ended up sharing the West

Sands with people and dogs and couples in love, and sweating jog-gers and kids, and fathers with swooping kites. They even watched some lunatic strip to his underwear and take a swim—

Something moved at his feet. The black labrador.

He scratched behind its ears as its tail brushed the long grass.

"Her name's Biddy," said the man in the yellow anorak.

Gilchrist scratched deeper. "That's a rare old name."

"That's what my father called my grandmother."

"He must have thought she gossiped too much, then?"

"Among other things." The man chuckled, held out his hand. "Charlie Blair."

The grip felt warm, hard, honest. "DCI Gilchrist."

Blair nodded. "Nice to meet you at last. I've seen your face around."

Gilchrist smiled. "In the bars, no doubt."

"On the telly." Blair nodded over his shoulder. "Quite gruesome," he said. "I don't think I would like your job. It must get to you."

You get used to it, Gilchrist wanted to say, but he would be lying. Instead, he said, "You found it? The hand, I mean."

"Just passing."

The significance of Blair's comment did not hit Gilchrist until Blair continued on his way and Biddy loped ahead, nose to the rough, tail like a black hand-brush sweeping the grass with canine pleasure. Gilchrist called out.

They met halfway, and Gilchrist asked what he meant by *just passing*.

"Exactly that. I saw Detective Watt standing at the bunker. At first I thought he was a drunk taking a leak, but then he called me over and asked me what I thought."

"What you thought?"

Blair nodded. "Of the hand."

"I see," said Gilchrist, and thanked him for his time.

"He's a strange one," said Blair as he strode off.

Gilchrist found Watt standing at the edge of the fairway,

and grabbed him by his coat lapels. "Why are you here?" he growled.

"What the fuck're you—"

"Why are you here? In St. Andrews."

A steel claw gripped his wrist. "Take your fucking hands off me."

Gilchrist glanced to his side, saw the SOCOs eye them with suspicion, as if undecided whether to separate them, or stand back and enjoy the fight. He tightened his grip. "Not until you tell me why you were up bright as a lark way before dawn this morning."

"I'm an early riser."

"Who told you the hand was here?"

"No one."

"Charlie Blair and his faithful mutt, Biddy, didn't find it. You did."

"Is that what he told you?" Watt sneered. "He doesn't want to be involved, does Charlie."

"I warned you, Ronnie. One step out of line and I'll have you kicked all the way back to Glasgow." He gritted his teeth. "Did somebody call you?"

"No."

"I swear I'll have your phone records examined."

Something went out of Watt at that moment, like a prisoner realising the futility of struggling against his shackles. Gilchrist responded by relaxing his grip. Then he let go and lowered his arm.

Watt straightened his lapels, shuffled his shoulders, smoothed his jacket. He pushed his hand into his pocket. "I got this." He pulled out a damp piece of paper that looked as if it had been ripped from an envelope.

Gilchrist read the pencilled words.

> right hand—principal's nose.

"Who gave you this?" he asked.

"It was stuck underneath my windscreen wiper." Watt's jaw was set as tight as rock. He widened his stance, and Gilchrist could almost taste the raw power of the guy.

"And you don't know who put it there?"

"Correct."

"Were you going to show me this?"

"Of course," Watt growled. "I never got a chance."

Gilchrist glared at him.

Watt shrugged. "You looked busy. I was taking a call. When I spoke to you, you ignored me. What do you expect me to do? Get down on my knees and fucking beg?"

Gilchrist narrowed his eyes. He held the damp scrap up between them. "Whoever wrote this," he said to Watt, "is playing games with us. A note for me. A message for you. Did it not cross your mind that we're being set up?"

Watt tightened his lips.

"What about Blair and his dog?" asked Gilchrist.

"What about them? He was walking down the fairway. I called him over, asked him to verify it."

"Why?"

"Thought I could use a witness."

"What for?"

"Protection."

"From what?"

Watt chewed his imaginary gum. "You're just itching to kick me out," he said.

Somehow hearing the truth of his own vendetta against Watt shamed Gilchrist. He needed to rise above it all. But damn it, what the hell had Greaves expected?

"Any other messages I need to see?"

Watt shook his head. "None."

Gilchrist was prepared to bet a month's salary that Watt was lying. But what could he do? Tie him to a rack? Hammer bamboo shoots under his fingernails? He raked his fingers through his hair. It felt damp. But the sea air had almost cleared his hangover. "After you removed the note from your windscreen," he said, "did you talk to anyone?"

"No."

"Call anyone?"

"No."

"You came straight here?"

"That's right."

Watt could be lying, but how could he prove it? "Get hold of Nance," he said. "Get her down here. With Bert. There's paint under the fingernails. I want Bert to tell us what it is. And if Brenda from the Procurator Fiscal's Office turns up, keep your hands off her. She's married."

"What's that got to do with anything?"

"Everything," he said, and walked away. It was corny, he knew, but he counted off seven steps then stopped. "Tell me this," he said to Watt. "Where's the Valley of Sin?"

Watt stopped chewing. "The what?"

"The Valley of Sin."

Watt gave an uncertain smile, and said, "Between a pair of knockers?" He shrugged and half-laughed. "What kind of a question is that?"

Gilchrist had his answer. He strutted off, past the SOCO van, reached the boundary wall, and glanced back. Watt stood at the edge of the bunker. Beyond the dunes, a low sun pierced thinning clouds that stretched to the horizon. He leapt over the stone wall and put his head down for the walk back to his car.

He should send Watt packing. Get it over and done with. But he wondered if there might be something to be gained by not doing that. The killer was smart, cunning, and for some reason it seemed important to make sure Watt was one of the first on the scene.

Hence the note under the windscreen.

After finding the note, Watt said he had not spoken to anyone.

But he was lying. Why else had he crumbled at the mention of his phone records?

And then there was the Valley of Sin.

Not being a golfer and not raised in St. Andrews, Watt's local knowledge was limited. The Valley of Sin was a grass swale that fronted the eighteenth green of the Old Course, a dip in the fairway that punished weak approach shots. To the golfing world, the Valley of Sin was infamous. But if Watt had never heard of the Valley of Sin he sure as hell had not heard of the Principal's Nose. So, how had he known the Principal's Nose was a cluster of bunkers on the sixteenth fairway? It could have been the name of a pub, for all he knew. Had a fairy fluttered down and lit Watt's way with her magic wand?

Not a chance. Gilchrist did not believe in fairies.

But he did believe in phone calls and phone records.

He reached his Mercedes and glanced over at the dunes, to the spot that had held so much promise for Jack and Chloe. He had seen in Chloe a young woman who could settle the wild stallion of his son, who could pull in his reins and have him snorting with restive passion. And as he stared seaward, he wondered what memories of St. Andrews Chloe had taken with her. Iced champagne on wind-chilled dunes? Shoeless strolls on sun-soaked sands? Jokes and hugs and kisses and beer?

And what of his own memories of Chloe?

He would remember her as waif-like, with slender limbs and blonde hair and eyes and teeth that sparkled with the promise of life.

And hands as fine as those of any model.

He slid behind the wheel and closed the door. He knew what he had to do.

For Chloe. And for Jack.

Chapter 7

JACK STOOD OUTSIDE his tenement building.
His breath evaporated in drizzle as fine as haar. To his side, water dripped from a broken drainpipe, as steady as a metronome. Runoff trickled along granite curbs that edged North Gardner Street. He blew into his hands, tried to take the chill from his body, would have called for a taxi if he could afford it. But he had spent the last of his dole check on a tab of speed to keep him awake for his latest work, a life-sized figure sculpted from concrete and reinforcing steel rods finagled from a building site in Partick.

He could blame the sculpture for setting Chloe off. But if he was being honest, it was not the sculpture at all but the drugs that upset her. He saw that now. But he had taken her comments as a personal slight, and they had argued.

How could they have? Chloe loved his sculptures. And he loved her paintings. Together, they were a creative team. Apart, they were. . . .

He took a deep breath.

He missed Chloe so much. He never should have gone back on speed, and he never should have spent his dole money. What the hell had he been thinking? But now he was off the drugs. By God, was he off them. When Chloe came back he would tell her he was off them for good. He pulled his combat jacket collar tight to his neck, skipped down the worn steps, and started walking.

Chloe had been gone for four days now. *Four days*.

Amphetamines were great to keep you awake, but when you

came off them, watch out. He had not missed her the first two days, been asleep most of the time. But it had now been four days since she told him to sort himself out or she was through with him.

You're losing it, Jack. You can do better than this. I've seen you do better.

They argued. Man, did they argue. And the following morning she rose from bed and left. Just like that. But she never took her paintings. Which was her way of telling him she would be back. On the third day, he called her mobile phone ten times, and each time got the recorded message, *It has not been possible to connect your call. Please try again later.* He even tried her parents' home then hung up when her mother said she was now living in Glasgow, and who is this speaking please?

He turned into Hyndland Road, and the wind stiffened, hard and cold against him. He tucked his head and braced himself as he waded into it.

Chloe wasn't dead. The hand wasn't hers. She was staying with Jenny. That's where she was. With Jenny. Not that he had spoken to Jenny, just that he knew Chloe and Jenny were close. Not as close as they had been when Chloe had been dating Kevin. But close nonetheless.

Kevin's death had hurt Chloe, hurt her relationship with Jack, often came between them. Or it might be more accurate to say Kevin's *life* came between them. For Jack had always thought there was more to Kevin than met the eye. He had seen Chloe about town with Kevin, first caught her eye three years ago at some party on the South side, fancied her even then. It was not Kevin that concerned Jack, but the company he kept. Jack was off drugs back then, and trouble was how he would have described Kevin's friends.

By the time he reached Jenny's flat, his feet were soaked through. As he scanned the list of names on the doorframe, he realised he could not remember Jenny's surname. But her boyfriend's name was Roddy, an Englishman with an English name and Scottish accent who worked in the city centre. They had dated for years. Chloe told him they split up.

He stopped at J. Colvin & R. Braithwaite.

That was it. Jenny Colvin and Roddy Braithwaite.

He rang the bell, turned his back to the door and blew into his hands. He felt chilled to the bone, gave out a cough.

A tinny voice crackled from the speaker. "Who's this?"

"Jenny?"

"Who's this?"

"It's Jack Gilchrist." He thought he heard a low curse. "I need to talk to you. Can I come in?"

"D'you know what time it is?"

"It's about Chloe."

"Chloe?"

He wanted to ask if Chloe was there, tell her he needed to talk to her. But he thought Jenny might lie for her, keep her hidden. "It's freezing out here," he said.

The speaker buzzed, and Jenny said, "Come on up."

He pushed open the heavy entrance door and fought off the feeling that Chloe was not there. On the top landing, the door to Jenny's flat lay ajar. He stepped into a narrow hallway that smelled of burned toast. Jenny's voice came at him from a doorway on the far right.

"In the kitchen."

Jenny was dressed in a white baggy bathrobe that hung loose at the front and did little to hide the swell of her boobs. Her face looked tanned, as if she had returned from a winter holiday. She scowled when she saw him.

"Jeezo, Jack. What happened to you?"

"Chloe," he said.

"So you keep saying."

"Is she here?"

"I haven't seen Chloe in months."

"Haven't you heard from her?"

"Not since before Christmas. Why? What's happened?"

Jack felt the power go out of his legs. He stumbled to the kitchen table and sat. He fought back the tears, but could not stop himself.

He buried his face in his hands and sobbed.

BERT MACKIE CALLED Gilchrist shortly before 9:00 and confirmed he had found traces of oil paint under the nails of both hands and was waiting for results of a spectrographic analysis to determine the paint's chemical composition. Gilchrist then ordered Nance and Watt to continue their investigation of all things artsy.

Brenda McAllister from the Procurator Fiscal's Office instructed the examination of the second hand to be done under the supervision of two pathologists. Alec Simpson, from Ninewells Hospital in Dundee, was contracted to assist Bert Mackie.

Gilchrist assigned DS Stan Davidson to oversee a fresh search of the Old Course and environs and to interview the greenkeeping staff. Then he sent a trainee out shopping with instructions not to return until she had a map of the Old Course that detailed all features. Next, he called the Town Council and ordered the West Sands closed, including cancelling the beach-cleaning tractor, in case the killer had not taken the pathway route, but come in over the dunes.

Unlikely, he thought, but it kept the scene quiet.

He called Martin Coyle on his mobile not long after 9:00 with the intention of driving into Cupar to meet him. But Coyle was in St. Andrews checking out golf club sales, so they agreed to meet later in the Jigger Inn.

By lunchtime, the investigation was no further forward. Gilchrist's hangover had returned with a vengeance, and after popping a couple of Paracetemol he decided a hair of the dog was just what the doctor ordered. He arrived at the Jigger ten minutes early and ordered a pint of Guinness. Coyle walked into the lounge before he had a chance to take a sip.

They shook hands like long lost friends.

"Pint?" Gilchrist asked.

Coyle had one of those faces that always seemed to want to smile. When he spoke, his eyes creased and his lips parted in a gap-toothed grin. "Just a tonic and lemon."

"On a diet?" Gilchrist asked.

"Afraid not."

"The wagon?"

Coyle smiled. "Alkey."

Gilchrist thought he managed to keep his surprise hidden. He and Coyle used to run cross-country marathons together when Gilchrist joined the force and Coyle the Post Office as a telecommunications engineer. They would meet in the Whey Pat Tavern on a Saturday night at 5:00, and stagger home this side of midnight after sampling the wares of most of the bars in town. Coyle in a bar without a beer was like a golfer on the course without his clubs.

Gilchrist sipped his beer. "When did this happen?"

"Nine months ago. I woke up one morning with eyes like I had yellow fever. Doctor told me to give up the drink, or get measured for my coffin." Coyle smiled. "Well, I've got the grandkid to think of now. Not to mention Linda."

At the mention of Coyle's wife, Gilchrist knew where the conversation was heading. But he was helpless to stop it.

"Do you still hear from Gail?"

Gilchrist grimaced. "Indirectly."

"How is she?"

Gilchrist took another sip of Guinness, then, defeated, said, "She's got cancer."

"Christ, Andy, I'm really sorry to hear that." He paused, then ventured, "Is it. . . ?"

"It is."

Coyle smiled. "That's dreadful."

Gilchrist dreaded Coyle asking after Jack and Maureen and the conversation turning towards Chloe, so he said, "Listen, Martin. I need a favour. Got a mobile phone number here. I'd like to see records from the start of the year. Including calls made today."

Coyle whistled. "That's a toughie," he said. "Might need to wait a few days before today's calls log on."

Gilchrist nodded. A few days would be fine. As long as the wheels were turning. He handed the number over, and Coyle said, "I take it no one is to know about this."

Gilchrist put on his poker face. "Know about what?"

It took a full two seconds for Coyle to catch on. He gave out a quick laugh, and said, "I get it. I get it."

"Get what?"

Coyle slapped his thigh and chuckled some more.

Gilchrist bought lunch, two chicken sandwiches and chips, and managed to keep the conversation off Gail and his children. By 2:00 they were all talked out, having caught up mostly on Coyle's life, his mid-life crisis with his wife, and the pregnancy of their fifteen-year-old daughter who had given them a surprise grandchild. Coyle left with assurances that he would call in a few days.

Gilchrist tried Maureen again, and this time she answered on the fourth ring with a curt, "Hello?" He choked a laugh, felt a dead weight lift off his heart and soar skyward.

"Have you stopped returning calls?" he grumped.

"Oh, hi, Dad. I got your message."

"All ten of them?"

"I've been meaning to call. Sorry." She made a noise like a sponge being squidged. "But you know I love you."

And you've no idea how much I love you.

"I'll make a point of calling more often," she added.

"Well, that's a start," he said, then found himself asking the same question he always asked. "Any chance of you making it up this way?" and expecting the same answer.

"I think that might be possible."

What? He pressed the phone to his ear. "Did I hear you right?" Maureen laughed, a soft rumble that cast up an image of dark eyes and white teeth and asked him how long it had been since they last met. Just after New Year? Had it been that long? "That's wonderful, Mo," he said, and meant it. "Any idea when this great event might take place?"

"Well, Chris and I are thinking—"

"What happened to Larry?"

"That plonker?"

"I thought you and he were . . . you know."

"Were what?"

"I thought you, eh, loved each other."

"Correct, Dad. Past tense."

Gilchrist felt his face flush. He and Maureen never talked about her personal life, and his embarrassment reminded him how far he had drifted from her life. He made a mental note to try to sort things out when she came up.

"So, what's this Chris like?" he asked.

"You can find out for yourself next month."

"So soon?"

"That's what I was trying to tell you, Dad, before you cut me off with the Larry crap."

"You're both welcome to stay at my place," he said.

"Thanks, Dad. But Chris has friends up that way."

"Of course. Right."

As if sensing his disappointment, she added, "But I'll run it past him. Okay?"

"Sure," he said. "I spoke to Jack."

"Who?"

He struggled not to rise to the bait. If he had spent more time with his family instead of the case of the day, then maybe Gail would not have had an affair, and they would still be together as a family. He thought of telling her why he called Jack, of his fears for Chloe, his concern for her own safety. But it was early days and he could be wrong. Rather than scare her, he said, "Jack told me about Mum."

"Mum's not doing well," she said.

"Is there anything I can do?"

"No, Dad. She's got Harry," then added, "I'm sorry. I know how you feel about him."

Gilchrist eyed his pint. When he first met Gail, they would get drunk together, as if it was some rite of passage Scottish couples had to negotiate. Back then, Gail drank wine and the odd beer, but after nineteen years of a bitter marriage no longer drank. And she hated that Gilchrist continued. Dark beer especially riled her. He had never understood her rationale.

"By all accounts," he said, "Harry is a nice guy." He took a sip, waited for Maureen to speak, but his phone beeped. "Hang on, Mo. I've got another call."

"That's okay, Dad. I've got to go. I'll tell Mum we spoke. Talk to you later."

"Listen, Mo. Will you be careful?" But she had hung up. He switched lines, and said, "Gilchrist."

"Andy, it's me."

"Jack?"

"I'm at Leuchars station. Can you pick me up?"

Confused, Gilchrist felt his hopes rise, then stall. "You have Chloe?"

"That's why I'm here."

"I'm not sure I follow," Gilchrist said, although he thought he did.

"I need to look at the hand."

Chapter 8

JACK'S FACE LOOKED as grey as the sky. His hair stood in untidy clumps that gave the impression he had not showered in days. His combat jacket hung from shoulders as thin as bone and sported greasy stains at the cuffs and neck.

They shook hands with nothing more than a nod, and Gilchrist tried to hide his concern with a quick smile. But he was fooling no one. They had still not spoken by the time he veered left at the Guardbridge roundabout.

"You look as if you've lost weight," he tried.

Jack shrugged.

"Are you managing to sell any work?"

"Some."

"Keeping gainfully employed, are you?"

"You could say."

Gilchrist accelerated up the slight incline, felt the car respond with a beefy spurt of power. "Talk to me," he said.

Jack shrugged again. "What do you want to hear?"

"Tell me what happened."

"Chloe's gone. What can I say?"

"Define *gone*."

Jack glanced at him with a grimace filled with contempt. "What the hell do you mean by that?"

"Gone home? Gone away? Gone to Spain? What?"

"She's gone. All right?"

"As in, gone away from you?"

Jack tutted. "Don't treat me like an idiot, Andy. All right?"

Gilchrist swung out to pass a couple of cars, and eased back in when the road ahead was clear. It did not happen often, but when Jack behaved like this, he could be harder to break through to than Maureen. Gilchrist tried again.

"You said you needed to look at the hand."

"Yeah."

"To ID it?"

"Yeah."

"And put your mind at rest?"

From the corner of his eye, he watched Jack turn away and stare across the fields to the Eden Estuary. A solitary pig stood mud-stained and grumpy in a grassless sty. A pair of jets from RAF Leuchars raced into the sky like dark missiles then banked east and bulleted out across the North Sea.

"Why do you think you could ID Chloe from the hand?"

"Which hand is it?"

Gilchrist twisted his grip on the steering wheel. "We have two hands now."

Jack sank deeper into his seat and stared out the window. It took Gilchrist a few seconds to realise he was crying. He reached across, was about to place his hand on his knee, when he pulled back. "Are you up for this?"

Jack sniffed, and said, "I'll be all right."

Gilchrist detected an undercurrent of anger, reminding him of how Jack used to behave as a child when scolded. He and Gail would wait it out, say nothing until Jack's mood evaporated. Silent, Gilchrist eyed the road ahead.

Jack ran the palm of his hand across his eyes. "I loved Chloe," he said.

Gilchrist caught the past tense, felt his chest tighten.

"She had this phenomenal talent as an artist. Like she had all this creative power just bubbling inside her, waiting to erupt onto the canvas." Jack shook his head. "She made my sculptures look incomplete. She had this ability to humble me as an artist, make me realise there was so much more I still have to learn, you know, without knowing she was doing it." Jack stared off across the golf courses to the dunes beyond, and Gilchrist wondered if he was searching for their winter picnic spot, or remembering it was only January since they had all been together.

"That's why we argued," Jack went on. "Sometimes she would just go on at me, urge me to do better, like she knew I had it in me, but I couldn't get it out. It used to do my nut in. In the end we had this huge row. I just flipped." He shook his head, and it took a few seconds of silence for Gilchrist to realise Jack had said all he was going to say.

"I'm not sure if trying to ID the hands is a good idea."

Jack turned to him. "I need to know."

Gilchrist felt Jack's eyes on him, and made a conscious effort to speak in the present tense. "Does Chloe have any marks on her hands or fingers like moles or freckles or anything that would provide conclusive identification?"

"Yes."

Gilchrist felt his heart leap. He had seen no marks on either hand. In fact, both hands looked unblemished. Had he jumped to the wrong conclusion? Were the hands not Chloe's? For a fleeting moment, his mind nurtured that idea then thumped back with the question he could not answer—why was his name on the note? The victim had to be someone close to him. He struggled to keep his voice level. "Such as?" he asked.

"A scar at the base of her thumb."

A scar? Mackie hadn't mentioned any scars.

"Which hand?" he asked.

Jack seemed to think for a second. "Right, I think."

"You think?"

"No. Definitely the right hand."

"How big a scar?"

"Half-inch."

"Crooked? Straight? What?"

"Straight. She cut herself with a palette knife." He almost smiled. "Don't ask."

"Any other marks?"

"On her hands?"

"Anywhere."

Jack pulled up the front of his sweater. "One of these."

Gilchrist glanced to the side, but saw only white skin and felt a spurt of surprise flush through him at how thin Jack looked. Skinny verging on skeletal. "One of what?" he asked.

Jack twisted in his seat and fingered a tattoo that stained his skin like a tiny ink blot an inch or so above his belly button. "Love-heart."

"And Chloe had one, too?" Too late, he realised he had spoken as if she was no longer alive.

Jack seemed unaware of his blunder. "Last Christmas," he said, lowering his sweater. "To seal our love. Kind of stupid, I suppose. It was Chloe's idea."

Gilchrist stared at the road ahead. When he first met Gail, drunk and wild in the Whey Pat Tavern, up from Glasgow on her annual holiday, she had sworn at some American guy with a buzz-cut and two bared arms blue with tattoos and taut with muscles. Gilchrist had escorted her from the pub after that, tried to calm her down. But something about the tattoos had her wound up.

My uncle had a tattoo, she told him. *An anchor with a silly rope wound around it.*

What's so bad about that? he had asked.

He hit my aunt.

It hurt to think that when he first met Gail he was taken by her vivacity, her uncut love of life. Nothing seemed too big to take on. The whole world, if they wanted. He had never been able to work out the exact moment Gail changed, that instant in time when something inside her died. He struggled to force his thoughts back to Jack.

"Chloe's scar," he said. "Why do you remember it so clearly?"

"She needed a couple of stitches. I took her to the hospital."

"You and Chloe were dating?"

"Yeah."

"So, the scar's recent?"

"Last summer." He sniffed again, tugged a hand through clumped hair. "Is that important?"

"Could be." He dialled Mackie's number. It was answered on the second ring. "Bert. Andy here. Have you completed your examination?"

"Other than spectrographic analysis, yes, I'm more or less finished."

Gilchrist puffed out his cheeks, then let out his breath. "Find any scars?"

"One. On the right hand."

A bull butted him in the gut. "Whereabouts?"

"Base of the thumb. Fairly recent, I'd say."

Last summer? Gilchrist pressed his phone hard to his ear as Mackie confirmed size and angle, and concluded with, "It looks like a knife wound."

"How about an artist's palette knife?"

"That's an interesting suggestion. But, yes, any kind of knife would make sense. Why do you ask?"

"Jack's with me. He might be able to make an ID."

"Your son, Jack?"

"Yes."

"Good lord, Andy. Are you saying. . . ."

"Nothing definite, Bert. But we'd better take a look at it." He hung up and glanced at Jack. "I'm sorry, Jack," he said. "It's not looking good."

"It's Chloe. I know it is." His voice sounded steady, as if he was oblivious to the gruesome prospect of examining amputated extremities.

Gilchrist wondered how on earth he ever got himself into such a morbid job.

He felt his heart sink. He hated to admit it.

But Jack was right.

GILCHRIST FOUND MACKIE in the post-mortem room in the Bell Street mortuary, a woman's body on the stainless steel table in front of him, opened from sternum to pubis. Cruel looking surgical equipment lay on flat metal surfaces. Something wet and slimy and white as brain glistened by a set of scales. The air felt cold, and hinted of decaying flesh and formaldehyde that left an aftertaste on the tongue.

Mackie caught Gilchrist's eye, and stepped away from the table.

Gilchrist introduced Jack, then together they followed Mackie into another room.

Gurneys lined either side.

Mackie shuffled forward without a word, and halted at one of the gurneys halfway along on the left. He peeled back a cotton sheet to reveal two clear plastic bags. Through the plastic sheen, the amputated hands looked ghostlike, as if at any moment they could move of their own accord and crawl from their confines. If Gilchrist had any doubts they were from different bodies, they evaporated right then.

He stood beside Jack. "Ready?"

Tight-lipped, Jack nodded.

Gilchrist eyed Mackie.

Mackie opened one plastic bag, removed a hand, the left one, and placed it palm down on the gurney. Then he did the same with the right hand. He pushed the bags to the side and positioned the hands so they looked as if they were reaching out for Gilchrist.

Jack let out a rush of breath and took a step back.

Something clamped Gilchrist's chest. He stared at the hands, the claws, the lifeless things on the table. They had once belonged to a young woman, once touched and caressed and moved with life. An image of him holding those hands, looking down at those fingers, burst into his mind. He fought off an overpowering urge to take Jack by the arm and lead him from the room. But his pragmatic side kept him rooted. He had a victim to identify, a murder to solve, and he prayed to God that Jack would simply shake his head and tell him the hands could not be Chloe's, that they belonged to some other poor soul.

"The scar should be on the inside," Jack whispered, and held his own hand out and pointed to the base of his right thumb. "About here."

Mackie eyed Gilchrist with an intensity he had not seen in the old man's eyes since he performed the post-mortem of his own sister-in-law. Grim-faced, Mackie turned the right hand over and pointed a finger to a pink mark at the base of the thumb. "This is the only scar I detected."

Gilchrist felt his lungs deflate. He had his answer. His peripheral vision watched Jack's body sway as if buffeted by a wind. He grasped his arm, tightened his grip. "Jack," he said, "I need you to be sure."

"It's her," Jack whispered. "It's Chloe."

Gilchrist stared at Jack's face. For his own benefit, he needed to hear more. "No doubts?" he asked.

Jack opened his eyes. His cheeks glistened with tears. His breath shuddered as he stared at the hands, and he surprised Gilchrist by leaning closer and reaching out as if to lift the hand from the gurney. Instead, he tapped the back of his own hand. "When Chloe was ten years old she crushed a knuckle on her left hand. Her pinkie knuckle. Compared to the others, it looked flat when she made a fist."

Gilchrist glanced at Mackie. "Did you take x-rays?"

Mackie nodded. He replaced the right hand, picked up the left, and pointed to the small knuckle. "Fifth metacarpal shows evidence of having sustained a similar injury." He looked at Jack. "Did she say how it happened?"

"She'd been watching TV. Some judo expert. She tried to punch her fist through a block of wood." He gave a wan smile.

"She said that was a defining moment in her life, when she realised she would be an artist, not a martial arts expert."

Mackie returned his attention to the hand, giving Gilchrist the impression he was leaving the hard part to him.

"That's all for now, Bert." Gilchrist tugged Jack's arm, felt a moment's resistance, then Jack was by his side, out the refrigerated room, into a short corridor. They pushed through the door and stepped into the grey light and cold air of a late winter afternoon. They walked past Gilchrist's Merc and over to the edge of the car park. Then stopped.

Jack breathed hard through his nostrils. "I'm not mistaken," he said. "It's Chloe."

Gilchrist said nothing. Christ, what would he give for a cigarette at that moment? Fourteen years since he last had a smoke, and the need still hit him like an unscratchable itch deep in his gut. "Why don't you stay here for a couple of days?" he said. "I'll be instructing Forensics to examine your flat."

Jack turned to him, eyes burning. "You don't think I had—"

"No, Jack. I don't. It's standard procedure. We need samples of clothing, hair from Chloe's hairbrush, stuff like that, to check her DNA." He looked away, felt Jack's eyes on him. Christ. He had the scar, the crushed knuckle. They would lift Chloe's fingerprints from Jack's flat. How conclusive did identification have to be? He gave Jack's shoulder a quick squeeze, not sure if he was trying to be strong for Jack or himself.

"I'm sorry," he whispered. "I'm truly sorry."

Gilchrist watched his son walk to the car. Part of him was aching, too, for Chloe, for Jack. But his own pain seemed smothered in dread. The killer was clever. They would not find the rest of the body intact, Gilchrist knew. He knew that with certainty. All he could do was dig harder, look deeper, try to find some lead to work on. But his heart told him they were just waiting for the next body part to turn up.

And he was not sure he could take that.

Chapter 9

GILCHRIST CONTACTED DAINTY Small with confirmation of Jack's ID, and asked if Dainty could have someone keep an eye on Maureen for him.

"Bloody hell, Andy. We're stretched thin as it is. But I'll see what I can do."

Strathclyde Police visited Chloe's parents and informed them of their suspicions, always suspicions, nothing definite until they conclusively matched the DNA results or the fingerprints. He drove to Glasgow and assisted Forensics with their search of Jack's flat. Three pairs of Chloe's knickers were removed from the laundry basket and samples of her hair from a hairbrush in the bathroom. They also took tubes of oils from her studio and lifted a perfect set of fingerprints from a coffee mug on a table by her easel.

By 10:45, and back in St. Andrews, Gilchrist had done all he could, and drew his day to a close. He drove to Fisherman's Cottage, and arrived home this side of midnight to find Jack crashed out on the settee, TV still on, and a half finished bottle of Glenfiddich standing upright on the coffee table. He decided not to waken him, and went to bed, his heart torn for Chloe and hurting for Jack.

He slept in confusing fits and sweating starts, his mind firing images of Gail in tears, only to morph into a waif-like Chloe who turned away to swirl paint onto an upright canvas with handless stumps. He pulled himself from bed at 5:00 and checked on Jack, pleased to see he had made it to the spare bedroom, and the bottle of Glenfiddich still at half-mast.

On the drive to the Office, he called Forensics who confirmed the fingerprints from the coffee cup matched those of the amputated right hand, and an appeal for information on Chloe's whereabouts went out on the national and local news that day. Strathclyde Police had a young PW put on Chloe's clothes—black jeans, top, shoes, jacket—and walk from Jack's flat down to Byres Road then on to Great Western. Without knowing which route Chloe might have taken, they tried several. By the end of the day no one had come forward. It seemed as if Chloe had stepped from Jack's flat and vanished in broad daylight.

To make matters worse, Bertie McKinnon, a local hack with a pathological distrust of Fife Constabulary, and Gilchrist in particular, stirred up local discontent with a passion. The incompetence of the Crime Management Department was spread across the front pages for all to see, with photographs of Gilchrist, the hapless SIO, in an assortment of unflattering poses. One inflammatory photo showed him standing alone on the sixteenth fairway, looking at his feet, scratching his head, under the headline *WHAT TO DO?* Another caught him stepping out of Lafferty's with the caption *MURDER'S THIRSTY WORK*.

In support of Strathclyde's efforts, teams of plain-clothed detectives and uniformed constables from Fife Constabulary were dispatched throughout the east coast. Farms on the outskirts of St. Andrews were searched. Gardens, outhouses, sheds, huts, barns, stables, even pig sties and a child's tree-house were all turned over.

But they found nothing.

And nothing could be made of the two notes. It was a mathematical impossibility to find a sequence from only two words. No fingerprints were evident, as if the notes had been first cleaned then slipped between lifeless digits. Only Watt's fingerprints were found on the scrap of paper pulled from under his windscreen wipers. And Watt still maintained that he removed it without thinking, believing it to be nothing more than an advertising flyer.

By the end of the third day, the investigation appeared to be stalling. All they seemed to have was a list of names and addresses of artists and students, parents and cousins, shop owners and paint suppliers.

But no suspects. Not even close.

Although Gilchrist would never say it, he was praying the killer would feed them another body part with another note, just so he had something to go on. So, when Greaves called him into his office, he expected the worst.

Newspapers lay scattered across the surface of Greaves' desk.

Gilchrist closed the door with a firm click.

"What the hell's wrong with this bloody fool, McKinnon?" Greaves slapped the back of his hand across a front page photograph of the SOCO van on the sixteenth fairway. Three SOCOs, coverall hoods pulled back to reveal smiling faces, sipped tea from a silver flask and ate sandwiches. The caption *TEE BREAK* summed it up.

"He hates the local police," Gilchrist said.

"But you in particular, Andy." Greaves lowered his head, eyed Gilchrist over the rim of some imaginary specs. "What have you done to the man, for God's sake? Skipped your round? Buy him a pint. Buy him a dozen. Just get him off our backs."

"Not as simple as that."

"Quite." Greaves picked up a newspaper folded open to the photograph of Gilchrist stepping from the Dunvegan Hotel. He smacked the image with the back of his hand, as if clipping Gilchrist around the ears. "This does not present a good image of Fife Constabulary, Andy. I have to tell you that."

"I was interviewing Tam Dunn again."

"I'm sure you were."

"It was eleven thirty at night, and I wasn't exactly celebrating."

"That's not the point. The public doesn't expect to open

their newspapers at the breakfast table and be confronted with photographs of Senior Investigating Officers looking like they're out on the town when we've got such a bloody gruesome case to solve. Makes us look like the Keystone Cops, for God's sake."

"I really don't—"

Greaves held up his hand, as if stopping traffic head on. "I don't want excuses, Andy. I want results. And I want results *now*."

Gilchrist eyed Greaves. They were getting down to it, and he did not like where it was heading.

"And we can't have you and Watt bloody well squabbling in public."

Greaves was referring to an incident at the University yesterday where Gilchrist had grabbed Watt's arm and pulled him back from a heated interview with a student. The depth of Watt's anger had surprised him.

"Are you any further forward?" Greaves demanded.

"I would be lying if I said yes."

"Bloody hell, Andy. McVicar's been on the phone twice today. Heat's been turned up. Bloody flame's turned from orange to blue, and aimed in my direction. I don't like it, let me tell you." He leaned forward. "Tell me something I want to hear, Andy. Give me something to calm the man down."

Big Archie McVicar, Fife Constabulary's Assistant Chief Constable, was a staunch supporter of Gilchrist. But there had to be a limit to the man's patience. Gilchrist needed more than a pair of amputated hands and an army of police officers scouring the countryside. Like Greaves, he needed a result.

"Anything?" Greaves tried.

Gilchrist grimaced. Fabricating nonsense would help no one. "Nothing," he said.

"What the hell am I supposed to tell him, Andy?"

"That we're looking to increase manpower?"

"We've no one else to put on the bloody thing, for God's sake. We're stretched to the bloody limit as it is."

"Chloe Fullerton lived within the jurisdiction of Strathclyde Police. I would think a call from the ACC—"

"Don't," snapped Greaves. "The answer's an emphatic No."

Gilchrist had anticipated no support on the touchy subject of requesting assistance from outside sources. He had tried the back door himself. But even Dainty had given him a body-swerve, saying he was up to his oxters in alligators of his own. Police units throughout the nation had their own tight budgets to meet. "We're doing what we can," he said, "but without the rest of the body we can't expect much."

"Well, do something, Andy."

It was on the tip of Gilchrist's tongue to ask for Watt to be replaced, but he thought better of it. "We're widening our search," he said, "but the body's nowhere near here."

"Where then?"

Where indeed? "Glasgow," he said.

"You have proof?"

Gilchrist shook his head. "Just a hunch."

"For God's sake, Andy. I need more than just a hunch. I need evidence. I need results. I need. . . . Oh for God's sake, just get bloody well on with it, will you? I'll think of something to tell Archie."

Gilchrist felt his face flush as Greaves reached for his phone.

The meeting was over.

Outside, an easterly chill swept in from the sea and seemed to funnel its way along North Street. Overhead, gulls fought with the night storm, wings flashing white as they tumbled and swooped in the stiff gusts.

Gilchrist pulled his collar around his neck and walked towards College Street. The proverbial shit was piled at the fan and splattering through the system. First, ACC McVicar. Second, CS Greaves. Next, DCI Gilchrist, acting SIO in a case stacked against him. His name was printed on a note, and the press were baying for results. Thoughts of having it out with McKinnon surged through his mind for an angry moment, then he glanced at his watch.

Just after 8:00. To hell with it. He needed a pint.

He reached the corner of College and Market Streets and veered left into the Central Bar, promising to have greater willpower in matters of import. If McKinnon photographed him once more with a pint in his hand, well, that was just too damn bad.

The bar was redolent of cigarettes, beer, and warm food. The air swirled thick and blue under a high ceiling. Piped music competed with raucous laughter. High in the corner a television screen showed a muted football match. Rangers and Hibs, it looked like.

He found a vacant spot at the bar, close to the till, and managed to catch the barmaid's eye. She mouthed, *With you in a moment*. While he waited, he dialled his own home number to talk to Jack, but was shunted into voice mail. He left a message, telling Jack he would be home shortly, and keep your hands off the Glenfiddich. He glanced up to see Nance waving at him from the opposite end of the bar.

When he joined her, she said, "Caught."

"You or me?"

"Both of us."

Gilchrist smiled. Nance was hardworking and thorough. If she wanted to have a drink at the end of a day's shift, then who was he to question her?

"Pint?" she asked.

"You talked me into it."

She laughed, a staccato chuckle that almost took him by surprise. It had been some time since he had seen Nance happy. He had heard she had split from Gregg, her partner of eighteen months.

Nance ordered two pints of Eighty-Shilling.

"On your second already," Gilchrist said. "Must've been a hard day."

"Hard partner, more like."

"How are you getting along with my favourite DS?"

"Sarcasm doesn't become you."

Gilchrist scanned the faces around the bar. "He's not here, is he?"

Nance shook her head. "He's checking out a lead."

"Taking the dog for a walk?"

Nance chuckled. "I've stopped asking," then tipped the remains of her first pint to her lips. "Cheers."

Gilchrist did likewise, loving the beer's smoothness as the first mouthful slid down his throat. He returned his glass to the counter, ran his fingers across his lips. "Boy, was I ready for that."

"Have you heard about the sweepstake?" Nance asked.

"What sweepstake?"

"Watt's started a sweepstake on when the next body part will turn up, and which part it will be." She grimaced. "He's one disturbed human being, let me tell you."

An image of McKinnon writing a scathing article on Fife Constabulary's gambling over murder enquiries burst into Gilchrist's mind with the force of an electric strike. He felt his teeth clench. Watt had to go. The man was a liability. He made a mental note to have it out with him first thing in the morning and have all bets forfeited and the monies deposited into the charity box. Then the slimmest of ideas shimmered before him.

"Did Watt put on any money?" he asked.

"He led the way."

"Which body part?"

"Leg."

"Left or right?"

Nance looked at him as if he had sprouted horns. "I don't know."

"And when does he bet this leg is going to turn up?"

"Tomorrow," Nance said. "You're not suggesting. . . ."

"Not really. But it's an interesting thought all the same."

Gilchrist lifted his pint. He had not heard from Martin Coyle about Watt's phone records. Maybe Coyle could turn an interesting thought into something worthwhile.

"**HAUD ON THERE,** big man," said Wee Kenny. "Watch what you're doing."

Jimmy Reid grimaced. "Just hold the fucker steady. Is that too much to ask?"

Wee Kenny scowled as Jimmy placed the red-hot poker flat against the skin. Black smoke curled into the air as he pressed down and rolled his wrist to ensure a deep brand.

"What's the matter, wee man? Never smelt burning meat before?"

Wee Kenny put a hand to his mouth. "That's fucking honking, so it is."

Jimmy returned the poker to the brazier, slid grimy fingers across his forehead and licked the sweat from them. He seemed always to be sweating now. He had a touch of the flu. That was all. He hawked phlegm from the back of his throat and spat a gob of green into the brazier where it hit with a hard hiss then bubbled and popped. Then he removed a flat tin from his pocket and fingered tobacco onto a strip of Rizla paper. He evened it out, rolled the paper, ran his tongue along the edge. He pulled the poker from the fire and held it to his face. As he drew on his cigarette, acrid smoke forced his eyes to water, and he slapped the poker back onto the skin.

Wee Kenny jumped, but kept his grip.

Jimmy held his cigarette in one hand, stirred the poker in the brazier with the other. Cigarette smoke shifted in the still air. He half-closed his eyes. The heat from the brazier felt as hot as the Spanish sun. He hated the sun. The sun was no place for a man to sit out in. He stabbed the poker at the coals. Sparks flickered then died in the night air. He felt a sudden need to just get on with it, and drew the tip of the poker across the skin in a curve.

Curling fingers of black smoke rose into the darkness.

"What's it say, big man?"

For a moment, Jimmy thought of pressing the poker to Wee Kenny's face. That would shut the fucker up. But he gobbed again and worked in silence, laying the poker on the skin, twisting and branding, taking pleasure from Wee Kenny grimacing from the stench of burning skin and putrescent meat.

When it was done, he eyed his handiwork.

Wee Kenny squinted at it. "Blood-what?" he asked. "Is that how you spell blood?"

"It's not blood."

"I thought it said—"

"Don't be so fucking stupid," he snarled. "Just wrap the fucker up."

Wee Kenny pulled a polythene sheet from the box and did as he was ordered.

Jimmy took a final drag, the short stub crimped between the tips of his thumb and forefinger. He sucked in hard, felt the dowt's burning heat, then flicked it into the brazier.

Wee Kenny glanced up at him, then returned his frightened gaze to the poker, staring at the handle sticking out of the red coals, at the tip glowing white-red. He knew Wee Kenny was scared of him. That was the way it should be with goffers. Wee Kenny had seen him in action before, seen him with his brother, Bully. He told Wee Kenny that you could never tell with Bully. But you could never tell with himself either.

You just never knew the minute.

Wee Kenny hugged his gruesome parcel to his chest. "Is that us?"

Jimmy hawked another gob onto the brazier. "That's it, wee man. Let's go."

Chapter 10

GILCHRIST PEERED AT the digital display.

5:01. Bloody hell. He reached for his mobile phone and pressed *Connect*.

"Gilchrist." He tried to sound awake, but his voice betrayed him.

"We've got another body part, sir. Report's just come in."

Gilchrist slid his feet from under the quilt. "Whereabouts?" he growled.

"Near the Golf Museum."

"On the Old Course?"

"No, sir. By Golf Place."

Opposite the R&A clubhouse. Not a bunker in sight. "Who's at the scene?"

"PW Lambert, sir. She called it in about a minute ago."

Dorothy Lambert. Dot to friends and colleagues. "Which part is it this time?"

"Leg, sir."

Gilchrist grimaced as Nance's words came back at him. *Watt's started a sweepstake.* "You called anyone else?" he asked.

"Not yet, sir."

"Have Nance meet me at the scene," he growled. "And don't call Watt until. . . ." He glanced at his watch. ". . . 5:45. On the button."

"Sir?"

"And get Bert Mackie and his team down there right away. I'm on my way."

He stumbled to the bathroom. Rain battered the frosted glass. He brushed his teeth, felt his stomach lurch, and coughed into the sink. Why had he let Jack persuade him to have a half? Just the one. But one always led to two. He tried to convince himself that he'd had a few to keep Jack company, get his mind off Chloe. At that thought he coughed again, spat out a dribble of bile. Jesus. Was he really about to see Chloe's hacked off leg?

He stared at the mirror, ran a hand over his face, felt the hard brush of stubble on his chin. Slivers of grey pressed by his ears. He tried a smile. It was a toss-up as to which was whiter, his teeth or his face. The bags under his eyes looked as dark as mascara. If he ever thought he was a looker, those days were gone. Maybe it was just as well Gail had found Harry. And how could he blame Beth for running off to Spain?

He shaved and showered, and as he stepped into a brisk east coast breeze he made a promise to himself that soon he would retire. He would take up photography again, be more serious this time, maybe turn the front room into a gallery, make a few bob selling framed photographs, just enough to supplement his pension. Much more sensible than running around at all hours of the day and night looking at body parts.

Twenty minutes later, he parked his Merc by the side of the R&A Clubhouse. The rain had stopped, the air as fresh and cold as ice. He removed a set of coveralls and gloves from the boot, put his head down, and marched into the wind. Winter on the Fife coast could be freezing cold. That morning was making no exceptions.

Ahead, the lone figure of PW Lambert stood as still as a silhouette by the dulled light from a streetlamp on the opposite side of the road, the area devoid of police tape and cones.

Gilchrist reached her. "Where is it, Dot?"

"This way, sir."

He thought her voice possessed a hint of a shiver, from the cold or her gruesome find, he could not say. She pointed to a rolled sheet of plastic that lay just off the back of the path, then stepped to the side, as if in deference to his seniority. The plastic sheet had split open to reveal the knee joint and a length of white calf.

Gilchrist slipped on his coveralls and gloves.

He eased back the sheet to reveal the painted toenails of a left foot. Rain dotted the plastic's grimy surface, but from the length of it, Gilchrist could tell it was a complete leg. He grimaced. *Left leg.*

Watt had won the sweepstake. A guess? Or had he known?

Gilchrist promised himself he would tear it out of him.

The package had been dumped on the grass next to the putting green, and by the way it had burst open Gilchrist would bet a month's wages that it had been thrown there.

Tossed from a passing car?

"How did you find it?" he asked Lambert.

"It was just lying there, sir."

"Which way were you walking?"

She glanced over his shoulder, away from the beach, past the R&A Clubhouse. "From that way, sir."

"Did you walk along the Links Road?"

"Yes, sir."

"From the pathway by the Jigger Inn?"

"Yes, sir."

"So, from the Jigger it would take you what, five to ten minutes to walk from there to here?"

"About that, sir. Yes."

"During which time this road"—he swept an arm from the seafront to Auchterlonies, down past Tom Morris's to the house at the end of the terrace that overlooked the eighteenth tee— "would have been in your view."

"Yes, sir."

It would have been dark, too. But still. . . .

"Did you see anyone?" he asked.

"No, sir."

"Any cars? Anything?"

"Sorry, sir. I was just walking past when I happened to look over and see it."

Gilchrist nodded. At night, this was a quiet part of town. No reason for anyone to walk or drive that way, unless they were heading to the beach. And who would do that in the pre-dawn hours of a winter morning? He turned to The Scores, the road that ran uphill at right angles to Golf Place. Hotels lined one side and overlooked an expanse of grass that fell away to rocks and the beach below. Martyrs' Monument stood dark and tall as a silent sentinel.

Gilchrist eyed the hotel windows. Most lay in blackness, but beyond The Scores Hotel a few rectangles of light spilled into the pre-dawn gloom. Had someone glanced out one of those windows? Had anyone heard anything, seen anything?

He shifted his gaze to the junction at the top of the hill. If you turned right at the Dunvegan, then through the mini-roundabout, that put you on the road out of St. Andrews. And he saw in his mind's eye that the car had come from Glasgow. That was where Chloe and Jack lived. Why hide her body anywhere else? He would challenge Greaves again on working closer with Strathclyde Police.

From somewhere beyond the buildings that bordered the eighteenth, he heard the unsteady rumble of a car's exhaust. He eyed the road out of town and caught the shiver of parting head-lights beyond the hedgerows and shrubs.

But at that time in the morning it could be anyone.

He turned his attention back to the polythene package. Through the sheeting, the leg was slim, verging on the skinny. It lay at an angle, so the inner thigh lay exposed. A lump choked his throat. Had Jack's hand caressed that leg in moments of intimacy? How could he let Jack see this? He was torturing himself. What the hell would it do to Jack?

He kneeled. The grass felt cold through his coveralls. The leg had been amputated at the top of the thigh, cut at an angle. He tugged the sheeting, eased it back. The wind shifted at that moment, and he thought he caught the smell of burning. He looked up, sniffed the air.

Maybe he'd imagined it.

He shifted the sheet a touch more.

From the marks on the thigh bone and the roughness of the meat where the skin had been cut he guessed the leg had been amputated with a saw.

Mackie would be the one to make that call.

It struck him all of a sudden that there was no note. Which puzzled him. Was that not what this was about? The killer taunting Gilchrist, torturing him, making him pay for the wrong some lunatic conceived had been done against him? And with that, he gripped the plastic and pulled it back.

A rush of ice chilled his blood.

Dear God. There it was. His note. Branded into the skin.

He let go of the plastic, slipped on the wet grass, landed on his rump, and scrambled back, back with his elbows, away from the leg, away from the message that—

"Sir?"

He looked up at Lambert and forced a smile. But his lips jerked instead. "Slipped," he said. She helped him to his feet. He brushed a hand over his coveralls, tried to convince himself he had seen worse. The five-year-old girl they pulled from the mud of the Kinness Burn four years ago. Even Mackie had gagged when her head slipped through his fingers, leaving him holding her peeled off face as her skull bounced and skittered on the post-mortem slab. But it had still not been as bad as this. This was personal. Chloe had been murdered so her hacked off body parts could be sent to Gilchrist as some kind of morbid message.

He gritted his teeth, held his breath as he bent down to the amputated limb. Christ, just get on with it. He lifted the plastic so the leg could slide free. But it stuck for a second before ripping free and rolling onto the grass to reveal a mass of blackened scars that ran from the top of the outer thigh to halfway down the calf.

He stared at the disfigured letters, at first unable to make sense of the mess, then deciphered the single word.

BLUDGEON.

The smell hit him again, a warm guff that rose from the blackened skin like a pall of invisible smoke that found its way into his mouth and lungs—the stench of the burned flesh of his son's girlfriend. He felt his stomach lurch, and he stumbled to the side. He bumped into the wooden fence, hung over it, and dry-heaved onto the grass.

Then Lambert was by his side. "Sir?"

He straightened, dragged his hand across his mouth. "Jesus, Dot. Sorry." He closed his lips, faced the wind, took a deep breath. The air smelled clear, cold, devoid of the stench of cooked meat that lay like a coating of filth on his tongue. He coughed, tried to clear his throat, but resisted spitting in front of Lambert.

"Sir?"

"I'm fine, Dot."

"It's not that, sir." Her eyes glistened in the cold, like those of a child reflecting her hidden fears. "I think I remember seeing a car."

"You *think*?"

She nodded.

"I don't follow."

"It was parked on The Links Road. I remember seeing it as I walked past. It was there five or ten minutes ago, but it's not there now."

Gilchrist followed her line of sight. "Five or ten minutes ago?" he said. "When I was looking at the. . . ."

"Yes, sir. It was parked at the corner."

"Did you get its registration number?"

"No, sir. But it was a Vauxhall. A Vauxhall Astra."

"You sure?"

"Yes, sir. I've been thinking of buying one, and I—"

"Colour?"

"Dark-blue. Black, maybe."

Gilchrist eyed the corner of The Links Road that paralleled the eighteenth fairway, and realised what the earlier sound of the engine had been. "Facing downhill?"

She thought for a moment, then nodded. "Yes."

Gilchrist stripped off his gloves and coveralls, threw them to the ground, pulled out his phone. "Stay here," he ordered. "Nance is on her way." He ran to his car, had his keys in his hand and the Office on his mobile by the time he opened the door.

"Crime Management."

"Call Cupar Division," he ordered. "Tell them to set up a road block and stop all cars out of St. Andrews." He switched on his engine. "We're looking for a Vauxhall Astra, dark-blue, black, or any other car that looks like it. All occupants are to be considered armed and dangerous." He pulled into reverse, hit the pedal, and tugged the wheel.

The Merc's tyres squealed as it raced up Golf Place. Cupar was about ten miles west of St. Andrews on the A91, the main road to Stirling. And Glasgow.

It was a long shot. Maybe his longest yet.

But if they were quick enough. . . .

Chapter 11

GILCHRIST PASSED **T**HE Links Road and noted the spot where the Vauxhall Astra had parked, a dry patch on the road, darkening by the second from a steady drizzle moving in from the sea.

He played out the scene in his mind's eye.

Car parked at the corner, its occupants peering through the windows to make sure their grisly package was found. Then releasing the handbrake and cruising downhill, into gear and the clutch out.

That was the sound he had heard, the Astra bump-starting.

He powered through the mini-roundabout and raced out of town. The clock on the dashboard read 5:43. Ahead, the Roadster's twin beams pierced the darkness. The rain had almost stopped, and the road glimmered with beads of water as bright as ice.

He roared past the Old Course Hotel to his right, its tan façade alight from an array of spotlights, then on to open countryside, all zipping past unseen in the pre-dawn dark, like nighttime memories.

He glanced at the dashboard—5:46. When had he heard the bump-starting? Fifteen minutes? Ten? Less? At sixty miles an hour, fifteen minutes would put the Vauxhall fifteen miles away. Through Cupar. And he would be too late.

Ten would be too late, too.

He grabbed his phone, poked in Nance's mobile number from his list of contacts.

She answered with a snappy, "Hold your horses, big boy. I'm on my way."

"Get onto the PNC and do a search for Vauxhall Astras," he said. "Dark-blue or black. I want names and addresses of all owners living in Glasgow."

"Care to tell me what's going on?"

"We have another body part down by the Golf Museum."

"The Office already called," she said. "The left leg."

"Surprise, surprise," he hissed. He felt his teeth grind. "When Watt shows up, make sure you nail his feet to the ground until I get back."

"Got it."

Another glance at the dashboard. Almost ninety. If the Astra was doing sixty, he was making up a mile every two minutes. If it had a ten-minute start on him, it would take twenty minutes to catch up. By which time he could have reached Cupar and had a cup of tea and a sandwich. That thought settled him down. No need to kill himself hounding the rabbit into the snare.

He eased his foot from the pedal and called the Office. As soon as he was connected, he said, "Has Cupar Division been called?"

"One minute, sir."

"Don't put me on. . . ." *Shit*. He pulled out to overtake a van, caught a glimpse of an angry face as he shot past. What were these people doing up at this time? Back into the inside lane, dabbed the brake for the left-hand bend, through it and foot to the floor again.

Seventy-plus. Still too fast.

He eased back.

"I have Cupar Division on the phone for you, sir."

"That's not what—"

"DC Grant Neville. How can I help?"

Gilchrist felt his jaw clench. Nothing had been done about setting up the road block. Not a damn bloody thing. He should have called himself. *Shit*. And *damn it*. He felt his foot pressing to the floor again. "This is DCI Gilchrist of St. Andrews Division," he said, struggling to keep his tone level. "I asked for a road block to be set up on—"

"Yes, sir. We're taking care of that."

Gilchrist felt a surge of regret at his misplaced assumption. Maybe he needed a refresher course on anger management. "That's good," was all he could think to say.

"The occupants are armed and dangerous," continued DC Neville. "What are we looking at here?"

All of a sudden, Gilchrist felt like the boy who cried wolf. What could he say? That it was a spur of the moment thing? That it was only a hunch? Greaves' voice came back at him, ingratiating as ever. *I need more than just a hunch. I need results.* Why the hell could he not keep his thoughts to himself?

"Sir?"

Gilchrist cleared his throat. "I'm SIO on the body part investigation in St. Andrews. A limb turned up half an hour ago. We believe the occupants of the Vauxhall can help in our investigation. We need to apprehend them for questioning."

"Do you have the registration number?"

"No."

"How many occupants?"

"Don't know."

"Male or female?"

"Don't know."

"Do you know if they're armed?"

Bloody hell. This was as bad as being cross-examined. "We don't know for certain," he said, "but he, she, or they should be approached with caution. Is that clear enough?"

"Very good, sir. Anything else I need to know?"

Gilchrist's mind turned up a blank. "I'll be with you in five minutes. Don't let any cars through until I get there."

"Very good, sir."

Gilchrist offered curt thanks and hung up.

He neared the Guardbridge roundabout, shot through it at

sixty-plus, and up the hill towards Dairsie. He tried to rationalise his thought process, but that niggling gut feeling of his was telling him to keep going, keep chasing, you've got them trapped.

At 5:54 he reached the roadblock, no more than twenty cars end to end in a line that stopped at a police car with blue twirling lights. He pulled his Merc onto the pavement, and switched off the engine. The ground felt dry, the air fresh and crisp. The rain had somehow missed Cupar. He walked past the end car, a yellow Fiat, then on past a white Lexus, then a tired-silver Jaguar XJ-12 with an unfinished repair to the boot lid. Under the streetlights the red-oxide patch looked like blood, which had him thinking what Chloe's last thoughts had been as she watched her lifeblood leave her.

Jesus, he was torturing himself. But images of Chloe's body lying in a pool of blood kept stirring in his mind. He thrust his hands into his jacket pockets and kept walking, past a decrepit pick-up with a ladder strapped to its roof, onto a Ford, past a Transit van, another Ford, and a—

The black Astra sat four cars from the front.

He forced himself to keep walking.

Exhaust fumes rose from idling engines like steam from panting horses. He felt his pulse quicken as he neared the Vauxhall. Almost on it. For one moment he toyed with the idea of just opening the driver's door and dragging whoever was inside onto the ground.

He drew level, threw a glance inside. The windows were misted.

But through the steamed glass he saw two passengers. Both male.

Then he was past it, fighting the urge to glance back.

He kept walking until he reached the police car, its lights rotating in the night air. Two uniformed constables stood with their backs to their car. He stepped up to the taller of the two, a smooth-faced hulk of a man, about an inch or so taller than himself. He flashed his warrant card and introduced himself.

The tall constable was Mark Graham. The other, Vic MacKay.

"Where's DC Neville?" Gilchrist asked.

"On his way, sir," Graham replied.

"Did he tell you what we're looking for?"

"Vauxhall Astra. Dark blue or black." Graham nodded over Gilchrist's shoulder and, with all the stiff-lipped subtlety of a trainee ventriloquist, added, "Like the Vauxhall four from the front, sir?"

"We've checked with PNC," MacKay said. "It's registered to a James Fletcher."

"Address?"

"Ardmore Street, Glasgow."

Glasgow. Was his hunch right? Was his sixth sense doing the impossible? He told Constables Graham and MacKay how he wanted to handle it. They nodded in understanding.

"Right," Gilchrist said. "Let's get on with it."

He turned to the first car, a glistening black BMW 531, and stepped onto the road. He waited until the driver opened his window, then said, "Sorry to keep you waiting, sir. You can drive on now."

The driver frowned, as if undecided whether to be annoyed at the delay or relieved it was over, then spurted through the gap between the police cars with a squeal from the tyres.

Gilchrist did the same with the next vehicle, an ageing Ford Capri and a carefree farmer, then the next, a Landrover and a platinum blonde in her seventies, two dogs in her lap. She had to be violating some traffic law, but he waved her on.

The Astra pulled level and drew to a halt as he held up his hand.

Graham and MacKay stepped onto the road in front of it.

Gilchrist tapped the window, leaned forward as it opened.

The driver tried a smile. "Any problems?"

Even from those two words, Gilchrist detected the hard Glasgow accent, the street-wise manner. Not your upper-class citizen. He eyed the passenger who sat with his face to the front, as if he could not look the law in the eye. "Pull off to the side of the road, sir."

The driver grimaced, swarthy features gaunt and rough from a couple of days' growth. "What's this in aid of?"

"Pull in over there, sir." Harder that time.

The driver bumped the Astra onto the pavement with a squeal of rubber that had MacKay reaching for his truncheon.

Gilchrist waved the remaining cars through while Graham stood next to the Astra and MacKay returned to his vehicle to carry out preliminary checks. When the traffic cleared, Gilchrist walked over to MacKay and pushed his head through the open window.

MacKay was seated, the driver's licence in one hand, his radio in the other.

"Does it check out?" Gilchrist asked.

"It checks. James Fletcher. The Vauxhall's registered in his name."

"And the other guy?"

MacKay shook his head. "Says his name is Joe Smith. I was thinking nothing out of ten for originality, then he hands me a passport." He held the burgundy-coloured passport up and gave a wry smile. "Joseph Smith."

Gilchrist frowned, doubts already niggling at him. Who carried their passport around with them? "Right," he said, and walked over to the Astra. He nodded to Graham. Like a choreographed act, he and Graham gripped opposite door handles and opened the passenger and driver doors in unison.

"Could you please step out, sir," Graham said.

Gilchrist smiled down at the upturned face, then stepped back as Fletcher slid out.

"Will someone tell me what the fuck's going on?"

"No need to use foul language, Mr. Fletcher." Gilchrist watched a mixture of anger and surprise shift behind the man's dark eyes. "Where are you driving to?"

"Glasgow Airport."

"From?"

"St. Andrews."

"Both of you?"

"Yeah. Me and my mate, Joe."

"Why?"

"What do you mean *why*? Because I like him. That's why."

"I meant, why are you driving to Glasgow Airport? Do you have a plane to catch?"

"Yeah," growled Fletcher. "We were going on our holidays until you lot stopped us."

Hence the passport. "Spain, is it?"

"Cyprus. Like to see the tickets?"

Gilchrist gave a short smile, doubt swelling in his mind. "Not at the moment," he said, then added, "Your car was spotted this morning parked adjacent to the Old Course."

"So?"

"What was it doing there?"

"That's where I park it."

"Overnight?"

"Yeah."

And at that instant, Gilchrist saw his error. The dry patch on the road surface. The storm had lasted the best part of an hour. The Vauxhall must have been parked longer than that, and he felt the beginnings of a flush warm his neck and work its way to his cheeks.

"Your licence has your address in Glasgow," he tried.

"We've just moved up here."

"To do what?"

"Look for work."

"As what?"

"Caddies."

"Where are you staying?"

"At a friend's flat."

"Student?"

"Yeah."

"Address?"

"A dump in Howard Place."

The Links was no more than a couple of hundred yards from Howard Place. "Why park in The Links?" Gilchrist asked.

"Starter motor's shot. Park at the top of the hill, so I can get a good run."

"For a bump-start?"

"Is that against the law?"

"Not yet," said Gilchrist, and tried another smile. *Shit.* How could he have been so blinkered? He had it wrong. Or was he missing something? He was about to buy Fletcher's story, when he frowned. "How long are you staying in Cyprus?"

"Nine days."

"Nicosia?"

"Limassol."

"Where are your suitcases?"

"In the boot. Where'd you think?"

If Fletcher was telling the truth, then either Gilchrist or Lambert should have heard the boot being closed. "This morning, did you?"

"Huh?"

"Put your suitcases in the boot this morning?"

"Last night. So we'd get a quick start." Fletcher must have seen the despair in Gilchrist's face, for he said, "Look, pal, we really do have a plane to catch. Do you mind?"

Gilchrist tried one final question. "When you fly back from Cyprus," he said, "how are you going to start your car at the airport?"

"Jump leads." Fletcher looked at his watch. "Why don't you look in the boot?" He held up his keys. "Here," he said. "Let me show you."

He raised the boot lid, pulled one of the cases out, and thudded it to the ground. Then he slipped his hands down the side of the other. "Look," he said, holding up a pair of jump leads. "Believe me now?" He threw them back into the boot with a whispered curse, and said, "Joe's got the tickets."

"Thank you for helping us with our enquiries, Mr. Fletcher." He tried a smile. What a fuck up. "Have a good holiday."

"Is that it?"

"It is."

Fletcher grunted and heaved the suitcase into the boot.

Gilchrist gave Graham a quick shake of his head, and heard the boot lid close with a force that made him think Fletcher imagined decapitating him.

Before the Astra drove off, Gilchrist called Nance. "Forget the PNC," he said. "It's the wrong car."

"There is a God after all."

"Praying for a break, were you?"

"Something like that."

"If you're going to pray for anything, Nance, pray that we find this guy. I think we're in for a rough ride."

He hung up and watched the Astra pull to a halt at the traffic lights. Maybe it was something in the heat of the moment, some surge of adrenaline in the anticipation of making an arrest that triggered his thought process. Or maybe not. Whatever it was, he had learned over the years to trust it.

Murder.

Massacre.

Now *Bludgeon.*

He whispered the words, rolled them around his mouth, not liking the feel of them, liking even less the dread surging through him like a wave of despair. Three. That was the magic number, the minimum needed to create a sequence. And he thought he saw the start of some sequence, some reason for the order in which the words were being fed to him.

But he could be wrong.

He dabbed his forehead. It felt sweaty and cold.

Which told him he was worried. He was worried sick.

His hunch with the Astra had been wrong. So wrong.

And he prayed to God that the thoughts stirring in his mind to reach their numbing conclusion were wrong, too.

But he could not rid himself of the fear that this time he was right.

"NEXT TIME I tell you to fill it up with petrol, you fill it up with petrol. You got that?"

"Yeah, big man."

Jimmy clipped the side of Wee Kenny's head.

"I hear you, big man, I hear you."

He clipped Wee Kenny's head again, once, twice, then balled his hand into a fist and thudded it into Wee Kenny's head with two quick hits.

Wee Kenny howled. Tears filled his eyes. But Jimmy knew Wee Kenny would not retaliate. That would make it worse. Wee Kenny had fucked up.

Jimmy punched him again, this time caught him on the ear.

Wee Kenny squealed. "Sorry, big man. Sorry. It'll no happen again."

"You're fucking right it'll no happen again."

His next punch glanced off the back of Wee Kenny's head. "Stupid wee fucker," he growled. "That could have been us back there. Done and fucking dusted. D'you fucking understand?"

Wee Kenny looked up with a silent plea, and Jimmy timed a punch to his mouth that cracked his lips and cut short any thoughts he might have had of trying to explain. "And how often have I told you to get the boot painted?" Jimmy roared.

"A lot of times, big man."

"That's right. A fucking lot of times." Jimmy leaned across and punched Wee Kenny in the mouth again, pleased to see that he had drawn blood at last. Then he pressed himself into his seat and gripped the steering wheel. The first thing he would do when he got back to Glasgow was organise a respray. Maybe change the colour. But he liked silver. The paint might look a bit dull. But it gave the Jaguar some class.

Except that dent on the boot still needed doing.

And after the respray he would take care of Kenny.

The wee man was becoming a fucking liability. Thicker than two short planks, so he was. He would talk to his brother, convince him that Wee Kenny was no longer fit for the job. Bully would understand, then give the thumbs-up. Or was it thumbs-down? He bet the wee man would bleed like a pig. Squeal like one, too. He smiled at that thought and reached over to Wee Kenny's shoulder.

"You all right, wee man?"

"I'm fine, Jimmy. I'm fine."

"Sit up, then. I'm not going to hit you."

"You sure?"

"Anyone can make a mistake." Jimmy smiled. "Don't worry about a thing, wee man. I'm going to look after you."

Chapter 12

GILCHRIST RETURNED TO the scene of the crime. Yellow tape stretched the width of Golf Place, and traffic cones diverted beach-bound traffic onto The Scores. The SOCO tent was erected, the van parked in the centre of the road, doors open. The wind had died, and dawn was peeling back a cloudless sky, as if the early morning storm had been only a dream.

He parked his Mercedes next to Mackie's Volvo Estate. He walked towards the tent where DC Alan Bowers, the Crime Scene Manager, was talking to Lambert. He saw no sign of Watt. He caught up with Nance scribbling in her notebook.

"Have you seen Watt?" he asked her.

"Been and gone."

"Did you tell him I wanted to talk to him?"

"Of course."

Gilchrist tightened his lips. Watt's insubordination stiffened his resolve to have it out with Greaves. But he needed to get moving with his investigation.

He nodded to the row of hotels and guest houses that ran along The Scores. "Before anyone has a chance to check out," he said to Nance, "I want you and Lambert to go to every door along The Scores. Find out which guests occupy the seafront rooms. Maybe one of them saw something." He glanced at his watch. "You don't have much time, so split up. You start with the Scores Hotel. Have Lambert take the one next to it. Then alternate after that. Get back to me by mid-morning."

Nance walked away as Mackie emerged from the SOCO tent

peeling his coveralls from his head. "Getting too old for this," he said to Gilchrist, unzipping his coveralls. He stepped out of them, ran a liver-spotted hand over a balding pate. "Bludgeon?" He eyed Gilchrist, his sandy eyes creasing against a brightening sky. "Any idea what it means?"

Yes, Gilchrist wanted to say. *And it frightens me to death*. "Not yet."

"Murder, massacre, bludgeon?" Mackie scratched his head. "What's this sick bastard trying to tell us? Tell you?" His gaze fixed on Gilchrist with a directness that could unsettle judge-hardened prosecutors, and for one moment, Gilchrist felt certain Mackie could see through his lie.

"The leg's a mess," Mackie continued. "The branding's uneven, probably as a result of not being consistently hot or applied with even pressure. You know what I'm saying?"

"A DIY job?"

Mackie almost smiled, a quick tug of the lips. "Starts off with the letters being over-branded," he went on. "Too deep. Too long. Running into each other. By the end, it seems as if he has it about right."

"Practice makes perfect?"

"That's one way of looking at it."

"And another way?"

"Anger."

Gilchrist waited for Mackie to continue. But the old man stared over his shoulder. Gilchrist had come to understand Mackie's periods of silence, when he gave the impression of being inattentive, but in reality was deep in thought.

"It's as if he was angry to start with," Mackie went on. "Then calmed down as he progressed."

"Worked his anger out?"

"Precisely."

"A sadist?"

"Definitely." Mackie raised an eyebrow. "Among other things."

"Such as?"

Mackie exhaled a long puff of air, and Gilchrist was almost wishing he had not asked the question. "I'm not a psychologist, of course. It's just a feeling." Mackie's jowls jiggled as he shook his head. "It takes a certain kind of mental dysfunction to cope with cutting up a human body," he said. "And an even greater insanity to brand words onto it. I would say whoever did this had to be more than cruel. He had to be devoid of feeling. No sense of compassion, no sense of ethics, moral or otherwise, an abject failure to consider the difference between right and wrong."

"Psychopath?" Gilchrist tried.

Mackie nodded. "At a minimum."

Gilchrist took a deep breath. He had dealt with a number of psychopaths in his day, had seen enough MRI scans on the brains of an assortment of criminals to know the neural activity in the pre-frontal lobe, that part of the brain that controlled impulsiveness, was lower in the brains of psychopaths than in normal humans. And without that ability to stop and think, to give consideration to the consequence of their actions, some psychopaths turned to murder.

Mackie cleared his throat. "This someone needs to be in control. The notes to you. The delay in the leg turning up. He's keeping you guessing, letting you know he's in control, or put another way, that you're *not* in control. And if I had to guess, I would say he's sexually deviant."

"Why do you say that?"

Mackie shrugged. "Another feeling."

Gilchrist thought he detected a hint of regret. "And?"

"This case is personal to you."

"Let's have it, Bert."

Mackie frowned. "Whoever is doing this gains little or no pleasure from normal sexual activity. At a guess I'd say he's into necrophilia."

Necrophilia? Gilchrist felt his lips tighten. For God's sake.

What could he say to Jack? He closed his eyes and in his mind's eye saw Chloe naked, her eyes staring blind-sighted to the ceiling, her small breasts shuddering from rhythmic thudding. . . .

Dear Jesus. He opened his eyes, gulped some air.

"Live bodies. Dead bodies." Mackie's jowls shivered. "I don't think it matters which to this demented creep."

Gilchrist stared off to the horizon. The sun was shooting pink streaks across the sky. How could the beauty of nature be spoiled by the rotten-to-the-core creature known as *homo sapiens*, who killed its own species for . . . for. . . .

For what?

Pleasure? Sexual satisfaction? Dead or otherwise?

He knew of no other species that killed for sexual pleasure. But maybe they were out there, hidden deep in some undiscovered tropical forest. Or at the microscopic level, where the struggle of life and death took on a—

"I'm sorry, Andy. I shouldn't have. . . ."

Gilchrist shook his head. "I need to know your thoughts, Bert."

Mackie reached for Gilchrist's shoulder, and squeezed. "How's Jack?"

Gilchrist thought back to last night, at Jack's show of bravado, at eyes that lay dead behind a forced smile. "Having a tough time."

"And you?" Mackie asked. "You look as though you've been out on the binge."

Gilchrist could use a pint right there and then, but was not sure he could keep it down. "Tired," he said.

Mackie gave Gilchrist one of his direct stares. "Any suspects? Any ideas?"

Gilchrist shrugged. "Working on it."

"I think the answer's in your past, Andy. Maybe someone you put away, someone vindictive enough to get even with you. Maybe someone recently released from prison."

Gilchrist's own thoughts had already paralleled Mackie's. Whoever was doing this wanted to get even for some reason, likely because Gilchrist's investigation had put him behind bars. He already knew that.

He had just not wanted to believe it.

"And cut back on the booze," said Mackie.

Gilchrist walked towards the seafront, the breeze refreshing on his face. He inhaled, tried to clear his thoughts, chase his fears away. *Cut back on the booze.* What was the point of that? So he could be stone-cold sober when he next witnessed the sickest depravities of mankind? He reached the seafront. Several joggers were already running along the West Sands. A woman slipped onto the beach from between dunes and marched across the sand with arm-swinging strides. He followed her progress, felt his mind pull him back to the cryptic notes.

Murder. Massacre. Bludgeon.

He saw a sequence. But it was too vague. He could be wrong. *Dear God. Tell me I'm wrong.*

He inhaled the sea breeze, reached for his phone. He was wrong. He had to be.

He needed to hear her voice, needed to know she was all right. He dialled her number and eyed the black silhouette of a ship sliding over the horizon.

"Hello?"

Maureen's voice sounded tired and heavy, and he pulled up an old image of a sleepy-headed toddler. He used to waken her with, *Wakey wakey let's get shaky*, and bounce her bed with a roughness that always pulled a smile to her face. Then she would reach up to him with tired little arms, and he would lift her from bed and carry her downstairs, the smell of sleep in her hair like her personal morning fragrance.

"Wakey wakey let's get shaky," he whispered.

"Dad?"

"The one and only."

A rustling of covers, then a tired chuckle. "It's been years since I've heard that."

"I love you, Mo."

A pause, then, "Where are you?"

"Looking out over the West Sands. It's going to be a beautiful day. Cold. But beautiful. A lovely day for a walk along the beach. Care to join me?"

Another chuckle. "Mum never said you were a romantic."

Something turned over in his stomach at that comment. He used to send flowers to Gail, leave silly little love notes on her bedside table or pinned to the fridge when he was out on a case. And it struck him that he could not recall when he had stopped doing that. And Gail, too. When had she changed? When was the exact moment she stopped loving him? And why did he still struggle with her not being in his life? Was it because she had taken Jack and Maureen with her? Or was jealousy still smothering his emotions? And as a dark shadow worked its way through his mind he wondered how much longer Gail had to live.

"How's Mum?" he asked.

"I saw her last night."

Gilchrist stared off across the water of the Eden Estuary, not trusting his voice.

"She's not well," Maureen said. "I mean, she's, she's desperately ill. . . ."

"She's not in any. . . ."

"She's on a morphine drip, Dad. It's only a matter of time."

Only a matter of time. Dear Jesus. When he and Gail married he would never have predicted this was how it would end. He had imagined they would grow old together, walk the beach with their grandchildren together. Not like this. Bitter and apart.

"Is there anything, I mean, can I do anything. . . ."

"I don't think so, Dad. I'm sorry."

He felt his head nod.

"Have you heard from Jack?" Maureen asked.

"He's here at the moment. Staying at the cottage."

A pause, then, "Is it true about Chloe?"

"It's looking that way."

"Oh, God," she whispered. "That's awful."

It's worse than awful, he almost said. *Necrophilia*? Surely Mackie was wrong. "Did you know Chloe?" he asked.

"Met her a few times."

"Recently?" he tried.

"A couple of months back."

"Before Christmas?"

"Yes."

"At Jack's?"

"In town. How's Jack taking it?"

"You know Jack. Doesn't say much," he said. "Keeps it to himself." He felt a sudden need to change the subject. "Will you be seeing Mum again?"

"I see Mum every day now. But with the drugs and stuff she's mostly out of it."

He hated asking, but the words were out before he could stop himself. "Do you think she might . . . she might want to see me?"

"Oh, Dad."

"Well then, if you can," he said. "If you get a chance, Mo, will you tell her I love her?" Maureen's silence only cut him deeper, made him feel the need to say more. "Will you tell her I've always loved her?"

"Oh, Dad."

The words were whispered, and in her whisper he heard the echo of his own pain. He watched a pair of labradors splash into the sea and wondered why he had been against buying a puppy for Jack. "Listen, Mo," he said, fighting to liven up. "Why don't you come up to St. Andrews this weekend? I could maybe wangle an early night, take you out for an Indian—"

"I'd love to, Dad. But I've got stuff to do. You know. With Mum. And work and stuff."

Her answer did not surprise him, but hearing her say she had work to do somehow settled his mind. "Sure, Mo. Love you."

"Love you, too, Dad."

He wanted to tell her his fears about the case. But how could he? He could be wrong, so wrong, and doing so would only frighten her. "Take care now," he said.

"Don't I always?"

"And call me."

"Sure."

"No. I mean it, Mo. Call me."

"Dad?"

"More often, I mean. We should talk to each other more often."

"Okay, Dad. But I've got to go. Love you," and hung up before he could respond.

He held onto the phone, listened to the echo of her voice in his mind, and worried that he should have been more direct with her. He felt that familiar need to fight off the dark feelings, heard his mind whisper, *Focus on work. It's how you've coped over the years. Cut everything else out and focus. On work.* So he called Stan and asked him to track down anyone recently released from prison, who had been put away by Gilchrist years ago. But only those who had killed before, on the theory that revenge by itself was not reason enough to kill for the first time.

Or was it? Well, it was as good a place as any to start.

He walked from the seafront, back to DC Bowers. "Who's checked in at the scene?"

Bowers opened his book. "Right here."

Gilchrist scanned the signatures. His own was not there because he had arrived before Bowers, although a note had been added by Lambert that *DCI Gilchrist arrived at the scene at 5:27 and thereafter identified the body part as a left leg.* Gilchrist calculated that by the time he had donned his coveralls and carried out a preliminary inspection it had probably been close to 5:35, 5:40, when he left the scene. Nance's signature was first after Lambert's at 5:44, then Watt's at 5:48.

Gilchrist thanked Bowers and walked past the R&A Clubhouse.

He reached his Mercedes and called the Office. "When was DS Ronnie Watt informed of the body part at the Golf Museum?" he asked.

"That would be, ah, here it is. 5:46, sir. You asked that we didn't inform him before 5:45."

Not quite, he wanted to say, but chose not to get into it. "Did you make the call?"

"I did."

"How did he respond?"

"He just said he would be on his way, sir."

Gilchrist snapped his phone shut.

Watt had arrived at the scene two minutes after the Office called, which meant he must have been on his way when they rang. Why would he be out and about at that time in the morning? He had guessed the correct body part. Had he also known when and where? It seemed that Watt knew more about the body parts than he should. Had someone called him before the Office had? If so, who? And why was Greaves hell-bent on having Watt on Gilchrist's team when he knew about their past?

Too many questions. Too few answers.

Gilchrist promised himself he would change that.

Chapter 13

"**MARTIN. ANDY HERE.** Any luck?"

"It's just come in. Like me to post it to you?"

Gilchrist accelerated out of Golf Place. "I'll pick it up." He confirmed Coyle's home address and assigned the directions to memory.

Twenty-five minutes later, after taking a wrong turn, he drove up to Coyle's home, a detached stone mansion that sat on the outskirts of Cupar. Coyle met him at the front door, wearing a dressing-gown that looked as if it should be binned. White legs as bare as sticks dangled to a pair of scuffed slippers. He smiled at Gilchrist. "Stop in for a cuppa?"

Gilchrist found it impossible to resist Coyle's gormless charm. "Why not?"

Inside, Coyle led him along a hallway with high-gloss doors that seemed out of character with the stone structure, and into a kitchen with grimy linoleum tiles centred by a beaten pine table. The room was redolent of coffee and toast, tainted by a musty fragrance that seemed to come at him from his side.

Two ageing dogs, a clot-haired collie and a matted wire-haired terrier, looked up at him with hound dog eyes, then rose from battered wicker baskets and kowtowed towards him, tails brushing the tiles. He leaned down, dug in his fingers behind the collie's ears, and said, "Names?"

"Jack and Jill," Coyle replied.

"Which is which?"

"Basket."

Both dogs skulked to their baskets, leaving Gilchrist to wipe his fingers on his trousers. As they stepped up and over the wicker edges, he could not help but notice how both of them were hung.

He raised an eyebrow at Coyle. "Jill?"

"They can't speak English." Coyle shrugged. "Linda's idea. Don't ask." Then he reached for a large envelope on the shelf and held it out. "This what you're after?"

Gilchrist thanked him, was about to open the envelope when the kitchen door swung open and Linda walked in wearing a threadbare bathrobe. A thatch of witch-grey hair looked as if it had not seen a brush for a month. She rushed over, put her arms around him. "Andy, love. How nice to see you again."

She felt soft and fat and smelled of bedclothes and dogs. He responded with, "Nice to see you, too," and was squeezed with a big-breasted bear-hug.

"We're so sorry to hear about Gail," Linda said, relaxing her grip. "Aren't we, Martin?"

Coyle smiled.

"How are you coping, love?"

Gilchrist felt his face flush. "Fine," he said.

"And the kids? Jack and Maureen, isn't it?"

"They're fine, too."

"Poor souls. I always think it's those that have to live on that suffer the most." She placed her lips to his cheek and kissed him. "God bless you, love." Then she stepped back. "Have you eaten?"

Gilchrist patted his stomach. "Had something earlier," he lied.

Linda scowled at the wicker baskets. "Who's a pair of lovely wonders, then? Eh?"

Gilchrist smiled as both dogs' back ends twitched with measured pleasure. Then he turned to Coyle and waved the envelope. "If you don't mind, Martin, I'll skip the cuppa. I really should get going."

Linda kissed Gilchrist on the cheek again, then Coyle led him to the door.

They promised to keep in touch.

Gilchrist waited until he could no longer see the mansion in his rear-view mirror before pulling off the road. He opened the envelope and removed fifteen pages of computer print-out that listed in columns from left to right across the page, date, telephone number, time of call, duration, and cost.

He checked the last call—outgoing to a mobile phone number he failed to recognise. Three days ago. At 22:54. Lasting two minutes. He found the first outgoing call that day at 04:49, and felt his brow furrow.

One minute only.

Watt had said he had risen early. To make a call? Who would he call at that time in the morning? Then he noticed it was the same phone number as the last call. So, the first and last calls of that day were both to the same mobile number. Which meant. . . ?

Gilchrist flipped through the rest of the pages, checked the very first call on the list.

Same number. 07:51. Three minutes long.

And the last call that day.

Same number. 23:03. Two minutes.

Gilchrist searched the lists for the same number, and found it. Three more calls had been made three days ago. He found a pencil and circled each of the numbers, ending up with five circles three days ago. And five again, the day before.

He worked his way back.

Watt's records never had fewer than a dozen calls on any given day, but always a minimum of three to that same mobile number, and almost always the first and last calls of the day. And the earliest time of any of the morning calls was seven days ago, at 04:07.

Gilchrist opened his mobile phone and punched in 141, which prevented the recipient from tracing the incoming call, then tapped in the number. He pressed the phone to his ear, not wanting to miss the slightest sound.

Fifteen rings later, he hung up.

He checked the print-out and tried again. He counted twenty rings, then hung up.

He could think of any number of reasons why the call would not be answered, but he worried that a sequence had to be followed, that perhaps it had to ring an agreed number of times, then hung up and tried again. If that was the case, then he had already blown it, and Watt was being warned off at that moment.

Gilchrist dialled the Office. "Put me through to Dick," he ordered.

Several seconds later, an upbeat voice chirped, "Hey, Andy. Long time."

"Can you do a reverse number check on a mobile phone number for me?"

A sharp intake of breath, then, "Could do. But it depends on which company. Some of them spring up out of nowhere, do the biz, then pow, just evaporate. Sometimes you can't get a damn thing. But I'll give it a go. Looking for a name and address?"

"At least."

"Need bank account details, driver's licence?"

"Give me what you can." Gilchrist recited the number, and said, "And as soon as."

"You got it."

Working back from the most recent date, Gilchrist looked for numbers he recognised. On the page that listed Watt's outgoing calls the day before he returned to Fife Constabulary, he came across a number that reverberated in the depths of his memory banks. He had seen that number before, but could not recall whose it was. He opened his mobile and ran through its memorised numbers.

Thirty seconds later he had a name.

His lips moved in silence as he compared the number, one digit after another, taking care to make sure it was correct, then failing to understand how it could be on Watt's records in the first place. He checked other pages, flipped the records over and over then back to the beginning to make sure the number on Watt's record, the number that should not be there, was the number he was reading.

But he was not mistaken. The number was right.

Starting with 0141, the code for Glasgow.

He ran through every page, but found it recorded only once. As if that would lessen the anger that swelled in his throat and stifled his breath. The call, the one call, the only call to that number he could find, had lasted all of sixteen minutes.

Which could mean only one thing.

She had answered. And Watt had spoken to her.

For sixteen minutes, a full sixteen minutes, DS Ronnie Watt had spoken to Maureen Gillian Gilchrist.

An image of Watt's bloodied face flashed into his mind with the force of a lightning strike. Then Maureen, face tearful and twisted with anger, burst through. He remembered how they had argued and, after calming down, how he thought he had talked sense into her. She promised she would never speak to Watt again. But now her promise had been broken.

And by Christ, she would tell him why.

He dialled Maureen's number, and counted ten rings before it struck him that he had checked Watt's records for her home number only, not her mobile. He hung up and searched his memorised numbers again until he found her mobile number. Then he searched Watt's records and found Maureen's number on five separate dates and circled every one of them. The calls ranged from twenty-six minutes, to the shortest at two minutes, three weeks ago, after which Watt had not called her mobile number again.

Did that mean Maureen and Watt had an affair that ended? That she wanted nothing more to do with him? Or was it worse than that? Was she calling Watt? Again, thoughts of having it out with her fired through his mind, until he saw that it was not his daughter he needed to talk to.

He crumpled the print-out into a ball, and threw it into the passenger seat.

"You bastard," he hissed, and thudded into gear.

The Merc's tires cut into the asphalt with a tight squeal. Only once before had his control failed him. And that was against Watt. He had almost lost his job over that incident. But back then, he'd had two children and a wife to consider. Now none of that mattered.

He had heard criminals say they would swing for the bastard. Now he knew how they felt.

SHE KICKED OUT, thought she hit a thigh, and tried again.

"Fuck—"

Another pair of hands gripped her ankles, and a man's voice, damp with spittle and stale with the smell of cigarette smoke, hissed in her ear.

"Steady, steady. . . ."

Already her peripheral vision was dimming. She tried to shake her head, break free from the rough hand that pinched her nose and pressed as hard as wood across her mouth. She screamed, but could only mumble, and knew she was using up the last of her breath.

Her lips felt as if they could burst under the pressure. Her lungs burned.

She tried another kick, but her legs could be wrapped in lead. She snapped her head back, thought she connected, but her heart felt as if it was about to explode. She thought she heard a voice mumble, "No," but it could have been the rush of blood in her ears.

The room darkened, the walls tilted, and the floor came up and pressed its woven carpet against her back.

Chapter 14

As Gilchrist neared the Old Course Hotel, all thoughts of choking the truth from Watt were put on hold. Two SOCOs were erecting an *Incitent* on the other side of the stone wall that bounded the hotel grounds. Had they found another body part? But no one had called him. As he reached for his mobile phone it rang. He expected it to be the Office, but it was Mackie.

"They said they couldn't find you."

"I'm almost with you, Bert. What've you got?"

"The other leg."

"And a note?"

"Cut into the flesh. Gouged out more like."

Gilchrist slowed down. Up ahead, the *Incitent* shivered in the breeze. Would this note confirm his theory? If the order was wrong, the cryptic message might not make sense.

"What word this time?"

"Matricide."

Gilchrist took a few seconds to go through the letters, then felt something heavy slap over in his gut. *Murder. Massacre. Bludgeon. And now Matricide.*

He hung up, stared off to the horizon, pressed his mobile to his lips.

He had his message.

He had known. He had known as soon as he had the third word.

And he had failed to act.

Two hands. Two legs. Four body parts. Four notes.

And he saw how the order could not be mistaken.

Left hand, right hand. Left leg, right leg.

The notes were being delivered in a specific order so the message was clear, with the simplest of codes so that he could not fail to work it out. He now knew he would be given three more body parts, all the killer would need to send his entire message. But it was worse than that. Much worse. If the killer planned on Gilchrist solving the puzzle, then he reasoned that it would be too late for him to be able to do anything about it when he did.

He parked on the expanse of grass that separated the Old Course Hotel from the main road, tried Maureen again, and cursed when it rang out. He should have been shunted into voice mail. He tried her mobile, but again could not get through.

Christ, it was happening. It was really happening.

He punched in the number for Strathclyde Police Headquarters and asked for Dainty.

"DCI Small speaking." The voice sounded thin, just like the man.

"Pete, it's Andy Gilchrist. I need your help."

"If I can, Andy."

"It's Maureen." He tried to sound calm, but could not control a quiver that seemed to catch the back of his throat. "Did you assign someone to watch her?"

"PC Tom Russell. He's a good guy."

"Can you have him bring her in?"

A moment's pause, then, "Care to explain?"

Gilchrist did, and Dainty reassured him that Maureen must be all right, or he would have already heard from PC Russell. But when he hung up, Gilchrist could not rid himself of the gut-sinking feeling that he was too late. It was her answering machine being switched off that worried him. Whenever Maureen was out, her answering machine was always on. It seemed to be how they communicated.

Now he was too late. And seventy miles too far north.

But Dainty was a good detective, and a good man, and Gilchrist took comfort from the thought that he would treat Gilchrist's request as if Maureen were his own daughter. And maybe, just maybe, Gilchrist could do something at this end.

Mackie greeted him with a hardened face and a spare set of coveralls and gloves.

Gilchrist pulled them on and entered the SOCO tent.

A faint yellow light spread over the scene, making the leg look as if it was made of plastic. Gilchrist kneeled. MATRICIDE was cut along the length of the inner thigh and calf. Although the curves of the R, C and D looked irregular, he thought the word had been formed with some care. The leg had been amputated at the top of the thigh, with a clean cut. But the cut had been made too high, and a thin strip of pubic hair trimmed the edge like the beginnings of a weak moustache.

Gilchrist felt his throat constrict. This was the leg of a young woman he had spoken to, laughed with, had a drink with, someone who shared a life with his son with all the youthful aspirations of the future.

What could he tell Jack?

"Same method of amputation," Mackie mumbled. "Some sort of saw. See here?" He pointed at the cut through the bone. "You can see the curved marks on the femur. See? And where it cuts into the skin. Here." He ran a pointed finger along the edge.

Gilchrist nodded.

"I would say circular saw. We may be looking for a workshop of sorts."

"Like a home workshop?"

"Could be."

Gilchrist frowned. He was looking at too wide a target. Anyone could install a workshop in their attic, garden shed, or God only knew where. He needed to refine it. "How about the saw marks?" he said. "Can we tell the size of the blade from the curve?"

"Might do," said Mackie. "But I wouldn't want to bank on a high level of accuracy."

"You might be able to define some diametrical limits."

"Possible."

Gilchrist eyed the leg, resisted touching the skin. "Why the different techniques?" he asked. "The first two notes were printed. The next two by mutilation."

"To make us think there's worse to come?" Mackie offered.

Gilchrist grimaced. Mackie had a point. If each body part was presented with a hand-printed note, where were the scare tactics? The purpose was to frighten him, let him solve the cryptic clues, so he would know revenge was being sought. He swallowed the lump in his throat, dabbed at the cold sweat on his brow. The tactics were working. He knew what the killer had planned, and now he needed a break in his investigation before, before. . . .

Jesus. It didn't bear thinking about.

Think. Damn it. Think.

But his mind refused to work.

"This guy's one sick bastard," he said, and pushed past Mackie, out into the open.

He freed his hair from the coveralls and peeled off the gloves. The cold air carried the tangy taste of kelp. He breathed it in, almost revelled in the light-headedness of the moment. He unzipped the coveralls, removed his phone to try Maureen again, and was about to punch in the number when Mackie said, "Andy?"

Gilchrist snapped his phone shut and faced Mackie. Deep intelligence hewn from a lifetime of pathology shifted like a shadow behind the old man's eyes.

"You know," Mackie said. "You know what the killer is saying."

Gilchrist felt his lips tighten. *Did* he know? Did he *really* know? He could be wrong. He hoped to God he was wrong. But every nerve in his body told him he was not. He shook his head. "I'm not sure, Bert," he said. "It's just a thought."

"Share it with me."

Gilchrist stared off past the hotel, across the fairways to the grass-covered mounds of the dunes where they had sat on the windswept sands drinking ice-cold champagne.

First Chloe. And now. . . .

"I think Maureen's next."

Silent, Mackie returned his stare.

"I think that's what the notes are trying to tell me."

"Why do you think that?" Mackie's voice resonated deep and calm. He placed his hand on Gilchrist's shoulder, and squeezed. "Run it past me."

"First note, Murder. First letter, *M*.

"Second note, Massacre. Second letter, *A*.

"Third note, Bludgeon. Third letter, *U*.

"Fourth note, Matricide. Fourth letter, *R*."

Gilchrist watched the meaning of his words work through the old man's mind.

"M, A, U, R," Mackie said.

"E, E, N," added Gilchrist. "Three more body parts." He watched Mackie's head turn to the side and his eyes stare at the tent, as if trying to imagine how he would feel if that leg belonged to his own daughter.

"I don't want anyone to know, Bert."

Mackie turned back to him, eyes creased against the sunlight. "Can I ask why?"

"I want whoever's doing this to think we don't know what's going on."

"Playing for time?"

Playing for time. What a way to put it. It sounded like a game. But it was no game. And Gilchrist saw then how he had run out of time. He should have had a couple of minders watch her round the clock earlier. But maybe he had it wrong. He stepped away from Mackie and opened his mobile. But he could still not get through.

He tried his cottage.

Three rings and he was through. He could not mention the latest leg to Jack. "I need to get hold of Maureen." He struggled to sound calm. "Do you know where she is?"

"Probably with Chris."

Gilchrist's hopes soared. "You have a number for him?"

"Sorry."

"Home number?"

"No."

"Address?"

"Never met the guy."

"You wouldn't happen to know his surname, would you?"

"Sorry."

"Thanks, Jack. You're a great help."

"Why don't you try Mo on her mobile?"

"Why didn't I think of that?" he said, and hung up.

He stared at his phone. When he had been Jack's age, had he been as uninterested in family? He saw, as if for the first time, how like Gail Jack was. And Maureen, too. Had he contributed nothing to the gene banks of his children?

He struggled to refocus.

Despite the obvious, he tried Maureen's mobile again, once, twice, then her home, counting twenty-two rings before hanging up. He glanced at his watch. Even if he jumped into his Merc at that moment, it would take him the best part of an hour and a half to drive to Maureen's. But what would that achieve? And that thought made him realise that he had to place his trust in Dainty. Dainty would call as soon as he found Maureen. In the meantime, Gilchrist would do what he could to move his investigation forward, and pray that he had it all wrong.

But if his worst fears were realised, even God could not help him.

SHE CAME TO, her face pressed against carpet pile as short and rough as sandpaper.

She opened her eyes, but in the darkness she could have been blind. She moved her arms, and realised with a spurt of panic that she was bound, her hands tied behind her back. She gasped, but a gag as tight as binding tape pressed her lips shut. She breathed in through her nostrils, hard, struggling to stay calm as other senses stirred awake.

The smell of dirt and petrol. . . .

The thrum of speeding tires. . . .

Her stomach lurched at that moment, from movement that told her she was in the boot of some car. And again, as they crested a hill at speed and another fear hit her in a cold wave as she fought off the dizzying sensation of motion sickness.

She could not throw up. Her lips were sealed.

If she vomited, she would choke to death.

No. Not this, not this. Concentrate. . . .

Her throat constricted as her stomach spasmed.

Dear God, no. . . .

Chapter 15

GILCHRIST CORNERED NANCE at Golf Place.

"Find anything?" he asked.

She opened her notebook to a tabbed page. "A Mr. Fraser Crowley, staying at the Glen Eden Guest House, saw a car race out of Golf Place at around 4:00 this morning."

"Details?"

"Not a lot, I'm afraid."

"Make? Model? Colour? Registration number? What?"

"Hold your horses. The elderly Mr. Crowley—"

"Elderly?" Gilchrist groaned.

"Fraser is seventy-two with a mind as sharp as a tack."

"First name terms, are we?"

"He's quite the lad."

Even so, Gilchrist felt a rush of disappointment. The elderly often proved unreliable witnesses and could break down in court under relentless cross-examination. Just how sharp was a tack at seventy-two?

"He thought the car was being driven erratically," Nance continued. "Before passing the R&A clubhouse it swerved across the road then sped uphill."

Gilchrist eyed the lone stone building. The car could have crossed the road so the driver could throw the package beyond the footpath. Had Crowley witnessed the leg being dumped?

"A Jaguar," Nance pronounced. "XJ-12 with silver paintwork."

Gilchrist blinked once, twice. He had seen a Jaguar just like that. It took him several seconds to remember where. The road-block in Cupar. He had walked past it, more focused on the Vauxhall Astra. Damn. Had that been *the* XJ-12? Was there any difference between the body of an XJ-12 and an XJ-6? If so, could Crowley have noticed it at that time in the morning? And from a hotel room window?

"Where was Crowley when he saw the car?" he asked.

"Martyrs' Monument."

"At four in the morning?"

"Said he had an upset stomach and went outside for a breath of fresh air."

Martyrs' Monument stood on the hill at the crest of the Scores. Which meant that Crowley would have been about a hundred yards away.

"Where is this Crowley?" Gilchrist asked.

LIGHT EXPLODED, BLINDING her.

Fingers as sharp as talons dug into her hair, pulled her upright, dragged her from the boot. The sudden movement, the brightness, the sense of freedom—

Her stomach pumped.

Vomit surged into her throat, choking her airways, squirting from her nostrils.

"Ah, fuck," and a hand as hard as a board sent her tumbling to the ground.

Fingers tore the tape free, letting vomit splash from her mouth.

She spat it out, gulped in lungfuls of cool clean air. But any thoughts of calling for help thudded into darkness as a fist as hard as stone cracked the side of her head.

IT TOOK THEM two hours to find Crowley by the rocks that fronted the Scores, kneeling by one of the sea pools, nothing more than puddles of seawater trapped by the receding tide.

Crowley looked up as they approached, then stood with barely a grimace. "Ah," he said with a grin. "The lovely Nancy Wilson." He came towards them, stepping over rocks with the sure-footed agility of a man half his age. Sunlight sparkled in eyes as blue as bleached denim. His teeth were gap-spaced, long and white. "We meet again," he said.

"This is DCI Gilchrist," Nance said. "My boss."

Crowley nodded, as if he was a competitor about to post a challenge for Nance's hand. "A pleasure," he said.

"You don't wear glasses," Gilchrist said.

"I'm a retired pilot. My eyesight has always been excellent."

"The Jaguar," Gilchrist went on. "You sure it was an XJ-12?"

"You can tell from the front grille."

"Expert on cars, are you?"

"Cars no, Jaguars yes."

"Own one, do you?"

"I own several. The pride of my fleet is a '73 convertible E-type V12. Rarely drive the thing, of course."

"Of course." Gilchrist felt a smile tug at his lips. Crowley looked like one of those individuals with a panache for life, who earned big money, drank fine wine, made love to beautiful women. And drove fast cars. "It was silver," he said to Crowley. "What else can you tell me about it?"

"1988-ish, I'd say. Run down. Not well looked after. Original paint job. Could do with a respray."

"And all this at 4:00 in the morning?"

"Not at all. I'd seen it before."

Nance pressed forward. "You didn't tell me that."

"You never asked, dear Nancy."

Nance glanced at Gilchrist. He took over. "Where exactly did you see it before?"

"Market Street. By the fountain. Last Tuesday."

"You're clear on that?"

"I visit the bank every Tuesday."

"What time was this?"

"Around 2:00 in the afternoon."

"Did you see the driver?"

"No."

"Any passenger?"

"Couldn't say."

"Eighty-eightish?"

Crowley's eyes creased, and Gilchrist caught an image of the younger man as a dashing pilot. "About that, I would say."

"Did you see the registration number?"

"I'm hopeless now with numbers," Crowley said. "Memory's not as good as it used to be."

"But you might have seen the number and associated that with a year of registration, then forgotten the number?"

Crowley shook his head.

"We'll run a search on PNC," Gilchrist said to Nance. "Every silver Jaguar XJ-12 from '86 through '90."

Nance scribbled it down.

"Would you recognise it again?" Gilchrist asked.

"Absolutely."

"When you saw it at that bank, how close were you?"

"Close enough to see the tax disc had expired."

"Did you note the month?"

"Now you're asking."

"See anything on any of the seats?"

Crowley shook his head.

"Papers? Documents? Umbrellas? Jackets?"

"Anything?" Nance chipped in.

"I wasn't looking."

"Spotless, was it?" Gilchrist tried.

"I wouldn't say that."

"What would you say?"

"Once I saw it was run down, I didn't give it too much attention. That's a big no-no for a Jaguar enthusiast." Crowley grimaced. "Tires were worn. Blisters of rust on the wheel arches.

The whole thing needed a good wash, wax and polish. Inside and out. It's a disgrace that a car so majestic could be treated with such disdain—"

"Any stickers? Aerials? That sort of thing?"

"The boot lid had been patch-painted."

Gilchrist stiffened. "Painted?"

"With red lead. Poorly, I might add."

Red lead. An undercoat used as rust prohibitor on metal. Gilchrist remembered the Jaguar in the roadblock, its boot as dark as spilled blood. "How long do you intend to stay in St. Andrews?" he asked Crowley.

"Until the end of the month."

"Then?"

"Spring in upstate New York with my brother."

"No Mrs. Crowley?"

"She passed away six years ago."

"I'm sorry," Gilchrist said, regretting having raised the subject of wives. Time to leave. "Give your full contact details to DS Wilson," he added. "And don't leave town without letting us know."

"Is that necessary?"

But Gilchrist was walking up the path towards Martyrs' Monument.

Crowley's sighting of the Jaguar last Tuesday troubled him. If it was the same Jaguar used to dump the leg, why had it been in town then? On the other hand, why not? The killer could have driven from Glasgow for a number of reasons. And Gilchrist felt something jar at that thought. The killer knew Gilchrist. Did he also know Watt?

When he thought about it, it seemed odd that on the day Watt returned to St. Andrews the hand was discovered. And Watt was first on the scene. First day on the job, first on the scene? Was that coincidence? But Gilchrist did not believe in coincidence. When things happened together they were connected. Believe that, and everything else fell into place.

He now saw the flaw in his earlier rationale. The killer had known Gilchrist would solve the cryptic clues. It then followed that Maureen would be taken long before the last body part turned up. Leaving it any later would risk Gilchrist's securing her safety. Maureen lived in Glasgow. And the Jaguar would be registered in Glasgow. On that he would bet his life. But he had taken no action. How could he have been so stupid? He looked down at the black rocks, at Nance still in conversation with Crowley, and saw he had to take action now.

He shouted, pointed to Golf Place, then ran.

He ran in that long-legged stride of his that had served him well on cross-country runs at school, and in later years through days of personal training. His gangly build would never permit him to be a sprinter, but he could jog at a steady pace for hours.

He had the Merc's engine started and the gear lever slotted before he closed the door.

He floored the pedal, reversed into Golf Place, and skidded to a halt.

Nance grabbed the door handle and jumped in as the tires squealed. The quick dash and the urgency with which Gilchrist had rushed into action had her breath pumping with excitement. She clicked on her seatbelt as the Merc accelerated up the hill. She knew him well enough not to press for details, and quipped, "Forgot a clean pair of underpants?"

Gilchrist turned right, raced across oncoming traffic.

Tires screeched. Horns blared.

Two pedestrians jumped back as if the road surface had scorched their feet.

Nance pressed her hands against the dashboard as the Merc tore across the roundabout at Pilmour Links and City Road. She had heard of Gilchrist's relentlessness on the job, but never experienced it first-hand. Now the set of his jaw, the look in his eyes, told her just how focused he could be.

"Call the Office and have someone check up on Jack," he ordered.

Nance put two and two together, and gasped, "First Chloe, now Jack?"

He shook his head. "Maureen."

The reality of Gilchrist's dilemma hit her like a punch to the chest. The case had just turned personal in a major way. She stared at him, watched him eye the road ahead with cold determination, but thought she caught the look of something else in his face—fear.

"Start praying," he said to her, as he pulled out and overtook three cars.

"For good brakes?"

"That we're not too late."

Chapter 16

O N THE OTHER side of Cupar, Dainty called Gilchrist.

"Maureen's slipped us."

"What about your man—"

"That's another bloody matter," Dainty growled. "Followed her from her flat. On her way to work, he assumed. And lost her. In the city centre? It beggars fucking belief."

Gilchrist gritted his teeth. All his senses were screaming at him.

Too damn late. And stupid. So fucking stupid.

"Do you know where she works?" Dainty asked.

"Let me get back to you."

Gilchrist twisted his hands on the steering wheel. The problem was that he did not know where she worked. He'd never had a reason to call her at work, called her only on her mobile or at home. Wouldn't any normal father know where his daughter worked? Had he failed his family so completely that Maureen could not discuss her life with him? And it struck him that Jack might know.

He caught him on his mobile phone.

"Hey, Andy. How's it going?"

Jack's upbeat tone surprised Gilchrist, until he caught the hubbub in the background. "Which pub?" he asked.

"Quit playing Sherlock Holmes, Andy," Jack said. "But if you must know, it's the Whey Pat."

The Whey Pat Tavern. The pub where he and Gail first met. He had not set foot in it since Gail left, as if to do so was a violation of his memories of her, of his family, of how it used to be when they were in love, before his career and her infidelity destroyed what they had.

"You don't know where Maureen works, do you?"

"Changed jobs about six months back. Works in some big-shot agency in the city centre. Don't ask me where. Got the job through her latest boyfriend."

"Chris?"

"That's the one."

"And you've never met him?" he tried.

"Just the once. Utter plonker. Wads of cash. Buys every round. You know the kind. I hated him the instant I set eyes on his alligator-skin wallet."

Gilchrist felt himself deflate. Jack knew as little about Maureen's personal life as he did, which only compounded his feelings of failure. When he stumbled across Gail's affair with Harry, all he had wanted to do as a father was to convince Gail to stay with him. *Stay together for the sake of the children.* Is that not what parents did? But not Gail. At the first confrontation, she rushed off to Glasgow with Harry and the kids faster than a skelped cat.

"Mum wouldn't know where Mo works, would she?" Gilchrist asked.

"Not a chance, Andy. Sorry."

Well, that was that. He closed his phone. "No one knows where she is," he said.

"Maybe she's out shopping. You know, that thing women like to do."

Gilchrist tried a smile. But what was the point of faking despair? He should have acted sooner, instead of waiting for the next body part to turn up.

Murder. Massacre.

Even with those two words, he had seen something, been suspicious of the letters M and A being first and second in their respective notes. But two letters were not enough for a progression. And that was his mistake. He had known, God damn it. He had known.

But had failed to act.

And now he was acting, he was terrified he was too late.

On the unlikely off-chance that Maureen had phoned the Office, he called for his messages. None. Not from Maureen, not from Watt, not from anyone else. He asked for Chief Super Greaves, but was told he was unavailable. Jesus, he felt as if he was becoming obsolete. He drove on in silence, deep in the pit of his misery.

DARKNESS AGAIN, BUT this time not total.

Wooden floorboards, rough and grainy, pressed against her face.

Even lying on her side, she could make out the dark shape of a curtained window next to a narrow door rimmed with grey light. Dark shadows of four walls told her the room was small. She lay still, let her eyes adjust, worried at pulsing cramps in her stomach. If no one came soon, she would have to. . . .

She forced her mind off the body's natural urge, shifted her weight—

And froze at the rattle of a chain.

She choked back a gasp, and realised her mouth was gagged.

A cold frisson chilled her neck, ran the length of both arms, and turned into a tremor that shivered her body and caused tears to sting her eyes.

She held her breath, concentrated on catching the slightest sound.

Was she not alone?

MAUREEN LIVED IN a modernised apartment building in Glasgow's Merchant City. Once derelict and soot-covered, the brick and sandstone tenements had been refurbished and converted into low-tech office space and luxury residential flats.

Gilchrist parked his Roadster on a double yellow line.

He stepped into a grey Glasgow drizzle, and upped his collar to ward off the cold. The upmarket area surprised him. What had he expected? He eyed the sand-blasted façade, the pedestrianised streets, the painted bollards, the shining pub sign at the end of the road, all painted, all new. Even the cobbled walkway seemed to glisten in the rain.

"You never told me your daughter was a high earner."

"I never knew."

"What does she do for a living?"

"Last I heard she was studying to be a physiotherapist," he said, and puzzled once more at his failure to follow her career. He was about to push the entrance door open when he noticed it lay ajar. "Not as upmarket as we thought," he said, then felt a cold rush as he saw the lock was damaged, the wood splintered where it had been jimmied off.

His peripheral vision sensed movement to the side. He turned, watched a red Mini Cooper pull up with a sharp stop at the far end of the street. Something about the driver's look, a furtive glance his way, told Gilchrist he was watching out for someone.

And waiting?

On instinct, he walked towards the car. From that angle he could not read the number plate. He was halfway across the road when the Cooper's engine burst into life with a growl.

"Nance." He started running. "The number plate."

Nance surprised him by sprinting ahead.

The Cooper took off, front wheels spinning, and bullied its way down Candleriggs. He caught up with Nance in time to see its disappearing tail-end as it zipped from sight into Argyle Street. Nance had her mobile phone in her hand.

"Got it." She poked at the pad of her phone.

"I don't like this," he said, and jogged back towards Maureen's flat. Nance jogged alongside him, and he was surprised by how fit she seemed, how fluid her movement was.

"Run a check on PNC for me," she ordered into her mobile. "One of the new Mini Coopers. Red with a white roof." She recited the registration number.

Through the entrance door the clamour of their feet echoed off the walls. Maureen's flat was on the top floor, and Gilchrist took the stairs three at a time, Nance so close behind him that he swore he felt the heat of her breath on his neck.

They reached the landing together.

Gilchrist gasped for breath, tried to still the pounding in his chest. He thought he kept himself fit, but Nance was barely breathing.

"Is this it?" she asked.

He could only nod.

She gripped the handle. "Locked."

For a moment he thought he had screwed up, that the Mini was nothing to do with Maureen's flat, that he had it all wrong. Then an image of Maureen as a child crying flashed into his mind, and he remembered promising to do whatever it took to protect her.

He thudded his shoulder to the door. Solid. He tried again. It barely budged.

He stood back, lifted his foot, and heeled it hard against the lock.

The door rattled, maybe moved. But not much.

He kicked again.

"Almost there," Nance said, and kicked at the door in time with Gilchrist.

The lock burst open, and Nance beat him inside.

"*Police*," she shouted, and raced down the short hallway.

Gilchrist followed, opened a door on the left. Bedroom. No curtains. No furniture.

Ahead, Nance crashed through the door at the end of the hallway.

Gilchrist watched her fall off to her right, then leap backwards in a move that defied the laws of physics. Glass smashed. He rushed to her aid, burst into the room, and charged at the body as a foot lifted and caught him a fraction too high to threaten his manhood.

He grunted from the blow, pulled his handcuffs out, whipped them like a chain at a gloved fist that caught him on the chin and snapped his head back. He hit the edge of the door as his knees cracked the floor, and he reached out at the departing figure. His fingers touched fabric, caught it, gripped tight. A black leather boot buried its toe into his shoulder. It swung again, connected with his chin.

He felt his teeth crack and his grip slip free, and he grunted in despair as long legs strode off and slipped through the door. He pulled himself to his feet, flapped a hand at the wall, missed it, and stumbled across the room. By the time he reached the window and fumbled with the blinds, the figure, a tall man dressed all in black, was running across the cobbled street, phone to his ear. At the corner, he waved an outstretched arm as the Mini Cooper pulled level. He opened the door and jumped in as the Cooper sped away.

Gilchrist retreated from the window, relieved to feel his teeth intact.

Nance had her hand to her stomach. "Caught me where it would hurt if I was a man," she grimaced. "Wasn't expecting it." She reached over her shoulder. "And my back hurts."

"Let me look."

She surprised him by lifting her blouse. Her skin looked white, her waist slim, her physique more athletic than he imagined. "See anything?"

He eased her blouse up her back to reveal a black sports bra.

She twisted an arm behind her and tapped with her finger. "Just about there."

He eyed an angry welt at the base of her shoulder blade, already darkening to a bruise. "The skin's not broken," he said, "but it could hurt for a while." He thumbed the bruise, felt her body jerk. "Sorry," he said.

"Remind me never to come back to your surgery."

"Nothing's broken," he said, and noticed a short-legged coffee table twisted askew on the rug, the remains of a glass tumbler in the corner near the stereo set. "I'd say you hit the corner of the table." He let her blouse drop, and she surprised him once more by unzipping and tucking it in, giving him a glimpse of skimpy underwear.

Then she lifted her hand to his temple. "You're bleeding."

He almost pulled away. "Will I live?"

"Regrettably." Then she stepped back. "Just a graze." She looked around the tidy room and grimaced. "I'd say we got here before he had time to steal anything."

"Who said anything about stealing?"

"What do you think he was doing? Choosing furniture?"

"Looking for something."

Nance raised an eyebrow. "Looking for something?"

Gilchrist moved through the room, fingered a pile of CDs on a shelf, an eclectic mix of old and new—Marti Pellow, Elton John, Nelly Furtado, Lionel Ritchie—and he saw in Maureen's collection the wants and longings of a young woman searching for love.

"Notice anything?" he asked Nance.

"Like what?"

"The walls." He looked around the room. "And the shelves."

"I'm not sure I'd choose the colour scheme."

"No photographs," he said.

"Is that odd?"

"Maureen was a keen photographer. I bought her a camera for her thirteenth birthday. Back then she was going to be a photo-journalist."

"What happened?"

"She met men."

"Figures."

It struck Gilchrist then that he had never been invited to Maureen's flat. He would meet her in Glasgow on the odd occasion, take her out for a drink and a meal, but she would never invite him back. *You wouldn't want to see it. It's too messy.* So he never pushed.

Other than an archway into a modern kitchen-dining room, one other door opened off the living room, to the hallway. The flat was small, probably too small to share. Somewhere in the back of his mind he heard Maureen say that one day she would have a place of her own, no one to pick up her dirty knickers, tell her what to do, how to run her life. He wondered if this was it.

"It's not too messy," Nance said.

Gilchrist was not sure if she meant Maureen kept her place tidy, or the intruder had not done much damage. He chose the latter. "We caught him in the act," he said. "But what's odd about the break-in? What do you see?"

"I don't get it."

He let his silence do the asking.

"This place isn't crawling with people," she tried. "Did you notice anybody checking out the commotion? We weren't exactly quiet breaking in here."

Gilchrist nodded. The flats were probably owned by young professionals with careers and money, who worked hard and socialised harder still. No time for kids. During the day the building would be deserted. But something else did not fit.

"The outside door was jimmied," he said. "But the door to Maureen's flat wasn't."

"So he let himself in?"

"Maybe."

"With a key?"

"Maybe."

Nance eyed him. "Maybe he was an expert lock-picker?"

"So why jimmy the outside door?"

"It takes time to pick a lock. He couldn't risk being seen fiddling with it."

"So he jimmied it instead?" Gilchrist eyed the CDs, the shelves, the walls. And why no photographs? What was he missing?

Nance's mobile rang. She took the call, then said, "Mini Cooper belongs to a Tony Brenton. Lives with his mother in Edinburgh."

"Right," said Gilchrist. "Let's pay him a visit."

"Won't help. Yesterday morning he reported it stolen."

As Gilchrist's mind worked through the rationale, he struggled to keep his emotions in check. The stakes had just been raised. If he had any doubts about the danger Maureen was in, they were dispelled at that moment. The fact that someone stole a car in Edinburgh to break into a flat in Glasgow put the crime in a different league. He was no longer dealing with local criminals, but with someone higher up the food chain, with money and contacts and power, and crews who worked the streets, and the criminal wherewithal to lead Gilchrist by the nose and make sure he would never find his daughter.

Even though this was Maureen's flat, and he was standing on her rug, looking at her tables and chairs and shelves filled with CDs, personal effects she had touched and listened to and sat upon, he did not feel close to her. At that moment he felt farther from her than at any time in his life. He thought he caught a glimpse of what his life would be like without his daughter in it.

And it felt lonely and cold and dark.

Chapter 17

GILCHRIST CALLED FOR a Lookout Request for the Mini Cooper. It was stolen, almost certain to be abandoned now, but you could never tell. He elected not to report the break-in to Dainty, deciding instead to do some investigation of his own first. This was his daughter's home, after all.

The flat had two bedrooms; one unfurnished that smelled of fresh paint and plaster. Surprisingly, he thought, Maureen's room was clean, with the Queen-sized bed made. He pulled back the duvet cover and confirmed only one side had been slept in.

Sweaters, jeans, socks, lay folded on open Formica shelves that took up most of one wall. In a fitted cupboard, he found a selection of silk blouses, mostly white, and expensive-looking jackets hanging on cedar coat-hangers. A dozen pairs of shoes sat in formation on the floor. Again, expensive-looking.

One thing continued to trouble him. Maureen had a computer. But other than a plug in a socket close to the bed, the flat seemed devoid of all things electrical.

"Maybe she has a laptop and has it with her," Nance said.

"Maybe." But he thought it odd that they found nothing computer-like—no discs, no software, no electrical leads. A more careful search under the bed uncovered two deep fitted-drawers either side, which he had mistaken for part of the bed-frame. With the fitted sheets and valance on, the drawers were hidden.

Nance was almost right. Maureen did have a laptop, but not with her. He found it in the under-bed drawer next to the headboard end, and a filing box that held a number of CDs. He read Maureen's scribbled label on one—*Short Stories*.

And on another—*Mystery Novels 1 & 2*.

It surprised him that Maureen would write not just one novel, but two, and he felt dismayed that he knew nothing about her literary efforts. Other CDs confirmed she had written six novels. Was she published? Was that how she could afford this flat?

The feeling that Maureen was so far removed from his life rushed through him in a warm flush. She wanted little to do with her father. She was growing up, *had* grown up, and wanted a life free of parental ties.

He plugged in her laptop, struggling to smother the feeling of guilt that he was about to violate her privacy. What right did he have to read her personal writings? The hard-drive hummed alive. If her laptop was password-protected he would have to take it to the experts, the computer geeks who would—

The screen flickered, went blank, then recovered to settle at Maureen's desktop.

Well, he was in, which pleased him in one way, but disappointed him in another. Maureen might be wise to many things in life, but personal security was not one of them.

He clicked *start*, moved the cursor to—

"You want me to report the break-in?"

Strictly speaking, Maureen's flat was a crime scene. Removing her laptop and CDs was a serious violation of scene of crime protocol. But what would Strathclyde Division find? Better that he explained it to Dainty directly, he thought.

"Let's get out of here first," he said to Nance, and powered down the laptop.

They drove to Pitt Street, but Dainty was tied up in a major interrogation and could spare only a few minutes, time enough for Gilchrist to tell him about Maureen's flat and the Mini Cooper, but nothing about her laptop and CDs. Dainty ordered

Gilchrist to write a full report, then assigned a scar-faced detective to the case, who introduced himself as Tony and insisted he be given a blow-by-blow account. Once Tony was dealt with, Gilchrist took over a desk and two phones.

The remainder of the day was a mess of phone calls and paperwork.

In amongst all the calls, Gilchrist called Watt on his mobile several times, before concluding that Watt must have removed his SIM card or powered it down. Had his own calls to the number on Watt's records alerted the man? He surprised himself by getting through to Watt on the Office phone.

"I hear you started an Office sweepstake," he said to him.

"So?"

"And you guessed—"

Watt hung up.

Gilchrist tried again, but was informed that Watt had left the building, which had Gilchrist promising himself he would fire Watt on the spot the next time they met.

He would take his chances with Greaves.

Meanwhile, the Mini Cooper was found abandoned in St. Enoch's carpark, doors unlocked, keys in the ignition, all surfaces wiped clean. And Stan confirmed that only three criminals put away by Gilchrist had been released within the last year, none of whom could be involved in Chloe's murder. One had died four months ago from a heart attack; one was in a hospice waiting to die; and the third was in Portugal lapping up the sun and the booze.

By 8:00 P.M. they were no farther forward.

"My stomach's rumbling," said Nance. "Fancy a bite?"

Gilchrist tried to remember when he had last eaten, and thought a pint and a bite might uplift his spirits and re-energise his sense of detection.

"We could go out for your favourite," Nance pressed on.

"Which is?"

"A pint of real ale?"

"And a bridie, chips and beans. With HP Sauce?"

"I know just the place."

THE HORSESHOE BAR in Drury Street—a narrow lane running between West Nile and Renfield Streets—was one of Glasgow's more famous pubs. The bar itself, shaped more like a circle than a horseshoe, had once been listed in the Guinness Book of Records as the longest in Great Britain at one hundred and four feet.

Gilchrist ordered two Eighty-Shillings that came still and creamy with a hint of spillage. He lifted his glass to Nance's, took that first mouthful, cold and smooth, and could have purred with pleasure.

The bar buzzed with the hubbub of a Glasgow evening. A powerful fragrance of second-hand smoke tainted with the faintest aroma of cooked meat filled the air. Gilchrist eyed the crowd. It felt good to be out, to let his mental powers relax and recover, if only for an hour or so.

"How did you know about this place?" he asked Nance.

"Spent two years at Strathclyde studying biology."

"I never knew that," which had him thinking that he also seemed not to know much about Maureen. Or even Gail. His thoughts darkened as his mind cast up his parting image of his ex-wife, teary-eyed and pale, and bitter beyond reason.

"There's a lot you don't know about me," she said.

Gilchrist was not sure how to take that remark. Nance had a reputation as a bit of a teaser, but had kept all relationships off her own doorstep, so to speak. But the beer was hitting the spot, so he said, "Like what?"

"What would you like to know?"

"Why give up biology and join the police?"

She almost sneered. "Biology gave me up. I lost interest. Spent too much time in places like this. Met the wrong guy. Failed my exams. More or less in that order. Give or take the odd shag or three on the side."

All of a sudden, Gilchrist felt unsure of himself. Nance seemed different, as if being in a bar in Glasgow gave her thoughts of re-enacting her student days, guzzling beer and screwing men. She had developed a devil-may-care attitude in the space of one pint, and a hint of sexual mischief sparkled in her eyes, which had him trying to shift his own thoughts. He eyed the black and white framed pictures, the massive mirrors on the back wall, thought the motif on one of them looked like a horsewhip twisted into the shape of an S.

"You wouldn't happen to know what that letter S stands for?" he tried.

"Scouller. The original owner in the late eighteen-hundreds. He also owned another couple of bars named after horsey stuff. The Snaffle Bit was one. And The Spur."

Gilchrist tipped his beer. "I'm impressed."

"Don't be. I have a good memory. That's all."

He nodded to other initials. "And JYW?"

"John Whyte, I think. He took over in the early nineteen-hundreds." She glanced at him, her pint poised at her lips. "And no," she said, "I don't know what the Y stands for."

Letters. Gilchrist sipped his pint, troubled by his thoughts. Letters defied time. A century ago, two pub-owners, Scouller and Whyte, immortalised themselves in Glasgow's pub-lore by having their initials imprinted on bar memorabilia. Was that what would happen to Chloe's case? A hundred years from now, would someone browse through police records and come across the words *Murder, Massacre, Bludgeon, Matricide,* then the letters M, A, U, R, and ridicule the SIO for his inability to jump-start such an obvious case? Which thought brought with it the need to find out what was on Maureen's laptop.

He downed his pint with a rush.

"Hold your horses, Andy," Nance said, and had a twenty-pound note in her hand.

"I'm getting these," he protested. "This is my treat."

"Your treat comes later," she replied with a wink, and ordered two more pints.

Gilchrist knew it was a mistake not to leave. He tried to convince himself he would not be tempted, that he was mature enough to resist, had done so in the past. Not with Nance, but with others. But two pints later, with not too much to eat, they traipsed into Drury Street.

In West Nile Street Nance slipped her arm through his, and Gilchrist let her, telling himself it would be rude to pull free. Besides, it was cold. He could feel her body shiver, as their breaths puffed in unison in the damp air. As they crossed St. Vincent Street her thigh bumped against his, and he caught her fragrance as she swept her free hand through her hair. And all of a sudden it struck him that without discussing it they seemed to have decided to spend the night together.

Not so fast, he thought.

He considered driving to St. Andrews. But the earlier adrenaline rush from searching for Maureen, plus three pints in under two hours, had left him far from his brightest. A night in Glasgow would have to do. Besides, he had Maureen's laptop to go through.

He clicked his remote. The Merc's lights blinked. Like the gentleman he knew he should be, he held the passenger door open as Nance slid inside. He was conscious of her eyes on him as he sat behind the wheel and slipped the key into the ignition.

As he eased into traffic, Nance said, "Where are you taking me?"

Even though four weeks had passed since Beth ended their relationship once and for all, he said, "I'm not sure this is a good idea."

"No one's forcing you."

"I have a spare key for Jack's flat," he said. "It's a bit rough at the edges, but at least it's got two beds."

"Good," she said. "Then that's settled."

• • •

JIMMY SQUEEZED WEE Kenny's shoulder.

Wee Kenny looked at the hard hand only inches from his neck.

"You look worried, wee man."

Wee Kenny shook his head. "No me, Jimmy."

"You done a good job there."

Relief flooded through Wee Kenny in a rush so strong that for one crazy second he thought he was going to piss in his pants. "I done my best, Jimmy." He tried to force a laugh, conscious of the fingers digging into his collarbone, but it fell flat.

"It's looking good."

Wee Kenny eyed the Jaguar's boot lid. He had never spray-painted a car before, and paint rippled like orange peel in parts where he'd sprayed it too thick. But overall, he thought he done a good job.

"It'll be dry for the morra," he said.

Jimmy took a deep draw of his cigarette. Thin cheeks pulled thinner. Eyes as dark as coal closed for a moment's pleasure. Smoke curled from nostrils thick with hair that leaked into a dank moustache. In the dim light, Wee Kenny thought Jimmy's mouth looked like one more scar on a face creased with scars.

Jimmy kept a permanent week-old growth to hide his scars. Black stubble, a quarter of an inch long, hid the worst of them, a jagged welt that ran from the corner of his right lip to the lower jaw, the result of a broken bottle to his face. And Wee Kenny remembered what happened to big Archie Chalmers, the punter who done it to him.

It was years ago. Jimmy was fifteen. Not much more. Archie in his early twenties, a small-time thug making a name for himself as a hard-man to be reckoned with. Even though Jimmy still had the stitches in his face, he and his big brother, Bully, goes to see Archie at his home on the fourteenth floor in Red Road. Jimmy stands out of sight while Bully knuckles the door. Archie's mother opens up. Bully smiles and asks for Archie. But when Archie turns up, Bully steps back, Jimmy steps in, open razors slashing up and down, left and right, like a drummer gone wild. The story goes that the slashing was so bad, even Bully almost threw up.

One slash cut Archie's left eyeball in half. Another almost had his nose off. Bully had to stick the head on Jimmy to stop him cutting Archie to death, and ended up with sixteen stitches himself from a cut that opened his palm. From that day on, no one messed with the Reid brothers.

But Bully was now in the Bar-L serving fifteen years for manslaughter. The charges should have been murder, but even the Procurator Fiscal seemed too afraid to go for the max. The Bar-L should have been enough to keep Bully out of the picture, but he was keeping busy behind bars, having Jimmy do his legwork.

And rumour had it that something big was about to break, and that Bully was filing an appeal. But Wee Kenny knew better than to ask Jimmy what it was. No way would he ask.

If he did, that would be the end of him.

Chapter 18

GILCHRIST STUMBLED ACROSS Jack's makeshift cocktail cabinet on the bottom shelf of the food cupboard—a Glenfiddich single malt that looked tempting enough, but contained less than an inch of whisky; or a ten-year-old Longrow, which he remembered gifting to Jack on one of his infrequent visits. He removed it from its burgundy gift box and confirmed it was almost half-full. Perfect.

He picked up a tumbler and walked along the hall to Jack's bedroom, the bottle of Longrow in hand. As he passed the bathroom he heard the rattle of glass and the sound of running water.

"Goodnight," he called out.

Nance did not reply.

In Jack's bedroom, he poured himself a large one and powered up Maureen's laptop. He double-clicked *My Documents*, and a screen flashed up with a list of *Folder* icons entitled *Novels*, *Letters*, *Research*, *Databases*, and the last one, *Spreadsheets*. The toilet flushed, and the bathroom door opened and closed with a quiet double click. A shadow drifted by the gap at the bottom of the door like a spectral image, then vanished as the hall light was switched off. He clicked his bedside lamp off and took a sip of whisky, feeling its fiery warmth work through his system. The only light in the room came from the laptop's screen. He took another sip then clicked on *Letters*.

The screen flashed up a fresh page that contained a list of files with names such as *royalbank—12-01-03*, *dkerr—29-09-02*. He double-clicked one to confirm the simple filing system.

jstevens—11-02-03 was a letter to Joyce Stevens dated 11th February 2003. He dug deeper, did an automatic search for files that contained the title *rwatt*, but found none. He tried rearranging the lists alphabetically, then checked the Rs for Ronnie, the Ws for Watt, but came up empty, which pleased him.

Next, he clicked his way into the *Novels* folder to reveal more *Folder* icons entitled by novel. He clicked on *Novel 1* to find yet more folders and files that contained research notes, character traits, synopses, and even one that listed titles. He clicked on *Correspondence* and spent the next twenty minutes discovering that Maureen had written to over thirty literary agents in London and sent another twenty query letters to agents in the States.

He felt as if his daughter was a stranger to him. How long had she wanted to be a novelist? Why had she never mentioned it to him? And what about her photography? Had she given that up? He took another sip of whisky, worked his way out of *Correspondence*, and jerked his head to the side as the bedroom door clicked open.

Light from the front lounge cast a faint glow along the hallway, exposing Nance in the doorway. A blanket draped around her shoulders hung almost to the floor. Her feet and ankles were bare. "I can't sleep," she said.

"That makes two of us."

She eased into the room. "Do you mind?"

Gilchrist tilted his glass to her. "Like a half?"

"You rat," she said. "Where did that come from?"

He eyed her over a pair of imaginary spectacles, and said in a ridiculous German accent, "I haf my sourses."

Nance flitted towards him like a shrouded ghost and sat on the edge of the bed. The laptop lay between them like some tech-age chastity belt. She eased the tumbler from his fingers and took a sip.

From the way her lips puckered, Gilchrist could tell she was not a whisky drinker.

"Like it?" he asked.

"The occasional sip."

He finished the glass and poured another. Three pints and two large measures was not the recipe for feeling great in the morning, but sometimes stuff happened. Besides, alcohol helped his powers of deductive reasoning. Or so he told himself.

"Any luck?" she asked. In the faint light, her cheeks looked sunken, her chin square. Her eyes lay hidden in pools of shadow, as if shielding her thoughts from him.

"Most of it is innocent enough," he said. "Daily correspondence. That sort of thing."

"Know what you're looking for?"

"Any connection to Ronnie Watt for starters. But I haven't found it yet."

"You hate him, don't you."

"Oh, much worse than that."

"Care to tell me why?"

"Not really."

Nance reached for the glass again. Her fingers wrapped around his as they clutched the tumbler together. She leaned forward, took a sip, and the blanket fell away, just sufficient for the blue-white light of the computer screen to reveal the round swell of her right breast, the nipple hidden in shadow. "That tasted better," she said, and pulled the blanket back around her as if warding off a light chill.

Gilchrist felt something shift deep in his groin. Nance had removed her make-up. In the glow from the laptop her face looked pale and smooth, her eyes dark and large, as if the absence of all things unnatural allowed her own beauty to shine through. But the alcohol and long hours were finally taking their toll, and he felt a wave of sleep fold over him. Or maybe it was Nance prying into his hatred of Watt that had him wanting to end the day.

"I'm done in," he said, and powered down the laptop.

"Me too."

"I thought you couldn't sleep."

The room fell into darkness. Light glowed from the open doorway.

Nance lowered the laptop to the floor, then stood, the blanket hugging her body. She removed the tumbler from his grip and laid it on the bedside table.

"I was enjoying that," he said.

The blanket slipped to the floor.

Other than the briefest of knickers, she stood naked, her body a grey silhouette against the soft light from the hall. Her pubic mound, hidden in shadow, lay level with his face and acted like a magnet to his eyes. He forced himself to look up, and in doing so, scanned the length of her.

Even in the dark, as naked as she was, he could see she was slim and fit. Her pinched waist made her hips look large, her thighs long and lean. She stared off to the side, and he caught a glint in her eyes that told him she was pleased to see her body excited him.

"I'm not sure this is a good idea," he tried, but his heart wasn't in it.

She leaned down, pulled the cover from his light grip. Her breasts hung as firm as half-melons as she slid in beside him. "You can tell me to leave anytime."

Her feet felt as cold as ice against his legs. With a familiarity that surprised him, she turned on her side, threw a leg and an arm over his body, and snuggled in.

"You're all lovely and warm," she said. She kissed his shoulder, buried her head into the crook of his neck. "Do you mind if I go to sleep?" she whispered.

"You're quite the woman of contradictions."

"Is that a yes or a no?"

For an instant, he was confused as to how to respond, then said, "No. I don't mind if you sleep."

"Good." She pulled closer.

Gilchrist felt the lump of her pubis on his thigh, the swell of her breasts on his chest, the warmth of her breath on his neck. He lay still, staring blind-eyed at the ceiling, and wondered what Greaves would do to them if he ever got wind of this.

Within seconds, it seemed, sleep pulled Nance down. He felt her muscles twitch as she faded away. He turned his face to her and brushed his lips through hair as soft as merino. He felt his own fatigue overpower him and pull him down into the dark unconsciousness of troubled sleep.

Then he fell away.

Twisted images of amputated body parts swelled in his mind then manifested into the body of a female. She held her arms out to him. He recognised her, knew she was calling to him for help. He tried to fight his way towards her, but failed, trapped by a dead weight that clung to his body as she pulled away from him.

Maureen, he tried to call. *Maureen*.

But she could not hear him.

JIMMY EYED THE paint-job. What a fucking mess. He'd have to get someone else to sort it out. Which made up his mind for him. The wee man had to go. He took one last draw, deep and hot, felt the fire burn his lips, and flicked the dowt away.

"Fancy a pint, wee man?"

Wee Kenny cringed as Jimmy clasped his shoulder. "I'm skint," he said.

"Consider it payment for painting the car."

"You gonnie buy the beer?"

"A couple of pints for the job you done."

Although Wee Kenny smiled, Jimmy seen the fear in his eyes. The wee man was thinking something was not right. In the four years since he'd took Wee Kenny under his wing as his goffer, he never once bought the wee man a pint. And even though the Jag was Wee Kenny's, he never let him drive it. Wee Kenny paid for all the petrol, tax, insurance, repairs. It was his car after all. Well, fuck it, times were about to change.

"You drive, wee man."

"You sure, Jimmy? I mean. . . ."

"I already said you done a good job."

Without another word, Wee Kenny took his seat behind the wheel. In the mirror, he watched Jimmy walk around to the passenger side. He turned the key, gripped the steering wheel as the engine roared to life, and for one crazy moment thought of just booting it. But Jimmy would come after him. Then what? No, he would do as he always done. He would do as he was told. That's what goffers were for.

The big car leaned to the side as Jimmy slid into the passenger seat. Wee Kenny could feel the presence of the man, the heavy heat from his body, which told him Jimmy was not well. He was sure of it. The big man looked rough as fuck some mornings. He winced as the door slammed shut with a hard thud.

"Where to, Jimmy?"

"Just drive."

Wee Kenny dared a glance. "Like, just anywhere?"

"Don't make me have to tell you again."

Wee Kenny eased the Jaguar from the derelict warehouse into the unlit streets of the abandoned business park. It was too soon to take the Jag out for a drive. His paint job was too fresh. No sooner had those thoughts crossed his mind when the skies opened, and he knew his paintwork was fucked. He would need to do it all over again.

But no when Jimmy was looking.

"Drive, wee man. I'm thirsty."

"Right, Jimmy. Where to?" He darted a glance. "I didnae mean that, Jimmy. Slip of the tongue."

"Just drive, wee man."

So he drove. He had no idea where to, only that he had to keep going.

"Get onto the M80, wee man."

He did as he was told, pleased that at last Jimmy was giving directions. That usually meant Jimmy had business to attend to. Not that he ever asked what kind of business, but he heard about some stuff in the pub a few days earlier. Some punter with their head smashed in. Or their throat cut. Beads of perspiration gathered on his lips, and he ran a hand behind his neck, surprised to find it damp.

Getting your throat cut must be a right sore way to go, he thought. But Jimmy's business was not deadly that night. He felt sure of that, because he had not seen Jimmy's ten-inch butcher's knife. He drove on in silence, and forty minutes later said, "Is it much further, Jimmy? It's just that I need to fill it up."

Jimmy twisted his head, looked out the back. "No much further, wee man," then ahead out the windscreen. "Here it's now. Take this exit on the left."

Wee Kenny did as he was told.

"Turn right at the top of the hill," Jimmy said. "Then go for about a mile and you'll come to a bridge. Cross it and take the next left."

"Nae bother."

After the bridge, the road narrowed. Wee Kenny peered ahead as he searched for the next turning. The Jaguar's headlights pierced the night rain. The skies pelted down as he pulled into a narrow lane that was no more than two wheel ruts overgrown with grass.

Fifty bumpy yards later, they arrived at a closed gate.

"Douse the lights, wee man, and give me a hand to open the gate."

Wee Kenny stepped into the rain, and wondered why Jimmy had asked him to switch off the headlights. It would be easier to open the gate if he left the lights on.

"Over here, wee man."

He stumbled towards Jimmy's lean figure in the shadows.

"The key's down there."

"What key?"

"The key for the padlock. Fuck sake, wee man, don't annoy me. It's down there. Under a stone. Get it."

Wee Kenny wondered how Jimmy knew the key was under a stone, but he stepped past him and pushed his hands into the dripping bushes.

"Where abouts, Jimmy. It's dark."

"Here, wee man. Let me show you the way."

As Wee Kenny stood, a couple of things struck him—that it was more painful having your hair grabbed and your head twisted than it was having your throat cut. And having your throat cut was not sore at all, more like not being able to catch your breath. But the sound of blood spurting over the bushes confused him.

"Down you go, wee man," as a hard hand kept a grip of his hair, and lowered his head to the ground.

The grass felt cold and soaking wet. He tried to lift his hands to feel the slit in his throat, but he had lost all strength, just wanted to close his eyes, go to sleep. He heard the Jaguar's engine roar into life, and for a fleeting moment his world exploded with light.

Then that, too, faded, until all that was left was darkness and the sound of rain.

And his own bubbling whimpers.

GILCHRIST WAKENED WITH a start.

He lay still for several seconds, confused as to where he was and who he was with. They had turned from each other in their sleep, and he felt a shiver of surprise as his fingers found, then touched, bare skin.

Nance moaned, a soft sound that hinted of consent and compliance, and she rolled her body into his. An arm slid over his chest, a leg over his thighs. He felt the press of her pubis and the heat of her breath as her lips worked up his neck like damp fingers, searching for him.

They found each other.

His body pulled towards her while his mind flew away, as if some sensual part of him had been released from his physical being and was floating, looking down at what was left of him. From somewhere deep in the logical part of his brain he heard a whisper call out to him, a sound that was almost indistinguishable from the rush of blood in his ear. Then the whisper took on an urgency that ordered him to stop.

He came to with a jolt.

"Nance," he said. "I'm—"

"Sshh." Her finger pressed against his lips. "You don't have to say a thing."

"I—"

"Not a thing." She kissed him then, her lips swollen and soft, like flesh of the sweetest fruit peeling apart. Then she pulled back. "Would you like me to stop?"

Gilchrist felt his heart bound in his chest like some caged animal. *Yes, I would like you to stop. But make love to me first. Please stop.*

"No," he said.

"Are you all right?" she whispered.

"Yes."

That was how he should have answered her first question. *Yes,* he should have said. *Yes, I would like you to stop.* But now it was too late. He felt as if some part of him that had lain dormant for too long had resurfaced in all its sensual libidinous glory. He felt, too, that he was breaking the rules. Not just constabulary rules, but his own unwritten code of ethics that had guided him since his affair with Alyson Baird several years earlier. He had made a promise to himself to keep sexual relationships remote from the Office.

"Kiss me again," she said.

Her lips tasted as moist as mango, and when he opened his

mouth her tongue powered inside like some living thing driven to search out every sensual nerve of his being.

Her fingers slid down his chest. His breath caught.

Her hand found him, slid down the base of him, cupped him in its warm grip. He heard someone groan, then let himself freefall into the dream.

Was he dreaming?

She seemed to be all around him, in his mouth, against his chest, his thighs. Fingers of the lightest silk slid over him, down and under to hold him, rubbing, stretching, then up again, caressing the head of him.

Then she pulled away from him.

He lay there, confused for a moment as to what he had done wrong, then felt his desire surge to a new high as he heard the soft rustle of her thong being slipped off.

When she returned to him, she slid a leg over his thigh, and straddled him. Her fingers took hold of him, guided him, and he opened his mouth to afford her one last opportunity to stop.

We shouldn't, his mind whispered.

She set herself down on him and he slid into the depths of her. She eased herself up, as if riding the lazy waves of a Caribbean surf. With each slow mounting, she leaned farther forward, falling closer to him, until her arms reached around his neck and he took hold of her breasts.

Her wetness ran onto his aching sac and down and over the top of his thighs. He took control then, placed his hands on her buttocks, pulled her onto him, her rhythmic surfing more frantic with each rising thrust.

Still, his personal turmoil persisted.

Please stop, he wanted to say. *No, make love to me. Let me make love to you. No. You. Me. Please. No.*

Yes. . . .

His breath caught in his throat, gave out tiny gasps that hardened as she impaled herself onto him again and again. The waves rose and fell, the seas roughened, the swell deepened, falling lower, rising higher, climbing, peaking, then crashing onto the warm shores of their drenched bodies to ebb and flow with a force that almost sucked the heart out of him.

She lay on top of him, her body writhing, squeezing every last ounce of pleasure from the moment. And Gilchrist wanted to thank her for what she had given him, but could not find the words. Instead, he drifted off and dreamed the dream of the dead.

Chapter 19

GILCHRIST WAKENED TO the whisper of rain on glass, then realised it was Nance having a shower. He raised the white-cotton Roman blinds to the pale grey of a Glasgow morning, then tried Maureen's mobile, but got no connection. He called Dainty for an update, only to be told they had uncovered nothing overnight.

The unequivocal fact that his daughter was missing hit him like a blow to the gut. A cold sweat came over him, and he brushed his forehead surprised to see his fingers tremble. He had never felt such helplessness. He forced his mind to think, to come up with something, some intangible clue that might lead him to her, or at least point him in the right direction.

But what? And how?

He powered up her laptop, then entered *My Documents* and tried the *Research* folder, and into more subfolders, working through one branch, then back out and down another, but coming up with nothing, until an idea stopped him. Was Maureen's laptop wi-fi enabled? Even if it was, Jack would not have wireless Internet, of that he felt certain. A short search located the Ethernet cable, but plugging it in gave him no connection, and he had to switch the power off. Within four minutes of restarting, he had an Internet connection and found himself at the BBC home page—another surprise. He typed *hotmail.com* and in the Sign In page entered Maureen's email address. For her password, he typed *Blackie1980*—the name of her first cat and the year of her birth—and prayed she had not changed it since she last told him. He held his breath while the screen opened to her Hotmail account.

He was in.

He read the folders listed in a column that ran down the left side of the screen, searching for something that might lead him to Ronnie Watt, until his eye tripped up on Topley. He had heard that name somewhere before. Topley. But where, he could not recall.

He opened it to a screen that contained no emails, and wondered why Maureen had emptied that folder. He eyed the column list again and stopped at *Chris*.

Was this Maureen's boyfriend?

He opened that folder, surprised to find a list of emails that ran to five pages and dated back to January two years earlier.

Two years? But was Chris not Maureen's latest boyfriend? Despite the distancing in their relationship, Gilchrist knew Maureen well enough to know that two years was too long for her to keep any romance secret. Ergo, Chris could not be her latest boyfriend.

Or could he?

He chose the most recent email, dated six weeks ago.

The screen opened to a short message from Maureen Gilchrist to Chris—no second name—titled Incoming.

> As requested, written confirmation has been sought for incoming order expected to arrive within the week.

How harmless was that? It was so harmless it rattled alarm bells.

Then the Topley name came to him with a chill that iced his spine. Was the message recipient Chris Topley?

And what was the *incoming order*?

He clicked through several older emails, but at first glance they offered nothing more.

He exited and eyed the column of folders, this time focusing on *Kevin*.

The name niggled at him. He had come across it last year on a visit to Jack's flat in Hillhead. Chloe's paintings had struck him as not only vivid and colourful, but tempestuous and wild, verging on the surreal. Chloe told him she had painted that series to work through the sudden death of her friend, Kevin.

Didn't Chris Topley have a brother called Kevin? He seemed to remember that. But the likelihood of Chloe's Kevin and Maureen's Kevin being Kevin Topley, or even the same Kevin, was almost laughable. Still, the name would not leave. He opened the folder to a single email, dated about four weeks ago, and stared in disbelief at the screen, at an untitled message from Maureen Gilchrist to Ronald Watt. Had Maureen mistakenly filed this in the wrong folder after deleting all emails to Kevin? He gritted his teeth and read on.

> Hi Ron,
> I'm sorry I haven't written since before Christmas, but I've been busy. Work is hectic. You know how it is. And Chris can be a real slave-master. But you know that, too. I've missed you, and I look forward to seeing you again at Glenorra, if only to say farewell. I'm sorry things haven't worked out between us the way you would have liked, but that's life. You have yours, and I have mine. Let's live and let live. And let bygones be bygones.
> Love.
> M xx

He was not sure if he was angered by Maureen's feelings for Watt, or embarrassed at reading her personal correspondence. However he felt, he could not dispute the fact that she had resurrected her relationship with DS Ronald Watt, transferred from Fife Constabulary's Crime Management Department to some outpost in the city of Glasgow all those years ago.

And now Watt was back in Fife, and Maureen was seeing him. Again.

Gilchrist seethed. This was betrayal at its worst. Maureen had lost her virginity one month after her fifteenth birthday, had since renewed her affair with the culprit, a man ten years her senior. Now after eight years, after all that time, here was written proof that she had reneged on the promise she made to her father.

He eyed the email.

I've missed you.

Gilchrist squeezed the bridge of his nose. Christ, Mo, what were you thinking? How could you let the man back into your life? He grimaced at the screen.

I'm sorry things haven't worked out between us the way you would have liked.

He read that line again, then once more, and felt his heart grasp onto that slice of hope and cling to it. Watt wanted to keep the relationship alive. Not Maureen.

. . . let bygones be bygones.

Gilchrist clenched his jaw. How could she ever forgive the man? And in his mind's eye, Watt pulled himself from bed and staggered to the bathroom, crumpled bed-sheets pressed to his bloodied face.

Gilchrist had moved towards Maureen then.

Stay away from me.

The words had been screamed. Even now, he flinched at the memory.

He remembered his breath rushing in and out in short hits, as if his body had forgotten how its lungs worked. He was as fit as he had ever been, but his burst of anger had carried him beyond some physical limit.

"You *hit* him," she shouted. "You beat him up."

"What did you expect?" he shouted back at her.

"Not that."

At fifteen, Maureen had the verbal alacrity to argue with her elders. Rationale and logic were not necessary prerequisites, of course, and even Gail had a tough time withstanding the occasional verbal lashing.

It seemed surreal to be talking to his naked daughter, her eyes defiant, her clothes clutched to her body.

"He raped you."

"He didn't rape me."

"That's not what it looked like to me."

"Was I screaming for help?"

"That's not the point," he shouted. "Having sex with a minor is against the law."

"Not if I wanted to."

Gilchrist felt a pain stab his chest. "It doesn't matter if you wanted to or not. You're fifteen. It's against the law."

"I don't care what the law—"

"You're *underage*."

She turned her back to him then, took hold of her knickers, and he had to avert his eyes from the swell of her vulva as she leaned forward and stepped into them, one leg, two legs, then up. And something about the way she did that reminded him of Gail all those years ago. "So?" she said.

"So you could be charged," he tried.

"Charge me."

Gilchrist remembered feeling stunned. It seemed such a challenging thing for any daughter to say. "You don't understand what—"

"I understand perfectly well. You hit him. You hit a defenceless man who—"

"He was having sex with a minor, for God's sake. That is rape. It is against the law. Can I make it any clearer than that?"

She slipped her bra over her tight breasts. "Minor?"

"Yes. Minor. Now get dressed." He had turned then, not knowing what to do, what to say. His knuckles were bloodied from battering Watt. The sound of water running in the bathroom had him fighting off the ridiculous urge to apologise to the man. But his dilemma was clear. Charge Watt with rape, and

Watt would reciprocate by charging him with assault. Which was why Watt had not fought back. He had been caught breaking the law, could lose his job in a heartbeat, and had egged Gilchrist on simply by smiling at—

The door clicked.

Gilchrist exited the file.

Nance walked into the bedroom, her hair a glistening mass of blackened curls, a cream cotton bath towel around her body. She gave a white smile, and Gilchrist tried to reciprocate.

"What's got you upset?" she asked.

"Maureen's seeing Ronnie Watt."

"Tell me you're joking." She slipped off the bath towel and dried her hair as she walked towards him, firm breasts bouncing from the effort. Her pubic hair stood at the joint of her thighs, as trim and tidy as a black exclamation mark. "What've you got?"

Gilchrist struggled to concentrate. "Some emails," he said.

"From Watt?"

Gilchrist bit his tongue. Just the thought of Watt contacting his daughter riled him. He should have charged Watt for all he was worth, taken his chances with his own assault charges. Instead he had let Gail talk him out of it.

What would the gossip do, for goodness sake? She's only a child. And there's your career to think about. You might lose your pension. And what about the mortgage? Think about someone other than yourself for once in your life. Damn you to hell if you do this.

So he had not pressed charges, instead worked a deal with the powers that be to have Watt transferred out of St. Andrews. Now eight years on, Watt had the audacity to be seeing Maureen behind his back. And back in St. Andrews. It did not bear thinking about—

His mobile rang. He turned from Nance's nudity.

"Bad news, Boss. We got an arm this morning."

"Left arm, Stan?"

"Correct, Boss."

The left arm was significant, because whoever was feeding Chloe to him needed to keep the sequence in order. Left right, left right. Like marching, he thought. Was that significant? Was the killer in the military? Was that part of the message?

"Any note?"

"Yes, Boss. Felt-tip pen printed along its length."

Thank God for small mercies.

"Dismember, Boss."

The fifth note. He spelled it in his head to the fifth letter—E. M A U R E. Christ, how clear could it be?

"Where was it found?"

"Lying on Grannie Clark's Wynd on the eighteenth fairway, wrapped in plastic."

"Close to the boundary fence?"

"About ten yards in."

"Thrown there?"

"Bert thinks it was placed, Boss."

Gilchrist puzzled over the killer's fascination with the Old Course. But it was open to the public and almost impossible to monitor around the clock. At night, it would be the simplest thing to drop an amputated limb in the passing.

But surely someone somewhere must have seen something.

"Tell me we've got a witness, Stan."

"Afraid not, Boss."

"Don't we have the place flooded with uniforms?"

"No one saw a thing."

How could someone drop an arm on a golf course in the middle of the night and not be seen? They were supposed to be patrolling the place, for God's sake.

"Where's Ronnie Watt?" he demanded.

"Haven't seen him today."

"When was the last time anyone saw him?" he asked.

"Yesterday afternoon, Boss."

Gilchrist's mind crackled with possibilities. Maureen had been corresponding with Watt, ending their affair. The logic seemed improbable, but Maureen's recent email would have given Watt time to set things in motion, if that had been his intention. First Chloe, then Mo. Revenge for Gilchrist kicking him out of St. Andrews, and for Maureen dumping him? Was that possible? Had the man they chased from her flat been searching for Maureen's laptop so he could delete any reference to *Ronnie*?

Gilchrist decided to take the beast by the balls. If he had acted on his hunch sooner, Maureen might be safe. Now he could no longer afford to wait. "Stan," he ordered. "Get a warrant for Watt's arrest."

A pause, then, "On what charge, Boss?"

"On suspicion of murder."

"You sure, Boss?"

No, he wanted to say, *I'm not sure. But I need to take action.* "He's been seeing Maureen again," he said. "Now Maureen's missing and I can't get hold of Watt."

Stan whistled. "Greaves'll blow a fuse, Boss."

Gilchrist thought it an odd thing for Stan to say. "If Greaves has a problem with that, he can talk to me."

"Okay, Boss."

Gilchrist hung up.

"I suppose that makes a quickie out of the question."

Nance had partially dressed and stood in thong knickers, the skimpiest of material that bulged with the lump of her pubis. Stubble speckled the tops of her thighs. Her breasts stood proud-nippled, and for one disorienting moment Gilchrist was back in his bedroom facing a fifteen-year-old Maureen.

"Get dressed," he said, then tried to soften it with, "We've got work to do."

But from the way Nance turned away, he knew he had not pulled it off.

Chapter 20

BY MID AFTERNOON, Gilchrist established that Maureen was employed as a marketing representative with the Topley Agency, a company owned and run by Chris Topley, an ex-hard-man from the Gorbals, now in his mid-thirties, who spent three years in Barlinnie for beating up his neighbour over a pint of beer. According to Dainty, the neighbour committed suicide the week before Topley was to be released. Rumour had it that if the man had not taken his own life, Topley had promised to take it for him.

The Topley Agency was housed on the fourth floor of a glass and steel building that overlooked the River Clyde. The reception area glistened with bronze statuettes and towering plants that had Gilchrist wondering just how much Maureen was earning. The receptionist asked them to wait while she paged Mr. Topley. Nance took one of the deep leather chairs. Gilchrist remained standing.

Fifteen minutes later, they were ushered into an office that looked as if it had been furnished by a minimalist. Two small black and white photographs in silver frames hung on otherwise bare walls. An expansive desk lay devoid of clutter. Gilchrist saw no filing cabinets or anything else that would suggest the room was ever used.

The door clicked.

Gilchrist and Nance turned like a choreographed act.

Despite the dark-blue suit with silver shirt and matching tie, Chris Topley had failed to lose his bruiser image. As he stood framed by the doorway, it did not take much to imagine him booting someone to death in the wet streets of Glasgow.

The door closed behind him with a dull thud.

Gilchrist stood a good six inches taller than Topley's squat figure. From that vantage point, Topley's sandy hair, shorn to the bone, looked like roughened wood grain.

"Chris Topley?"

Topley eyed Gilchrist with the look of a businessman undecided if this was an opportunity about to blossom into cash or some past deal come back to haunt him. "And you are?" His accent was hard Glaswegian softened to a low growl.

"Detective Chief Inspector Andy Gilchrist." Gilchrist declined to show his warrant card or tell Topley they were from Fife Constabulary. He had the impression that neither would matter to a man of Topley's background. Instead, he offered his hand.

Topley's grip felt hard and moist, like roughened leather greased smooth. An overpowering fragrance of aftershave hung around him, and his gaze slid off to the side as he eyed Nance from top to toe. By the time he offered her a gold-toothed grin, Gilchrist felt as if she had been stripped and abused before his eyes.

Topley held out his hand to her.

Gilchrist almost smiled when Nance ignored it.

"You have a name?" Topley asked her.

"Yes."

Topley oozed charm like a snake in an alligator pool. His face had the hardened look of a street fighter and bore the faded scars of past disputes—a nick on the forehead; dotted line on the right cheek; disfigured knuckles on bunched fists.

"Well well well," he growled. "Two detectives. I must say I'm honoured. How can I help you?"

"Maureen Gilchrist is one of your employees," said Gilchrist.

"A lovely girl," he said. "What about her?"

"She's missing."

Topley scrubbed the back of his hand under his chin, the sound like sandpaper on wood. Then he pointed a finger at Gilchrist. "Now I get it. You're the old man." He walked around his desk, and Gilchrist had the distinct impression that few paper trails were left in the company. Topley stood behind his high-backed leather chair, his right arm along the top. In the light from the glass wall, his eyes took on a hunted look, like a guilty man waiting for the damning question.

Gilchrist kept his voice level. "Do you know where she is?"

"Could do."

For a moment, Gilchrist toyed with the idea of leaning across the desk and grabbing him by the throat. "I'm not here to play games," he said. "Just answer the question."

"Should I be talking to my solicitor?"

"That's your prerogative." It was Nance.

Gold fillings glinted either side of front incisors. "She speaks," he said.

"She also arrests," said Nance.

Topley held out his arms, wrists together. "Please. It's been a while since I've been handcuffed by someone so pretty."

And at that moment, Gilchrist knew Chris Topley was not Maureen's boyfriend. Of that fact, he would bet his life. "We can cuff you later," he said, "but for now we're trying to establish if you can help with our enquiries, when you last saw Maureen, who you last saw her with, where she might be. That sort of thing."

Topley lowered his arms. "Maureen told me I wouldn't like you."

The sound of his daughter's name coming from the mouth of an ex-convict sent the chill of horripilation through Gilchrist. "Why would she say that?"

"Because she cares for you."

Topley's use of the present tense sent some signal buzzing through Gilchrist's system. Maureen was alive. Was that what he was saying? And if so, how did he know?

"As an employee, what does Maureen do?" Nance again.

"Marketing."

"Marketing what?"

"Topley clients."

"Who are?"

"The rich and the famous."

"And the infamous?" Gilchrist tried.

"I'm clean," Topley growled. "The past is past. This business is legit."

"Why don't I believe you?"

Topley's eyes flashed, nothing more than a widening of the pupils. But for a fraction of a second Gilchrist caught a glimpse of the wilder version of the man. "I couldn't give a monkey's toss what you believe."

"How long has Maureen been employed here?" Nance again.

Topley puffed his cheeks. "Less than a year."

"The job pay well?"

"Basic of sixty to seventy. Then a bonus that usually doubles it." He flashed some more gold. "At Christmas."

Maureen earning upwards of a hundred-thousand at the age of twenty-three did not sit well with Gilchrist. Why had she never told him about this job? Had Gail known? Had Harry? Or Jack?

"When did you last see Maureen?" Nance asked.

Topley turned to the tinted glass panels that ran from floor to ceiling and wall to wall. Beyond, the Clyde slid past like some dirt-caked beast, its murky waters a silent reminder of Glasgow's industrial past. He stood with his back to the room, hands clasped behind him so that Gilchrist caught the blue lines of some tattoo on the inside of his left wrist. The twin-tipped tail of a swallow, he thought.

"Two nights ago," Topley said. "We went out for a drink after work."

"Just the two of you?" Nance had her notebook out.

"Yes."

"Like on a date?"

"I wouldn't put it that way."

"What way would you put it?" Gilchrist interrupted.

"Two friends having a drink."

The emphasis on *friends* rankled Gilchrist, but he nodded to Nance to continue.

"Anyone see you?" she asked.

"See us?" Topley shrugged his shoulders. "Of course they saw us. We weren't hiding."

"Who saw you?"

"Other than everyone in the pub?"

"At work, I mean."

"Most of the office staff."

"You make a habit of going out for a drink with your employees?"

"Just the good-looking ones."

Gilchrist tightened his lips, thought it better to let Nance get on with it.

Nance seemed to sense his discomfort. "Where did you and Maureen go?" she asked.

"Had a glass of wine in Arta."

"Where's that?"

"Not far from where she lives."

"You know where she lives, do you?"

Topley chuckled. "Of course I do. I own the place."

"She rents it from you?"

"In a way."

"What kind of a way?"

"The flat comes with the job. It's a perk."

"Any other perks come with the job?"

Topley turned at that question. His eyes creased in a knowing smile. "Depends on how hard-working my staff are. How far up the ladder they want to climb." He flicked an ophidian glance at Gilchrist. "Know what I mean?"

Nance scribbled hard into her notebook as if trying to lead Gilchrist away from the trap. But it was no use. "No," he said. "Why don't you tell me?"

Topley turned to the window again, and Gilchrist sensed the man was not as tough as he liked people to think. "She does stuff for me," Topley went on.

"What sort of stuff?" Gilchrist pressed.

"Stuff stuff."

"Illegal stuff stuff?"

Topley shook his head, gave a dry chuckle. "She told me about you."

"Why would she do that? She expecting me to visit you some-time?"

Silence.

"What else did she say about me?"

Topley turned then, and any thoughts Gilchrist might have had of the man losing his hardness evaporated. "That you're a fucking cunt," he said. "And a wanker. A fucking wanker." He smiled. "That's what she said about you."

"Those her exact words?" Gilchrist asked. "Fucking cunt? Fucking wanker? She say that, did she?"

"More or less."

"So, she never said those words. Not exactly," he added.

"If it makes you happy, those were her exact words."

Gilchrist almost smiled. In all the time he had known Maureen, the use of that single word, *cunt*, had never passed her lips. "So," he continued, "after Arta, where did you go?"

Topley tilted his chin, as if to look at Gilchrist down the length of his flattened nose. "Babbity Bowster."

"How do you spell that?" Nance asked.

"Any way you like, sweetheart."

Nance shook her head, scribbled in her notebook.

"What did you have to drink there?" Gilchrist asked.

"More wine."

"A glass?"

"A bottle."

"Or two?"

"Probably."

"Pay by cash?"

"How else?"

How else indeed?

"Maureen likes her wine," Topley continued, as if warming to the idea of being interrogated. "It loosens her up, if you catch my drift."

Gilchrist ignored the taunt. "What kind of wine?" he asked. "House? White? Red?"

"Red."

"Red?"

"Yeah. Red. I'm sure you've heard of it."

Got you, you plonker. Gilchrist had no doubt Maureen frequented those pubs. They were both within walking distance of her home. But why would Topley lie? Or was he just stringing them along for the hell of it? "Two bottles of red between the two of you?" he went on.

"We might have left the second one unfinished."

"Might?"

"Yeah. I think we did."

"Red wine? Like a Cabernet?"

"Yeah. That's the one. Cabernet."

"Sauvignon?"

"Yeah. Cabernet Sauvignon."

"Did you have a meal?"

"No. We drank."

"More red wine?"

"Gin."

Maureen liked the occasional gin and tonic, so Topley was telling him a mixture of lies and truth. "Then what?"

"We went back to her place and fucked each other senseless."

Nance giggled, God bless her. She shook her head, slapped her notebook shut. "In your dreams, big boy."

Topley seemed not to have heard. He glared at Gilchrist, his eyes like blue burning beads. "She likes it up the arse. Hard and fast. She swears when she's getting fucked. Did you know that? She swears like a trooper. Fuck me harder, Chris baby, she says. Go on. Deeper. Harder. Fuck me. Fuck me." Topley stopped his billy-goat thrusts then, and lowered his arms. He ran the back of his hand across his lips, as if out of breath.

Gilchrist smiled. "Finished?"

Topley frowned.

"Would you like me to charge you with obstructing a criminal investigation?"

"I'm obstructing nothing. You're asking questions. I'm giving answers."

"You're lying."

"Prove it."

"Maureen doesn't drink red wine."

"Do what?"

"Red wine makes her sick." Gilchrist stepped towards the door.

"Maybe it was white, then."

"Maybe you weren't even with her."

Topley's face deadpanned.

"Thanks for your time," Gilchrist said. "I've enjoyed myself." He gripped the door handle, then hesitated. "If I were you I'd make sure my books were in order."

"I'm legit."

"You'd better be," said Gilchrist, and raised his wrist. "Because in about twenty-four hours this place is going to be crawling with inspectors from the Inland Revenue and Her Majesty's Customs and Excise. Wouldn't you say, Nance?"

Nance shook her head. "Wouldn't think it would take them that long."

Gilchrist opened the door. "And one other thing." He turned to Topley, pleased in some cruel way to see his fists bunching. "Maureen's never liked it up the arse. She prefers to be on top."

Topley unclenched his fists, then closed them in a white-knuckled crush.

Gilchrist pulled the door shut. His stomach churned. He should not have mentioned Maureen, but he had caught an image of her turning, dismounting from Watt, and the words had slipped from his lips before he could stop himself.

Outside, Nance said, "He's lying through his back teeth. There's no way Maureen would let him touch her with a barge pole. And what's with the gold fillings? Did you see them?" She shivered her shoulders. "Was it true about the red wine?"

Gilchrist nodded.

"So, what's he up to?"

Gilchrist had no answer. Topley's hatred had been revealed to him with such intensity that he felt the man had to be holding some grudge. He might have served time in Barlinnie, but as far as Gilchrist knew their paths had never crossed.

But one thing Gilchrist did know.

His daughter was in grave danger.

Chapter 21

GILCHRIST WAS ABOUT to step into Babbity Bowster when his phone rang. It was Dick.

"That mobile number you asked me to do a reverse check on," Dick said. "It's listed to a Peggy Linnet."

"Got an address?"

"That's where it gets complicated. According to the company's records she lives in Dundee. In one of those high-rise flats. But the council has it belonging to a Jerry McPhail, who works as an engineer in Saudi—"

"And he hasn't been in the country for months, right?"

"First time."

"Renting it out?"

"Maybe."

"Can you have someone in the Office check it out for me, Dick? Let's try to find this Peggy Linnet."

"Will do."

Gilchrist hung up. Who was Peggy Linnet? And why did Watt call her at such odd times of the day and night? He could confront Watt, have it out with him, then thought it better to have some facts first.

At the bar, he removed a passport-sized photo from his wallet. A young woman, fiercely attractive, the fire of defiance burning her dark-brown eyes, looked as if she was daring the camera to take her picture.

He held it out to Nance. "Maureen with her hair short."

"She looks angry."

"She has Gail's temperament."

"Ouch."

Gilchrist offered the photograph to the barman. "Have you seen this woman in here recently?"

The barman glanced at it. "I'm only part-time."

"That's not what I asked. Take a good look."

The barman eyed the image, shook his head.

"What about the others?"

The barman turned to a skinny guy stacking glasses. "Hey, Brian. Someone wants to speak to you."

Brian slid the last of the glasses onto the shelf and walked from behind the bar, drying his hands on his apron. A silver ring in his left eyebrow looked tarnished. He eyed the photograph and nodded. "She's a regular."

"Define regular."

"Comes in every other day or so. Mostly early, doesn't stay long."

"Like after work?"

"Yes."

"Alone?"

"Sometimes she's with someone."

"Male? Female?"

"Both."

Gilchrist exhaled. He was getting nowhere, confirming only what he already knew, that Maureen had the occasional after-work drink in one of her local pubs, sometimes by herself, sometimes with a work associate, male or female.

"When did you last see her?" Gilchrist asked.

Brian shook his head. "Couldn't say."

"Have a guess."

"Last week, maybe."

"But not since?"

Brian shrugged. "She could have been here and I might not have noticed." He stared at Gilchrist for several seconds, then said, "Look, I'm sorry. I get paid to work here. Not eye the talent. When this place gets busy, it's heaving. Know what I'm saying?"

Gilchrist was about to slip the photograph back into his wallet, when he said, "Do you know Chris Topley?"

"Who doesn't around here?"

"What's he like?"

"Spends cash like it's going out of fashion."

"Wealthy, is he?"

"Loaded."

"And?"

"And he shows off. Fancies himself as the brain of Britain, too. Always giving his opinion about this and that. But he's thick as shite. Don't tell him I said that."

"Did you ever see him with Maureen?"

"With who?"

"The girl in the photograph."

"I thought you didn't know her name."

"I didn't say that."

"He's her father," Nance said.

"Did you ever see her with Chris Topley?" Gilchrist pressed.

Beads of sweat glistened on Brian's forehead. He blinked once, twice, as if his brain was having trouble coming up with an answer.

Nance flashed her warrant card.

"You're police?"

"Why don't you let us ask the questions?"

"Is she in trouble?"

"You're not listening."

Brian's lips tightened.

"She's missing," Gilchrist said.

"That's why we're asking the questions," Nance followed.

"Look," Brian said. "I only know Topley because he comes in here now and again. He's Mr. Big around here. His friends come and go. You don't see them for months on end, then in they come, all grins and cash and fancy cars."

"From out of town?" Nance said.

Brian sneered. "Try Barlinnie."

"You know that for a fact?"

"That's the pub scoop."

Brian ran the back of his hand under his nose, then sniffed. And that simple action told Gilchrist what Brian's problem was. He took drugs. And Topley supplied him.

"Did Maureen ever take drugs?" he asked Brian.

Brian tried to hide his surprise, but failed. "No."

"I thought you didn't know her." It was Nance.

"I don't."

"But you know she doesn't take drugs?"

"Yeah."

"You sure about that?"

"I'm sure."

Gilchrist and Nance said nothing, just waited for Brian to continue. It worked.

"She doesn't look the kind," he continued. "Know what I'm saying?"

"What kind does she look like?" Nance again.

"She's classy." He risked a glance at Gilchrist. "She's way above the likes of Topley and his hangers-on."

Hearing those words sent pride surging through Gilchrist. Maureen did not do drugs and was perceived as classy, and someone who would not associate with the wrong kind of guys. Which did not explain why she was employed by Topley. Was it for money? Over a hundred thousand pounds a year kind of money? Plus a flat as a perk? Surely she could not know about his criminal past. And once again, he felt as if so much water had passed under the bridge of his daughter's life that he was left standing high and dry on the banks of the memories of her life.

"Look," said Brian. "I've got work to do."

"You never answered the question," Gilchrist said.

"What question?"

"Did you ever see Chris Topley with Maureen?"

Brian shook his head. "Can't say that I did. Look, I'm telling the truth. He's not her type, is all."

Gilchrist wondered why he had not thought of asking the question until then. "Did you ever see her with Ronnie?"

"Ronnie Watt?"

Gilchrist tried to hide his surprise.

Brian nodded. "Once or twice."

"Twice? Once?"

"Several times, then."

"Like they were regular boyfriend-girlfriend?"

"Not really."

"Why not really?"

"They didn't look close, like. They argued."

"Argued? About what?"

"How would I know? I work the bar."

"You couldn't hear them?"

"No."

"So how do you know they argued?"

Brian shrugged. "She looked unhappy. Like she didn't want to be in his company. And one time she just got up and left him sitting there. Know what I'm saying?"

Fuck you, Ronnie, flitted through Gilchrist's mind, followed by, *That's my girl*.

Nance said, "And did you ever see Ronnie Watt with Chris Topley?"

Gilchrist almost smiled. Nance was beginning to make jumps in logic on her own, jumps that could catch someone cold, himself included.

"Once or twice," Brian said.

What? "When?" Gilchrist snapped.

Brian held up his hands. "Hey, man. Steady on."

Gilchrist was breathing hard. The whole thing with Maureen

and Watt was getting to him. And now a link to Topley. "Do you know what Topley and Watt talk about?" he asked.

Brian shook his head.

"Think about it." He slid Maureen's photo back into his wallet, then handed over a business card. "And when you've worked it out, give me a call."

Outside, the sky had darkened. Swollen clouds hugged the skyline, low and dark.

"Let's try Arta."

But after showing Maureen's photo around the place, they called it a day. She might have been seen, she might not, she looked familiar, but then again, did not. As they stepped outside, Gilchrist pulled out his phone and searched its memory. He found the number he was looking for.

It rang four times before being answered.

Gilchrist said, "Terry Leighton?"

"Speaking."

"DCI Gilchrist. You did some work for me last year."

A pause, then "Oh, yes, I remember. How can I help you?"

"I have a laptop I'd like you to take a look at. I want you to print out every file in it."

"Every file?"

"Just your common or garden Microsoft Word files."

"Oh, I see. That should be quite easy." A pause, then, "When do you need them?"

"I'll be with you in a couple of hours." He hung up before Leighton could object.

"What a pity we're heading back to St. Andrews," Nance said.

"Why's that?"

"I was looking forward to another treat."

From the look in her dark eyes, Gilchrist realised she was serious. Why would she want to get involved with someone like him? He was twenty years her senior, drank too much, spent too many hours at the Office, and seemed incapable of sustaining any relationship with the opposite sex. All she had to do was talk to Beth.

She lifted her hand to his face. "You look sad," she said. "And vulnerable. Not like the fearsome crime-buster of legendary fame."

"Who writes that stuff, anyway?" he said. "Come on," he growled. "We have work to do."

Nance shoved her hands into her pockets and strode alongside. "You can be a real bastard at times, Andy."

"I've been called worse."

"I wonder why."

Gilchrist grabbed her by the arm.

She stopped, frozen in mid-step, and glared at him until he released his grip.

"I'm sorry," he said. "I didn't mean it that way."

Anger danced behind her eyes, as if she was preparing to let him have it. Then she shook her head. "You're an easy man to like, Andy. But a difficult man to get to know."

"You got to know me last night," he tried.

"Fleetingly."

He was not sure how to take that remark. Was she letting him know he had been too selfish? Could he be blamed for that? It had been almost a year since he had last been with a woman. And with Chloe's murder and Maureen's disappearance, it was a wonder he'd been aroused at all. He felt something touch his hand, and looked down to see Nance's fingers entwine with his.

"Come on," she said. "We really do have work to do."

He let her lead him back to his car.

Chapter 22

AT STRATHCLYDE POLICE Headquarters in Pitt Street, Gilchrist pulled in an old favour by having Dainty put out another appeal on national television. Dainty was all hard handshakes and curt commands, with nothing being too much for the search for an associate's daughter, not even a follow up call with Chris Topley, which he seemed pleased to offer.

"It'll keep the cheeky bastard on his toes, let him know we've got our eyes on him."

"Getting too big for his boots?" Gilchrist asked.

"That's one way of putting it."

The appeal was set for the evening news, targeted for Glasgow and the surrounding areas. Gilchrist watched it with Nance in a bar off Charing Cross, and found himself holding his breath when Maureen's face filled the screen. But no one seemed to take notice—*Any person knowing the whereabouts of Maureen Gillian Gilchrist, twenty-three, slim-built, five ten, shoulder-length dark hair, last seen having a drink in Babbity Bowster in Merchant City several nights ago, should contact Strathclyde Police*. A number was given for callers to use with anonymity.

Gilchrist pushed his unfinished pint across the bar and stomped out, Nance close behind him.

On the drive back to St. Andrews, he called Jack. Although Jack had not heard from Maureen, he sounded upbeat. Gilchrist took advantage of his cavalier mood and asked if he would call Mum, find out when she last spoke to Maureen.

Ten minutes later Jack called back.

"Mum was asleep, but Harry says he hasn't spoken to Maureen since last week."

"Did he mention the news? We put out an appeal."

"He never said a word, Andy."

Gilchrist felt his lips tighten. This was his and Gail's daughter, Jack's sister, Harry's step-daughter, for crying out loud, and no one seemed to—

"I tried Jenny again, on the off-chance. But she hasn't heard from her either."

"Jenny?"

"Jenny Colvin. A friend of Chloe's."

At the mention of Chloe's name, Gilchrist felt his lips purse. He had not told Jack about the left arm. Now was not the time to bring it up.

"Jenny saw Chloe last year. Way before Christmas. We would sometimes go out with her."

"You and Chloe?"

"Sometimes Maureen, too."

"I didn't know you and Maureen went out together."

"Not often. Maureen's got her own circle of friends."

"How about boyfriends? Did you meet any of them?"

"That's how I met Chloe."

Things always seemed confused with Jack.

"Jenny's boyfriend knew Kevin."

Kevin. Chloe's boyfriend before Jack. Out of nothing comes something. "I'm listening," he said.

"Jenny used to go out with Roddy. Roddy knew Kevin. We went to a party in the south side. I was with Sheila. Chloe was with Kevin. That's where we met. Me and Chloe. . . ."

Gilchrist caught the saddening in Jack's tone, thought he should end the call before the conversation turned to his investigation. But he still had a couple of questions left. "Whose house was the party in?" he asked.

"Kevin's."

"You wouldn't know where Glenorra is?"

"Who?"

"I thought not. Did Maureen ever mention Glenorra?"

"Not that I remember."

Gilchrist felt powerless to lift Jack's spirits and now regretted having called. "Listen, Jack, I've got to go. Call you later."

"Yeah." And with that, Jack hung up.

Gilchrist sat his mobile phone in the centre console. What the hell was he doing? Have a chat with Dad and ruin your day? When was the last time he had spoken to Jack without picking his brain?

"Do you ever feel you're losing control?" he said to Nance.

Nance placed her hand on his thigh and squeezed. "You give the impression of always being in control."

He eyed the road ahead. Always in control? Of what? His family? His career? His life? That was a laugh. He felt as if he was hanging on by his fingernails while the stallion of life galloped off like some untamed beast. And Nance's hand on his thigh had his thoughts reverting to other problems. If Greaves found out, he would—

"Penny for your thoughts."

Gilchrist gave a defeated shrug.

"Don't worry," she said. "No one'll find out about last night."

Gilchrist eased the Merc through a sweeping corner. "And here was me thinking I was the one with the sixth sense."

"I can read you like a book, Andy."

"What am I thinking right now?"

"About how much you enjoyed last night, but don't know how to tell me you don't want it to continue." Her hand gave a quick squeeze. He glanced at her, but she was staring out the side, into the darkness of the passing fields.

"It's not that I don't want it to continue," he said. "It's . . . I'm not sure I'm ready for a relationship."

"A bit presumptuous, don't you think?"

"In what way?"

"That I would want us to have a relationship."

"Isn't that what this is about?"

"This?"

Gilchrist twisted his hands on the steering wheel. Why do women have the ability to flip the simplest of comments? "Well, isn't it?" It was all he could think to say.

Nance eyed the road ahead.

"I'm sorry," he said, "for being presumptuous."

"I'm sorry, too," she said, "for making you sweat."

"Who's sweating?"

She laughed, a long chuckle that let him know the air was cleared. "I think that's what I've always liked about you," she said. "Your honesty."

"It's nice to know someone thinks I'm telling the truth."

"Aren't you?"

It seemed as if their convoluted conversation was some form of verbal foreplay. And he found himself wanting to move on. "So, tell me. What are you looking for?"

"In a man?"

"In a relationship."

Nance turned her head to the side window again. Beyond, the countryside passed by unseen, like grey shadows shifting through the night. She stared out the window for what seemed like a minute, and Gilchrist was thinking he had offended her, when she said, "Affection," then added, "and kindness."

"Anything else?"

"And sex."

"That sounds undemanding enough."

"Especially the sex?"

"The affection."

Nance slapped his thigh. "You smarmy bugger."

"What about trust?" he asked.

"Kindness covers trust. If you're kind to someone, you

wouldn't want to do anything to upset them. Therefore you can be trusted."

"Touché."

"Is it a deal?"

A deal? Gilchrist was on the verge of reiterating the bit about presumption, when he heard her chuckle. With women, he could never be unkind, which he supposed satisfied one of the criteria. "Let me think about it," he tried.

Nance shook her head. "Men and commitment. Never the twain shall meet."

"That sounds like a quote."

"It is."

"Who said it?"

"Detective Constable Nancy Wilson."

Gilchrist gave a chuckle of his own. "I thought you didn't want commitment."

"Only to affection, kindness, and sex. The rest will follow."

"The rest of what?"

"You'll have to be affectionate and kind to find out."

"What about the sex?"

"You've already passed that test."

Gilchrist stared at the road ahead as an odd tranquillity settled over him. Nance was under his skin. She was under his skin from the moment she entered his bedroom last night. She had known he would not say no. And he had known that, too. But he could also see she had the ability to control him sans sex, twiddle him around her tongue with barely a flicker.

As they drove towards St. Andrews, he wondered if that was how he had behaved with Gail. Back then had he been as malleable? Was that why his marriage had failed? How was it possible to be so wrapped up in a career that more important issues slipped by? Was that the reason Maureen had drifted away from him? Had he spent too much time concentrating on issues of lesser import?

Family mattered. Family had always mattered.

Jack mattered. Maureen mattered. He just had not paid enough attention to that basic tenet. God, he prayed he was not too late to change that.

Maureen meant so much to him, he would die for her.

And he realised that without his children in his life he was dead anyway.

Chapter 23

THEY FOUND LEIGHTON'S terraced house at the end of the lane, bordered by a six-foot stone wall draped in branches of clematis as twisted as shrivelled veins. A brass coach lamp, polished like new, hung by a gleaming door. Tiny flies, tricked into life by the warmth of the sheltered spot, orbited the lamp like minuscule satellites. In the lambent light the windows glistened spotless.

The doorbell chimed from deep within.

Ten seconds later the door opened with a sticky slap.

Leighton frowned down on them, a crimson cravat stuffed into the neck of a starched white cotton shirt. Black trousers covered thighs joined at the knees, it seemed, and a shiny black leather belt with a silver buckle circled a fifty-plus waist.

"You're late," he said.

"Traffic," Gilchrist offered.

"We had to cancel our dinner reservation."

"Sorry." Gilchrist held up Maureen's computer. "This is the laptop I mentioned. And some CDs." He pushed the lot into Leighton's hands. "I haven't looked at all of them, but I think they're mostly manuscripts." He pulled a folded A4 sheet from his pocket, on which he had printed the names of some files. "You'll find this useful to start with. Get on the Internet and go to Hotmail. I've given you an email address and password. Print out every email in the account."

"When do you need this?"

"As soon as."

"We haven't discussed payment," Leighton said. "I would propose hourly, same rate as last time, plus moderate expenses. Paper, printer cartridges, delivery, etcetera."

"Don't bother with delivery. Call me when it's ready. I'll pick it up."

"Why me?"

It was Gilchrist's turn to frown. "What do you mean?"

"Fife Constabulary has its own computer experts. Why not use them?"

Gilchrist nodded to the laptop. "Some of the files may be personal in nature."

Nance stepped in. "What DCI Gilchrist is omitting to tell you, Mr. Leighton, is that the laptop belongs to his daughter. He doesn't want anyone at the Office to read his daughter's private writings."

"She's missing," Gilchrist added. "Her files might help us locate her and solve an ongoing murder investigation."

Leighton's eyes widened. "The body part case?"

Gilchrist nodded, disappointed that it had to take the notoriety of a murder enquiry to arouse interest.

Leighton pulled the laptop to his chest. "I'll call you tomorrow."

The lane slipped into darkness as the door closed.

When they reached the Mercedes, Nance said, "Where to?"

"It's almost ten." Gilchrist pressed the remote. "I've got an early rise and a busy day ahead of me. If you'd like, I could drop you off."

"Trying to get rid of me?"

"Jack's at my place," he said. "It's not a good idea."

"There's that presumption again."

Gilchrist drove through the back streets in silence and pulled to a halt in front of a row of three-story terraced apartments. Parked cars lined both sides of the street.

Nance gripped the door handle. "You needn't worry," she said. "Your secret's safe."

In the dim light, he thought she might not see his smile, so he said, "Thanks," and before he could stop himself added, "For last night."

She hesitated, as if reconsidering whether to stay or leave. "No commitment," she said. "Just affection, kindness, and the occasional session. That way no one gets hurt. How does that sound?"

Impractical? Impossible? "Impressive."

She chuckled and stepped into the night. A cold breeze brushed his face. Before he could say, "Goodnight," she closed the door.

She skipped up a short flight of steps. The key must have been in her hand, or the door unlocked, for she seemed to vanish without missing a beat or giving a backward glance.

INSIDE, NANCE THREW her jacket over the back of the sofa, and ran a bath.

Water drummed in the background as she removed a bottle of Cava from the fridge and poured herself a large glass. The wine tasted chilled and fresh and mellowed her senses, like water in whisky, smoothing the rough edges off a hard couple of days.

She smiled, unbuttoned her blouse, took another sip.

Affection, kindness. . . .

And the occasional session. . . .

To most women she knew that Gilchrist seemed an enigma—distant, but friendly; all work, but approachable; and never one to mix business with pleasure.

Until last night.

Last night she had caught him in a moment of weakness. But the echo of his hard words that morning came back to her. She had let the sensual torrent carry them along, with herself at the rudder. She had done nothing to stop it, just taken advantage of the situation, taken advantage of him. And she saw in the gathering of her thoughts how unprofessional she had been. His daughter was missing, and here she was, coming on to him.

She resolved to change her attitude. She had a murder to solve, was a member of its investigation team, and needed to push personal feelings aside until. . . .

Until later.

GILCHRIST'S THOUGHTS HAMMERED back to Maureen as he accelerated down Abbey Walk on his way to Crail. It was his helplessness that hit the hardest, the fact that he could do nothing to ensure her safety. Where was she? Was she all right? Christ, he didn't even know if she was alive or. . . .

She was alive.

She had to be. He had to believe that.

He had to, because he would not let her die.

He reached Crail and parked in Castle Street. Although the rain had stayed off, the wind had risen, carrying with it an icy chill off the sea. By the time he reached Fisherman's Cottage he brushed off the cold with a shiver.

Inside, the heat hit him. The thermostat had been adjusted to thirty. When good old Dad was paying, cost did not matter. A goal-scoring roar came from a half-opened door off the hallway. When he entered the lounge, Jack twisted in his seat. Even from one glance, Gilchrist could tell he was well on his way.

"Heh, Andy. Didn't hear you come in."

"I wonder why."

"Liverpool and Man U." Jack pointed the remote at the TV, and the noise dropped. "Giggs's just been booked."

"Good game?"

"Seen better." Jack held up a glass of whisky, swirled it about. "Afraid your Johnny Walker's taken a beating."

"The Black?"

"Of course."

It pleased Gilchrist in some paternal way that Jack drank his whisky. Jack's life as a freelance artist-slash-sculptor did not pay well, and he could not hold a grudge if his only son overindulged when he visited. But demolishing a bottle of Walker Black did not suggest a sober face-to-face, so he decided not to mention Maureen's flat.

Defeated, he said, "I'm for a Sam Adams."

"I'll join you."

"That took a lot of persuasion."

"You know me," Jack said. "I'm fussy what I drink. It's got to be liquid."

Even though he had heard Jack cough out that phrase a thousand times, he smiled. It always irritated Maureen, and an image of her frowning at Jack entered his mind with such clarity that he caught his breath. He cleared his throat. "Frosted glass?"

"By the neck'll do."

He strode along the hall and into the kitchen, thankful that Jack seemed to have put the horror of Chloe behind him, if only for the evening. The television was back off mute, and he closed the hatch. The previous owner had done away with the door between the kitchen and the front room, and several other ill-advised modifications had enabled Gilchrist to buy the cottage at a knock-down price with the intention of making improvements of his own. But for the last five years he had lived in the cottage just as he had bought it.

When Gail left, Gilchrist stayed in the family home for almost eighteen months. But with his children gone the place lost its heart, no longer a home, just somewhere in which to sleep. He replaced none of the furniture Gail had taken with her, and he felt as if his life was stagnating until he woke up one Sunday morning to find a woman in his bed, a friend of a friend, who had taken pity on him the previous drunken night.

"Are you just moving in?" she had asked him.

"No," he replied. "I'm just moving out."

Decision made, he put the family home on the market the following month, bought Fisherman's Cottage and moved ten miles down the coast to Crail. The lengthened commute was not a problem, the only downside being that he could not spend as long in the pub after work. But now and again he paid a fortune for a taxi home.

He removed two bottles of Sam Adams from the fridge and carried them through to the front room. He handed Jack one and took a seat opposite the fireplace. The microbrew tasted cold and soothed the fire in his throat from some bug. Or maybe he was just burning out. He was getting too old for all this shit anymore. He tried to redirect his thoughts by asking Jack, "How long do you intend to stay? I mean, stay as long as you like. It's great that you're here."

Jack tipped his Sam Adams at him. "Cheers. But I'm not sure how long. I'm kind of keen to start on something new."

Gilchrist nodded. Jack had inherited the trait from Gail that when she was unhappy she worked harder. Maureen was the same. Not that Gilchrist could put in more hours even if he tried. "How was Harry?" he asked.

"The usual."

"Which is?"

"Bit of a diddy."

Gilchrist frowned. "You don't like him?"

"He's all right. He looks after Mum."

Somehow hearing how Harry and Gail interacted did not sit right with him. He had never fully understood why he had been so upset about their break-up. Had it been the loss of his children to another man? Or the mental image of Gail making love to Harry? Or was it because he thought he still loved Gail, even after what she had done, and the fact that their marriage had died years before the split?

As he sipped his beer and watched the football the heat and the alcohol took their toll. Within minutes he was asleep, dreaming of wakening up in a coffin, finding he was sharing it with a woman who turned out to be Maureen. Except that it wasn't Maureen, but Chloe with her body parts stitched together.

He woke up sweating to a dark room and black television screen and an empty chair vacated by Jack. By the time he pulled himself to bed, he would be back on his feet in less than three hours.

Chapter 24

"**A** WARRANT FOR **WATT'S** arrest for murder?" Greaves blasted. "What in God's name's gotten into you, man?"

"For *suspicion* of murder," Gilchrist corrected.

"Cut the semantics, Andy. It's not on."

"Why did you assign Watt to my investigation?"

Greaves' anger dissipated to annoyance. "We've been over this already."

"I never asked for Watt. He wasn't needed."

"That's for me to decide," Greaves said. "Not you."

Gilchrist pushed his fingers through his hair. He had come up against Greaves in this mood before, once when he had argued for extra compensation for his staff. He had lost then. And he was losing now. Then it struck him like a slap to the head, and he wondered why he had not thought of it earlier. "It's out of your hands. Isn't it?"

"Don't push it, Andy."

"Push what, Tom?" Gilchrist stepped closer. But Greaves stood six-two and was not a man to be intimidated. "My son's girlfriend has been murdered and is being fed to me in bits. Not to you. Not to anyone else. To me. Her left arm was found yesterday." From the look on Greaves' face Gilchrist thought he had just given him some news. "Now my own daughter's missing and I'm terrified she's going to be served up to me in bits as well."

Greaves' eyes narrowed, showing in their damp reflection the tiniest glimmer of compassion. "Very well, Andy." He returned to his seat, stared hard at his desk for several seconds, then looked up. "Ronnie's with Strathclyde Drug Squad." He held up his hands. "I can't give you details, for the simple reason that I don't know. My remit was to find him a position in this Division and make it look as if he was back with Fife Constabulary."

"That doesn't explain why you assigned him to me."

"It was a perfect arrangement."

"What are you talking about?"

Greaves gave a tiny smirk. "You hate the man. Can't say I blame you. So, I knew you would do your damnedest to keep him out the picture."

"I don't follow."

"Oh, do come along, Andy. It's a bit late in the day to play dumb."

Gilchrist wondered why he had never before noticed the cruelty reflected in Greaves' eyes. But he was still missing something. Then he thought he saw it, and wondered if Greaves could really be that devious.

"You knew I would keep Watt busy," he said. "You knew I would bury him in the investigation, have him go off on his own, effectively give him the means to carry out his Drug Squad business."

Greaves gave a tight smile.

But Gilchrist was in no mood to let him off. "Did you know Watt was seeing my daughter in Glasgow?"

Greaves frowned. "What?"

"Soon after Watt arrives back in St. Andrews, Maureen goes missing." He leaned closer. "Does that not make you suspicious?"

"Of what?"

"Now who's acting dumb?"

"Watch that tongue of yours."

Gilchrist struggled to keep his voice steady. "If I ever find out that Watt is involved with Maureen's disappearance, I swear to God, Tom, I'll hold you personally responsible for interfering with my investigation."

"I'll pretend I didn't hear that."

"Don't pretend. Pray." And with that, Gilchrist strode from Greaves' office.

Outside on North Street he thrust his hands into his pockets. His outburst had drained him. He felt emptied, flattened, beyond anger. He imagined Greaves on the phone with ACC McVicar, demanding his resignation. McVicar had stood up for him in the past, but there were only so many rules a man could break, and his final threat to Greaves might have broken the lot.

He pulled out his mobile, called Watt's number, but it was unobtainable, or his mobile was dead. He tried Nance, and she picked up on the third ring.

"Have you seen Watt?" he asked her.

"Good morning to you, too," she said. "He's standing right beside me."

"Put him on."

"He's on his mobile."

Gilchrist almost cursed, then realised that his calling Peggy Linnet's number earlier had warned Watt off, forced him to change his SIM card, or use another phone. For all he knew, Watt might be on his new mobile to Greaves, listening to his confession that he had to let the SIO know about Watt's connection to the Drug Squad.

"Where are you?" he asked Nance.

"Outside the University Library."

"Nail that bastard to the wall. I'll be there in five minutes."

By the time he entered the University grounds, he had cooled off some, but not by much. Watt grinned at him as he approached, his lips lopsided from chewing gum, and Gilchrist had a sense of Nance backing away.

He reached Watt, grabbed his shirt at the throat. "I warned you," he growled.

Watt dead-eyed him. "Don't make me have to break your arm."

"I should kick you off the—"

"You can't kick me anywhere," Watt said. "This goes higher than you, higher than Greaves, higher than McVicar."

Gilchrist tightened his grip. "I'm not talking about that," he snarled. "When did you last see Maureen?"

Watt seemed to freeze, but only for a second. Then he lifted his hand and took hold of Gilchrist's bunched fist. "I told you I didn't want to break—"

"Give it up, boys," Nance interrupted. "You're causing a scene."

Gilchrist relaxed his grip. Watt pushed his hand away, tugged at his collar.

"I won't ask you to kiss and make up," Nance said. "That might scare the students even more."

All of a sudden, Gilchrist was aware of young men and women standing in silent groups, watching them. "Outside," he growled at Watt.

On North Street, Nance had the sense to keep out of earshot while Gilchrist had a face-to-face with Watt. "Does Nance know?"

"Only you and Greaves. The silly fucker shouldn't have told you."

"Then you'd have no excuse not to be kicked back to Glasgow."

Watt grimaced at Gilchrist's logic.

"How about Maureen?" Gilchrist pressed on. "Does she know?"

"Not a chance."

"I know you're seeing her."

"Not any more," Watt said. "It's over." He shoved his hands into his pockets. "And so is this half-arsed interrogation."

"Not so fast, Ronnie. When did you last see Maureen?"

"About three weeks ago."

"And the last time you spoke to her?"

"About a week ago."

"And what about her job with Chris Topley?"

"What about it?"

"Why is she working there?"

"A job's a job."

"And you know Topley."

"In Glasgow, who doesn't?"

"Who's Peggy Linnet?"

"Never heard of her."

Gilchrist knew he was being stone-walled.

"Are we through?" Watt said.

If Watt's authority was higher than McVicar, then the chances of Gilchrist being made privy to an on-going drug operation ranged from zero to one hundred below. Watt would tell him nothing, and he would just have to live with it, work alongside the man. But now he had confronted Watt, he could think of no reason for him to be lying about Maureen.

"Make sure Nance has your new mobile number," he growled, and stomped off.

Past the Dunvegan Hotel, he turned into Grannie Clark's Wynd, then veered onto the Old Course, oblivious to the golfers. A cold wind hit him, bringing with it the smell of a brisk sea. The Old Course seemed such an important part of the killer's plan that he felt an almost irresistible need to walk the links.

Was the Old Course itself significant? Or was it being used simply to gather media attention? He walked past the Road Hole Bunker kicking his feet through the rough that bordered the fairway's length. He continued alongside the sixteenth. From there, the course ran all the way out to the Eden Estuary. He plodded on in his solitary search, criss-crossing the dunes like some game-dog, groping as far as he could into gorse bushes that cluttered the rough. He had to dislodge himself from a bristling clump off the fourteenth fairway to answer his phone.

The rush of Jack's voice had him pressing his mobile tight to his ear.

"Why didn't you tell me about Maureen?"

The question almost threw him, but he recovered with, "It's early days, and I—"

"What's that supposed to mean? Harry told me there's an appeal on the TV for information on Maureen's whereabouts. That doesn't sound like early days to me."

"I'm sorry, Jack. I didn't want to say anything until I knew for sure."

The fight seemed to go out of Jack then. "Don't tell me Mo's next," he said, and before Gilchrist could offer anything, he hung up.

Gilchrist folded his mobile and eyed the grass and gorse around him. How could he go on with this? How could he search for Chloe when his own daughter was missing? But even as he asked that question of himself, he knew the answer to Maureen's disappearance would be delivered through the remaining parts of Chloe's body.

He hung his head and struggled on.

By the time he reached the twelfth tee he had found nothing. The tide was out and the flat sands of the Eden Estuary stretched before him as uninviting as mud. Overhead, clouds tumbled like windblown cotton. He decided to cut across the Jubilee and the New Course onto the West Sands and walk back to town along the beach.

When he ducked through the wire fence that bordered the links, his mobile rang.

"No luck," said Dick without introduction. "Peggy Linnet is one of three students who rent the flat from McPhail. The number belongs to her ex-boyfriend who used her address for billing purposes."

"Got a name?"

"Joe."

"Joe who?"

"That's the problem. She only ever knew him as Joe."

"How long had she been going out with the guy?"

"Three months."

"And she never knew his name?"

"Looks like it."

"Are they all covering for him?"

"Don't think so. Apparently he's a nasty piece of work. Drank too much. Argued all the time. Left without paying his share of the rent. Peggy says she keeps getting his bills and keeps sending them back. They would all shop him if they could."

"Description?"

"Slim. Dark hair. Five-eight. Thirty-something going on fifty. Rolls his own. Born in Glasgow. Rough as they come."

Gilchrist dug his thumb and forefinger into his eyes. A thousand Glaswegians would fit that description. "Keep at it, Dick," he said, even though it was probably useless.

He slid down a worn path between two dunes.

The West Sands stretched before him, copper and gold bordered by the dark waters of the North Sea. Multi-coloured kites of reds, yellows, blues, dipped and swooped then soared high. In the distance he noticed a gathering crowd and wondered if a busload of day-trippers had offloaded and spilled onto the sands, or if someone was having a party, a student perhaps, celebrating God only knew what excuse for a drunken orgy.

By the time he figured it out, his feet were pounding the firm sands at the water's edge, his breath coming at him in hard hits. He heard his own whimper burst from his mouth with the certain knowledge that after a few more minutes he would have only one more body part to find. And then. . . .

"Dear God, no."

Chapter 25

GILCHRIST ORDERED EVERYONE to, "Step back. Police. Step back."

And louder. "*Sir*. Back from the body."

He had used the word *body*, even though it was not a complete body, but a mostly limbless torso. As he stood by the white thing that lay before him like a lump of bloodless meat, his lungs seemed unable to pull in air. He stumbled to his knees. Seawater soaked through his trousers.

He stared at it, at the headless torso with no legs, and only one arm—without a hand—which shifted on the sands with each incoming wave. Ruddied pockmarks dotted the skin where gulls and other seabirds had pecked through.

He brushed sand from the flat swell of the stomach, revealing what looked like a black stain above the belly-button. He cupped seawater with his hands, spilled it over the torso, and a tiny love-heart swam into view.

He pushed himself to his feet, brushed his hands on his thighs. Despite himself, he could not take his eyes off the blackened nipples of her small breasts. It struck him then that her nakedness was exposed for all to see, and he snapped at the onlookers, "Go on. Get out of here. What are you looking at?"

With hesitant reluctance the crowd backed up.

He slapped his mobile to his ear, ordered the SOCOs, and gave directions. But it was not until he closed his mobile and stared at the blonde pubis that lay between twin circles of butchered meat that he realised something was missing.

Curiosity overpowered his revulsion. He kneeled again, and studied the love-heart. The finest of blonde hairs, dried by the sun, stood proud, as if refusing to give up life. His gaze shifted on to bony shoulders made all the more narrow by the missing left arm, down across a rippled ribcage to a wasp-like waist that made Chloe's torso seem strangely thin and frail. The gulls had not done too much harm. Open pits around the upper chest looked more like unhealed sores than carrion food-spots. But other than the tattoo and the peck-holes the torso was unblemished.

A wave rushed the shore and a hacked hip bumped against his arm before he could move. He choked back the urge to throw up, trying to convince himself it was the personal nature of the torso that was making him gag. But he saw with a clarity that stunned him that it was more than that. For once, he was on the receiving end, the relative of a murder victim, the person left to cope with death. How heartless he must have appeared to relatives of other victims. And he saw that no amount of whispered condolences or words of kindness could ever salve their loss.

He forced himself to concentrate on the task at hand, see this as just another murder. And that thought stopped him. *Just* another murder? How had he ever let himself become this cold? He took a deep breath, gripped Chloe's right arm, pulled her up and over, surprised by how light she felt. Her torso slapped onto the sand, and a muted gasp rushed from the onlookers as they took another step back.

He had his sixth note. Gouged into the back with vee-shaped cuts deep enough to show bone. *BUTCHER.*

And the sixth letter. E.

It could not be clearer.

M. A. U. R. E. E.

His daughter was next. And she was missing.

"HEY."

Gilchrist pressed his phone to his ear, stared out to sea. "Jack?"

"Hey, Andy, listen, I'm sorry about earlier. I just—"

"Jack."

A pause, then, "It's Chloe, isn't it?"

Gilchrist dragged a hand over his face. Two SOCOs in white coveralls were rolling her torso into a body-bag. A yellow cordon did little to separate the scene from onlookers. Uniformed policemen were interviewing individuals from the dwindling crowd.

"Tell it to me straight, Andy."

Straight? What could he say? He stepped away as the SOCOs lifted the body-bagged torso and carried it dripping with seawater to the back of their van for Mackie to examine at Ninewells.

"I'm sorry, Jack. It's Chloe. That's all I can tell you."

"Jesus." And from that one word Gilchrist could almost feel Jack's utter despair.

He wondered if he should have spoken to Jack face-to-face rather than tell him over the phone. He had handled his marriage all wrong, the break-up, too. Now he was handling his son wrong.

"Jack. Listen," he said. "We will solve this. I promise you." He tried to force all thoughts of failing from his mind. But you could never tell with a murder enquiry. "Where are you?" he asked.

"Down by the harbour. It's where we used to walk. Chloe loved the sea. Did she tell you that?"

He was about to say yes, then realised Jack needed to air his grief. "No, she didn't."

"Chloe had something about not being able to paint the ocean, about it being too wild and beautiful. *The ocean represents life in its perpetual evolution*, she said. She refused to paint seascapes because she said she could never capture its beauty in its stillness. You had to see it moving to appreciate the ocean's true beauty." A rush of breath, then, "I tell you, Andy, Chloe was something else. She was special, man."

"I know she was." It was all he could think to say. The SOCO van roared into life and eased along the sands. Onlookers drifted away. Already Chloe's mutilated torso on the beach was being assigned to history.

"I feel like, you know . . . helpless, Andy. Just out-and-out helpless."

Like father like son, he thought.

"Do you, uh, do you need me to do anything?"

Gilchrist knew what Jack was asking. But how could he have his son identify his girlfriend's hacked up torso? "No," he said, and thought he caught a sigh of relief.

"You haven't heard from Maureen yet, have you?" Jack asked.

"I was hoping you had."

"You really don't think anything's happened to her, do you?"

Jack's question confirmed he was in denial. First his girlfriend, then his sister. It was too much for anyone to handle emotionally. But Jack did not need to hear that his sister was next to be hacked to pieces. "I'm sure there's a simple explanation," he tried. "You know Mo. She's probably gone away for a few days.

"Remember that time she ran off to Spain for a month without telling you or Mum? You went ballistic, man. Through the roof." Jack chuckled. "Maybe she's gone there again. Do you think?"

Gilchrist kept the deception alive. Having Jack do something was better than him doing nothing. "Maybe," he said, and tried to sound upbeat. "Why don't you look into that, Jack? Call a few friends. Find out if they know anything."

"Yeah. I'll do that."

"And when you get hold of her," Gilchrist said, "give her an earful and tell her to call her old Dad."

Jack forced a chuckle down the line. "Will do, Andy."

By nightfall Gilchrist had not heard from Maureen.

But he had not expected to.

MAUREEN STARTLED AT the scraping sound.

Someone was outside.

She heard it again.

A key? A knife?

She peered into the darkness, but saw only the shape of the door and the curtained window of the hut she was in. She struggled to move, but the knots bit into her skin, brought tears to her eyes again. She fought them back, bit down on the gag, and breathed through her nose. She had worried about the gag, worried that if her nose blocked she would be unable to breathe. It had happened once, two nights ago, and she had passed out from lack of air. But she wakened later, her nasal passageways clear again.

Another scrape. A key that time. No doubt about it.

The door opened and in the dim greyness she could make out the dark silhouette of his figure. She felt wetness spread between her legs, and tears well at her inability to contain her fear. The warm smell of urine lifted off the wooden floorboards.

She felt the floorboards shiver from the heels of his boots, smelled the stale tobacco that clung to his body like his personal scent. Despite hating that smell, it gave a welcome respite from the stench of defecation that had filled her senses for days.

An explosion of light hit her like a blow to the head.

She squeezed her eyes shut.

"It's fucking honking in here," his voice growled.

Footsteps thudded across the floorboards. A tremor took hold of her then.

Don't let him touch me. Don't let him come near me.

The footsteps stopped. She knew he was standing in front of her. She heard a rustle of cloth, jacket rubbing jeans, perhaps, the sound of a bottle being opened. She eased her eyes open, squinted against the harsh light.

He squatted no more than three feet from her, his filthy moustache thick and dark over lips as tight and narrow as a scar. He smiled a slow smile that exposed cracked and yellow teeth, then held a plastic bottle out to her.

"Want some?"

She tried to say yes, but managed only a groan from behind the gag. She shifted herself on the floor, felt the damp squelch of her own defecation as it squeezed thick in the folds of her underwear.

"Want me to take that off?"

She closed her eyes in a long blink.

Please, take it off. Please. I won't do anything. I promise.

She held her breath as he tilted the bottle to her upturned face and dribbled water onto her gag. She worked her tongue, sucked at the cool liquid.

Then the bottle tilted upright, and he waved it in front of her. "Some more?" He grinned at her, his eyes dark and feral, his hand lowering to his zip. "This first."

She turned her head away, closed her eyes.

I can't, I can't. Don't make me do this. I can't.

She heard his zip being pulled down, some rustling, a grunt.

Fingers dug into her hair, twisted her head to face him, face it. "Open your eyes."

She started to cry then, her breath rushing in and out of her nasal passages, short sharp blasts that made her think she might pass out. She had read somewhere that hyperventilation could make you faint. She shortened her breaths, prayed she would pass out.

His grip tightened. She whimpered from the pain.

"Open your eyes, bitch."

Quick breaths. Fast and hard.

"Open them, you fucking bitch."

Please God. Don't let him. Not again. I'll spew and choke. I know I will.

He was close. She could tell by the way his breath rasped, the way his grip clutched and scratched her hair. She had looked once, had opened her eyes the first time, had seen how his face twisted in an ugly grimace as he climaxed.

Dear God. He's coming. He's coming.

She squeezed her eyes, heard him groan as sperm hit her forehead in a warm squirt. Another over her cheek. And one more. Then drips like syrup that oozed down her cheek and threatened to slide behind the gag and over her lips. She lowered her head, felt his sperm slither over her chin and drip free.

She had not done as he had asked. She had not opened her eyes. He would give her no water. Which was now what she wanted.

Without water, she would die.

Please God, let me die. Just let me die.

Chapter 26

BUT SHE DID not die.

Instead, she was photographed.

He took the Polaroid prints into another room, from where she heard the metallic click of a staple gun. When he came back, she tried to stare him out. But a glob of sperm slipped into the corner of her right eye, and she closed it, losing her short-lived resistance.

"Get up."

She cut back her cry as he grabbed her by the hair and pulled her upright.

"I said get up."

She tried to stand, she truly did, but her legs gave out. She shook her head, felt slime by her eye drip free, then gagged a scream as a knife flashed in front of her. She whimpered as the blade pressed against her calf, then watched in disbelief as it sliced through the cords around her ankles. She tried to turn as he walked behind her, but a heavy boot against her shoulder forced her face against the wall as the rope that had held her hands behind her back for the last three days and kept her captive to an iron ring on the wall, was cut. Another slice, this time at the back of her neck, and the gag slipped loose.

She gulped in lungfuls of air, lolling her tongue like a panting dog.

"Get up."

She pulled her hands from behind her back and grimaced from a pain that burned like fire in her shoulders. She gripped the gag, used it to wipe sperm from her eyes and face. Her fingers felt thick and stiff, as if they belonged to someone else. She twisted into a sitting position, but slumped to the floor. Her head hit the floorboards, but she felt no pain, only a numbing sense of relief at being able to move her arms, her legs, breathe unrestricted.

"Don't make me have to say it again."

"Water." But the voice that cracked from her dried throat did not sound like her own.

He held the bottle out.

She grabbed it, forced herself upright, ignoring the clotty dampness at her rump, and drank. Long glorious gulps of cool clean water that overflowed from her mouth and spilled down her chin. She coughed, almost choked, took another mouthful then remembered reading somewhere that too much water after a time without could make you sick.

"For the last time," he snarled, "get up."

She pressed a hand to the floor and rolled over onto her knees. A bit wobbly, but the benefit of fluids in her system was already doing wonders for her strength and morale. She wondered for one crazy moment if she could make a run for it, but knew she would not manage ten feet without being caught.

She flapped a hand at the wall, and steadied herself, then held her head as high as she could. "I'm up."

"Strip."

"Fuck off." Her tongue was not working the way it should, but it felt good cursing.

He leaned to the side, opened a holdall that she had not noticed, reached inside, and removed a handful of crumpled clothes. He dropped them to the floor.

"Now take off your fucking clothes and get into these."

"In case it's escaped your attention," she said, "I'm covered in shit."

He backed up to the door and stepped outside, then reappeared in the doorway with a garden hose in his hands. "We can do this in there or out here. I don't give a fuck."

Maureen blinked, fighting back tears of hope. Was she being set free? It seemed impossible. But he was giving her clean clothes, offering her a wash.

"Outside," she whispered.

"Strip first," he ordered.

Sweet fresh air wafted into the hut on a chilling breeze. If she did as she was told, she could be washed and wearing clean clothes and underwear in a few minutes. That thought alone was almost enough to make her move. She caught the sound of traffic somewhere off in the distance, the scent of cooked meat on the wind, and felt her stomach knot with hunger. When had she last eaten? Three days ago? She was weak, did not have the strength to fight back or make a sustained run for it.

Even if she knew where to run to.

She made her decision.

She crossed her arms, flinched with the pain of flexing stiffened muscles, grimaced at the sight of bloodied and bruised wrists, and tugged her top up and over and dropped it to the floor. Undid her zip at the side, and let her skirt fall off. She choked at the sight of her inner thighs, coated with faeces and glistening damp from fresh urine. She had become inured to the stench, but against the fresh air the rancid guff hit her with renewed strength.

Hands behind her back, off with her bra.

Oh, God. Just do it.

Thumbs hooked in her knickers, dropped to the floor.

She fought back a choke of disgust and staggered outside into the night air.

Cold water hit her with a shock that trapped her breath. She gasped, turned, felt the jet hit her backside, and she faced him again, to hide her mess from him. Her hands slid over her body, her thighs, her behind, her filth washing through her fingers like wet mud.

"Don't you have any soap?"

"Think you're at the fucking Hilton? Get on with it before I switch it off."

She swept her hands over her skin, rubbing and brushing.

The jet stopped.

"I'm not clean," she pleaded, then shielded her face as a blast hit her again.

"Fucking hurry up then."

When she pushed her hands through her hair the jet stopped.

She stood shivering from the cold, watching his dark eyes study her nakedness.

"Get the clothes."

Back inside the hut, the fetid air almost choked her. She pressed her hand to her nose, amazed that she had breathed in that vile stench for so long. She picked up the bundle and rushed outside.

He stood on a slabbed path that slipped between bushes at the side of a bungalow that looked vaguely familiar. She assumed that had to be the way out, but in the darkness could not be sure. And she could not stop a tremor that now gripped her limbs. Running was out of the question.

She tugged at the clothing. "Do you have a towel?"

"Get the fuck dressed before I change my mind."

She separated the bundle to find it consisted of only a skirt and a sweater.

"There's no underwear," she said.

He looked away, gobbed off to the side.

She turned her back to him and slipped on the skirt. It felt tight, too tight to fasten at the waist. But it was long and black and woollen soft. She pulled on the top, a black woollen sweater, thin at the elbows, with cuffs frayed and stained with paint. It felt tight around her boobs, but she felt warmth seep through her system, despite being wet.

Then a hand gripped her hair, twisted her head, and she

gasped as the cold steel of a blade pressed to her throat. "One squeak and I'll slit you from ear to fucking ear." Breath as stale as cigarette ash warmed her face. "Now start walking."

She was prodded along a slabbed pathway, between bushes to the dark hulk of a car she recognised as a BMW. The boot was already open.

"Get in."

"You're hurting me."

"Get the fuck in."

At least he was not going to gag her, or tie her hands and feet. She lifted one leg over the rim, then the other, and ducked just in time as the boot lid slammed shut. She listened to the sound of footsteps fading, and imagined him returning to the shed to put out the light and lock the door. Cover their tracks? Why would he do that if she was being set free? And if she was being freed, why would he lock her in the boot of his car?

Oh, God, I'm wrong, I'm wrong. He's going to kill me.

But her rationale insisted he would not have had her clean herself if he was going to kill her. Confused, she lay on her back, pleased to feel her thighs clear of the tackiness of the last few days. But the cold shower had not rid her skin of the smell of defecation that clung to her like smoke to clothing. She fumbled around, but the darkness was total and the boot-space solid. She lay still. Where had he gone? Was she to be freed? *Dear God, tell me he's going to let me go. Tell me he's not going to do any more of that to me. . . .*

But the truth sank inside her like an anchor into dark waters, pulling hope down with it. She had seen his face and knew he would not let witnesses to his sadistic crimes roam the streets. *He's going to kill me. He's going to take me away somewhere and slit my throat.* Her eyes strained into the darkness. She had never been scared of the dark before, but as she lay there in the black silence she felt the warm sting of tears in her eyes—

Footsteps.

She held her breath as they stopped at the back of the BMW. The lock popped, and she shielded her face as the boot lid opened.

It was him again. Smiling. Something in his hand.

He leaned into the boot, placed it by her face.

"Look after this," he said.

She stared at it.

Horror seared her throat in a voiceless scream.

She scrambled away from it, pushed herself back, felt her head hit metal, her legs kick like a trapped swimmer, her arms flail the air for some way out.

The boot lid slammed with a thud.

She screamed then. A primal scream that reflected the terror she had seen in Chloe's sightless eyes.

GILCHRIST WAKENED WITH a start.

He had been dreaming, more nightmare than dream.

Maureen had been speaking to him in a language he knew but could not place. Then he realised she was speaking the language of the dead. He had reached for her then, but with every step she seemed to fade away, so that when he grabbed her she was nothing more than a shadow dancing in the mirror of his imagination, weak and faint as the vaguest remnants of his oldest dream.

That was when he came to.

His T-shirt clung to his skin like damp cloth. He struggled to still the jackhammer pounding in his chest. He glanced at his radio clock—3:33.

He breathed in, almost sobbed. *Dear God, tell me this isn't happening. Tell me that if I had never joined the force Maureen's life would not now be in danger.* His head slumped into his hands and he choked back a sob. He clenched his jaw and looked up. He had to get a grip. He had to get on with it. Moping around wasn't going to solve a damn thing. But how was he supposed to think, when his daughter was next in line to be served up to him in bits?

He staggered into the shower, scrubbed himself with soap as if he wanted to rip his skin from his bones. An early morning shower often brought his thoughts into focus, but ten minutes later he stepped from the cubicle none the wiser.

In the kitchen he poured a glass of orange juice, then checked with the Office. But no one had any news for him. He tried Dainty on his mobile, but it rang out. He got through to Pitt Street, but was told Dainty would not be in until 8:00. He asked for a home number but the receptionist declined to give it out. He next called Directory Enquiries for Strathclyde Drug Squad, but when he asked for Watt he was surprised to be told they had no record of a Ronnie Watt, Ron Watt, Ronald Watt, or any variation of that name, either at Detective Sergeant or Constable level.

Gilchrist gave a whispered curse as he hung up.

What the hell was going on? If Strathclyde had no record of Watt, did that mean Watt had pulled one over on Greaves? Watt would be transferred to Fife only on written authority. Had Watt faked the transfer, or was Greaves in on it? Or was he just pissing up against the wrong tree?

He checked his watch. He would make one more call.

"This is DCI Gilchrist," he said. "How much have you printed?"

"Mr. Gilchrist?" grumbled Leighton. "It's 5:00 in the morning."

"You said you would call."

"I've been quite busy working on them."

"In that case, I'll be there in twenty minutes. Give me what you've got."

He pulled on his black leather jacket and stepped out into a cold east coast morning.

Today he would find his daughter.

Even if he had to die doing so.

Chapter 27

LEIGHTON SCOWLED AT him. "Through there," he said, and pointed to a door at the end of the hallway. "I don't like being wakened at this time of the morning."

"Neither do I."

Gilchrist brushed past and entered the room. An oak dining table with folded leaves, reminiscent of the one his grand-mother used to have, centred the cramped space. Reams of printed paper stacked the table's polished surface. On a cof-fee table to the side, Maureen's laptop sat hooked to an HP DeskJet printer. Two opened boxes of copier paper squatted on the carpet.

"Is this it?" Gilchrist asked.

"As much as I've printed thus far."

Gilchrist flipped through several pages. Leighton had printed them in chronological order and divided them into piles by year. A single sheet listed the file names in each stack.

"Is there much more?" he asked.

"That's only one day's printing."

Gilchrist removed his wallet. "Ten hours cover it so far?"

Leighton did not hesitate. "That should just about do it."

Gilchrist knew he was being ripped off, but peeled ten twen-ties from his wallet and passed them to Leighton. He picked up the printed reams. "How soon until you print the rest?"

Leighton shrugged. "Another day or so?"

"Too long. I need them tonight."

"I can only print out as fast as my printer will allow."

"Get another printer," he snapped. "Get two. I'm paying your expenses. I need them tonight, no later than seven."

"That doesn't give me much time."

"You'd better get on with it then," he said, and strode down the hall.

THE BMW DREW to a halt.

Its engine purred in the quiet of some deserted spot. Maureen knew it was deserted, because the sound of traffic had stopped fifteen minutes earlier. They were in the countryside somewhere. But even if she knew how far they had travelled, she did not know the starting point, or in which direction they had come. They could be anywhere.

The engine died.

She listened to the sounds of the door opening, closing, then footsteps crunching the length of the car. The footsteps stopped.

The boot lid popped open.

Before she had time to move, fingers as tight as talons grabbed her by the hair.

"Don't even think about it."

He pulled her upright, and she squealed, "You're hurting me."

A blow to the side of her head sent her slamming into the dark confines of the boot.

Warm breath by her ear. "If you want to see your old man again, shut the fuck up, and do as you're told."

Hope and fear surged through her in a confusing wave. If she did as she was told, she would see her father again. But why mention her father, not her mother? Did he know her mother was ill? If he knew that, what else did he know?

"Sign this."

She peered up. The sky was still dark, but she caught the high-pitched chatter of birdsong. A blackbird? A starling? Did that mean it was morning, not night?

A beam of light pierced the darkness, and she glimpsed the

back of Chloe's head. When they had driven off, Chloe's head had rolled into her. She had screamed then, pushed the thing away, hating the feel of Chloe's hair on her bare skin, just managing to keep down the vomit that threatened to erupt from her throat. She must have jammed it into a hole or something, for the head had not moved for the rest of the journey.

"Here."

She stared at a pen and a rough-edged piece of paper.

"Sign."

"Why?"

"Don't play the silly cunt." He leaned down, picked up Chloe's head, and she gagged back a scream. "If you don't want this to happen to you," he growled, "you'd better sign."

Once more, hope soared within her.

If she signed, would he let her go? She took the paper, noticed something was printed on it. "What's it say?"

The beam of light shivered across the paper.

"Vengeance? What's that supposed to mean?"

"Just sign the fucking thing."

"You'll let me go then?"

"I won't slit your throat, you stupid bitch."

Maureen stared at his lantern jaw, made all the more gaunt by several days' growth, at his filthy moustache yellowed from tobacco smoke. Where was his knife? Could she make a run for it? And once again that thought flew from her mind. She would not stand a chance. She turned to the note and pretended to have difficulty holding the pen. But between looking up at him, then down at the pen, she glanced past him to the bushes by the wall.

It was morning. She knew by the way the sky was lightening.

And that was when she saw it, when it hit her that he had no intention of letting her live. She felt the warm release of urine as a tremor gripped her hands. She almost dropped the pen. "Please," she whimpered. "Please let me go."

His face darkened. "Aw, you bitch, you pissed in my car. I should slit your fucking throat for that. Get out."

She tried to pull herself to her feet, but her legs gave way. She did not even have the strength to scream as he hauled her out by her hair.

She slumped onto hard asphalt.

"Now sign that fucking paper or I'll rip your fucking head off." He gobbed off to the side, a thick lump of green phlegm that anger had released from his throat.

Through the blur of her tears, she tried to make sense of the single word.

VENGEANCE.

What did it mean? But it was pointless asking. She was going to be killed. Maybe by signing she could leave a message to her parents, let them know she had remained defiant to the last. She almost choked a laugh at the thought. How could she even think that, when she wet herself with every spurt of fear?

She gripped the pen, signed beneath the single word.

Mo, she wrote. That was all.

He snatched the paper from her, stuffed it into his pocket.

She felt herself freeze as he reached behind him. He was going for his knife. That was where he kept it. In a leather sheath on his belt. She stared at the bushes, or what she had mistaken for bushes. Now morning was dawning, the old stone wall and the headstones behind it had taken shape. And the oddest thought coursed through her mind.

A cemetery seemed such an appropriate place in which to be killed.

"ANDY. IT'S PETE Small. You tried to reach me?"

Gilchrist dug his thumb and forefinger into his eyes. "Ronnie Watt," he said. "He's not one of yours. Is he?"

"You know I can't talk about that, Andy. Is that why you called?"

Gilchrist caught the anger in Dainty's voice. The man might be small in stature, but that did little to lessen his presence. "There used to be a time when we worked hand in hand."

"Don't play with words, Andy. You know the rules."

Gilchrist stared at Leighton's printouts on his desk. He'd been reading his way through them for the last four hours, but come up with nothing. "Watt knows Chris Topley. Did you know that?"

"Yes."

"They were seen having a drink together. Does that not interest you?"

"I've had the odd pint with a criminal or two. So has half the force."

Gilchrist could not argue with that. "Where did Topley get the money to start his business?"

"Topley's clean. We've checked him out. He might have an eponymous agency, but it's part of a larger holding group. Some international company with too much money."

"Does it have a name?"

"W something Holdings International."

"Can you find out?"

"Can do."

"And where it's based?"

"Can do. Why?"

He had no clear idea why his interest was piqued, other than his sixth sense telling him something did not ring true. "Just a hunch," he said.

Dainty grunted, then said, "One other thing."

Gilchrist caught the bite in Dainty's voice. "I'm all ears."

"A body was found in a farm lane on the outskirts of Castlecary, off the M80 on the way to Stirling. Male, early thirties, throat cut. Being treated as murder, obviously."

"Anyone we know?"

"Kenneth Finnigan. Wee Kenny to his friends. But for the last two or three years was Jimmy Reid's goffer."

Jimmy Reid? Why was Dainty telling him this? Reid? Then Gilchrist felt the hairs on the nape of his neck stir. "Bully's brother?"

"The one and only."

Christ. "What does Jimmy have to say about it?"

"Jimmy's shot the crow. We raided his house this morning, but he's packed up and left. Spain, probably. Has a villa there. We've already been onto the airlines and the Spanish Police."

Gilchrist could tell from Dainty's tone that Jimmy's disappearance was not the crux of the matter. "What aren't you telling me?"

"Wee Kenny's car was discovered twenty miles away, burned to a shell."

"A Jaguar?"

"Right first time."

"How badly burned?"

"Nothing left of it."

Gilchrist knew they would not be able to tell from the paintwork if the boot of the Jaguar had been patch-painted. But they might from the metalwork. "The boot," he said. "Any damage done to it?"

Dainty chuckled. "You don't miss a thing, do you?"

And neither do you, Gilchrist thought.

"Repaired pockmarks were found on the boot. Possible bullet holes. Six in total. Which might suggest an old-fashioned revolver."

"For an old-fashioned gangland war."

"Could be. Jimmy was involved in some turf war about eight years ago."

"About the time Bully was put behind bars?"

"Some time after that. Rumour had it he was looking after the family business."

Bully had been sent down on charges of manslaughter. Fifteen years, with no chance of parole—supposedly. Was it possible he was still pulling the strings from behind bars?

"Bully's still in prison, right?" Gilchrist asked.

"Bar-L. The one and only."

"He's not getting out any time soon, is he?"

"He's hired one of the top legal firms in town."

"Meaning?"

"They're pushing to have him out in maybe two years."

"You're joking."

"Afraid not."

The Jaguar. Burned to a cinder. Kenny Finnigan. Dead in a farm lane. Ronnie Watt. Back in Fife. Maureen. Vanished. Jimmy Reid. Gone to Spain. And Bully. Getting out in two years. Did it add up to something Gilchrist should be able to see? He hated to say it, but only one person was available to him. "I need to talk to Bully," he said. "Can you set it up for me?"

"This afternoon do?"

"Perfect," he said, and closed his mobile.

Gilchrist had once prayed that he would never have to face hatred like Bully's again. Now he had arranged to meet with the psycho. Just the thought that Bully might be involved with Maureen's disappearance had his heart racing. Christ, anyone but Bully.

But he knew Bully was involved. Bully would *always* be involved.

He did not need his sixth sense to tell him that.

For years he had dreaded this day coming.

Now it had, he prayed he was up to the task.

Chapter 28

GILCHRIST REMEMBERED IT as if it were yesterday.

He closed his eyes, saw spittle splutter from Bully's mouth as he was dragged away, handcuffed, screaming a vindictive diatribe that had Sheriff MacFarlane thumping his gavel with the energy of a piecework blacksmith.

Fuck you, Gilchrist. Fuck you. I'm going to have you for this. D'you hear, you fucking cunt? You'll regret this, Gilchrist. To your dying fucking day you're going to regret this. D'you hear?

Gilchrist heard all right. He had turned away as Bully was led from the dock. Had he shown weakness by doing so? Should he have stared the man out, smiled and mouthed *Goodbye*? And here he was again, after all these years.

He pulled his Roadster into the car park that fronted the stone monolith of Glasgow's Barlinnie Prison. He had not set foot in the Bar-L for ten years, when he had visited Donnie Crawford, a petty crook serving twenty years for murder. Accompanied by Donnie's court-appointed solicitor, Gilchrist asked specific questions that had proven Donnie's innocence. He remained proud of his efforts that day. Donnie had joined the Army six months later, ending his life of crime before it started in earnest. The last Gilchrist heard, Donnie had married and was now the father of two young daughters.

But Bully was a different animal altogether, *animal* being the operative word. Bully was beyond salvation. And had been ever since the murderous age of ten.

Gilchrist signed in and was escorted through a series of

steel-barred doors, along a corridor with breezeblock walls painted prison-grey, and into a square room furnished with one table and two chairs opposite each other.

He sat.

The sour smell of urine filled his senses. He found his hands patting his pockets for his cigarettes, recalling that when he first came up against Bully he'd been smoking thirty a day. Christ, he could do with one right now. He forced himself to focus on why he was there. If Bully was somehow involved, he might be able to glean something from him, some tiny detail that could lead him to Maureen. Bully's cockiness had been his downfall in the past. It could be again.

The door opened.

There stood Bully, six-foot-one of him, street-fighter-thin and prison-hard. He paused at the doorway before being pushed into the room, arms and legs shackled. The guard manacled the chains to a metal ring on the floor.

"Sit."

Bully sat. Sweat glistened his brow. A yellow tint in the whites of his eyes hinted at a prison illness. Gilchrist found himself surprised by an odd reluctance to lock eyes with the man. Even after eight years.

The guard stood with his back to the door.

Bully broke the verbal standoff.

"I've been expecting you." His deep voice echoed off the block walls, thick with the guttural accent of a Glasgow hard-man grown old.

Gilchrist focused on his hands on the table. He wanted to give Bully the impression that his words had slipped over his head.

But he had heard. And he understood.

I've been expecting you. Why?

Because I knew you would work out who was behind Chloe's death.

Gilchrist looked across at Bully, at eyes that sparkled with the anticipation of revenge. "Why?" was all he said.

Bully chuckled.

Gilchrist caught the stale scent of sweat from pockmarked skin. His rationale was screaming at him—Bully must know. But did he know? Gilchrist forced himself to control his voice. "Why were you expecting me?"

Bully's eyes flickered with a crazed look. "You think I know where your daughter is," he said.

"Who told you she was missing?"

"Word gets around."

"So you know where she is."

"That's for you to find out."

"I'm not here to play games."

"You're free to leave."

"You don't want me to leave."

"I'm not stopping you."

Gilchrist felt the tiniest of tremors take over his left leg. Fear. Of all the criminals he had come up against, Bully was the only one who scared him. All of a sudden he was not sure he could tackle him about his daughter. But, Christ, he had to.

"What's wrong, Mr. Gilchrist? Are you thinking playing games might not be such a bad idea?" Bully laughed, a dry chuckle that sounded forced.

"Where is she?"

"I don't like that game."

"Where is she?"

"Don't you want to play?"

"*Where is she?*"

Bully's face deadpanned. "Do you think I'd tell *you*?"

"So you know."

"*Hah*." The word was barked. Spittle formed at the corners of thin lips. "You're not a stupid man, Mr. Gilchrist. But you're coming across as one."

"Where is my daughter?"

"I haven't the fucking foggiest."

"So why were you expecting me?"

Bully seemed lost at the snap question, but Gilchrist wanted to keep the momentum going.

"I can have you charged with complicity in murder."

"You'd never fucking prove it."

No denial. Was that as good as a confession?

"In case you haven't noticed," Bully said. "I'm inside."

"You are indeed."

Bully glared at him. "I told you I'd get even with you."

"No you didn't. You said I'd regret it."

Bully looked confused for a moment, then revealed white teeth that looked at odds with the hard-man image. "You always were the cocky cunt."

"Well now's your chance to make me regret it."

Bully tilted his head. "Look at you," he said. "The best of gear. What'd the leather jacket sting you? Four hundred? Five? More? Yeah, I bet it was more. And the shirt." He tutted. "You're spoiling the image without a tie."

"You're spoiling my day, Bully. And talking shite."

Bully seemed unfazed. "You must be worth a few bob."

Gilchrist struggled to hold Bully's eyes. Was he hinting at a ransom? But money was not the object of Bully's exercise. Getting even was. Hitting Gilchrist where it hurt the most. Not his pocket—his family.

"And look at poor old me," Bully pressed on. "Dressed in the best of prison rags." Anger shifted like ripples in his jaw. "You put me here."

"You put yourself here," Gilchrist snapped. "If you hadn't massacred that family, you and I would never have met."

"They were asking for it."

"What's your point?"

"You wanted to see me."

"And you've been expecting me. Why?"

Bully glared at him. "D'you know what pleasures I have in life now?"

Silent, Gilchrist waited.

"Writing."

"Sold anything to the Beano yet?"

Bully tried a grin, but his eyes died. "I could fuck your life like that." He snapped his fingers with a hard flick.

Gilchrist pushed his chair back. "You're wasting my time."

"Got things to do? More criminals to put away?"

Gilchrist nodded to the guard who moved towards Bully.

"Missing your *princess*?" Bully hissed.

Ice fingered Gilchrist's spine. He raised his hand to the guard. "What did you say?"

Bully side-nodded. "Get rid of the monkey."

They had discussed this possibility, Gilchrist and Bully being left alone in the same room. The Prison Director had not liked it. But Gilchrist had insisted. He gave a tiny nod, and the guard stepped from the room.

"I'll be right outside if you need me, sir."

Gilchrist waited until the door was closed, then said, "Talk. Or I'm walking, and you're never going to hear from me again."

"You're a brainy bastard," Bully said. "And you're smart."

Gilchrist had no idea where Bully was going, so he waited.

"But I'm smarter. I'm smarter than you. I'm smarter than ape-face out there. I'm smarter than the whole fucking lot of you piled together."

Gilchrist said nothing. He sensed Bully was leading the conversation to what he wanted to talk about, what game he wanted Gilchrist to play.

"Wee, sleekit, cowerin, timorous beastie." Bully's smile darkened his face and warned Gilchrist to beware. "Oh what a panic's in thy breastie."

Cowering? Timorous? Panic? Was that Bully's game? Was he trying to sow the seed of fear into Gilchrist's mind? If so, he needn't bother. Fear was well and truly planted where Bully was concerned. "Didn't know you were a Burns aficionado," he tried.

Bully chuckled. "You shitting yourself yet?"

Not quite. "What's your point?"

"His knife see rustic Labour dight, an' cut you up wi' ready slight, trenching your gushing entrails bright."

Gilchrist had been to enough Burns Suppers to know Bully was reciting from *To a Haggis*. But the reference to gushing entrails had him worried. He tried to redirect the flow with, "You're talking in riddles."

"I'm talking in poems, Mr. Gilchrist. Father of Jack. Protector of Maureen. Poems." He tapped the side of his head. "It's what makes me smarter than the rest of the bozos in here. Poems."

Gilchrist tried again. "Why did you ask if I was missing my princess?"

"That's what you called Maureen when she was young. Your little princess."

Gilchrist felt his breath leave him. Hearing Maureen's name being uttered from the mouth of a convicted killer hit some point deep within him. How did Bully know Maureen was his princess? She was five when he called her that. *Time to go to bed, my little princess.* Then he would lift her up and carry her upstairs—

"Inhuman man! Curse on thy barb'rous art, and blasted be thy murder-aiming eye."

The words sounded like Burns, but they were unfamiliar to Gilchrist.

"May never pity soothe thee with a sigh, nor ever pleasure glad thy cruel heart."

More unfamiliar verses, but he could not fail to catch the emphasis on *cruel*. Was Bully talking about himself, or suggesting something else? *Inhuman man!* That would certainly describe Bully.

As if reading Gilchrist's confusion, Bully said, "Do you know what's good about being in this place?"

"You not being outside."

"You always were a cheeky bastard. But I'm too old in the

tooth to rise to your petty baiting now." Bully narrowed his eyes. "Honesty," he said. "That's what you get when you're in here. Honesty."

Gilchrist puzzled at the words. He could not think of a more dishonest bunch of souls than those incarcerated in Barlinnie. "Now you've lost me."

Bully chuckled, a hacking cackle that came from deep inside his lungs. "No one tells lies in here," he said. "Why should they? They've got nothing to lie for. Not like the world you live in."

"So you're trying to tell me that you've seen the error of your ways?"

Something dark shifted behind Bully's eyes at that moment. "Three lawyers' tongues turned inside out," he growled, "wi' lies seamed like a beggar's clout. Three priests' hearts, rotten, black as muck, lay stinking, vile in every neuk." Bully's lips parted in an ugly smile. "Even back in Burns' day, lawyers and priests were the same lying fucking shites they are today."

"And your point is?"

"I would have thought a brainy bastard like you would work it out."

Work what out? The verses? The reference to lawyers and priests? The lies? The truth? What? But what Gilchrist *had* worked out was that Bully was behind Maureen's disappearance. Of that he was certain.

He tried again. "Where is my daughter?"

Bully held his gaze for a long moment, then glanced at the door, and Gilchrist felt his hopes soar at the possibility that Bully was about to tell him. Then Bully's eyes gleamed with victory. "Oh princess, by thy watchtower be, it is the wished, the trysted hour. Those smiles and glances let me see, that makes the miser's treasure poor," and with an abruptness that had Gilchrist on full alert, Bully pushed back and stood. He raised his hands, shackles jangling, then brought them down on the table with such force that Gilchrist was sure he must have cracked several bones.

The guard burst in. "*You. Sit.*"

Bully held out his hands, and Gilchrist saw the disfigured fingers of crushed joints.

"Take me." Bully shuffled towards the guard, as if the act of smashing his hands had drained him of all energy. But at the door, he halted. "Vengeance, Mr. Gilchrist. You put me away eight years ago. And through every second of every minute of every hour of every one of those eight years, vengeance has kept me going."

Gilchrist saw that Bully had said all he was going to say. But he could not let him just walk away. He had to give it one last shot. "My daughter's done nothing to harm you," he tried. "Let her go." It was pointless negotiating with a psychopath, he knew that, but he tried anyway. "Please," he added. "What's she ever done to you?"

Bully glared at him for a full ten seconds, then said, "The wind blew as twad blawn its last. The rattling showers rose on the blast. The speedy gleams the darkness swallowed. Loud, deep and lang the thunder bellowed. That night, a child might understand, the Deil had business on his hand, Mr. Gilchrist." Then Bully tilted his head back and let out an ear-piercing howl like a demented wolf.

Even the guard looked taken aback.

Gilchrist stared at the man, knowing he was being toyed with. Another howl raised the hairs on his neck, followed by a crazed laugh that cut to the heart of his soul.

Then Bully stepped into the corridor.

The door closed with a metallic clang.

Gilchrist sat stunned, listening to the sound of Bully's laughter and wolf-howls fade, until all that was left was the silent echo of prison life. He opened his jacket and removed his recorder. He replayed their conversation, recognised some of the words, excerpts from poems by Robert Burns. But what did they mean? Was Bully giving him more clues? Or just playing with him?

On the way out, he checked with the prison doctor, who confirmed Bully was not on medication.

"What about his health? Any sweats, yellow eyes, that sort of thing?"

"We have the occasional viral infection passing through the prison population. Much like the real world. According to my records, Mr. Reid has not had any serious illness for five years."

"And five years ago, what happened?"

"The flu." He cocked his head. "I'm sorry to disappoint you, Inspector, but Mr. Reid has enjoyed, and continues to enjoy, excellent health."

Driving back to St. Andrews, Gilchrist let his thoughts run their convoluted course.

Bully was not being prescribed medication. Was he having drugs smuggled in? Hard to do, but not impossible. He could not say. But one thing he could say was that Bully's gibberish had to mean something. Of that, he was certain.

But what?

And if he found out, could he save Maureen?

MAUREEN GROANED FROM a dull pain at the nape of her neck.

That was where he had hit her, knocked her unconscious.

Since coming to, she had spent the last thirty minutes kicking the wooden door that was the only exit from her chamber. But her efforts had resulted only in bruised and bloodied feet. Her mouth was gagged with duct tape that ran around the back of her head, pulled her hair tight, made breathing difficult. Her ankles were bound with the same tape. Behind her back, her hands were, too. Every joint in her body seemed to ache.

She shuffled across the concrete floor on her rump until her back hit the stone wall. As best she could work out in the pitch darkness, the chamber was no more than six feet square. The ceiling was low, barely high enough to allow her to sit. The air smelled dusty and dry, and she worried that the oxygen might run out. The tape was wound four or five times around her limbs, letting her know she was not meant to escape.

And she knew, too, that he was not coming back.

She was all alone. No water. No food.

She was going to die. This chamber was to be her final resting place. And it pained her to think that no one would find her, no one would visit her once she was gone.

The tears came then, racking sobs that threatened to steal the air from her lungs. Thoughts of all she had done wrong in her life—the indifference she had shown her parents, the disregard she had shown her brother, the recklessness she had developed of late—swirled around her mind in dizzying waves. Oddly, it was the thought of dying that stopped her crying. She sniffed, tried to blink her eyes dry. She was not dead yet.

She would not lie down and die. She would not let that happen.

She wriggled to the door, turned her back to it, felt her fingers fumble over the wooden surface, work their way around the edge, searching for a splinter of wood that might have broken off during her attempts to break free. But the door was solid. She twisted her body, tried to reach higher, the fire in her shoulders and arms forcing a gasp from her aching throat. She fought to ignore the pain, and pressed harder, pushing, pushing, until—

She scraped against something.

An edge of the concrete wall, a bit that was chipped, maybe sharp enough to cut.

She gritted her teeth, pressed the tape to the wall.

She would not die. She would not let him win.

She rubbed her wrists up and down.

Up and down.

Chapter 29

JACK SAID, "THAT'S scary, man. What the hell does it mean?"

Gilchrist had asked that same question a hundred times. And a hundred times he had come up with the same answer. *I don't know.* On the drive back to St. Andrews, the word *watchtower* had prompted him to call Stan to initiate a search of the West Port, St. Rules Tower, St. Salvator's, and any other tower-like structure in the St. Andrews area. But so far, no one had found a damn thing. Maureen no longer lived in Fife, so how many other towers were there in Glasgow, or Scotland, or the British Isles for that matter? A similar call to Dainty had resulted in a curt lack of manpower response, and a snide remark that left Gilchrist wondering if it was all just a hoax. Had Bully been teasing him, letting him think he was giving him clues, knowing they meant nothing? Now that would be Bully, devious and cruel to the point of mental sickness.

Bully's voice came back to him.

I'm smarter than the whole fucking lot of you piled together.

And because Bully believed he was smarter, he had left clues. Gilchrist was certain of that. If Bully's recitals had not been intended as clues, then what the hell did they mean?

Which brought him full circle.

He fingered the recorder. "Let's go through it again."

Jack seemed to have come to terms with Chloe's murder, and had offered to help in Maureen's disappearance. Trying to decipher Bully's madness was a good start. He stared at the recorder, hand poised with pencil. Bully's metallic voice whispered at them.

Jack hit the button, scribbled on his notepad.

"Wee, sleekit, cowerin, timorous beastie," he said. "That's the start of *To a Mouse*. Right?" He clicked the recorder on, then off again. "Which one's that from?"

"*To a Haggis*."

"Yeah, well, whatever. Maybe the clues are in the following lines, or something."

Gilchrist had already thought of that, and more. Perhaps the clues were in the number of the verses within the poem, or in the date the poem was written, or in the number of words in the verse. Or in any other millions of different ways a nutcase like Bully could screw with your brain. But in the end he had come to see that Bully had wanted his body-part clues to be worked out, so that Gilchrist would come to him. So whatever clues he was giving needed to be tricky, not impossible—

"And this one?"

"Don't know."

Another click of the recorder. "This?"

"*Tam O'Shanter*."

When Jack had all the verses down, he read them out, line after line.

Then he handed them over. "Any clearer?"

Gilchrist stared at the verses. No, God damn it. He was not any clearer. He was less clear. And what if the clues were in the next verses? That would be typical Bully. Plant the seed, and grow the wrong crop. But that would be too complicated. Whatever Bully was trying to tell him had to be in these verses.

His gaze returned to *Oh princess, by thy watchtower be*, the first verse Bully recited after Gilchrist asked where Maureen was. Was the secret to her disappearance hidden within that single line? He read it again. But he could think of nothing.

"I could search the Internet," Jack said.

"Please do."

"Just one thing."

"What's that?"

"You don't have a computer."

Gilchrist blinked. For Christ's sake. He'd never had a computer at home because he used one at the Office. He reached for his mobile phone and got through in seconds.

"Nance," he said. "Where are you?"

"At the other end of this line."

"I need assistance."

Serious now. "Shoot."

"Can you get onto the Internet and download Robert Burns' poems 'To a Mouse,' 'To a Haggis,' and 'Tam O'Shanter'?"

"Can I ask why?"

"It's important."

"I gathered that."

"And also the poem that contains the verse *Oh princess, by thy watchtower be.* And another that contains the verse *Inhuman man! Curse on thy barb'rous art.*"

"'The Wounded Hare'?"

"The what?"

"*Inhuman man!* It's the opening line of 'The Wounded Hare.'"

Was Bully trying to scare him into believing Maureen was in some way wounded? But if so, how wounded? Before he could stop himself, he said, "Does it die?"

"The hare? Not that I remember. More like it was about to die."

Gilchrist felt his breath leave him. That was it. Bully was telling him Maureen was about to die and there was bugger all he could do to prevent it—

"Hang on. Let me look it up."

"You on the Internet?"

"Yep," she said. "Ah, here we are. The second verse is, *Go live poor wand'rer of the wood and field!*"

Go live? Hope swelled—

"*The bitter little that of life remains.*"

Something slumped deep in the pit of his stomach. Well, there he had it. The hare will die. So would Maureen. And he could do nothing to stop it.

"I'm sorry, Andy," Nance said. "Is it to do with Maureen?"

"Afraid so."

"We'll find her, Andy. We have to."

Gilchrist puzzled at how close he felt to Nance. She seemed to be able to reach him with barely a murmur. "Can you read out the whole poem, while I write it down?"

When he hung up he read it from start to finish, returning to *Ah, helpless nurslings, who will now provide that life a mother only can bestow?*

He felt his lips tighten, his eyes nip. Would Maureen ever become a mother? Would she survive to have children of her own? He read the poem again, but came up with nothing new. Did he have it all wrong? Were there really clues in the verses? Or was Bully setting him off on the wrong track?

But his sixth sense was stirring.

Bully had been expecting him. And he had turned up at Barlinnie. Which meant that Bully's scheme was working to plan. The notes on Chloe's body parts, sent to Gilchrist, and from which Bully knew Gilchrist would work out that Maureen was next. But were these lines now Bully's clue for Gilchrist to save Maureen?

They had to be. Why else would Bully have recited them?

Then he realised that he could read these verses until he was blue in the face. He needed help. He dialled Nance's number again.

"This is becoming a habit I could enjoy," she said.

"Do you know if Hammie's still around?" he asked her. "I need him to decipher some of this stuff."

"I'm a detective. Not a psychic. Care to explain?"

Gilchrist gave her a rundown of his meeting with Bully, asked her to write down the lines Bully had recited, then said, "Maybe

Hammie can make some sense of them. He was one of the best cryptologists I ever worked with."

"I'll get back to you."

"Tonight, Nance. I need it tonight."

When he hung up, Jack said, "You look knackered, Andy. You need a break. I'm going to think about it over a pint. Like to join me?"

Gilchrist eyed the printouts. "I'd love to," he said. "But I can't."

"Anything else I can do to help?"

He shook his head. "Have a pint for me."

With Jack gone, he started sifting through the printouts. Some were printed emails, others copies of typed letters. He had no idea what he was looking for, then realised he had forgotten to collect the rest from Leighton. But even if he had them all in front of him there was nothing more he could do. He had only one pair of hands, one pair of eyes. He glanced at his watch—22:09. In less than two hours, Maureen would have been missing for one more day, and he was no further forward. He pressed on with reading her correspondence, but half an hour later took a break to call Nance.

"Any luck tracking down Hammie?" he asked her.

"Moved to the Borders. But I've got him working on it."

"How did you manage that?"

"I recited the verses over the phone. That was what you wanted, right?"

It took a full two seconds for Gilchrist to realise the folly of his thinking. He'd had it in his mind that the verses needed to be hand-delivered. Maybe Jack was right. He really was knackered. Nance's voice came at him as if from a distance. "What's that?" he said.

"I was asking if you've eaten." He hesitated long enough for her to say, "Why don't I nip down to the chippie and bring you out your favourite?"

"It's really no—"

"I'm on my way." The line went dead.

Gilchrist closed his mobile then removed a letter from the next pile.

A note to Tracy. Never heard of her. He eyed the date. Two years ago. Then the address. West end of Glasgow. He lifted others, reading, but not reading, scanning for key words. Ten minutes later, he wished he had gone to the pub with Jack. One pint would—

He frowned at an addressee's name.

Kevin Topley. Chris Topley's brother?

Then the address. Christ.

He grabbed his mobile, called Nance's number. "Where are you?"

"PM's."

"Stay there. I'm on my way."

It was a long shot, but a shot nevertheless. He dialled Dainty's mobile.

"Small speaking."

"Dainty. It's Andy. Can you get a hostage team together at short notice?"

"Is this to do with Maureen?"

"It is."

"You know where she is?"

He wanted to hold back, say he was not sure, but instead said, "Yes. I do."

THE COLD HURT.

It bit through her skin, wormed deep into her core, dug into the marrow of her bones. She pulled her legs to her chest, wrapped her arms around them, tried to stop shivering. But the cold cut through her woollen skirt and top as if she was naked.

Her breath rasped in grunts that stung. The pain in her chest was greater than the pain in her torn wrists. Her efforts to cut through the duct tape had caused the skin to rub off from the inside of her forearms, leaving gashes of raw flesh. She had ignored the pain, just kept driving her arms up and down. But when she managed to rip the tape off, the sight of her bloodied skin almost made her faint.

With her arms freed, she ripped the tape from her mouth, then her legs. Only then did she realise the seriousness of her predicament. She thumped the wooden door, appalled by its strength. She scraped at the hinges, dark and rough with rust. She eyed the keyhole, but saw nothing in the darkness of her tomb. A small gap at the bottom allowed her to slip her fingers under. But she felt only the dustiness of cold concrete. She shouted and screamed until her throat ached. She battered the door until she could no longer stand the pain in her fists. She scraped at the stone around the hinges until her fingernails bled.

Then the cold hit her.

Her chamber felt as cold as a morgue. Which was what this stone tomb was about to become. She saw that now.

Her own personal sarcophagus.

Chapter 30

GILCHRIST SQUEALED TO a stop at PM's fish and chip shop. Nance jumped in and pulled the door shut as he floored the pedal. "I'd like to eat this from the wrapper," she said. "Not off the back window."

He powered the Roadster onto North Street.

"Open wide." Nance slipped a piece of battered cod into his mouth, did the same with a couple of chips, then waited until they cleared the town before saying, "Care to tell me where we're going?"

"Glenorra."

"Ah, yes, Glenorra. I've always wanted to go there." She popped another piece of fish into his mouth. "Haven't packed a bikini or brought my passport. Is that a problem?"

"Very funny."

"So, where is Glenorra?"

"You should be asking, what is Glenorra?"

"Sorry, Andy, but you have me at a disadvantage here."

"It's Kevin Topley's home address."

Nance mouthed an Ah-hah. "Mister big-shot Chris's brother. That Kevin Topley?"

"The very one. And Chloe had a boyfriend called Kevin."

"The same Kevin?"

"Could be."

"But you don't know?"

"No. But Maureen wrote to Kevin several years ago."

"She did?"

"Chloe's Kevin's dead. And Dainty confirmed that Chris Topley lost his brother a few years back."

"How old was he?"

"Early thirties. From a drug overdose, according to Dainty. Before Chloe met Jack, she had a flat in the south side of Glasgow. Her relationship with Kevin was in the south side also. She frequented pubs there. They both did. That's where Jack met her."

"In a pub?"

"At a party. But I'm sure drink was involved, if that's what you're implying."

"Must run in the family." She slid another piece of fish into his mouth.

Five minutes later, with the suppers finished, Nance scrunched up the wrapping. "Where can I put this?"

"Not outside."

"Of course." She dropped it on the floor, nudged it into the depths of the footwell with her shoe.

"Here." Gilchrist held out a cloth. "For your fingers."

"A gentleman to the end." She cleaned her hands, held up the cloth. "Floor, too?"

"What can I tell you?"

Nance dropped the cloth between her feet. "So, what's so special about Glenorra?"

"It's also the place where Maureen said she and Watt would meet. In an email she wrote to him."

"So we're driving to the late Kevin Topley's house to do . . . what, exactly?"

"I think Maureen might be there."

"You think?"

He caught the hint of incredulity in her voice, and gripped the steering wheel. "I can't sit back and do nothing," he said. "Talk to me. What am I missing? What do Burns' poems have to do with anything?"

He removed the letter to Kevin and the scribbled verses from his pocket, and handed them to her.

She tugged the visor, switched on the mirror light. "The letter's three years old."

"Correct."

"Dear Kevin. Thanks for the party. Larry and I really enjoyed ourselves. Who's Larry?"

"One of Maureen's conquests?"

Nance read on. "It's a thank-you letter."

"So?"

"The only questions this raises are, has Maureen never heard of thank-you cards? And why would she not write it by hand?"

"She's a wannabe novelist. Maybe sitting at her computer is easier. Maybe she's lost her handwriting skills." He shrugged. "I don't know. Does it matter?"

Nance studied the sheet of verses. "Does any of this mean anything to you?"

"The reference to princess. That's what I called Maureen as a child."

"And Bully knew that?"

Gilchrist twisted the steering wheel. "That's what worries me."

"How accurate are these?"

"I taped our meeting. Why?"

"I'm not sure." She removed a piece of paper from her own pocket. "I did a search on first lines, and variations of that first line, thinking that perhaps Bully had got them wrong, maybe forgot the words."

Gilchrist shook his head. "Bully thinks he's smarter than us. It's characteristic of a psychopath." He overtook a slow plug of cars. "He's playing some kind of game," he went on. "Bully was expecting me. It's the first thing he said. Don't you want to play? He said that, too. Read it out again. The verse about the princess."

"*Oh princess, by thy watchtower be, it is the wished the trysted hour*," she said, then added, "As far as I could find out, Burns never used the word *princess* or *watchtower* in any of his poems."

Ice chilled Gilchrist's neck. Was this Bully's clue? Had he slipped them into a poem by Burns? Princess for Maureen. Watchtower for. . . ? For what? And a thought struck him.

"What if that line is not by Burns?"

Nance shook her head. "Google would have picked it up, no matter who wrote it. That line does not appear in anything written by anyone."

Gilchrist let the logic of her words work into his mind. This was Bully's clue. It had to be. Why else would he say these words? But he had recited other verses. Would he find more clues in these? "Call Jack," he ordered, "and tell him to check the other verses, make sure they match Bully's lines. And get him to call back the instant he finds something." He gripped the steering wheel. "Maureen's alive," he urged. "She's alive. I know she is."

As he powered into the night, he prayed he was right.

And that he would not be too late.

SHE DID NOT know how long she cried.

But even when she tried to stop, heavy sobs came at her in nervous spasms that tore the air from her lungs. In the cold darkness of her death chamber, her sightless eyes nipped from dust and lack of tears. Her throat ached, and her tongue felt thick and dry as she tried to work up saliva.

She could not survive long without water.

She thumped her hand at the door again, nothing more than a heavy slap, a feeble effort that told her that the last of her energy was spent. She had nothing left.

She was going to die.

But she could not die. Not now. Not here.

"No," she screamed. But the dry hack that coughed from her throat sounded like the voice of someone who was already dead.

GILCHRIST PARKED ON the pavement.

From the activity around the house he knew they were too late. A SOCO van, with its door open to reveal an array of equipment, sat parked as if abandoned.

He found Dainty in coveralls, phone pressed to his ear. When he saw Gilchrist, he slapped his phone shut.

They gripped hands in grim silence.

Then Dainty said, "Maureen was here. But we're too late."

The power to stand almost deserted Gilchrist. "Too late?"

"She's been moved. We found a shed in the back."

Gilchrist pushed past, but Dainty gripped his arm.

"It's not pretty, Andy."

"I need to see."

Dainty squeezed his lips together, then said, "Put on your coveralls."

The back garden looked like a film set. Dragonlights lit the scene like a stage. An unkempt beech hedge pushed branches over a pathway overgrown with weeds. Beyond, a light shone from the open doorway of a wooden building at the bottom of the garden.

Together, they stepped down the pathway. SOCOs shuffled in silence, tagging and bagging. Someone was pouring a milky looking substance onto the ground, making a cast.

"We found a bare footprint." Dainty pointed. "Over there. The grass is covered in shite. We think it's human."

Gilchrist followed in silence. His tongue felt hard, his mouth dry. He stopped on the threshold, gripped the doorframe for support. The stench had him almost backing up.

In the near corner, discarded underwear lay knotted and thick with fecal matter. Close by, a bra, a skirt, a white blouse, dirty and bloodied. But no shoes. Gilchrist ordered his memory to call up an image of Maureen. Was the blouse hers? The skirt, too? But it was useless. He forced himself to analyse the facts as if he was looking at the crime scene of a stranger. He stared at bloodied smears on the floor and walls. Was that Maureen's blood? A chain fetter lay coiled on the floor, next to a stain that had him gritting his teeth. The chain ran up the wall to an iron ring bolted to the wood near waist height.

Dainty's voice snapped him back.

"Through here."

He entered another room, not much larger than the one with the metal shackles. The air was thick enough to taste, a cloying stench of fat and meat that stuck to the tongue, a rich fleshy smell that reminded him of the butcher's shop on Market Street. A table as thick as a workbench lined one wall. His eyes took in the instruments of torture—the circular saw with its twelve-inch blade that Mackie had calculated, three hacksaws, blades dark with blood or rust. The bench was scarred with a history of cuts and scrapes clogged with dried blood. Bits of flesh or skin lay curled on the clatty surface like tiny scraps, and Gilchrist wondered if they would find slivers of fingernails embedded in the sides. Beneath the table, the floorboards lay stained black. Flies stirred from the mess with a noisy rush.

To his side, dull wooden walls brightened with a display of stapled photographs.

He stepped towards them, felt his breath catch.

He stared at the closest image—Chloe's white face. Her eyes stared at him with the vacant look of the dead. It took Gilchrist a full second to work out that the slime on her lips was sperm. Another next to it—Chloe on the floor, naked. Breasts as flat as a child's. *Mons veneris* lined with a pathetic strip of blonde hair that did little to hide her vagina.

Around her ankles, Gilchrist recognised the shackles.

He peered closer. Was that the toe of a boot?

Closer still. It was.

"There's two of them," he said to Dainty.

Dainty pressed in beside him.

Gilchrist pointed at the image. "Can we get an enhancement on that boot?"

"Can do."

"What do you think, Nance?" he asked, and saw from her tight lips that the worst was yet to come. A glance at Dainty revealed he knew that, too.

Then his eyes settled on a group of six photographs. Even from where he stood, he recognised Maureen. Her bloodied blouse, the abandoned garment in the adjacent room, reflected the glare of the flashlight. Her bare legs looked thinner than he remembered.

"Don't touch," Dainty snapped.

Gilchrist had to force himself not to rip the lot from the wall. The photographs could provide clues, could be used as evidence, dusted for prints, analysed for age. But who had taken them? And when? And how long since Maureen had lain chained to the wall?

He tried to study the images with professional detachment. He was a DCI with Fife Constabulary, in charge of a murder investigation. The fact that the victim was known to him should be of no significance, so that his powers of detection remained uninhibited, his sense of reasoning unimpeded, his—

"I'm sorry, Andy." It was Dainty.

Gilchrist stared at the images the same way he had stared at the images of a hundred dead bodies before. He felt an odd sense of satisfaction that Maureen had been alive at the taking the photographs. But he had seen that red-rimmed look of fear locked in the eyes of too many victims for him to be mistaken. Maureen had known she was going to die.

He felt his lips tighten as he struggled to comprehend the sperm splattered on her forehead, dripping from her chin, creeping into her eyes. He tried to see past that, focus on what any normal detective would. He struggled to reason the facts like an impartial investigator. But it was no use.

He pressed his hand to his mouth, bit down on his knuckles. Tears came at him in gasping sobs, and a fire that he had not felt since he had been bullied with a leather strap at the age of twelve, rose from somewhere deep within him and emerged in a choked curse.

Dainty's hand squeezed his shoulder.

He shook it off, and thudded from the shed into the cold morning air, past the SOCOs, the flickering camera, the murmuring voices, and strode down the slabbed path.

He was going to have Bully.

He was going to have him with his bare hands.

He was going to tear him limb from limb.

If Maureen's body was served up to him in bits, he would kill Bully.

By Christ, he promised himself that treat.

Chapter 31

IT TOOK THE realization that Glenorra had to be the key to finding Maureen—it just had to be—to force Gilchrist back to the crime scene.

"Our best guess is that she was taken from here within the last twenty-four hours," Dainty said to him. "Her underwear may help determine when. We'll need to run DNA tests. Could you give a blood sample?"

"Of course."

Dainty nodded.

Gilchrist read the pain in Dainty's eyes. He knew how Dainty was thinking, how he would feel if it were his own daughter's life on the line, how he could ask the unanswerable question—how could any father be asked to carry out his professional duties as if the victim was not related to him? It would be too much for Dainty. Gilchrist saw that.

And he saw, too, that it was too much for himself.

He stepped into a kitchen commandeered by Dainty's team. Muddled voices and the crackle of radio static filled the air. He pushed through an open door into the relative quiet of the hall. He forced himself to concentrate, fight his way back into his investigation. If he had any hope of saving Maureen, he had to think.

Topley. Glenorra. Bully.

Think, God damn it, think.

How were they connected?

Had Chloe visited Glenorra when she dated Kevin Topley?

Had she walked along this hallway, stepped into that kitchen? And Maureen, too? She had been at Topley's party. Had she once stood on this same spot, maybe eyed the same rooms? Had she been here with Chris Topley? Gilchrist looked around him, at cobwebbed cornicing, at a dusty balustrade that led up a staircase of bare floorboards to an upper hallway that seemed to swim with motes of dust. Once-white wallpaper hung from the stairwell in dried strips.

Why had the house been allowed to fall into such a state? And why hack Chloe to pieces here? Why keep Maureen chained in the garden shed? Was Bully trying to make it look as if Chris Topley was involved in Chloe's murder?

Chris Topley had shared a cell with Bully. Gilchrist had established that fact. And Chris Topley had employed Maureen. Chloe had dated Kevin Topley then dumped him for Jack. Was that part of a twisted plot dreamed up by Bully in the cells of Barlinnie? To set Gilchrist's son up with his cellmate's brother's ex? Then kill her?

It seemed too complex by far. Or was it?

Gilchrist stepped from the hall into a darkened lounge. Heavy floral curtains were still drawn. He opened them. Light slid into the room on dusty beams. Another day was dawning. Would he find Maureen alive by the end of this day? Or was she already dead? He tried to bury that thought, and peered out the window.

Glenorra stood at the end of a narrow road lined by mature trees. The footpath opposite was edged by a privet hedge, behind which an open field rose into the daybreak gloom. Fifty yards to his left, the grey hulk of the only neighbouring house seemed to manifest in the lightening skies.

Who lived there? Had they seen anything? Heard anything?

He faced the room again. Light patches on the flocked wallpaper were ghostly reminders of removed pictures. What had these pictures shown?

Upstairs, the same questions worried away at him. Why this

house? Why here? Why use the garden shed to hack up a murder victim, and why keep another one captive? But the house stood in a tranquil country setting, so why not?

On the ceiling, in an oversized cupboard off the upper landing, he found the entrance hatch to the attic. He reached up and pulled it down to reveal a sliding ladder. He waggled it to the floor then clambered up the wooden treads.

He stood with his head and shoulders in the confines of the attic. In the darkness the air smelled dry and musty. His fingers found a light-switch close to the entrance hatch, but the electricity had been disconnected. He called for a torch.

Two minutes later, Nance obliged. "See anything?" she asked.

"Not yet."

Gilchrist ran the beam around the attic space. What was he looking for?

He guessed no one had been in the attic for years. The space was small, the angle of the ceiling restrictive to someone his height. Planks of wood ran at right angles across the roof beams, creating a floored area about ten by. Beyond, rafters ran into the darkness like ship's ribbing. Two suitcases lay one on top of the other. From the hollow sound they made when he tapped them, he could tell they contained nothing. Four tea chests lined one edge of the attic flooring.

He pulled himself up and into the attic.

Nance scrambled in after him. "Looking for anything in particular?" she asked.

"Just sniffing." From the top of the chest, he removed an item wrapped in newspaper. He unravelled it to reveal a bone-china teacup. He was not an expert in antiques but had the distinct feeling that he was holding something of value. "Why leave this stuff here?" He shone his torch across the broadsheet. "The Herald," he said. "January 1993."

Nance dug into the adjacent tea chest. "Has the house been deserted that long?"

"We can have it checked out." The rest of the tea chest uncovered more crockery, but nothing of any interest. "Is this stuff expensive?" he asked Nance.

"You're asking the wrong person. My grannie wanted to leave me her china set and got upset when I told her I didn't want it. I prefer Mikasa."

"Whatever."

"Oh, shit."

Gilchrist shone the torch at her.

"Is this what I think it is?"

Gilchrist trained the beam on an urn that gleamed like polished copper. Although it had been wrapped in newspaper, he caught the green stain of verdigris around the base.

"Betsy Cunningham Topley," she said. "Born 5th of June 1932, died 1st of December 1997." She looked at him. "Topley's mother? Why keep her here?"

Gilchrist had no answer for that. His own parents were dead, and their funerals had been carried out in accordance with their wishes. Both had been cremated, and their ashes interred in a small plot in the local cemetery. It sometimes embarrassed him to think how seldom he visited.

Other tea chests revealed nothing of interest. He left the hatch open, the access ladder down, and had Nance notify the crime scene manager. Not that the stuff in the attic was relevant, he supposed.

In the back garden, SOCOs still combed the grounds. The dawn light flickered with the staccato flare of the police photographer's flashlight.

"Has anyone interviewed the neighbours?" he asked Dainty.

"Not yet."

Gilchrist was out of his jurisdiction, but he had a sense that Dainty was overwhelmed with the mass of evidence being gathered. "I can make a start," he said.

Dainty poked at the pad on his mobile. "Make sure you give me a typed report," then turned away to make the call.

The street surface was littered with potholes that glistened black with rainwater. A heavy dew painted the lawn in a transparent white. He caught movement behind an upper curtain as he and Nance approached the house, a smallholding with roughcast walls in dire need of paint. He glanced at his watch—6:15—then at the nameplate—Hutchison.

He rang the doorbell.

It took no more than five seconds for the door to crack open. An elderly woman with white hair as wild as candyfloss faced them. A blue housecoat stained from overuse covered a pink nightgown. Worn slippers warmed blue-veined feet as white as porcelain.

"Mrs. Hutchison?" Gilchrist asked.

"Yes?"

"We're with the police. May we come in?"

"Is it to do with the Topley's old house?" she asked.

"It is."

"Well, thank goodness. You'd better come in."

Gilchrist followed her tiny frame down a dark hall and into a dull kitchen that needed to be gutted. Cupboard doors hung from hinges long past their sell-by date. Woodchip wallpaper painted deep yellow was blackened with grease above the oven. A white tablecloth covered a small table in the centre of the room.

"Would you like some tea? I always have a pot brewing."

"That would be nice," Nance said.

"Do you live alone?" Gilchrist tried.

"For the last eleven years."

"I'm sorry to hear that."

"Cancer done it. That's what took my Tom. I told him to give up the smoking. But he never listened." She smiled, an odd crinkling of her lined face. "It's what I liked most about him," she went on, "that he took no one's advice but his own. Milk, love?"

Nance nodded. Gilchrist did likewise.

She handed Gilchrist a chipped cup with tea like melted

Caramac and speckles of soured milk spinning in it like dandruff. He took a polite sip through closed lips, then said, "Why were you so pleased to invite us in?"

"The old Topley house has been empty for years," she said. "Then all of a sudden it's like Sauchiehall Street."

"You saw someone go into it?" Nance asked.

"Two of them. Like tinkers. Scruffy they was."

"Did you call the police?" Gilchrist asked.

"Oh, dear, no. I didn't like to. I try to mind my own business."

"Could you describe them?"

She gave Gilchrist's question some thought, then shook her head. "My eyesight isn't what it used to be, you know. I need a new prescription." She scanned the kitchen with a worried frown. "Where did I put my glasses?"

"Tall, small? Fat, thin? Male, female?"

"Oh," she said. "One was tall and gangly." She screwed up her face. "I've never liked that in a man. The other was small. With short legs. Like Tom."

"Could you see what they were doing?" Nance asked.

"Doing, love?"

"Were they carrying anything?"

"I don't think so. They were just going in and out. Making a nuisance of themselves. Slamming car doors. My sight might not be as good as it used to be. But there's nothing wrong with my hearing."

"And when did all this going in and out take place?"

"Last week."

"And before that?"

She shook her head. "Oh, dear. Not for a while."

"Did they come by car?" Nance asked.

"Yes, love."

Gilchrist was sure he was about to waste his breath. "Did you get the number plate? The make of car?"

"Goodness gracious me. No. Tom was the man for the cars.

Not me. He always used to say he would buy me a big car so he could drive me to the shops—"

"Can you remember the colour?"

"Shiny. Like metal."

Gilchrist remembered the Jaguar with the paint repair on the boot. "Silver, perhaps?"

"I think so."

"Did it have any scratches or dents? Blotches of paint a different colour?"

"Oh, dear. I couldn't say. I've no idea about that."

Gilchrist and Nance continued to grill Mrs. Hutchison in a gentle round-about fashion, getting nowhere, learning nothing, until Gilchrist asked about Topley Senior.

"He was a strange one." She twisted her lips as if she had bitten into a rotten apple. "And a loud drunk. Singing and shouting all those religious songs. But Betsy was nice. I don't think John done her any harm. But I never understood why she went and married him. I think it was the children that done her in in the end."

"Done her in?"

"Wore her out." She shook her head. "A disappointment to her, they was. Two boys. But that was two too many, if you ask me. Poor Betsy. She lost their first child, you know. A girl. She died at birth. She's buried in the family plot in Maryhill. Betsy used to place flowers by her grave every year. November the eighth."

"You have a good memory."

"I used to. I remember it well because it was three days after Guy Fawkes." She smiled. "Remember remember, the fifth of November."

"What were the two boys like?"

Her smile evaporated. "Horrible."

That would certainly describe Chris Topley, Gilchrist thought.

"Cheeky cheeky cheeky. They used to break the heads off my

roses. And when they kicked their football into my garden, they would just run in and pick it up. They never asked permission." She bit into the apple again.

"And what about their father? Did you see much of him?"

"No. He died from a heart attack."

"When would that be?"

"Ten years ago."

"You remember it, do you?"

"It was the year after Tom. But Tom had been ill for a while."

"I'm sorry to hear that," said Gilchrist.

"It was so sad when Betsy passed away." Her face seemed to fail her then. "I went to John's funeral. But I didn't go to hers. Never even got a chance to pay my last respects."

"Why not?" Nance asked.

"The boys didn't want me to."

"Kevin and Chris?"

"Not so much Kevin. But that Chris. Horrible, he was. He swore at me."

"Why?"

"Called me an old cow. It was terrible what he done."

"What did he do?"

"Betsy wanted John to be laid to rest in the family plot in Maryhill. But he wouldn't have none of it, that Chris. He had John buried somewhere else. Betsy was in a terrible state about it. But she could never stand up to those boys. And when she died, I couldn't believe it. They had her cremated at Daldowie." Tears welled in her rheumy eyes. "Betsy didn't want that. She wanted the family to be laid to rest together."

Gilchrist decided not to mention the urn in the attic. "Do you know why he did that?"

She shook her head, tears close to the surface.

"Where's John buried?"

"In a cemetery in Kirkintilloch. His home town."

Gilchrist had never heard of the place, but made a mental note to check with Dainty. Not that it mattered, he supposed, but he said, "Do you know which cemetery?"

"The Auld Aisle," she said. "I remember thinking it was a nice name for a cemetery." Then she frowned. "But I never understood why there."

"You said Kirkintilloch was his home town."

"But that was years ago. When he was a little boy. Betsy told me. They moved to Milngavie at first, then bought the house up the road. All his family are buried in Maryhill. His mother and father. His brother, too. And little Betty."

Gilchrist watched reminiscence cross her face then fade to a look of loss. For her own family, or her past, he could not say. He reached inside his jacket, felt his lips tighten as he held out Maureen's photograph. "Have you ever seen this woman before?"

The old lady looked around her, and Nance walked to the window ledge and picked up a pair of spectacles. "Are these what you're looking for?"

"Yes, dear. Where did you find them?" She slid them over her ears then peered long-armed at the photograph. "What a beautiful face," she said. "Such lovely eyes. Tom always wanted a girl. It's funny that, don't you think? Most men want boys."

"Have you seen her before?" Nance nudged.

She shook her head.

Gilchrist then showed her a photograph of Chloe.

"She reminds me of my sister Aggie. Such lovely eyes. I miss her, you know."

Gilchrist retrieved the photographs and pushed himself to his feet. "You've been very helpful, Mrs. Hutchison."

"Stay for another cup of tea," she said. "Please?"

"We really must be going."

At the door the old lady said, "My, that was a strange kafuffle last night."

"Pardon?"

"With that car parked outside. I thought he was up to no good."

"He? Can you describe him?"

"It was too dark, dear. But I think it might have been the tall skinny one."

Gilchrist's mobile rang, and he excused himself.

"What time last night?" Nance asked.

"After midnight. When I looked out later, the car was gone."

"Was it the same silver-coloured car?"

"I don't think so. It looked darker. I'm not very good with cars."

"Don't worry," Nance said. "And thanks for the tea."

When Nance turned she could tell from the look on Gilchrist's face that the last body part had turned up. She ran after him as he jogged towards his Mercedes, and caught up as he jumped into the driver's seat.

"It's Chloe," he said to her, and jerked the ignition key.

The engine started with a hard roar that had two constables looking their way. But he did not shift into gear, just sat there, eyes glazed, staring straight ahead.

After thirty seconds, she leaned across and switched off the engine.

"What's wrong, Andy?"

Gilchrist looked away from her then. "I haven't the faintest idea where Maureen is," he whispered. "I hear her voice in my head. I close my eyes and I see her. But I can't reach her. I can't help her. I feel helpless."

"You said it was Chloe."

He faced her. "They found her head."

Nance pressed her hand to her mouth. She had seen only one dacapitated head before, and the memory still stuck with her. She reached out, touched his arm, and he looked down at it, as if surprised to see it there. She wanted to ask if the final note had been found, what it said, but dreaded being told how it had been sent. Surely not branded onto Chloe's face. Or cut into her skin like scars. No one could be that cruel.

Instead, she squeezed his arm, and waited.

"The final word is *vengeance*," he finally said. "And just in case we couldn't work it out, he had Maureen sign the note. Stuffed into Chloe's mouth."

Nance felt her eyes burn as her mind cast up that image. She struggled to hold back her tears. She could not cry. She had to be strong for herself. And strong for Andy.

"The bastard had Maureen sign it. *Mo*," Gilchrist gasped.

Then her eyes filled as Gilchrist buried his head in his hands and cried.

Chapter 32

"**I**'M SORRY, JACK,** but Chloe's body won't be released until Bert's done."

Jack stared out the windscreen in silence, while Gilchrist brought him up to date with the rest of his investigation. But he mentioned nothing of Maureen's note.

Deep in his own misery, Gilchrist drove through the back streets of St. Andrews. Jack confirmed that Bully's bastardised line was the opening line of Robert Burns' poem "Mary Morison." Instead of, *Oh Mary, at thy window be*, Bully had changed it to, *Oh princess, by thy watchtower be*, which told Gilchrist that Bully was responsible for Maureen's disappearance, and that somehow, somewhere, a tower had something to do with it. Or maybe not.

Gilchrist pulled the Roadster off the road, switched off the engine. He opened the door, turned to Jack. "You offered to help? Well, here we are."

Leighton looked tired. His jowls shivered with irritation. "It's taken me longer than I thought it would," he grumbled. "Even with three printers. But I've finished it now." He lumbered down the hallway and into the front room.

Gilchrist and Jack followed.

Five stacks of printed paper stood on the carpet.

Gilchrist picked up two, while Jack took the rest. As they walked back outside, Gilchrist said, "Send me the bill."

That seemed to please Leighton, for he smiled and tugged at his belt.

Driving back to Crail he said to Jack, "I'd like you to go

through Maureen's stuff. Put a Post-it at anything that references Watt, Glenorra, Topley, and anyone or anything else you don't understand, or that seems suspicious."

"I was dreading you asking me to do that."

"You did offer."

"Yeah, I suppose I did."

GILCHRIST DID NOT find Maureen by the end of that day.

Nor by the end of the next.

Strathclyde's Forensic teams confirmed that the discarded clothes belonged to Maureen. Blood, bone and skin tissue recovered from the butcher's bench confirmed that Chloe had been dismembered in the shed. Chris Topley, registered owner of Glenorra, was grilled in person by Dainty for four hours, but denied being within ten miles of the house. Alibis were presented and checked, and Topley walked away as clean as his laundered suit.

Gilchrist's search of towers in towns along the east coast—Crail, Anstruther, Pittenweem to the south, and as far as Newport-on-Tay to the north—had offered him nothing more except late nights and less sleep. At his frantic persistence Dainty had finally relented and organised a small team to investigate towers in Glasgow, beginning in Easterhouse, where Bully last lived, then stretching farther in a widening circle. But nothing came of it.

Bully was interrogated in Barlinnie by Strathclyde's top negotiators for ten straight hours. They even hinted at the possibility of a deal. *Just tell us what you know, where you've instructed the body to be hidden, and we'll look to get you a pardon.*

But Bully said, "It couldn't have happened to a nicer bastard," after which he refused to utter another word. And for ten straight hours, he sat and smiled at them.

By the morning of the following day Gilchrist had come to realise that no one would find Maureen. That was Bully's revenge. It mattered not that he had murdered a family of six, including a five-year-old child. A typical psychopath, Bully had no conscience, moral or ethical, no sense of remorse or compassion, took no responsibility for his actions, and could therefore suffer no emotional consequences for his misdeeds.

It was now clear to Gilchrist that Bully had planned to frighten him into believing Maureen was about to be served up to him in bits, and if he solved the clues he could ride in on his white stallion and save his princess. But he had not reckoned on Bully's trump card, that he had never planned to hack Maureen into pieces, but to have her kidnapped and killed, and her body buried where it would never be found. Gilchrist thought of interrogating Bully once more. But doing so would let Bully see his pain, give him another opportunity to taunt him with his secret knowledge.

So, he decided against it.

Hammie could offer nothing more than Gilchrist already knew. Bully's reference to Burns' words contained nothing mystical. The message was clear for all to see in Bully's bastardised line, *Oh princess, by thy watchtower be.*

According to Hammie, Bully was telling Gilchrist he knew where Maureen was, and his lips would be sealed until the day he died. And the use of the poem "Mary Morison" was significant as it was generally understood that the Mary Morison in Burns' poem was Alison Begbie, whom Burns dated when he was in his early twenties, but who refused to marry him. The psychological parallel being that where Burns had failed in his quest for a wife, so too would Gilchrist fail in his search for his daughter.

The other verses were nothing more than smokescreen.

Gilchrist had a different opinion, convinced that Bully had given him a clue, strong in his own twisted belief that he was smarter than everyone. But Gilchrist knew that Bully's ego would be his downfall. That was the flaw in his miserable scheming.

So, he went to see Chris Topley again.

Nance came with him.

Topley entered the room in a suit that looked like silver shards of herring-bone. It glittered like foil when he walked by the window. He stood on the opposite side of his desk, and gave Gilchrist a gold-toothed smile. "Nice jacket," he said. "Leather suits you."

"Wish I could say the same about your suit," Nance said.

Topley smiled at her. "Want me to throw you out now? Or fuck you later?"

"Try throwing me out now."

Topley widened his gold smile. "Maybe we'll just fuck later."

"You wouldn't get past Go."

Topley lowered his eyes and stared at Nance's crotch.

"Now we've got the foreplay out of the way," Gilchrist said, "I'd like to ask a few more questions."

Topley lifted his prurient gaze. "I don't feel like answering any questions today."

"Like us to arrest you instead?"

"I'd be interested to hear the charge."

"Attempted rape." Nance again.

"Do what?"

Nance stepped forward. She stood a couple of inches taller than Topley. "Believe me," she said, "my story will stick. If DCI Gilchrist hadn't arrived in the nick of time and pulled you off me, I do believe you might have scored."

"You wouldn't fucking dare."

"You'd better fucking believe it. Now answer the nice man's questions, or you're going back to your cage in the Bar-L zoo."

"Maybe I should call my solicitor."

"That's your prerogative," Gilchrist said. "But we can be out of here in a few minutes, or we can take the long road. Your choice."

"I'm clean," Topley sneered. "Let's have it. Anything to get rid of you lot."

"You shared a cell with Bully Reid," Gilchrist said. "For how long?"

"About a year."

"I heard eighteen months."

"If you know the answer, why ask the question?"

"To make sure you're telling no lies." Gilchrist caught a flush of anger wash across the hard face. "What did you and Bully talk about?"

"Are you joking, or what? How the fuck would I remember what we talked about?"

"Try."

"It was a while ago."

Gilchrist moved closer to the desk. "Did Bully ever mention my name?"

"Don't fucking flatter yourself."

"Did he ever mention my daughter's name?"

"No."

"Don't lie to me. I don't like it."

Topley narrowed his eyes. "He never mentioned your daughter's name."

"Did he mention any woman's name?"

"Sure he did. But I can't remember them all."

"But you remember he didn't mention Maureen."

"That's right."

"How did Maureen get a job with your company?"

"Replied to an ad. The same way every other bit of skirt gets a job here."

"I thought some of them had a horizontal interview," Nance chipped in.

Topley chuckled, his eyes flashing. "Want to apply?"

"Maureen's a compulsive saver," Gilchrist pressed on. "She's kept every bit of paper she's ever read, every letter she's ever received, written, or just thought of. And that includes job advertisements." He was lying now, just winging it, but sometimes you have to push. "We never found an ad for your firm in her papers. So, I'll ask you for the last time. How did she get the job?"

"Word of mouth."

"Whose mouth?"

"Now you really are pushing the boat out."

"Do you know something?" Nance said. "I'm hoping you don't answer the question, because I can't wait to face you in court."

Topley glared at Gilchrist. "Ronnie Watt," he said.

The name stung like a slap to the face. Gilchrist struggled to keep his voice even. "What did Ronnie say exactly?"

Topley smirked. "Said he was going out with a tidy bit of stuff, right classy looking, tight tits with nipples out to here, the kind punters love to rub their cocks over. Nice legs, too. And a muff so fine you could floss your teeth with it."

Gilchrist ignored the taunt. "And?"

"And she'd do anything to get a job."

"So you hired her."

"After the interview." Topley flashed gold at Nance. "If you get my meaning."

"When was this?"

"About a year ago."

"By which time you'd been out of prison, what, a year, give or take a month or two?"

"Yeah."

"Keep in contact with Bully, do you?"

"What for?"

"That's why I'm asking."

"No."

"Spoken to him since?"

"No."

"Written to him?"

"No."

"Contacted him in any way?"

"No."

"Not even one visit, one letter, one call, to let Bully know you'd hired Detective Chief Inspector Gilchrist's daughter?" His voice had risen in ridicule, and he struggled to smother his emotions. But he was almost asking too much of his nervous system.

As if sensing this, Topley turned to the window, placed his hands behind his back, revealing a swallow tattooed on the inside of his left wrist. "You're fucking fishing."

"I take it that's a *Yes*."

Topley faced Gilchrist again. "N - O." He etched the air with a pointed finger. "In huge big baby letters."

Gilchrist forced himself to stay calm. "What about Bully's brother?" he asked.

"What about him?"

"Talk to him?"

"Jimmy's a nutter. Bad for business." He hooked both thumbs under the lapel of his suit and hitched it up.

"So who's your go-between?"

"Do what?"

"Your go-between," Nance chipped in. "You know? The idiot who runs between you and Bully."

"Like I said, you're fishing."

"How about Glenorra?" Nance asked.

Topley's eyes narrowed. An arm searched for the back of his chair and rested against it in an air of casual indifference. But he would never pass an audition.

"We know you own it." Gilchrist again. "So be careful how you answer the question."

"What question?"

"Was it ever Kevin's?" Gilchrist asked.

"We used to have a half-share each."

"After your mother died?"

"Yeah."

"Then what?"

"Kevin died."

"And left Glenorra to you?"

"Yeah."

"So it's all yours?"

"You deaf or what?"

"And the hut at the back?" Nance said.

"What about it?"

"You own that, too, do you?"

"Yeah." A bit unsure.

"When were you last at Glenorra?"

"What the fuck's going on? I've explained all of this to that tiny fucker—"

"Just answer the lady's question, will you? There's a good boy."

A sniff. A tightening of his grip on the back of the chair. "About a year ago."

"Never been back since?"

"No."

"You still got a key to the hut?"

Topley shrugged. "Could do. It's been a while."

"Ever get another one cut?"

"What for?"

"Ever lend it to anyone?"

"Like I said, what for?"

"Why don't you let us ask the questions?"

Topley shifted his shoulders. "I never got a key cut and I never lent one out. That fucking good enough for you?"

Gilchrist smiled. "Book him," he said to Nance.

"Here. Hold on a fucking minute. Book me for what?"

"Accessory to murder."

"Do what?"

"You heard."

"You can't just come in here and fucking—"

"Oh yes I can sonny Jim, oh yes I can." Gilchrist leaned across the desk, glared hard into Topley's tight eyes with a hatred that worried him. How much more of this could he take before he flipped? How many more lies could he listen to before he took the law into his own hands?

He pulled back. "Book him," he said again.

Nance stepped forward.

"She warned me about you, she did," Topley complained. "Said you were a right evil fucker."

Gilchrist pushed Nance back on her heels, moved so close to Topley that he could see beads of sweat on the flattened nose. It would be so easy to wrap his fingers around his neck and press his thumbs into the windpipe. "*Evil?*" he growled. "You don't know the meaning of the word. You're nothing but a crook pretending to be straight."

Topley's eyes blazed. A chair bumped against the table.

"*Andy.*"

Gilchrist blinked, once, twice, as Topley's face twisted into an ugly grimace.

But Topley's hatred could never light a flame next to his own.

Chapter 33

*W*EAK NOW. *TOO* *weak to sit.*

She rolled over and her head thudded against the concrete floor.

But she felt no pain. She felt nothing. The pain had disappeared. The cold, too.

She fought off the urge to close her eyes, felt her body wallow in the slow motion of the moment, as if she was lying in a warm bed, or a hammock on the beach, the Caribbean, St. Maarten, where she and Larry spent a whole week, a lifetime ago. She was there again, and she turned her face to the sun, felt its rays on her face, her lips, tried to move her tongue over them. But it felt too thick, too heavy. Too dry.

Thirsty. So thirsty.

But it's late now. Time to go to bed.

To sleep. Close my eyes and just. . . .

. . . sleep.

So tired. . . .

Just want to lay my head on the pillow, pull the sheets over my warm skin, and fall asleep. Overhead, the ceiling fan swirls. Even with my eyes closed, I can see it.

Turning and turning. But it makes no sound.

It seems not to stir the air.

So tired. . . .

"I REALLY MUST object, Inspector. My client has rights—"

"And my daughter has rights, too. She has the right to marry, the right to be a mother, the right to live her life and grow old." Gilchrist slammed the table, splashing water from a polystyrene cup. He glared across the grey desk at Topley's narrowing eyes. "And so help me to God I'll have it out of you before the end of the day."

Jerry Foster looked as if his black pinstriped suit was about to burst. He wiped thick fingers over his lips. "That's all very well, Inspector, but my client has repeatedly said that he knows nothing of your daughter's disappearance."

"Your client's *lying*."

Foster turned to Topley. "Are you lying?"

"On my mother's grave."

Foster looked at Gilchrist. "On his mother's grave."

"His mother doesn't have a grave. Her ashes are in an urn in the attic. Ask him."

"I don't think that's—"

"Your client's lying. Now ask him."

"As I said—"

"*Ask him.*" Gilchrist was surprised to find he had almost crossed the table.

Foster pushed his chair back. Sweat glistened on his balled face. "I don't intend to have my client sit through—"

"Why did you have your mother cremated?" Gilchrist shouted. He had pressed so far forward that his face was inches from Topley's. "Why not have her buried with her husband? Why not grant an old lady her dying wish?"

Topley grinned at him.

Gilchrist pushed back and stood. "I'm having a coffee." He glared at Foster. "And when I come back I expect your client to be more forthcoming."

Foster fingered the knot in his tie.

At the coffee machine Gilchrist felt something touch his elbow. He turned. "What?"

Nance tried a weak smile. "I've never seen you like this before, Andy."

"I've never had a daughter missing before."

"Go easy. Will you?"

"Milk and sugar?"

Nance strutted off, her legs as stiff as a mannequin's.

Gilchrist felt the beginnings of a headache and wondered if it was all too much for him. Was Nance right? Was he out of control? But how the hell was he supposed to behave when that bastard smiled at him and whispered in his solicitor's ear? Dainty had taken some persuading before agreeing to provide an interview room. And Greaves, too, he had blown a fuse. Why all the fuss about jurisdiction and protocol? Could no one see the connection? In despair, he patted his pockets for his cigarettes, and gave a silent curse. Christ. Habits were hard to beat. Habits were things that made men behave like boys. Habits could—

Not habits. *Agreements.*

Silent compliance? Between Topley and Bully?

Was that it? Had Topley been compliant, agreed to do as Bully asked, so he could score a few more Brownie points for his hero? It seemed so simple he wondered why he had not thought of it sooner. Dainty had told him of Topley's early life, of how he had to prove his worth to Bully. Topley had been one of the tougher kids, who thought nothing of slicing off an opponent's ear to drop at his master's feet, a token of his worthiness.

And of Bully's parents, a father who ran away from a beaten life and a beaten wife, leaving her to raise six girls and two baby boys—Bully and Jimmy. What little money she mustered came from doing turns in tenement closes. She groomed her daughters, too, for the oldest profession, so that when Maggie reached twelve, money started to come in. Bully was only nine when Maggie and two other sisters ran off to London. He never heard from them again, and that seemed to signal the start of Bully's hatred of all things feminine.

Bully had been serving time when his mother passed away, and turned down a day on the outside to attend her funeral, a cremation at Daldowie. Which struck Gilchrist. Daldowie was the same crematorium where Topley had his mother cremated.

Was that the connection? A crematorium? And why Daldowie?

The closest crematorium to Glenorra was Maryhill. Not Daldowie. If Glasgow was a circle, Daldowie was more or less diametrically opposite Maryhill. So why would Topley have his mother cremated in Daldowie?

Because Bully told him to? Because they had an agreement?

In Bully's world, he was the leader, everyone else a follower— sheep herded to the cliff edge and ordered to jump. Or rob. Or murder. Or cremate your mother?

Bully the leader, the man of words, the poet.

Oh princess, by thy watchtower be.

Then it struck Gilchrist with a clarity that stunned him.

He threw his coffee away.

He asked a young sergeant at the front desk to check out something for him as a matter of urgency, and the instant, the absolute *instant* he had the result, to let him know.

"I'll be in Interview Room Two. Just say yes or no."

Gilchrist almost exploded into the room.

Topley stiffened, mouth frozen in the act of a whisper to Foster.

Gilchrist stepped past Nance, swept around the table, hauled Topley to his feet.

Foster pushed his chair back. "This is—"

"*Shut up.*"

The chair hit the floor with a hard clatter.

"I have to warn you that—"

"And I'm warning you," Gilchrist turned on Foster, "that if you are in any way responsible for letting this piece of shite keep information from me that could save my daughter's life then I'll hold you personally responsible."

"You can't do—"

"Do you have children?"

Foster's lips tightened. His throat bobbled.

Gilchrist secured his grip on Topley's suit lapels, pulled the man's muscled bulk up and over so the tips of their noses almost touched. Topley's arms dangled by his side, as if to tell Gilchrist that he knew he would not hit him. How wrong could he be?

"Why is your father buried in the Auld Aisle?" Gilchrist hissed.

"Where?"

"You heard. The Auld Aisle Cemetery. Why?"

"Why not?"

"The rest of his family's not buried there."

"So?"

"So why only him?" Gilchrist felt Topley shrug. "Did Bully tell you to do that?"

"Bully?"

"Yeah. Bully. You know, the guy who pulls the strings of puppets like you."

"Fuck you."

"Oh I'm just about to fuck *you*, don't you worry about that." He thrust Topley back onto his seat, turned to Foster. "I'm upping the charges."

"On what grounds?"

Gilchrist faced Topley. "I'm charging you, Christopher Topley, as an accessory in the murder of Maureen Gillian Gilchrist—"

"This is outrageous, a violation of my client's rights." Foster's colour had returned along with his power of speech. Anger danced like madness in button eyes. "What murder? Maureen Gilchrist isn't. . . ." He halted then, like a hunter realising he was about to set off his own baited trap.

"Maureen Gilchrist isn't dead?" Gilchrist said. "Is that what you wanted to say?" He felt his eyes blaze. "You forgot to add *yet*."

Foster looked away, as if law was something he no longer wanted to practise.

"You're a loopy one, that's for sure," Topley quipped.

"Loopy or not, you're going to jail." Gilchrist leaned towards him, fought off the almost overpowering urge to head butt the man. Topley's silvery suit looked out of place, as if he'd turned up at the wrong fancy-dress party. "And d'you know what Bully's going to do to you when you get back inside?"

Topley's eyes flickered.

That got your attention, thought Gilchrist.

"Me and Bully are mates."

"I thought you hadn't spoken to him in a year."

"Yeah, well, mates is mates."

"Bully's not well. He's ill."

"Says who?"

"Says me. I saw him."

"Yeah, I heard."

Gilchrist felt cheered by Topley's slip up. "Thought you didn't keep in touch."

"Yeah, well, someone in the pub told me."

"Got that, Nance?" Gilchrist shouted over his shoulder. "Someone in the pub told him." He eyed Topley. "Which pub?"

"Can't remember."

"Which someone?"

"Can't remember."

Gilchrist looked at Nance and nodded to the door. She frowned and stepped from the room, leaving the three of them. Topley ran his hand across his top lip, and Gilchrist leaned closer, almost kissed a scarred ear. "Just you and me," he whispered.

Topley said nothing as Gilchrist walked away and stood with his back to the far wall, arms crossed. It took Topley several slow seconds to turn to his solicitor. "Beat it, Jer. Go on. Skedaddle."

"I must advise against—"

"And don't bill me for your fucking time, you useless twat. It's a fucking crime what you lot charge. We're through. Got that?"

Foster spilled his papers into an opened briefcase, and snapped it shut. Then he eased his bulk upright, lumbered splay-footed to the door, and squeezed himself from the room.

Topley pushed back, stretched his arms behind his neck. "Fucking wanker."

Gilchrist returned to his chair, eyed the recorder that lay between them, and clicked it off. He hoped Topley would catch the sincerity in his words. "I only want to find my daughter," he said.

"You expect me to trust you?"

"It's your choice."

Topley pressed his elbows on the desk. "Or?"

"Or it's back inside." Gilchrist lowered his voice to that of a co-conspirator. "And believe me, I'll trump up the charges so much that you'll make Peter Manuel look like a virgin choirboy." He smiled. "Ready?"

Chapter 34

IS THIS WHAT death is like?

No sound. No feeling. No movement.

Just stillness. Like dreaming. Like floating on air.

She tried to sit up, move her neck, reach for the wall. But although she was no more than two feet from it, she could not find the strength to touch its roughened surface.

I have died. That is why I feel nothing, hear nothing, can move nothing.

Because I am dead. But if I am dead, why is it so cold?

So cold again. Freezing.

She managed to pull her legs up, tried to lock her knees against her chest, but toppled onto her side.

I am so weak, I don't know how. . . .

. . . I don't know . . .

. . . how long . . .

. . . I can . . .

. . . hold . . .

"BULLY'S GOT IT in for you," Topley said. "He hates you so much, he's forgotten why."

"Tell me what he said about Maureen."

Topley levelled his head, stared hard into Gilchrist's eyes. "I don't know a thing about that. And that's the truth."

Gilchrist felt a nip in his gut. Did he have it wrong? "What about Ronnie Watt?" he asked. "Did Ronnie ever talk to you about Bully?"

"Not a chance."

Gilchrist was not sure he believed that answer. But for the time being it would have to do. "How do you know Ronnie?"

"Does a bit of stuff for us."

"Us?"

"My company."

"What kind of stuff?"

"Stuff stuff."

Now where had he heard that before? "Did you know Watt's with Strathclyde Drug Squad?"

Topley's eyebrows shifted. "You're joking. Right?"

Ham actor of the century. Maybe even the universe. "Why did Bully want your father buried in the Auld Aisle?"

"Who says he did?"

"Me."

Topley paused, as if deciding whether or not to continue lying, then shrugged. "Don't know."

"Stop pulling my plonker."

"I'm telling you. I don't know why the fuck he wanted the old man buried there."

"But you did as he asked."

"Yeah."

"Why?"

"What the fuck's that supposed to mean?"

"He was *your* old man. Why let Bully get involved?"

"Why not?"

Gilchrist moved closer. "You scared of Bully?"

Topley cracked his knuckles. "I can look after myself."

"Why not tell him to bugger off?"

"What the fuck did I care? I mean, the old man's as stiff as a parrot. What the fuck difference does it make? He's gone. Out of it. Food for the worms."

"It made a difference to your mother."

"What the fuck is this? You'll be pulling the old violin out next."

"She cared."

"Yeah, well, she's gone where she doesn't need to care any more."

"Ashes in the attic?"

Topley looked off to the side, as if trying to avoid Gilchrist's eyes. But Gilchrist was having none of it. He fingered the recorder.

"Did Bully tell you *not* to bury her beside your father?"

Silence.

"Did you ever ask yourself why?"

Topley's flattened nose flared with anger.

Gilchrist pulled back. He was missing something. But what, he could not say. Did it matter that Bully had ordered Topley to bury his father in some cemetery far from the family plot? And then not to bury his mother there? Or was Gilchrist toddling up the wrong track? He did not know. But what he did know, from the heavy-lidded look in Topley's eyes, was that some impasse had been reached. Mrs. Hutchison had said ten years, but Gilchrist was interested in hearing how Topley would answer.

"When did your father die?" he asked.

"Fuck sake. How would I know? It was years ago."

"Twenty?"

"Not as long as that."

"Ten?"

"Yeah. About that."

"Were you in Barlinnie when he died?"

"Fuck off. I had a good job back then."

"Did you like your father?"

"Bad-tempered drunk, is what the old fucker was."

"Ever hit you?"

"That'd be the fucking day."

"How about Kevin? Your father hit him?"

"Kevin would have nailed him to the door."

Gilchrist frowned. Nothing seemed to fit. He had met Jack's girlfriend. And what had struck him about Chloe was her sensitivity, her artist's gentleness. Yet Kevin Topley had been her boyfriend before Jack. It seemed improbable. But there was Maureen, too, his own daughter, an employee of the likes of Topley. What the hell was the world coming to? Or more to the point, what the hell was he missing?

The door opened.

Gilchrist spun round.

"Sorry, sir. You did tell me to let you know."

"Well?"

"Yes. Sir."

Gilchrist succeeded in maintaining his composure in front of Topley. "Thank you," he said, and waited for the door to close. He wanted to ask Topley one more question, and leaned closer. "When was the last time you visited your father's grave?"

Topley shrugged.

"You've never visited it. Have you?"

Topley dead-eyed him. "Like I said. He's dead as a parrot. What's the fucking point?"

Gilchrist felt disappointment flush through him. Would anyone visit his own grave after he was dead? Had he made any impact on the world, left anything of any significance behind him? The futility of it all seemed insurmountable. The world was filled with villains much worse than Topley, who murdered without pity or compassion, the cruellest of human beings who took everything and gave nothing. And after trying to extract information from Topley, he now felt like a dog that had been scraping for a meatless bone in the wrong hole.

"You're free to go," he said.

"Didn't know I'd been arrested."

"Don't push it." Gilchrist tugged his hand through his hair. His fingers tined the thinning spot at the back of his crown. He gritted his teeth at the memory of Maureen teasing him. *Don't worry, Dad. I'll still love you when you're bald.* What would he give to hear her say those words again?

He waited until Topley's footfall faded before he stepped from the room. "Do you know how to get to Kirkintilloch?" he asked Nance.

"Not yet."

"And when you're at it, find out the location of John Topley's grave."

GILCHRIST DROVE HIS Roadster through the gateway of the Auld Aisle Cemetery. The watchtower stood in the oldest part of the graveyard. Beyond the old stone wall, rusting cages huddled over gravesites with tilted headstones weathered smooth.

He stood at the bottom of the watchtower's stairway. Behind him, high in the bared branches of a towering maple, a colony of crows watched his movement with black-eyed disinterest. A chill wind swept in from the north. He upped his collar, eyed the worn stairs. How many shoes had marched up and down that short flight? He had once read an article that alleged watchtower guards were often bought, and grave-robbing had not declined, but simply carried out with more care.

He eyed the ancient structure.

The base of the watchtower had an arched passage through it, the entrance to the original cemetery. Was this where he would find Maureen?

"Andy?" Nance's skin felt soft and warm. "Let me do this."

Gilchrist walked up the first six steps, then grabbed the walled stairway. The stone felt cold, and he took the steps one at a time, his heart heavy with the prospect of what he dreaded he would find.

He reached the top step. The watchtower's door had been boarded over. Scrapes on the wood looked as if they had been made by a claw-hammer. Was his daughter on the other side of that boarding? He resisted the urge to call out her name, afraid she could not answer. Instead, he pressed his ear against the unpainted surface.

He heard nothing.

He slapped his hand against the boarding, then thudded the heel of his hand hard against it. "Anyone?" he shouted, and gave a start when Nance joined him.

"Stand back." She leaned to the side, kicked out her foot.

The boarding wobbled.

She kicked again.

On the fourth kick, the boarding splintered along one edge.

Gilchrist thudded his shoulder against it, once, twice, then the nails gave out with a tearing crack. He stumbled into the dark interior.

"Maureen?"

Empty. Nothing but bare walls and boarded over openings.

Oh princess, by thy watchtower be.

Bully had him beaten, Burns' verses his way of making Gilchrist believe he had to solve a riddle to save his daughter's life. But it was a hoax, nothing more than Bully's self-satisfying ploy to build up Gilchrist's hopes. Then dash them. And he now saw that he would never find Maureen. She was gone.

"Andy?"

But he was already skipping down the steps.

He ran around the base like a demented lunatic, slapping his hands against the cold stone, hoping, praying he would find some secret door, some window, some opening that would validate his twisted theory that Bully had Maureen interred in some long-forgotten chamber.

But he found no such opening.

He pressed the flats of his hand to the cold stone walls and hung his head. It took him several seconds to realise Nance was not with him, but down by the new gate to the cemetery extension. He caught up with her as she strode along a gravel path lined by worn memorials. Headstones, darkened with age, spilled down the cemetery slopes to the Bothlyn Burn.

"Go back to the car," she said.

"I need to see for myself."

"We don't know for certain, Andy."

"No," he whispered. It was all he could hope for.

They found John Topley's grave in the newest part of the cemetery, which seemed brightened by shiny headstones of glossy grey and bituminous black, footed by wreaths that sprinkled the grass with pinks, reds, yellows, whites, like the leftovers from some garden party. Topley's grave was marked by a flat black headstone with an empty pewter flower-holder at its head. Shorn grass grew as tough as reeds around it.

Gilchrist read the chiselled epitaph.

Gone, but not forgotten.

How meaningless words could be.

But the turf that fronted the memorial looked sliced where the grass had been lifted and relaid. He checked the chiselled words. John Topley had died at the age of sixty-two, and been buried ten years earlier. Yet the turf that fronted his headstone had only recently been relaid.

Gilchrist now knew there was no hope.

He slipped his mobile into his hand and punched in the numbers. "Dainty," he said. "I need authorization to exhume a coffin." He listened to Dainty fire questions at him, then heard his own voice say, "I think we might have found her."

Chapter 35

IT TOOK LESS than two hours to uncover the coffin.

As Gilchrist had expected, it was not buried deep. Bully's men would have had little time in the space of a single night to bury it, and a shallow grave at least ensured it was out of sight. But the fact it was a coffin at all puzzled Gilchrist. Why not wrap Maureen's body in plastic sheeting instead, the same sheeting in which Chloe's left leg had been wrapped?

It made no sense to him. Or maybe it did.

Would lugging a coffin into a graveyard at night raise less suspicion? Or maybe Bully had known not to trust his men, that they might not follow his instructions to the letter but bury the body in a grave shallow enough for some feral dog to dig up. A coffin would at least offer the cadaver some protection.

But Gilchrist's rationale was muddled. Something did not fit. The coffin's surface looked scratched and worn, as if it had been in the ground for years, rather than days. One of the SOCOs unscrewed the brass holders and prepared to open the lid. Gilchrist glanced at Nance and caught the glitter of tears in the late afternoon sun.

Gloved hands gripped the coffin lid.

Gilchrist stopped breathing.

The lid was lifted and placed on the grass.

"Fucking hell."

"What's this then?"

"*Don't touch*."

Dainty stepped forward, his brow furrowed, and Gilchrist saw

Nance was just as puzzled. "There must be millions here," Dainty gasped. "Bloody hell. A fucking fortune is what we've got."

Gilchrist looked into the opened coffin, at bundles packed like icing sugar wrapped in polythene, the same material as that around Chloe's left leg, he would bet, crammed into the confines of a coffin stripped of silk and padding to make more room.

Dainty scratched his forehead. "I think our Mr. Topley's got a lot of answering to do. Wouldn't you say?"

Gilchrist should have been relieved that Maureen's body was not in the coffin, but it surprised him to feel disappointment flush through him. If Maureen had been buried there, then he had found her, could have tried to live with the horror of it all. But now she was still out there, somewhere, tied up, dead, buried, hacked to pieces, or God only knew what, her body planted for him to find, or not find, at Bully's dictate.

He now saw why Topley's mother's ashes were in the attic. The coffin was used for the temporary storage of drugs, which must have started after John Topley's death, but before Betsy's. Bully had instructed Topley not to bury his mother here. The grave-diggers would have unearthed an unrecorded coffin, and Bully's hidey-hole would have been lost, along with his millions in drugs.

Gilchrist held out his hand. "Gloves."

The nearest SOCO offered him a pair.

Gilchrist pulled them on and leaned into the coffin. He eased one bundle out, laid it to the side, then did the same with two others. But Bully would not risk contaminating his consignment by storing it with Maureen's body. Six packets later he knew he was right. He slipped off the gloves.

"What do you think?" Dainty asked him.

"When does Bully get out of Barlinnie?"

"With his appeal going ahead, two, three years, give or take six months or so. Why?"

"He must have known he would be the prime suspect in Maureen's murder."

"Come on, Andy, Bully's in a top security—"

"It's him—"

"You can't prove a—"

"I *will*," Gilchrist snarled. "Believe me, I will."

Dainty's eyes flared, then saddened. "You'll have a tough time, Andy. His brief's Rory Ingles. Solicitor to the mob. And the likes of Bully."

"Which means?"

"That he's never lost a case."

"And he costs a ton of money." Three SOCOs were dusting the coffin for prints, but they were wasting their time. "There's Bully's legal nest-egg for the next thirty years."

"So this is nothing to do with Topley, is what you're telling me."

"It's got Bully written all over it."

"Give it up, Andy. You've got Bully on the bloody brain." Dainty's mobile rang at that moment, and he seemed relieved to take the call.

Gilchrist choked back his anger, turned away, almost bumped into Nance.

"I don't know what to tell you," she said.

But he pushed past her, onto the asphalt path that led to the old part of the cemetery. Bully could not have anticipated the discovery of his drugs cache, which was a huge plus in Gilchrist's favour. Or was it? When Bully found out, he would go berserk. Then how could Gilchrist ever force Bully to confess to what he had done with Maureen? They had almost found her at Glenorra. But Bully had been one step ahead.

Why? Why had Maureen been moved?

Maybe that was the question he should be asking.

Not *where* had she been moved to, but *why* had she been moved.

Why that night? Why not earlier? Because the cryptic clues were simple, intended to be solved, and Bully would have known that Gilchrist was getting close, that he was pulling it all together. Were the clues provided not to solve the murder, but to ensure that Gilchrist would suspect Bully then meet him? So that Bully could gloat?

Was Bully only a red herring? Were the answers with Bully's brother, Jimmy? Was Maureen's body moved the night Wee Kenny was murdered? Was Jimmy already living it up in Spain, soaking up the sun, setting up the villa for Bully's release in three years, maybe less, with Rory Ingles, solicitor for the rich and infamous, handling his appeal?

Gilchrist removed his copy of Bully's lyrics, and studied that line again. He had spent almost twelve months bomb-proofing the case against Bully, had come to know the man as well as he would his own brother. So what was he missing?

Oh princess, by thy watchtower be.

He crushed the paper into a ball, his mind playing that line over and over.

Oh princess, by thy watchtower be.

He faced Topley's grave. The SOCOs were loading the drugs into their van. To the side, some forty feet away, Nance stood by another headstone. He walked towards her.

She surprised him by saying, "Joe Reid. Bully's father's grave."

Gilchrist almost smiled. In the process of locating Topley's grave, Nance had taken the initiative and found Bully's father's, too. He read the inscription.

> The honest man, though e'er sae poor
> Is king o' men for a' that.

He recognised the lines from Burns' poem *A Man's a Man for A' That*, and once again puzzled over the reference to Burns. "What's Bully's attraction to all things Burns?" he asked Nance.

"Maybe it was drummed into him at school?"

"Did he go to school?" His mobile rang. He flipped it open, and walked off.

"Hey, man, I went through the print-outs like you asked, and I found something."

Gilchrist's throat seemed to clamp at Jack's words. "I'm listening."

"Tried to check it out before I called, in case I'd got it wrong. But I got nowhere."

"Back up, Jack. You're losing me."

"It's Maureen's job, man. The Topley Company's just eye-wash."

"Are you saying she's employed by someone else?"

"The police."

Something thudded into Gilchrist's chest.

"I mean, who would've believed it? There's no contract or anything. Just two emails, the first confirming she would be available for employment, the second confirming the terms of their agreement."

"Who are they to and from?"

"DI Ronald Watt. You know him?"

Detective Inspector. Watt had lied to Maureen about his position, probably lied to her about the job. Watt had conned her, made up some bullshit story that had her drooling at the jowls, and in the end put her life in danger.

Watt would not have wanted correspondence mailed to his office. That would have blown his scheme. He would also have known Maureen kept a copy of all her emails on her computer. Which explained why her flat had been broken into.

"Does it say which division she was working for?" he asked.

"Strathclyde. And get this. The Drug Squad."

Gilchrist stopped walking. All of a sudden, a whole new line of reasoning opened up to him. "Don't let anyone see these letters, Jack. You got that?"

"I hear you."

Gilchrist was almost twitching to have it out with Watt. But phoning Watt first would steal his thunder, so he called the Topley Company, and got through to Topley on the first try.

"Maureen doesn't work for you, does she?" he growled.

"Mr. Gilchrist. Nice to hear from you—"

"*Does she?*"

"If that lovely daughter of yours doesn't show her tits around here any time soon, she won't be working for me any longer."

"Did you know she worked for Ronnie Watt?"

"Can't say that I did."

Gilchrist thought he caught the tiniest of hesitations. Surprised? Or lying? Gilchrist decided to go for it. "In about thirty seconds," he said, "Bully's going to be told you grassed on him to the Drug Squad."

"Is that supposed to scare me?"

Gilchrist eyed the SOCOs. The bags were stacking higher. Just how much cocaine did a coffin hold? "This afternoon," he said, "we found about thirty million pounds' worth of cocaine. All wrapped up in neat little bundles."

"Who's a lucky Detective Inspector then?"

"Buried in your old man's grave."

A pause, then, "I know fuck all about that."

"But you know Maureen worked with Watt."

"No chance. I swear. On my mother's grave."

Gilchrist could almost hear Topley sweating. "You've been seen talking to Watt."

"So?"

"Watt's with the Drug Squad."

Silence, as Topley put two and two together.

"How do you contact him?" Gilchrist asked. He listened to the digital ether fill the line, and an image of Topley trying to manufacture his next lie swelled in his mind.

"He'll know it's come from me," Topley said.

"Your choice. Bully or Watt. I really don't care."

"Look. If I tell you, you've got to help me."

"Keep talking."

"We have a deal?"

"Just cough it out, and I'll see what I can do."

It took so long for Topley to answer, that Gilchrist thought he had lost the connection. When Topley's voice came back at him, it growled low and guttural, letting him know there could be no compromise. "You didn't hear this from me. All right?" Another pause, then, "He drinks in the Dreel Tavern."

Gilchrist knew the east coast. "Anstruther?"

"Most nights between nine and ten."

"Who does he meet? I need a name."

"I don't know. I swear."

"No name, no deal."

"Fuck you, Gilchrist."

"No," Gilchrist snarled. "Fuck Watt. I need a name." He pressed on. "Give me a name, and it'll go no further. You have my word."

It took a full ten seconds before Topley said, "Bootsie. Real name's Joe Cobbler. But everyone calls him Bootsie."

Bootsie. Joe Cobbler. Joe. The same Joe who stole Peggy Linnet's phone?

"Got an address?" Gilchrist said.

Surprisingly, Topley did.

Chapter 36

WATT'S FACE DISPLAYED stubble that had not yet reached the curled stage. Another week and he would have a full beard. Gilchrist waited until Watt's fingers wrapped around his pint before he joined him.

"Mine's an Eighty."

Give Watt his due, he never so much as flinched. "An Eighty over here," he said to the barman. "Pubs in St. Andrews shut, are they?"

"You tricked Maureen," Gilchrist growled. "You tricked her into thinking she was working undercover for the police."

"Where do you get off?"

"Oh I'm staying on to the bitter end, you'd better believe it."

Although Gilchrist had not raised his voice, Watt picked up on the change in mood. He took a sip of beer. "If you must know," he said, "Maureen begged me to hire her."

The word *begged* did not conjure up an image of Maureen. He slapped a hand onto Watt's arm with a force that splashed beer over the counter and stopped the barman from pulling his pint. "She's missing," he hissed. "And you know who's behind it. You've known all along. But made no attempt to stop it. Why?"

Watt scowled until Gilchrist relaxed his grip. "Crap like that can get a lad like you hurt."

"Are you denying it?"

"What do *you* think?"

"Bootsie isn't coming tonight," Gilchrist tried.

"Who?"

"The Bootsie you used to phone first thing in the morning and last thing at night."

"Fifty quid says you never had a warrant to pull my phone records."

Gilchrist realised his attempts to call the number on Watt's records had succeeded only in alerting Watt. "You knew someone was onto you," he said. "So instead of calling Bootsie morning noon and night you meet him here."

"If you say so."

"Bootsie says so."

Watt sipped his beer like a lonely man.

"And Bootsie also says you're sniffing around the east coast waiting for some drug shipment from Europe. That's why you finagled a reassignment to Fife." Gilchrist leaned closer. "But there is no drug shipment."

Watt faced Gilchrist. "Says Bootsie? Bootsie knows the square root of fuck all."

"This didn't come from Bootsie."

Watt's eyes livened. "You always were a right cocky bastard."

Gilchrist struggled to hide his anxiety. Did he have it wrong? He had spent thirty minutes interrogating Bootsie, cutting it short to catch Watt before he left the Dreel. But now Watt was giving off the wrong signals. Had Bootsie told him a rat's nest of lies just to get rid of him? Nance was still interrogating him, and Gilchrist found himself wishing she was with him now, helping him pierce a way through Watt's deception.

"Maureen, Topley, Bully, Jimmy, you," Gilchrist said. "Took me a while to piece it all together. Bit of a Chinese puzzle, really. But it was the drug shipment that helped me work it out."

"And here was me thinking you were good at puzzles."

Gilchrist clenched his jaw. He had still not worked out the puzzle of where Maureen was. Bootsie had not been able to help them either. "Well, how's this for a puzzle?" he said. "How about I charge you as an accessory to murder?"

Watt smiled. He really smiled. "The Lone fucking Ranger," he growled. "That's you. You always get your man." He chewed imaginary gum, and something told Gilchrist that the worst was yet to come. "That's why Maureen hated you." Watt's teeth flashed a grin. "The most successful DCI in Fife Constabulary, but an abject failure as a father."

Something cold washed over Gilchrist then, and he had to look away.

He knew he had failed. He had failed as a father, failed as a husband. If he had been there for his wife, there for his children, would they have left him to live in Glasgow? In his mind's eye he watched the door open, the empty hallway appear before him, heard the thud of the door behind him as he stepped inside to his new life, all alone.

But Maureen *hated* him?

That could not be. *Hate* was too strong a word. No, it was *Watt* who hated him. And with that thought he saw it was time to tighten the screws.

"Bootsie's ready to tell all," he said.

"Fuck Bootsie. One wrong word from him and I'll put him away for life."

"Funny. That's what Bootsie said about you."

Watt's jaw ruminated, and Gilchrist knew his words had hit home at last.

Then Watt picked up his pint, downed it, and turned from the bar.

Gilchrist grabbed his arm. "Don't even think about it," he said. "Bootsie's safe and sound. Leave now and the next time you see him will be from behind bars. Not his. *Yours.*"

Watt tugged his arm free.

Gilchrist could almost see Watt's mind trying to work out what he had over him. But in reality, Watt had little to fear. Gilchrist needed him to fill in the gaps. He could not let Watt leave. Not just yet.

He turned to the bartender. "Same again," and waited until a glass was shoved under the tap before he said, "Talk to me, Ronnie. For Maureen's sake, talk to me."

Gilchrist thought he understood Watt's dilemma. Watt had a soft spot for Maureen, maybe even loved her in his own way. But nothing could come of their relationship because of the past. And behind his back Watt had resurrected their affair by tricking Maureen into working for him. Now she was missing and might never be found, Watt could deny it, talk his way out of it, lie himself clear. But Gilchrist suspected that Watt was up to his neck in unofficial police work, straddling the fine line between working inside or outside the law.

It would probably not take much to put him away.

"If Maureen dies," Gilchrist said to him, "I'll make it my life's mission to make sure you never see this side of a prison wall as long as you live. You got that?"

Watt's eyes blazed for a long moment, then softened. He took another sip of beer, and said, "That body they found?"

"What about it?"

"Bootsie says it's Wee Kenny."

Gilchrist remembered Dainty mentioning Wee Kenny, but the name meant nothing to him, so he waited.

"Bootsie used to live in Glasgow," Watt went on. "Left to start a new life. But some losers never change. With Bootsie gone, Jimmy Reid was looking for a new goffer." Watt returned his pint to the bartop. "So what's this about there being no drug shipment?"

The question threw Gilchrist, but he was not yet ready to give anything out. "Why the east coast?" he asked.

"Jimmy's ill."

Watt's answer made no sense to him, but he said, "Flu, cold, what?"

"Cancer."

Gilchrist felt a flush warm his face. His mind leapt to Gail, and he had to blink once, twice, three times to clear the image. "Terminal?"

"Word is he's got less than six months."

"So he'll be dead and buried by the time Bully's out."

"All his life he's lived in Bully's shadow. Even with Bully inside Jimmy still played second fiddle. But he can't wait for Bully to come out. He wants to reap the benefits of a life of crime before he dies." Watt took another sip of beer. "Jimmy'd been coming up this way several times a week. I figured he was getting ready to handle one final shipment."

Now it made some sense. Watt had assumed that Jimmy's visits to St. Andrews were to set up that final shipment. But he had it all wrong. The final shipment had already arrived, hidden in a coffin in the Auld Aisle Cemetery where it would remain until Bully got out of Barlinnie, or Jimmy shifted it before he died.

"Jimmy's made three trips to Spain this year alone," Watt said.

"Setting up his retirement villa?"

Watt nodded, sipped his beer.

According to Bootsie, he had told Watt when and where each body part was going to turn up, alerting Watt to Jimmy Reid's visits to St. Andrews so he could keep his eye on him. What Gilchrist could not rationalise was that Watt had known Jimmy Reid was involved in Chloe's murder, but had turned a blind eye for the sake of the discovery of a drug shipment.

"So how did Bootsie know when Jimmy was going to make a trip to St. Andrews?" Gilchrist asked.

"Wee Kenny."

"Jimmy's goffer was grassing on him?"

"Without realising it. Wee Kenny told Bootsie that Jimmy was about to hit pay dirt. And Bully's putting it about that he's going to be out in two and retire to Spain. I'd been keeping my eye on Jimmy for some time. He's a right bad bastard. Some say he's even worse than Bully."

Now it was beginning to make sense. With Jimmy dying, the

key was the next six months. For Bully to take his revenge on Gilchrist, what better way than to have Jimmy take care of it while he was still in prison? What did it matter to Jimmy if he killed a few more? But where was he now? In Spain? Hiding in Scotland? Waiting for the final shipment—

"You still haven't told me why you think there's no drug shipment," Watt said.

"We found it," Gilchrist said, and puzzled at the look of distress that passed over Watt's face.

"You found it?"

"All thirty million. Give or take a few."

"Where?"

"The Auld Aisle Cemetery. In Topley Senior's grave."

Watt placed his glass on the bartop with practiced calm, then faced Gilchrist. "Two years," he hissed. "Two years we've had our eye on that. Two years watching and waiting for the right moment."

For once Gilchrist's sense of logic left him. "You've lost me, Ronnie."

"The drug shipment was never coming from Europe. It was *going* to Europe."

Now Gilchrist understood. Topley's grave was being used as a holding spot.

"Two years I've been monitoring the European connection." The muscles on Watt's jaw rippled across his face. "Two years flushed down the toilet, all because of you and your fucking daughter."

Gilchrist hit him then, a straight-fingered punch to the solar plexus that had Watt gritting his teeth and gasping for breath. He caught the bartender's alarmed look, but Nance stepped to the bar and held up her warrant card.

"Mine's a pint of Eighty," she ordered.

The barman seemed relieved to oblige.

For a confusing moment, Gilchrist wondered what Nance

had done with Bootsie, then he pressed on with Watt. "So, with Jimmy's visits to St. Andrews you thought the shipment was about to be moved."

Watt straightened himself, tried to act as if nothing was hurting. But from the grey sheen around his eyes, Gilchrist knew he was struggling. "Through Topley's company."

Part of a larger holding group. Some international company with too much money.

"And you had Maureen spy on Topley and report back to you."

Watt almost smiled.

"You put Maureen's life at risk, you pompous prick. For what?" The strength of his anger stunned Gilchrist. For sixpence, he could rip Watt's heart from his chest with his bare hands. "Did you not think of telling her the danger she was in?"

Watt turned on him. "I tried to get her out," he growled. "But she was having none of it. She refused to meet me. What the hell could I do? I ended up pleading with her on the phone about a week ago."

The sixteen-minute call. "And?"

"She said she thought something was about to break."

"Damn it, Ronnie. You should have got her away—"

"You still don't get it." Watt's eyes burned. "It was Maureen who terminated our arrangement. I tried to warn her, but she wouldn't listen. In the end she told me to fuck off."

Gilchrist knew there was more than a hint of truth to Watt's words. Maureen was like her mother—stubborn beyond reason. Surely her obstinacy had not got her killed.

"She wanted to write crime novels." Watt tried a laugh. "Wanted firsthand experience, for fuck sake."

Christ. All Maureen had to do was ask her father. Was he so far out of her life that she could not ask him for help? He focused his mind, intent on keeping the pressure on Watt. "But you needed someone on the inside," he said. "So, you let her walk into the lion's den."

"She jumped at it."

"Didn't you tell her about Topley's criminal background?"

"Of course I did. That's why she fucking jumped." Watt tried a smile, but his lips seemed not to work. He pushed his beer away and covered his eyes, and it took Gilchrist a full ten seconds to realise Watt was struggling to hold back his tears. He glanced at Nance, but she looked as puzzled.

He gave Watt a moment before saying, "What aren't you telling me, Ronnie?"

Watt came to, stared at his pint. "Oh, she was a natural," he said. "She had them all fooled. Topley never suspected a fucking thing. The hours were long. Which was part of the cover. No one would notice her working late, digging up shit. I thought she was safe." He shook his head, lifted his beer. "I loved your daughter."

Gilchrist felt his heart stutter at the past tense.

"And I'll always wonder if I could have done more to prevent her being killed."

Gilchrist gripped Watt's arm. "What do you mean?"

"Mo's gone, Andy. Bully's closing shop. No one's ever going to find her. *Ever*." He tugged his arm free and turned to his glass. "I'm sorry," he gasped.

Chapter 37

GILCHRIST THOUGHT HE kept his emotions in check, but his stomach burned as if the beer was acid. Something flashed in his mind's eye, an image of Watt's bloodied face, Maureen's tortured grimace, her lips pulling back in a silent curse. She hated him then, at that instant, at the moment of his discovery. Had she died with those thoughts?

He pushed away from Watt and stepped from the bar.

"Andy."

Nance's voice came at him as if from a distance. Fingers gripped his arm, tight as talons. He looked down, then up, then off to a picture on the wall, the window. Darkness outside. Another night. One more night without Maureen. In his life? Or in this world? Was she dead? Was Maureen really dead?

"Andy." Fingers on his chin, turning his face.

"She's gone, Nance," he whispered.

Her eyes fired up. "You can't give up, Andy. Not now."

"No," he said. "I've lost her." The sound of his own voice puzzled him. Had he lost her? Or had she let him go? Was it as simple as that? Daughters fell out with their fathers, held grudges for days, weeks, months, could even hate their fathers.

Had Maureen hated *her* father?

How could she? When he sat her on his knee and pretended they were on a runaway horse together, he remembered how she had giggled and squealed and wrapped her arms around his neck. How could she hate him?

"Come on, Andy. Sit down."

His arm tugged. His feet lifted.

The bench seat thudded hard against his back.

The wooden table glistened with spillage, the ashtray grey with burned dust. He pulled out his wallet. "Here," he said, "get me a whisky. A large one."

"You need rest," Nance said to him.

"What for, Nance? What the hell for?" He struggled to his feet. Hard hands pulled him down. He slumped back onto the bench seat.

"Look at you," she said. "You're dead on your feet."

Dead on your feet. The irony of it brought a grin to his face. You had to be alive to be dead on your feet. "Good one, Nance. Good one."

She frowned again, as if not understanding. But what was there not to understand? Maureen was dead. And he had let it happen. Right under his nose, he had let it happen. He had ignored the warning signs, the notes, the cryptic clues, the crystal clear messages from Bully. Christ, how could he—

"*Andy.*" She tugged his sleeve. "Look at me. Don't listen to a word Watt says. He knows nothing, Andy. Nothing. Do you hear? Bootsie doesn't trust him."

"Where's Bootsie now?"

"In hiding."

"I know that. But where?"

Nance glanced at Watt as if to make sure he was out of earshot. "It doesn't matter."

Gilchrist could tell from the glitter in her eyes that she no longer trusted him. Is that how it begins? A little bit of distrust? A bit more, until all of a sudden the ground opens up and Hell swallows you whole?

Trust? Who knew what the fuck trust was any more?

He stood, the move so sudden that Nance gaped up at him.

He gave a twisted smirk. "I'm having a drink."

"Getting drunk's not the answer, Andy."

"D'you know what, Nance?" He saw uncertainty flicker in her eyes. She had never seen him this unhinged before. He was scaring her. If he wasn't so fucked up he would be scaring himself. "I'm not looking for any more answers," he said. "I've had it up to here with answers. I'm through with being lied to every minute of every day. So do you know what I'm going to do? I'm going to get drunk. That's what I'm going to do. If it's all right with you, that is."

Nance lowered her eyes as he brushed past.

He reached the bar and opened his wallet. He fingered a twenty, was about to remove it when it struck him what Nance had said. Had he misheard?

He returned to the table and leaned down to her, so close his lips were almost kissing her right ear. "Bootsie doesn't trust Watt?" he said.

Without looking at him, Nance smiled.

"What's Bootsie holding back?"

"Topley's mother."

"What about her?"

"And Wee Kenny's mother."

"Yes?"

"Were sisters."

Gilchrist slumped back into the bench seat. For the life of him he could not figure it out. "And?"

"Which makes Topley and Wee Kenny cousins."

Maybe Nance was right. Maybe he really was dead on his feet. "I'm listening."

"And family," Nance added.

Gilchrist narrowed his eyes. Family. *Now* he thought he understood. "And Topley knows Wee Kenny's dead, but doesn't know how or who?"

"He knows how. He suspects who."

Now he had it. "Jimmy Reid."

Nance tilted her beer to him.

"Which means. . . ?"

"Any allegiance Topley had to Jimmy and Bully," she said, "has just gone out the window."

"A new turf war?"

"And then some."

Gilchrist smiled, but only for a moment. Something was missing. "When did Topley find out it was Jimmy?" he asked.

"Oh . . ." Nance glanced at her watch. ". . . I'd say about ten minutes ago."

DESPITE THE TIREDNESS and the alcohol Gilchrist felt wide awake. As he gunned his Merc through the night, his mind sparked questions like a fired crackerjack.

Who would launder a coffin-load of drugs?

Chris Topley. Cleaner of all things dirty, with his *legit* Topley Company, shuffling money through offshore banks, business ventures, not to mention his own personal cut.

Why bury the drugs in Topley's grave? Why not hide them in Bully's father's grave?

Because if the drug cache were ever found, it would be a simple case for Bully to deny it. Topley would be blamed. Was that not the first person Dainty pointed to when the coffin was uncovered?

Will Bully be free in two years?

Maybe earlier. With his shite-hot solicitor, Bully could be walking the beaches of Spain next year.

Had Jimmy killed on Bully's orders? Would he do that?

You bet he would.

Why would Jimmy kill Wee Kenny?

Because Wee Kenny knew about Jimmy's involvement in Chloe's and Maureen's murders. Maybe even knew he had grassed to Bootsie. And Jimmy trusted no one. Alive, that is.

Why risk killing three people in the space of a month?

Because Jimmy's dying, with six months to live. That's why

he's buying property in Spain now, why he's closing shop, why he's clearing the decks.

But Bully and Jimmy had made a fatal mistake. They had not known, or had not cared, that Wee Kenny and Chris Topley were cousins, that they were family.

And family changes everything.

They reached Glasgow city centre before midnight. Gilchrist slipped off the M8 at Charing Cross, and powered down Sauchiehall Street. The one-way systems had him swearing under his breath, but Nance shouted directions.

They walked into Babbity Bowster at five to midnight.

The barman told them Topley had been in earlier, but had left with several others.

"Where to?"

The barman looked at them, dumb with confusion.

"Ask someone," snapped Gilchrist. "Hey. You."

A young girl with dirty-blonde hair in a loose ponytail almost jumped. The barman said something to her, but she shook her head. Without prompting, the barman stepped from the bar and returned a few minutes later. "They were heading for Truffles."

"What's that?"

"The Truffle Club. In Drury Street."

The street name tripped Gilchrist up. But Nance beat him to it. "Opposite the Horseshoe," she said.

It cost ten pounds each to enter.

Gilchrist stepped up a carpeted stairway to an upper level that glowed blue and red from the strip club's disco lighting. He thought of walking through the place and looking for Topley, but the aroma of the bar was too much for him, and he ordered a half for himself and a gin and tonic for Nance. He passed over a twenty then eyed the open floor.

Men in dull suits and sharp ties sat at tables in small groups. Some eyed the dancer on the stage, others drooled at bare breasts presented to them table-side. Notes were palmed with the legerdemain of men trained in marital deceit, and by the time their drinks came up Gilchrist had counted eighty pounds being disposed of at the table closest to him.

"He's over there," Nance said, nodding to a table near the stage.

Topley looked drunk, not happy, and proffered money into girls' hands with the disinterest of a financial glutton. A glass of something clear was tossed back and the empty tumbler returned to the table with a smack that Gilchrist heard above the ambient din. They did not have long before Topley would be beyond talking. If he was not there already.

Gilchrist threw back his whisky. "Let's go."

Topley did not notice them until Gilchrist squeezed his shoulder. A muscled man seated opposite slid a hand inside his suit jacket. Nance whispered in his ear, and the man's hand slipped to his knee.

Topley let out a guffaw then threw a pile of twenties onto the table. "A hundred quid for you, darling, if you pop them out for us. Go on. Let's have a goggle at those lovely tits of yours. What d'you say, Ray?" He nodded to the man opposite. "Fancy pushing your fat cock into that little lot?"

Topley struggled to pull himself upright then flopped back as if the act was beyond him. He laughed again. "Here," he said to Nance, and unfolded his wallet. He frowned as he rummaged inside it. "I thought I had a fifty in here." Then he looked up with a dazed smile. "Only hundreds." A single note flew from his hand and fluttered to the floor. "Tell you what, darling. I'll make it two hundred. How's that?" He raised his hands as if a gun had been placed to his skull. "I won't even try to touch them. House rules. How fair can a man get?"

Nance picked up the money, and for one confusing moment Gilchrist thought she was going to strip off her blouse. But she leaned forward, money held out, and said to Topley's spinning eyes, "Should you not be giving this to Wee Kenny's mother?"

Topley's face flattened. His eyes died. He lowered his hands, placed them on the table as if to prove he was unarmed.

Gilchrist readied himself to step in.

"Or do I get to keep it," Nance pressed on, "if I tell you where Jimmy Reid's at?"

Gilchrist knew she was bluffing. But it was lovely to watch the rationale of her words worm through the drunken fuzz of Topley's mind. Then Topley raised a hand, and Gilchrist realised with a spurt of surprise that four bouncers stood behind them.

Chapter 38

GILCHRIST FROZE. NANCE stood as stiff as a puppet. It felt as if the world was waiting for Topley to lower his hand. Even the music seemed silenced, the dancers stilled.

"Tell the heavies to vanish," Gilchrist said. He felt his muscles tense and wondered if Nance would take out the man to her side, or if she would expect him to do that. Or maybe both of them would be frog-marched from the Club and deposited into Drury Street.

Then, as if kick-started, Topley's head jerked with a drunken nod and the man called Ray pushed himself to his feet. Gilchrist sensed the space behind him clear. A gang of five men in suits as dark as their slicked-back hair trundled to the bar where they eyed Topley's table like a pack of dogs just itching to crunch their teeth through meat and bone.

Gilchrist took Ray's seat. It felt warm.

Nance pulled up the chair beside him.

Topley tried a smile, but some part of his nervous system was not working the way it should. On the stage by Topley's left shoulder a blonde in a thong, with breasts the colour of milked coffee, stretched into a backward crab and rolled onto the floor. A group of men at the table to Gilchrist's left huddled in conversation, oblivious to the torsioned nudity by their side. Another group seated to his right ordered drinks. The blonde skipped to the middle of the stage, breasts bouncing like water-filled balloons.

"You're a persistent bitch," Topley said to Nance.

"Nasty's my middle name."

Topley gave a gold-tooth grin then shoved the notes over to her. "Go on, take it," he said. "You can owe me a blow-job."

"You don't get it, do you?"

"Not yet." Topley grinned. "Maybe later?"

Gilchrist felt his eyebrows lift as Nance picked up the money. Then he smiled as she tapped the notes together like a pack of cards, ripped them in two, then again, and let the pieces flutter from her fingers onto the table.

Topley chuckled. But Gilchrist worried that some part of the man's psyche was about to crack and the bouncers would be called with the flicker of an irritated eyebrow. He tried to distract Topley's annoyance by leaning forward.

"You never told me your mother was Wee Kenny's aunt," Gilchrist said.

Topley turned dead eyes Gilchrist's way. In the shifting light, colours danced in time with the music, casting shadows that made Topley's face look as beaten as a boxer's. "So?"

"So you want to get even with Jimmy?" It was Nance.

"What's it to you?" Topley snarled.

"Tell us," she said.

"Tell you what, darling?"

"How to fuck Bully."

Topley pulled himself forward, pressed his chest against the table. "You don't look like you need a lesson in fucking anyone, darling."

Like a referee, Gilchrist stepped in. "We know you're getting ready to take on a big shipment," he said to Topley.

Topley turned the full heat of his leaden glare onto Gilchrist. Half-shut eyelids narrowed. Fingers balled into bruised-knuckle fists. If anything was going to happen, it would happen in the next few seconds.

"What the fuck're you talking about?"

"Drugs," Gilchrist said. "Isn't that what you do?"

Topley glanced over Gilchrist's shoulder. Had he just called his team over? Gilchrist readied himself for the thump of muscled hands.

"You're walking on thin ice, Mr. Gilchrist. You're talking about things that people like you do not talk to people like me about."

Gilchrist sensed it was now only a matter of time until Topley's bodyguards threw them out. "I'm not interested in your grubby little empire," he snarled, "or how you make your money. I only want to find my daughter."

Topley's half-shut eyes almost opened. "Well, Mr. Gilchrist, this may come as a surprise to you and your pretty sidekick with the big tits." He reached forward, gathered in the torn notes, then held them up. "But I *am* interested in making money. Lots of it." He balled his hand, crushed the notes, and deposited them into his pocket.

Gilchrist waited.

Topley sat back. "What's in it for me?"

"I won't press charges."

Topley guffawed, head back, eyes to the ceiling.

A waitress arrived, carrying a tray on which stood a bottle of champagne and three crystal flutes. She placed a glass in front of each of them and without a word topped them with fizzing champagne. Topley palmed her a single note as she left the table. Another hundred, Gilchrist thought.

"Charge me with what?" Topley said.

"Why don't you just cough up or shut up?" Nance said. She lifted her crystal glass and took a sip. "Not bad."

"Dom Perignon," Topley purred.

"I prefer Moët."

"I'll have a crate sent to your home, darling. All I need is your address."

"And if I give it to you?"

"Two crates of Moet would be delivered to your doorstep." Topley placed his hand to his chest. "With all my love."

"Who would do the delivering?"

"Whoever you want, darling."

"And would the delivery boy stay and help me polish off a bottle or two?"

Topley leaned forward, puzzled by the change in Nance's attitude. Gilchrist's ears were perked, too. "Whatever you like, darling, could be arranged." Topley reached across the table, and Nance took hold of his hand.

"Someone once told me," she said, "that men with money make the best lovers, because they can have all the toys they want, but can't buy a woman's love." She squeezed Topley's hand. "So, tell me, Chris. Just how much money do you have?"

"More than enough."

"More than enough to keep a girl happy?"

"More than enough to keep a girl *very* happy."

"Even someone who's difficult to please?"

"*Especially* someone who's difficult to please."

Nance leaned lower. Her breasts swelled against the table. "I'll make a deal."

Topley seemed to hold his breath. Nance had his full attention. Gilchrist's too.

"Do you have a good memory?" she asked.

"Why?"

She released his hand, then lifted her champagne to her lips. Over the rim, her eyes seemed to glitter with cheekiness. "I'll say my address once," she said, "and it'll be up to you to remember it."

Topley's lips twisted in a smirk of victory.

"But first." She took a sip, then said, "You have to answer some questions."

"How can I trust you?"

This time Nance smirked. "You can't."

Topley frowned and smiled at the same time, and Gilchrist caught the street cruelty of the man. Here was a man who could kick another man to death then hand his widow money at the funeral. Topley downed his champagne with barely a breath, then snapped his fingers over his head. Within seconds a bouncer as large as a lock forward stood at his side.

"Another bottle of this stuff," Topley ordered.

The bouncer retreated.

"Right, darling. You were saying?" Topley reclined in his chair, as if settling in for the evening. On the stage behind him, a dancer pirouetted like an ice skater, her arms almost clipping his shoulder, her body close enough for Gilchrist to smell her perfume.

Nance returned her glass to the table. "You spent eighteen months in Barlinnie."

"Don't tell me you hold that against me."

"And you shared a cell with Bully."

"Had to share with someone, darling. Bully's better than some. He's not into plugging holes, if you get my meaning."

"Bully mentioned Maureen's name."

Topley paused, as if trying to work out if she was telling or asking, and if giving the wrong answer would blow any chance of being given her address. Gilchrist realised with a spurt of disbelief that the man's brain was too far gone on drink and drugs to see Nance's scheming for what it was. He really thought he had a chance to get a leg over. Amazing.

Topley nodded. "He did."

"What did he say about her?" Nance asked.

"Are you sure you want to hear this?"

"I want to hear all of it."

Gilchrist felt a shiver tingle his spine. The thought of a convicted criminal talking about his daughter meant only one thing. Bully had been plotting his revenge for years.

Topley glanced at Gilchrist then grinned at Nance. "He told me how he'd love to tie her father down, nail him to the floor, then fuck her in front of him."

"Anything else?"

"Then he said he would make her watch while he did him in."
Topley grinned. "He's a bit sick that way, is Bully."

"Charming, is he?"

"Charming isn't what Bully's about, darling."

They sat tight-lipped while another waitress topped up three
more champagne flutes. Liquid frothed over the rims, puddled
on the tablecloth. To the side, a table-dancer straddled the thigh
of a bleary-eyed businessman and bunched her breasts together,
nipples as large and flat as saucers.

"He'd never seen Maureen, though," Nance said. "Right?"

"He had a photograph of her."

Gilchrist almost jolted. "Where did he get that?"

Topley shrugged. "You'd be surprised what you can get
inside. Nude books. Porno videos. The real thing if you know
who to ask and have the dosh to pay for it. A photo of your
favourite Detective Inspector's daughter is a piece of piss to
these guys."

"Would he still have the photograph?" Gilchrist asked.

"He wanked that much over it, it would have dissolved into
spunk by now."

Nance shook her head, and Gilchrist could tell she was having
a tough time keeping her tongue in place. "What else did he say
about my daughter?" he tried.

"That she was the way to get back at you for putting him
inside, the way to make you suffer for what you did to him."

Being beaten up by Bully was something Gilchrist could handle. It would not be the first time he'd taken a beating. But having
Maureen's life threatened was a different matter altogether. He
bristled, struggled to stay calm, took a sip of champagne. It tasted
sweet. He gulped a mouthful.

Topley chuckled. "Bully had it in for you. I can tell you that
much."

Gilchrist thudded his glass to the table. The champagne bubbled and fizzed. "Other than shooting his load over Maureen's

photo and nailing me to the floor," he growled, "did he ever tell you how he would make me suffer?"

"Can't say that he did."

Something in the way Topley quipped the denial told Gilchrist he was lying.

"Or when he planned to do it?" Nance added.

"No."

"He wouldn't want to do in someone the instant he came out of prison, would he?" Nance continued. "He'd be straight back inside."

"Bully's not scared of prison."

"But he likes his freedom."

"We all do."

"Did he tell you he wanted his brother, Jimmy, to do it?"

"No."

"So, he told you nothing?"

"About that subject. Yes. He told me nothing."

Nance sat back. Gilchrist leaned forward. "How about Robert Burns?"

Topley seemed puzzled by the question.

"What's Bully's obsession with Robert Burns?" Gilchrist asked.

"Never knew he had one."

"Come off it," Gilchrist snapped. "He's got an epitaph on his father's grave that's a direct quote from Burns. And he did nothing but quote Burns to me. He even rewrote one of his opening lines: "*Oh princess, by thy watchtower be.*"

At first he thought the change in Topley's face was anger, then realised something was working through the man's mind. He glanced at Nance and saw she had seen it, too.

"You've remembered something," Nance said.

Topley frowned, as if puzzled at finding himself in the company of two detectives. Then he said, "Bully read a lot of stuff. Jimmy would bring it in for him—books, tapes, CDs. And he was always writing poems. He let me read some of them."

Bully as a poet did not fit Gilchrist's image. "Can you remember what any of them were about?" he asked.

Topley shook his head. "Mostly about killing and raping and stuff like that."

Now they were getting back on track.

"But he did mention a watchtower," Topley added.

Gilchrist pulled himself forward. The bulging breasts on display over Topley's shoulder shifted from his peripheral vision. "I'm listening," he said.

"About a week before I got out."

Gilchrist held his breath.

"Said I should keep my eyes and ears open. That one of those days I was going to read about a killing. The watchtower killing, he told me."

"Were those his exact words?" Nance again.

"Can't remember. Bully ranted on about a lot of stuff. His mind was getting fucked with the drink and drugs and revenge and stuff." Topley fixed a dead-eyed stare on Gilchrist. "Told me you were going to rue the day you ever had a daughter. I remember that much. I remember thinking the two were linked. You know? Watchtower killing. Your daughter. Because he said he would send you a blank postcard and you would know it was from him."

"Why would I know?"

"Because it would have a watchtower on it."

"What kind of watchtower?" Nance asked.

"Like the old watchtowers in cemeteries."

Gilchrist felt his blood turn to ice. There, he had it. He'd been right all along. But was he right about the Auld Aisle? And what did it mean? Then a thought hit him, and he wondered if he was stretching his rationale too far.

"Did he ever tell you what he would do with the body?" he asked Topley.

Topley frowned. "What body? Bully wasn't going to kill her.

He wanted to bury her alive. That's what he told me. He wanted you to know he had buried her alive."

Gilchrist stilled, as if every molecule of muscle and fibre and sinew in his body was about to coil in, then unfold in fury against Bully.

"And he said something else I thought was odd," Topley added. "I never gave it a thought. Not one. Until you mentioned watchtower."

Gilchrist's lungs seemed to stop. His heart, too.

"He said that it was all ready, just waiting for her, as soon as he emptied it."

"Emptied it?" Nance asked. "The watchtower?"

"The coffin."

All of Gilchrist's senses fired alive, as if his mind and body were acting as one. He heard the breathing of the dancer as she writhed her sexual dance to his side, the soft shuffle of her shoes as she turned and shifted across the stage. The music seemed clearer, too, as if the instruments were whispering in his ear.

Buried alive. The coffin was ready. Those were the key words.

"The drug shipment," Gilchrist said. "When was it to be moved?"

Topley's face deadpanned, as if his dreams of sex with a full-chested policewoman had just evaporated. "I thought we agreed not to talk about that."

Gilchrist leaned closer. "I'm not interested in your drug-shipping empire," he said, and prayed Topley would believe him. He would get down on his knees and beg if that was what it would take. "Was it soon? Were the drugs to be moved in the next couple of days?"

Topley turned away, offered his heavy-lidded gaze to Nance.

"St. Andrews," she said. "One hundred North Street."

Gilchrist held his breath. Would Topley recognise the address of the Office? "She could still be alive," he urged.

Topley glanced left and right, as if to ensure no one was

listening. "Rumour has it something was going to happen tomorrow night. But I wouldn't know about that, of course."

Gilchrist pushed his chair back and stood. The coffin. They were not supposed to find it. But they had. Which could mean only one thing.

Maureen was no longer going to be buried alive.

She was going to be killed.

Chapter 39

GILCHRIST ENTERED THE Auld Aisle Cemetery from Woodilee Road.

He accelerated through the iron gate, sending it crashing to the side. He raced along asphalt pathways wide enough to accommodate a hearse. In the darkness, headstones passed in a shadowed blur. When he thought he was close enough, he veered onto the grass.

He left the engine running, the lights on, and stepped into the silence of the cemetery.

His feet slipped on the damp grass as he crossed beds of graves.

Nance reached him by the time he stood at Topley's grave.

"She's here," he said to her. "I know it. I feel it. She's here." He lifted the yellow police tape and peeled back the tarpaulin that covered the excavated pit. The coffin was gone, but the SOCOs had left the grave open for the cemetery staff to repair.

Gilchrist jumped into the grave. He stood waist deep. He stamped on the bottom, but the soil was firm. The coffin containing the body of John Topley would be a couple of feet beneath him. He kicked the sides of the grave, but they were solid.

Nance eyed him from a safe distance, as if watching the antics of a madman.

Gilchrist pulled himself from the pit. "She's here, Nance. I know it. She's here." He brushed soil from his clothes and scanned the dark shadows.

"*Maureen?*"

Nance shuffled her feet.

"*Maureen?*" Gilchrist cupped his hands to his mouth. "*Maureen?*"

"Andy."

Gilchrist faced her. His breath panted in the cold air. He had tried to explain his rationale on the drive from the city. But she seemed unconvinced. Did she not understand? Maureen was here. *Here.* In this cemetery. She had to be. That's what Bully had been telling him. It was simple.

"The coffin," he said.

"I know. You told me."

"That's why they moved her from Glenorra. To bring her here. Closer to the coffin." He lifted the yellow tape, stepped across the grass, marched along the pathway. "*Maureen?*"

The moon broke through the clouds and cast a ghostly glow across the cemetery. Headstones stood like silent bodyguards. A cold wind stirred in the passing, like the chilled breath of wraiths wakened by his calling.

"*Maureen?*"

Nance followed him through the opening in the stone wall that separated the old cemetery from the new. There, the headstones were larger, more ominous, the sky darker, too, as the moon settled behind a band of clouds.

"Why bring Maureen here?" she asked.

"It's closer to the coffin."

"I know that. But why here? Why not keep her in a house somewhere, and when they empty the coffin bring her then?"

"Why move her at all?" he replied. "Have you asked yourself that?"

"The neighbours were becoming suspicious? The hut in the back was becoming a liability? How would I know?"

"And from one house to another house?" Gilchrist shook his head.

"Maybe she's in a house nearby," Nance suggested.

"Maybe." Gilchrist marched on.

"You could be wrong, Andy."

Gilchrist stopped. "I'm not wrong, Nance. I know I'm not. I feel it here. Right here." He thumped his chest with a force that should have stopped his heart. "Bully might be a murdering psychopath, but he's not stupid. He had it planned. It was all ready. That's what Topley said. Maybe Bully's getting out in two years. Maybe sooner. Who knows? But with Jimmy dying, he couldn't wait. He needed Jimmy to do his dirty work. So he started the ball rolling."

"That's all very well," she said. "But—"

"Help me, Nance." He gripped her arms. "Help me find Maureen."

"Okay. Okay, Andy." She stared at him. "Okay."

Gilchrist released his grip. He knew from the tone of her voice that he was scaring her. If she did not want to help him he would find Maureen by himself. He stepped up the hill towards the oldest part of the cemetery, reached the old gate and pushed through. The watchtower stood like a miniature cathedral, an eerie grey in the moonlight. He reached its steps, bounded up them two at a time.

She was here. She had to be. Not here exactly. Not at the watchtower. But in this cemetery. Somewhere here, she was alive. Not buried. Not yet. But alive. Bully wanted to bury her alive in a coffin he had prepared for her, that would be ready after the drugs were removed. But with the coffin gone, Bully would now order Maureen to be killed instead of being buried alive.

If she was not already dead.

"*Maureen?*" The sound of his voice settled over the graveyard. High in the branches behind him, he heard the flutter of wings, the harsh caw of a crow. He cupped his hands again. "*Maureen?*"

Nance stared up at him from the bottom of the stone stairway. *Oh princess, by thy watchtower be.*

He gripped the cold stone. His breath clouded the night air. Christ, it was so cold. Who could survive in cold like this? Was he already too late? But Bully had not wanted her dead. He had wanted her alive.

To bury her.

"*Maureen?*"

Princess. Watchtower.

She was here. By the watchtower—

He stopped, frozen by a sudden thought that blew into his mind.

The poem. *Mary Morison*. Why that poem? Why not some other poem?

Had Bully left clues in the other verses? But they had not been changed.

He removed the crumpled sheet from his pocket, flattened it as best he could, and tried to read it from the light of the moon. Movement by his side startled him.

"Here," Nance said, and fingered her keyring. A weak light lit up the page.

He read out the verses. "Oh princess, by thy watchtower be, it is the wished, the trysted hour. Those smiles and glances let me see, that makes the miser's treasure poor." And underneath the first line, the original words printed in Jack's sprawling hand.

It took Gilchrist a full five seconds to realise what he had missed, what they had all missed, the one word that Bully had slipped in unnoticed. Until now.

He read the original line. "Oh Mary, at thy window be."

He read it again. "Christ," he whispered.

At. Not *by*.

It meant something. It had to. Why else would Bully have changed it?

He scanned the other lines, his gaze settling, then fixing on the words . . . *and glances let me see* . . .

Let me see. By thy watchtower.

At thy watchtower. *By* thy watchtower. Did it matter?

Let me see. Was that the key? He peered into the darkness, caught the frames of iron cages and lonely headstones that guarded graves targeted by nineteenth-century grave robbers on their nightly plunders—

He caught his breath. Was that it?

Nightly plunders. The graves were robbed at night.

When the guards were in the watchtower.

. . . let me see . . .

At night? From the watchtower?

What could he see from where he stood?

He scanned the graveyard, kept his focus on the wall within view, the headstones closest to him. But he saw nothing in which a body could be kept until the coffin was ready. He turned to the gate, the main entrance to the original cemetery, next to the caretaker's house—

Christ. The house. Why had he not noticed before?

Why had it taken until that moment for him to notice the house was derelict?

He ran down the steps and reached the front windows. A metal grille of sorts had been installed over them. He gripped it, but it was solid. He turned to the front door and shouldered it.

Solid, too.

He walked around the side, down a narrow alley that bordered the cemetery, and came to the back door. The air smelled of dampness and rotten leaves.

He gripped the door handle.

"What are you doing?"

Nance's voice jolted him. "She's here," he said.

"Andy, I think you need to consider what you're doing."

Gilchrist shouldered the door. The frame splintered.

"*Andy.*"

He shouldered it again.

The door burst open. The shattered frame clattered to the floor as Gilchrist stumbled into a dank hallway of bare floorboards and blistered walls.

"*Maureen?*" He ran into the first room, an empty room to the right. "*Are you here?*" He kicked something on the floor, almost tripped, but in the dark could tell only that it was low and wooden. A coffee table? A packing box?

The next room yielded the same result.

His shouts echoed off the walls. "*Maureen?*"

He tried another room.

Nothing.

Nance almost bumped into him in the centre of what Gilchrist took to be the living room. The realization that he had failed locked his breath in his throat. He felt a stab of pain in his chest, thought for one frightening moment that he was going to black out.

"Andy?"

"It's. . . . " He spun around, stared at the dark walls, the boarded windows. "It's. . . . " *It's useless*, he wanted to say. All around him only walls, stark and bare and black as night. It was useless. He was too late. *Too late*. He cupped his hands, screamed at the top of his voice. "*Maureen?*"

"She's not here, Andy."

The strength in Nance's voice hit him. "Maureen," he whispered to her. "Dear God, Maureen," then covered his mouth with his hands, felt his breath rush through his fingers, warm and wet. Jesus, how could he be so wrong? Why had he let himself believe in the slimmest of hopes?

Nance tugged his sleeve.

"No." He shook free, stepped to the side. "*Maureen?*" His breath came at him in waves that hit his lungs in gulping sobs. He felt his legs give out.

"Andy?"

He grunted as his knees hit the floor. He pressed his hands to his face, fought back the bile in his throat, felt Nance's hand on his shoulder, her fingers flex. He said nothing as she stood beside him. He had lost her. He had lost his daughter.

"Andy."

"I can't lose her," he gasped. "I can't, Nance. I just, I can't. . . . "

Nance's fingers tightened.

He looked to the floor, heard her shoes shuffle, except. . . .

Except. . . .

Except Nance had not moved.

He lifted her hand from his shoulder. "Did you hear that?"

"Hear what?"

"Shh." He tilted his head to the side. "Listen." He had gained his night-sight, but in the darkness all he saw were shapes. He peered to his right, to his left, twisted his head over his shoulder as—

Another shuffle.

He stared to his right, to the packing box on the floor.

A shuffle. But not a shuffle. More like. . . .

A scrape? From what?

A mouse? A rat? Something else?

Nance had heard it, too. He knew from the stiffness in her posture, the way her body turned to the wooden crate on the floor.

"*Maureen?*"

Silence.

"*Maureen? Are you there?*"

Another scrape.

By the box on the floor.

Beneath the box on the floor?

Nance beat him to it. She thudded the box out of the way and was tugging the carpet, peeling back the damp material. He thought she was ripping it into shreds, until he realised a rectangular piece had been cut from it. He gripped a corner, pulled it back—

"Bully warned me about you."

Gilchrist felt his body turn to ice, his blood to water. If he'd had anything in his stomach he would have dropped the lot there and then.

Light exploded in his brain like a kick to the teeth.

He had time only to cover his eyes and turn away from the boot coming his way, so that it caught him only a glancing blow on his ear. He roared as pain shot through him, and rolled into the darkness, hand pressed hard to the side of his head, half expecting to feel a bloody mess where his ear had once been.

But it was still intact.

A beam of light chased him as he dived to the side, felt the thud of something heavy and sharp shiver the floorboards by his head. A deep curse, a guttural scream, then a flurry of light around the room as the flashlight clattered to the floor.

Gilchrist lunged for it, felt the wind of something brush his ear, heard the metallic clatter on the wall behind him. He picked up the flashlight, trapped the shape of two figures in its beam, caught Nance beneath a raised arm, a sharp point—

He threw the flashlight.

The room flickered as wild as lightning then fell into darkness with a grunt as the flashlight bounced off bone. He heard the thud as the body hit the floor and had time only to dive at where he thought the figure had fallen.

Cuffs out. "You're under arrest," he shouted, then the hard clip of metal as he slipped them over a bony wrist.

"Fuck off," and a fist as hard as stone hit him on the jaw.

His head jerked and he almost lost his grip on the cuffs as another hammer blow hit the side of his head. In the blind darkness and the close struggle Gilchrist knew he could not trap the man's free arm long enough to cuff it, so he clipped the cuffs to his own wrist.

"Got you, you bastard."

He felt himself dragged to his feet, surprised by the animal strength of the man. He fought to grab the loose arm as it hit him on the neck like a poorly aimed rabbit punch, and felt his breath leave him as a knee came up between his legs. He smelled the stale tobacco stink of the man, felt the roughness

of stubble, the wet spray of spittle as the voice by his ear
cursed and spat.

But cuffed together, the man was going nowhere.

Arms as thin and strong as steel ropes wormed their way
around his ribcage.

Gilchrist tucked his left foot behind a leg and pushed.

They hit the floor like a loaded sack.

He heard the air go out of the man, but before he could overpower him a hand slapped onto his face, and fingers as hard and
sharp as steel claws dug into his skin.

Light again. A dancing beam.

"You're under arrest." Nance's voice, high, unsteady.

"Fuck off."

A roar, a grunt, and before Gilchrist could move, the man had
rolled on top of him, then over, body twisted to the wall.

The dancing flashlight caught the blade of the hunting knife at
the same instant Gilchrist saw Jimmy Reid's fingers fold around
the hilt and the knife rear into the darkness above his head.

"No!" he shouted, and caught the grim smile of victory as the
blade flashed down at him.

Chapter 40

THE KNIFE THUDDED into flesh.

But not Gilchrist's.

He heard Nance gasp, felt her body go limp, and realised she had dived at Reid and taken the blow meant for him.

Fire flashed through his mind.

Reid shifted his weight.

Nance's body tumbled off, and Gilchrist knew Reid had pulled the knife from her back. No time to think. Only to move.

And move *now*.

He gripped his cuffed wrist tight with his free hand, pulled his legs up and rolled heels over head. He heard a grunt of pain, a hard gasp of surprise. He tightened his grip, rolled in toward Reid, felt the pain as his own elbow twisted, the strain on his wrist as the cuff bit into his skin. His contorted move had Reid at a disadvantage. But he needed to move quickly. He pulled himself to his knees, felt Reid try to resist as he shoved his arm up his back.

Reid roared, "My arm."

Gilchrist pushed higher, heard the dry crunch of gristle tearing and the high-pitched scream like a pig being burned, then felt the loss of power as the strength went out of the guy.

On automatic now, he unclipped the cuff from his own wrist, pulled Reid's other arm behind his back, and clicked the wrists together. He pushed away, brushed the floor with his hands, found what he was looking for, and turned it on.

A beam of light shot out from his hand.

A quick flash at Reid to show him lying on his stomach, face twisted in pain, arms behind his back, the hunting knife with its serrated edge within easy reach.

Gilchrist kicked it to the corner.

He found Nance six feet away, on her front, her right shoulder a bloodied mess. But she was moving, pulling herself forward like some dying animal. He kneeled beside her, placed the flashlight on the floor, eased her jacket from her shoulder.

"Don't move," he ordered.

"I wasn't planning to."

He grimaced at her humour, but could tell she was hurting. He pushed his fingers through the bloodied cut in her blouse and ripped the material apart. In the flashlight's beam, the wound was wide, as if the blade had plunged into skin and been tugged back. But he saw, too, that it had not cut any major blood vessels, and that her sports bra was helping to hold the flesh together, keep the wound tight.

He pulled off his jacket, gripped his shirt, and almost tore it from his body. Shirt in teeth, he ripped off a sleeve and whipped it under her arm and around and over her shoulder. And again. He tied a quick knot. Could be better, he thought, but it would stanch the flow.

From behind, he heard a grunt.

Reid had twisted onto his side, his body long and lean, crawling out of the shadows like an alligator from a night swamp. From the way he was shifting, Gilchrist knew he was trying to find his feet.

Not so fast.

Gilchrist took one step, two, and booted him in the face. Reid grunted and slumped to the floor. Gilchrist stomped down hard on Reid's torn shoulder and almost flinched from the animal roar. "Stay put," he growled, then retrieved the flashlight.

The patch in the carpet had been cut and stitched like a proper opening. He could see the trapdoor, but no handle. He found

Reid's knife in the corner of the room and used it to jemmy the trapdoor open.

He pulled the wooden frame up and off and threw it to the side, stuck his head into the dusty underfloor space. He danced the beam beneath the floor, almost cried out in anguish as it flickered over four bare walls.

He pulled himself upright, shone the flashlight into Reid's eyes. "What have you done with her?" he shouted, and saw from their puzzled reflection that he was missing something.

Back under the floor.

This time he saw it.

What he had taken at first glance to be a solid wall was a piece of sheetrock cut to fit the space and jammed in to stay upright. He lowered himself through the opening, bent double in the tight space, pulled the sheetrock back, and exposed a small door.

Padlocked.

He thudded the heel of his fist against it. "*Maureen*?" But he heard nothing. He gripped the padlock and tugged. The hasp was secure. He thumped the door. "*Maureen*?" And again. But the wood was solid. Out with the knife, thudded down and behind the hasp, in as hard as he could, then pulled.

He grunted with effort, but the knife slipped free.

Down again. Harder that time. He tugged, felt the hasp pull from the wood, the screws or nails or whatever was holding it in draw out from the rough grain.

Slipped again. Damn it.

Another stab. Missed. Again. Got it that time.

He gritted his teeth, pulled hard, held it, pulled harder—

The hasp ripped off with splintering wood.

He opened the door, shone his flashlight in, saw her body curled in a foetal position, not moving, and knew from the way she was lying with one arm out that he was too late. He scrambled through the opening, his voice coming at him in whimpers he failed to recognise as his own.

He reached her, lifted her, cradled her in his arms, and watched in horror as her head lolled back and eyes as lifeless as death stared at nothing.

Oh, dear God, dear God.

No. . . .

Chapter 41

THE SMELL OF urine still hung in the cold room.

Gilchrist glanced at his watch—11:27. He removed her photograph from his jacket pocket, the same one he had passed around. Dark eyes smiled at him, filled with the youthful promise of life. He rubbed his thumb across her face and startled as the door opened.

A guard pushed at Bully as he shuffled in.

Gilchrist thought Bully had aged, as if a few more days in jail had added years to the man. Bully scowled as the guard shoved him onto his seat and shackled his legs to the floor. Then the guard stood and backed up to the door.

Bully's face broke into a cruel smile. "My oh my. How the mighty have fallen."

Gilchrist knew he looked a mess. His left cheek was swollen and bruised. Common sense told him he would need to have it x-rayed. His leather jacket was slashed at the sleeve where Reid had plunged his knife but failed to cut flesh. Underneath, his one-sleeved shirt was missing four buttons and stained with a mixture of his and Nance's blood. The knees of his jeans were caked with dirt. He placed Maureen's photograph on the table, as if laying down a trump card, then stood with his back against the opposite wall.

"You masturbate to my daughter," Gilchrist said.

Bully blinked, as slow as a reptile.

"You masturbate to my princess."

"Your princess?" Bully coughed a laugh. "I hear your princess is a good ride."

Gilchrist pushed off the wall and paced the short length of the room, eyes to the floor, away from Bully, always away, he thought, and felt wonder at the fear the man was able to instil in him. "We've contacted the Spanish authorities," he said to the floor. "Suggested it would be appropriate to impound your villas." He glanced at Bully. "They do that for drug-associated crimes these days."

The chains rattled.

He concentrated on the floor, did not want Bully to read anything from his eyes, to see how he scared him, even now. The chains clattered as Bully shuffled in his seat.

"We've also been in contact with your solicitor, Rory Ingles."

"You'll be hearing from Rory," Bully growled.

"Word on the street is that you think you're getting out in two years."

"Sooner, now you lot are fucking it up."

Gilchrist kept pacing. "I'm not here to argue that point."

"What the fuck're you here for then? To give me new wanking material?"

Gilchrist stepped to the table with a speed that almost had Bully tensing. He grabbed the photograph. "You could do yourself a favour," he said, and held it up for Bully to leer at. "And confess."

"To what?"

"That you ordered Chloe's murder. My daughter's, too. That you devised the whole scheme, the body parts, the notes, the kidnapping, all to satisfy your sick psycho needs."

Bully looked pleased to find himself back in control. "Not a fucking clue what you're on about," he said.

"That's a pity." Gilchrist slipped Maureen's photograph into his pocket, safe from Bully's lecherous eyes. He started pacing again. "We'll just have to let Jimmy tell us, then. Won't we?"

Bully hawked phlegm from the back of his throat. "In your dreams, big man."

"No dreams. Try nightmares." He gave Bully a passing glance. "Yours."

Bully smiled, an ugly grimace that settled somewhere between confusion and anger. "Jimmy'll tell you fuck all. He knows what would happen to him when I get out."

Gilchrist stopped. He faced Bully. "Don't you mean *if* you get out?"

Bully's eyes tightened. His lips pursed. Sweat dotted his upper lip. "Wait till I talk to Rory," he growled.

"Won't do you any good."

Bully's eyes flickered, as if he knew something was going on but could not figure it out. "You're at it," he said.

"Oh, Rory'll be talking to you all right. But it won't be about getting out in two years. More like breaking the news that you'll be spending the rest of your life in prison." He eyed the bare walls, faced the slit-window. "In this miserable hell-hole. Without the remotest chance of parole."

"What the fuck're you on about?"

Gilchrist leaned forward. That close, he could smell the prison stench of the man. If confinement and desperation had a scent, that was what he was smelling. "Oh princess, by thy watchtower be," he said.

Bully gave a smile of victory. "You worked it out yet?"

Gilchrist wanted Bully to think he had the upper hand. He wanted him to hold on to that belief for as long as possible, so that when he eventually told him the pain would be all the greater. For a moment he wondered if he had become as cruel as Bully, if recent events had snapped his mind and changed him. But what Bully had done to Chloe, to Maureen, violated all sense of conscience. And Gilchrist knew he could never be that cruel.

"Confess," he said to Bully. "Tell me how you commanded your brother to kill two women for you."

Bully smiled. "After I talk to Rory. Maybe I'll think about it. How does that sound?"

"I'll give you one last chance."

Bully chuckled. "You just fucking crack me up, Gilchrist. You know that?"

"We found the coffin."

Bully froze. Something dark shifted behind his feral eyes. Disbelief, perhaps. Or rising vitriol.

"And your secret stash."

Bully worked his jaw. From the look in his eyes he could have been chewing nails.

"Street rates put it at around thirty million, give or take a million or two."

Bully strained forward.

"We've got Jimmy, too."

The chain clattered as Bully shifted his feet. "You're at it, Gilchrist. You're fucking at it. I know you."

"Do you?"

Bully let Gilchrist's question hang in the air. Then he growled, "Jimmy's told you fuck all. I know Jimmy. He'd tell the fuzz to fuck off."

"And Maureen, too," Gilchrist added. "We found her."

Bully tried a tight grin. "Now I know you're at it."

Gilchrist returned to his place on the opposite wall. He stared at the pockmarked face, at demonic eyes that glared at him with madness, and felt a gut-sickening hatred simmer and boil and fill him with an almost irresistible desire to pull Bully across the table and bludgeon him to death with his bare hands. He fought against the moment, felt it pass, then in his softest voice said, "Maureen's in Stobhill Hospital."

The chains rattled. Bully clenched his fists.

Gilchrist felt his lips pull into a grin, then onto a heartfelt smile that tugged at his mouth and reached his eyes and made him want to laugh. "Despite what you had that psycho brother of yours do to her," he said, "to my daughter, to my princess, she survived." *Barely*, he thought. *But alive, thank God. Alive.* "She's expected to make a full recovery."

"Lies," hissed Bully. "It's all lies."

Gilchrist slipped his hand into his inside jacket pocket and removed a folder of photographs. "Jimmy's no longer afraid of you."

"I'll kill that bastard if he says a word."

"And do you know why Jimmy's not afraid of you?"

Bully's knuckles whitened. Spittle foamed at the corners of his mouth. "Jimmy knows he'll be dead fucking meat."

For a moment, Gilchrist wondered if Bully knew Jimmy had terminal cancer, or even if he cared. "Because Rory Ingles, your brief, your high-paid big-shot solicitor, on first-name terms, has now been hired by your brother, Jimmy."

"*Lies*." Clenched fists crashed onto the table. "Fucking *lies*." Bully reached for Gilchrist, but his fettered legs held him back.

Gilchrist threw the folder of photographs onto the table. It split open. Coloured images spilled out, sliding across the metal surface like a discarded pack of cards.

Bully glared at them.

"Taken early this morning," Gilchrist said. "At police headquarters in Pitt Street. Take a good look." He watched Bully finger through them. "That one is Rory talking to Jimmy, convincing him his best chance for a deal is to turn Queen's evidence."

"Lies," Bully hissed at the images. "Fucking lies."

"And here was me thinking the camera never lies."

Bully looked up. Anger danced like madness in eyes that burned. "Fuck you, Gilchrist." He slammed his fists to the table, swept the photographs to the floor. "Fuck you. It's lies. All of it. It's *lies. Fucking lies.*"

Gilchrist felt his lips pull into the tiniest of smiles. He nodded to the guard, who opened the door.

A short man with a balding head and thickening waist walked in, his pinstriped suit pristine next to Gilchrist's dishevelled figure. "William Thomson Reid," he said in a voice that sounded bored, "I am charging you with complicity in the murder of Chloe Fullerton, and conspiracy to abduct and murder Maureen Gillian Gilchrist. Charges will also be brought against you for drug-related offences. . . ."

As Bully was read his rights Gilchrist stared at him and hoped Bully could read from his eyes the hatred that pulsed beneath his skin in time with the beat of his heart. And as he watched the reality of Bully's dilemma settle into his twisted mind, Gilchrist came to realise that he was no longer afraid of the man, as if some road that had stretched out in front of him, once dark and ominous, now lay cleared to the horizon where he could see the safety of his own future.

It took three guards to haul Bully back to his cell, all the while struggling against his shackles and screaming like a demented lunatic. Gilchrist closed his eyes, let the diatribe vanish over his head.

I'll have you, Gilchrist, d'you hear? I'll fucking have you. I'm not through with you. The fucking lot of you are in for it now. You'd better believe it. You listening to me?

You're dead, Gilchrist.

You're fucking dead.

When all that was left was the echo of Bully's voice and the smell of stale urine, Gilchrist opened his eyes, pulled the recorder from his pocket, and switched it off. He had not been altogether honest about Jimmy turning Queen's evidence, but Bully's murderous threats would go a long way to convincing Jimmy to cooperate.

Gilchrist felt tired, and his body ached. He clawed his fingers through his hair, surprised by how grimy it felt. The thought of a long hot shower almost had him changing his mind, but he needed to make another visit.

● ● ●

HE FOUND HER still in Intensive Care, hooked up to a plethora of plastic tubes and full bottles and bags on wheeled stands. Surprisingly, he thought, she was awake. Well, her eyes were open, and swam in and out of focus as he approached.

He sat beside her, took hold of her hand. She tried to smile, but the effort seemed too much. Feeble fingers entwined with his, and he felt his eyes well as her cracked lips formed, "I'm sorry, Dad."

He leaned forward, pressed his lips to her damp cheek, not sure if the tears he tasted were from her eyes or his own.

"So am I," he whispered, then buried his face into the pillow beside her and let his tears flow.

Chapter 42

Two weeks later

JACK SURPRISED GILCHRIST.
Throughout Chloe's funeral, he stood upright and tight-lipped, blue eyes as clear as the sky through the crematory's stained-glass windows. Gilchrist, on the other hand, had to swallow the lump in his throat when commitment prayers were said and the velvet curtains closed on Chloe's coffin.

The mournful sound of some unfamiliar hymn swelled from the organ as Chloe's parents strode down the aisle, not holding hands, her mother's face tired and defeated, her father's tight and bitter. They did not wait at the entrance to accept condolences, but slipped into a glistening black limo that laid twin contrails of white exhaust in the still April air.

In the car park, Jack surprised Gilchrist again.

"I'm giving up sculpting," he said.

The unimaginable thought of Jack not working at what he lived for hit Gilchrist like a blow to the gut. "Is that what you want to do?" he asked.

Jack sniffed. "I've finally realised I'm no good at it, that my ideas are not original, that I've nothing to say that has not been said before."

"But your work. . . ."

"I'm going to concentrate on oils instead."

"So you're not getting a job," Gilchrist said, then chuckled. "Sorry. I didn't mean it the way it sounded."

Jack seemed unfazed by Gilchrist's gaffe. He stared off to the dark grey walls of the crematorium. "Chloe always liked my stuff," he said. "She thought I was a better artist than sculptor." His breath clouded in the cold air. "I wish I'd listened to her. Now I feel it's the least I can do for her. For her memory."

Gilchrist could only nod.

"She bequeathed me all of her canvases," he continued. "Her parents' solicitors have already challenged my right to have them."

Gilchrist did not like the sound of that. "Do you know why?"

"Money." Jack's gaze locked on his father's. "Can you believe that? They want to sell her paintings." He scowled. "They never supported her, you know. They never called to ask how she was getting on, or asked about her work. In the end, Chloe just closed the door on them. It upset her."

"I'm sorry." It was all Gilchrist could think to say.

Jack shrugged. "I've had a word with a friend who's eager to exhibit Chloe's work. None of her paintings will be up for sale, of course, but she's encouraged me to exhibit some work of my own. Oils and stuff. So I'll see how it goes."

Gilchrist gripped Jack's shoulder. "That's great news, Jack. I'll be rooting for you."

They stepped to the side as a stream of cars fled the crematorium grounds. When the final car passed, Gilchrist shielded his eyes from a burst of sunlight as he stared at the solitary figure at the far end of the car park, just about the last person he expected to see. The day was overflowing with surprises, he thought.

"Excuse me," he said. "Back in a tick."

He shoved his hands deep into his pockets and strode across the car park. As he approached, he thought the beard suited Watt. It hid most of his face.

Watt offered his hand.

Gilchrist ignored it. "Didn't expect to see you here," he said.

"Thought I'd pay my respects."

"You knew Chloe?"

"Our paths crossed way back. When she dated Kevin."

"Kevin Topley?"

Watt nodded. "She knew nothing of Kevin's background. Didn't know he was dealing drugs. Just let herself be lured by his masculine charm. Kevin could be like that."

"Like his brother, Chris, you mean."

Watt shook his head. "Different animal altogether," he said, then seemed to sense Gilchrist's unasked question. "Maureen and Topley were never an item. It was just a story put around to give Maureen cover and a bit of credibility about the office. It gave her access to places that might otherwise have been closed."

"And Topley went along with that?"

"Topley was on a tightrope, walking the fine line between keeping Bully and his mob happy, and feeding us crumbs. He's a pro, so he knew how to handle everyone."

"And if he stepped off the tightrope on the wrong side?"

"He would lose it all. The business. The money. The underworld respect he craved. Topley lives in a bit of a fantasy world. Sees himself as Glasgow's next Mr. Big. So he does as he's told, and keeps his ear to the ground."

Gilchrist shuffled his shoulders. "Did you never worry that Topley might take a dislike to being ordered about and try to snuff you from the picture? He has the pull."

Watt smirked. "Then he would be taken out. I told him that."

"And he believed you?"

"He believed me."

Something in the way Watt uttered these words had Gilchrist working through the rationale. Watt would have Topley killed if he didn't toe the line? Things might be different in Glasgow, but Gilchrist felt certain that Strathclyde Police would not entertain their officers threatening the life of any citizen, good or bad.

And then he thought he saw it.

"Kevin's death was no accident," he said.

Watt shrugged. "Some said he was getting too big for his boots. That Chris wanted to move in, take over. Who knows?"

"Chris had Kevin killed?"

Watt faked a smile.

And at that instant Gilchrist saw Watt for what he really was. "Not Chris," he said. "But you. To let Topley know the same thing could happen to him, if he ever misbehaved."

Watt narrowed his eyes.

"And Chloe?"

"Jimmy Reid," Watt said. "But we'll never know for sure."

Gilchrist worked through the logic. Bully wanted Jimmy to make Gilchrist believe he would kill Maureen and serve her up to him in pieces, but had him do Chloe first, so to speak, probably because he could never be sure how much Chloe knew of Kevin Topley's drug business and its connection to his own. It seemed as good an answer as any.

He eyed the crematorium gardens, settling on the skeletal branches of some vine or clematis, and felt sadness surge through him. Chloe would never see another flower bloom, another tree blossom, never enjoy the simplest pleasures of life. Her death seemed such a waste, such a needless act of cruelty. Someone other than the Reid brothers should pay.

"Chris Topley's not being charged," he snarled. "Why?"

"Bigger fish to catch."

"Don't tell me you're letting him off the hook."

"Topley doesn't know it yet, but he is the hook. And the bait." Watt chewed his gum. "He'll get what's coming to him in the end. I promise you. But we need to keep the status quo for a few more months."

Now Gilchrist was beginning to understand. Strathclyde's reaction to Watt's almost criminal activities had him baffled up until that moment. The answer seemed so simple he wondered why it had taken him so long to figure it out.

Watt was not with Strathclyde. He never had been. Watt was

some undercover agent battling the influx of drugs to the country. "I never believed your assignment to the London Met was for real," Gilchrist said. "That's cover, too."

"You're always digging, always looking for a reason. You never give up."

"I heard a rumour that MI5 and 6 had combined to bust some European drug cartel. Is that why you're moving to London?"

Watt stared off to some point in the distance. "Time to move on," he said. "There's nothing here for me."

Gilchrist needed more. "Define nothing."

Something in the way Watt returned Gilchrist's look told him he was about to hear the truth. "You know what I mean," Watt said.

"Nothing with Maureen?"

Watt breathed in the cold air, let it out in a white cloud. "I never knew her age," he said. "I met her in the pub. Thought she was eighteen. She said she was. And I believed her." He stared at Gilchrist for several long seconds. "If I had known, nothing would have happened. I'm sorry." He removed a hand from his pocket and offered it to Gilchrist.

This time Gilchrist took it.

"I'll miss her," Watt said. "Another time, another place."

"I'll make sure she never visits London."

Watt shook his head. "She wants to write about you. She admires you."

Admire was not the word Gilchrist would have used.

"Don't lose her again."

Gilchrist tightened his lips and watched Watt walk away. He waited until Watt's car slipped behind a copse of trees before he turned to Jack. Watt's words echoed in his mind.

Don't lose her again.

It seemed such an odd thing for Watt to say. But the truth of the matter was that he *had* lost Maureen, he had lost *both* his children. He eyed the opposite end of the car park.

Jack stood with his backside against the boot of his car.

Gilchrist felt a smile tug his lips. No, he thought. I won't lose her again. I won't lose either of them again.

He pulled his collar up and strode towards his son.

Acknowledgments

WRITING IS INDEED a lonely affair, but this book could not have been published without the help of the following: Gayle Richardson and Kenny Cameron of Fife Constabulary for police procedure. Forensic pathologist Doctor Marjorie Black for keeping me straight on the gruesome stuff. Everyone at Strathkelvin Writers' Group for continued support, despite my lengthy absence (I promise to return). Juliet Grames for terrific editorial input, and for taking a chance on publishing me. Bronwen Hruska, Rudy Martinez, Janine Agro, and Meredith Barnes of Soho Press for behind-the-scenes assistance. My literary agent, Al Zuckerman, for his sage advice and professional persistence. Other readers and friends, too many to mention, whose words of encouragement and support inspired me to continue. Many thanks to each and every one of you, especially Anne.

And finally, this book is fiction. Those readers familiar with St Andrews and the East Neuk may notice that I have taken creative license with respect to local geography.

Any and all mistakes are mine.

About the Author

BORN IN GLASGOW, Scotland, Frank was plagued from a young age with the urge to see more of the world than the rain sodden slopes of the Campsie Fells. By the time he graduated from University with a degree he hated, he'd already had more jobs than the River Clyde has bends. Short stints as a lumberjack in the Scottish Highlands and a moulder's laborer in the local foundry convinced Frank that his degree was not such a bad idea after all. Thirty-plus years of living and working overseas helped him appreciate the raw beauty of his home country. Now a dual US/UK citizen, Frank makes his home in the outskirts of Glasgow, from where he visits St. Andrews regularly to carry out some serious research in the old grey town's many pubs and restaurants. Frank is working hard on his next novel, another crime story suffused with dark alleyways and cobbled streets and some things gruesome.

Turn the page for a sneak preview of the next
Andy Gilchrist Investigation

TOOTH
FOR A
TOOTH

Chapter 1

October 2004

DETECTIVE **C**HIEF **I**NSPECTOR Andy Gilchrist stood alone at the back of the chapel as the curtains closed on the coffin of his ex-wife. He barely heard the prayer of committal as he watched his son, Jack, in the family group in the front pew, place an arm around Maureen. Beside them shuddered the grieving figure of their stepfather, Harry. Even now, at the moment of Gail's final parting, Gilchrist could not find it in his heart to forgive Harry.

As the chapel emptied, Gilchrist held back, tagging on to the end of the mourners, each giving their condolences to the family line as they shuffled through the vestibule.

Jack gave him a sad smile of surprise. "I didn't see you."

"Late as usual," Gilchrist offered.

Jack's grip was firm, a son-to-father handshake meant to assure Gilchrist that Jack would be strong for all of them. The tremor in his chin said otherwise.

Gilchrist pulled him closer, gave him a hug. "Mum's no longer suffering," he said.

Jack nodded, tight-lipped, as they parted.

Maureen went straight for a hug. "I wasn't sure you'd come."

Even through her heavy coat he could feel her bones, her body light enough to lift with ease, it seemed. She was thin, too thin. He tried to say something but found he could not trust his voice. Instead, he hugged her tighter, breathed her in, pressed his lips to her ear.

"We'll miss Mum," he managed to say.

"Oh, Dad."

He gave Harry a firm handshake and a wordless nod, conscious of Maureen's eyes on him, searching for signs of forgiveness. Then he was down the stone steps, marching across the car park, avoiding eye contact with family friends he did not know. From his car, he watched Jack and Maureen leave the chapel hand in hand, Harry in front, defeated, alone. Something in that simple formation told Gilchrist that Harry could never fill their paternal void.

He caught Maureen's eye as she prepared to step into the funeral car.

Are you coming back? she mouthed to him.

He nodded as she slipped from his view, then he powered up his mobile and saw he had two missed calls, both from Stan.

"What's up, Stan?" Gilchrist asked.

"Thought you might be interested in a skeleton, boss. Just been dug up."

Gilchrist switched on the ignition, slipped into Drive. "Keep going."

"In Dairsie Cemetery. Uncovered while the lair was being opened for another burial. No coffin and not six feet under, boss. So we're definitely thinking murder."

Gilchrist eased his Mercedes SLK Roadster forward. Ahead, the funeral car cruised through the crematorium grounds, gray exhaust swirling in the October chill. The wake was being held in Haggs Castle Clubhouse, the golf club where Harry was a member. Gilchrist knew he should attend, for Jack and Maureen, for Gail's memory, too. But the thought of faking a face for Harry decided it for him.

"I'm on my way, Stan."

GILCHRIST WALKED THROUGH the gate in the old stone wall and into the cemetery grounds.

The forensic tent was erected by a gnarled willow tree in the far corner. Yellow tape looped around it from headstone to headstone. As Gilchrist approached, Stan broke the connection on his mobile with a slap of its cover.

"This skeleton," Gilchrist said, as he pushed his feet into his coveralls. "Is it in good nick?"

"Right thigh bone chopped through by one of the gravediggers. But other than that, it seems perfect."

"Whose plot were they preparing?"

"A local by the name of Lorella McLeod. Fair old age of eighty-seven. Passed away at the weekend and was to be laid to rest in the family lair next to her husband, Hamish. He died in sixty-nine. So the grave's not been touched for thirty-odd years." Stan shook his head. "Already checked our misper files for sixty-eight to seventy-five and came up empty-handed."

"What about the PNC?"

"Got Nance doing that, even as we speak."

Gilchrist pulled his coveralls up and over his shoulders, his mind working through Stan's rationale. "Did the McLeods have children?" he asked.

"None. Mrs. McLeod lived alone."

"For the last what, thirty-five years?"

"So I'm told, boss. But I haven't confirmed that yet."

Gilchrist looked away. Tree-covered hills were already graying with the coming of winter. It seemed unimaginable for someone to live by themselves for that length of time, and he wondered if the end of his life would be as destitute. Sadness swept through him at that thought. *The end of his life*. Or more correctly, *part* of it. Gail was now gone, and he worried he would spend even less time with Jack and Maureen. He forced his mind to focus on the present and eyed the forensic tent.

"So, Stan, it looks like we're dealing with a thirty-five-year-old murder."

"Bit soon to jump to that conclusion, boss. The body could have been buried any time since the burial of Hamish McLeod."

Gilchrist zipped up his coveralls. "But why was it buried in *that* grave, Stan? Have you asked yourself that?"

Stan scratched his head. "It's difficult to imagine a more perfect place to hide a body. I mean, who would look for it in a cemetery?"

"But why that particular grave?"

"Boss?"

"Because it would have been *fresh*, that's why. And if there is no coffin, there was no funeral. And if there was no funeral, no one knew about it. Therefore, we have a thirty-five-year-old murder on our hands." He stared off to the edge of the cemetery and the open fields beyond. Scotland in the sun was like no other place on earth. But its blue skies offered only false promise of a fine day. "Not exactly thriving, is it, Stan?"

"Dead center of town, boss."

Gilchrist almost smiled. "Ever been here before, Stan? In this cemetery?"

"No."

"Neither have I. Which makes me think neither have a lot of people. So start off by making a list of all those who attended McLeod's funeral."

Stan livened. "I'll get onto it, boss. Door to door, discreet like, see who knows what," he said as he walked away.

From the outside, the *Incitent* gave the impression it would be cramped and dark, but the interior was suffused with a yellow light that seemed to lend a reverential quietness to the scene. Gilchrist counted four transparent plastic bags next to the open grave, each filled with bones the color of mud. A row of larger plastic bags full of earth lined one wall like a garden center. A camera sat on a silver metal case.

Four Scene of Crime Officers worked in silence while Gilchrist watched. One SOCO sifted through a heap of soil at the side of the grave. Another placed more muddied bones into a fifth bag, while two more scraped soil from the bottom of the open grave with the focused intensity of biblical archaeologists. As Gilchrist stepped forward, one of the SOCOs in the grave looked up. Despite coveralls that hid his balding pate and made his face look round and tight, Gilchrist recognized Bert Mackie, not a SOCO, but the police pathologist from Ninewells Hospital in Dundee.

"Any luck, Bert?" he asked.

"I expect you mean have we found any items of identification?"

"That'll do for starters."

"Afraid not, Andy. All we have at the moment are bones. And the clothes have deteriorated to rags. Looks like she was wearing some sort of nylon jacket, but it's difficult to say at this stage—"

"She?"

"The bra gives the game away. Unless *he* was trying it on for size. Interestingly," he added, scowling at a muddied bone, scraping at it with his thumb, "she appears not to have been wearing any knickers."

"Could they have rotted away?"

"I'd expect to find traces of elastic." Mackie shook his head. "None so far."

Gilchrist wondered if that was important. Why wear a bra, but no knickers? Had she just had sex, perhaps a quickie, and something was said that ended in violence? Had she been raped then murdered? Or did she simply like to walk around feeling free and airy, so to speak? "Any ideas on her age?" he asked.

"I'll be in a better position to confirm that after a full postmortem, of course. But if I was pushed, I'd say late teens, early twenties."

Gilchrist squatted by the open grave. "This no knickers thing," he persisted. "Any thoughts?"

"Sex is always a grand motive," said Mackie. "He wants some. She doesn't. He's drunk. They argue. Turns into a fight, and before you know where you are, he has a fit and batters her to death."

Mackie's explanation seemed brutally simplified, but Gilchrist had heard of less compelling motives. "Too early to have a stab at cause of death?"

"Neil," snapped Mackie. "Skull."

The SOCO by the plastic bags removed a dirty-brown skull from one of them and handed it to Mackie as if passing over the Crown Jewels.

Mackie took it without a word, and Gilchrist noted that the teeth looked perfect. The skull's deformed shape confirmed the cause of death as blunt trauma. "See here," said Mackie, pointing to a jagged hole in front of where the right ear would have been. The skull was indented and networked with cracks. "Best guess would be a single blow to the temple. And to crush the skull like that, she was most likely dead when she hit the deck. Definitely unconscious. From the damage here," he said and ran his finger over the bone, "to here, I'd say not a hammer. The impact dent would have been more circular. And not an axe. The skull's been crushed, not cut."

"Blunt axe?" offered Gilchrist.

Mackie shook his head. "Something broader, more rounded. If she was killed at home, perhaps the base of a heavy table lamp. Now that would do it." Seemingly satisfied with his theory, Mackie offered the skull to Gilchrist.

Gilchrist folded his arms. He had never been comfortable handling human remains. Not long after joining the Force, he had held the skull of a man shot through the head and found himself struggling to control his emotions as he visualized the bullet thudding into the forehead, ripping through the brain, and exiting in an eruption of blood and gore. Had the man felt any pain? Or just a numbing thud, followed by blind confusion then death? At what point in the bullet's passing had the man died? Gilchrist had managed to hand back the skull before vomiting on the mortuary floor. From that point on, he made sure to keep a safe distance.

"It's a classic wound for someone murdered on the spur of the moment," said Mackie. "Face to face. A heavy blow that crushed her skull and sent her flying, either dead or dying." He gave a slow-motion demonstration, holding an imaginary weapon and striking at the skull.

"Left-handed, I see," said Gilchrist. "Unless she was struck from behind, of course."

"Of course," said Mackie.

Gilchrist stared at the battered skull. Had sex been the motive behind this young woman's murder? Had she put up a fight that ended in her death? Regardless of how she was killed, her disappearance would not have gone unreported. Someone would have missed her—her parents, boyfriend, sister, brother. She could not have vanished without some stirring in the local press. Gilchrist had been with Fife Constabulary nigh on thirty years and had come across only two unsolved misper cases, neither of which involved a woman, young or old. And Stan had found nothing up to '75. Maybe Nance would have better luck with the Police National Computer.

Mackie handed the skull back to the SOCO.

"Dr. Mackie, sir?" shouted the other SOCO, scraping around the exposed ribcage.

Gilchrist found himself on hands and knees, leaning into the grave.

"It looks like a metal case, sir."

"Camera," ordered Mackie. He flapped a hand to his side.

The SOCO by the plastic bags obliged.

The camera flashed as Mackie pried more soil loose and eased a rusted lump of metal from the rotted remains of clothing. "Aha," he said, holding it to his face. "Looks like we've found ourselves a cigarette lighter." Mackie rubbed the lighter's rusted surface with his thumb, holding it as if about to light up. "Don't suppose it works," he said.

"Shouldn't think so."

Mackie reached for a metal box beside the moss-covered head-stone and removed a magnifying glass. He turned his attention to the lighter. "Looks as if there's some marks here," he mumbled. "It's scratched on the side. Difficult to say. Could be damage to the case, of course. Or just natural deterioration."

"May I?" asked Gilchrist.

The case was about three inches long by two wide, scarred black with rust. Gilchrist supposed it had been silver coated at one time. He studied it through the magnifier and tried to make sense of the markings, but the metal was too rusted. "It could be anything," he said, and handed the magnifying glass and lighter back to Mackie. "Can you clean it up?" he asked. "I'd like to know if it means anything. You never know."

"Let me see what I can come up with."

Gilchrist thanked Mackie and stepped from the tent.

Outside, the crisp air and bright sunlight failed to lift his spirits. Somehow, the discovery of the cigarette lighter troubled him. Seven years earlier, a child's body had been discovered on a stretch of dunes, a pair of matching footprints stamped into the sand close by. Gilchrist's suspicion that they had been set there to lead them away from the murderer had proven to be correct in the end. And now he had that same feeling with the cigarette lighter.

It seemed so innocent that it rattled alarm bells. They had found no watch or jewelry of any kind on the woman. Only the lighter. If the killer had removed her jewelry, if in fact she had ever worn any, why leave the lighter? Gilchrist grimaced at the thought. Had the lighter been overlooked? Or was he searching for clues where there were none?

As he unzipped his coveralls, he struggled through his ratio-nale.

Was it possible the lighter had been deliberately left in the woman's clothing? If so, did that mean the killer had known Hamish McLeod, had known that the family plot would be reopened in the future to bury Lorella, and the body found? It all seemed possible. But more troubling was the thought that for thirty-five years the murder had gone unnoticed, as if the young woman had simply been forgotten by all who had ever known her.

Had her parents been alive? Would they not have missed their own child?

And now that her remains had been found, would her killer worry about her murder investigation commencing?

What secrets from the past was he about to uncover?

OTHER TITLES IN THE SOHO CRIME SERIES

Quentin Bates
(Iceland)
Frozen Assets
Cold Comfort
Chilled to the Bone

Cheryl Benard
(Pakistan)
Moghul Buffet

James R. Benn
(World War II Europe)
Billy Boyle
The First Wave
Blood Alone
Evil for Evil
Rag & Bone
A Mortal Terror
Death's Door
A Blind Goddess

Cara Black
(Paris, France)
Murder in the Marais
Murder in Belleville
Murder in the Sentier
Murder in the Bastille
Murder in Clichy
Murder in Montmartre
Murder on the Ile Saint-Louis
Murder in the Rue de Paradis
Murder in the Latin Quarter
Murder in the Palais Royal
Murder in Passy
Murder at the Lanterne Rouge
Murder Below Montparnasse
Murder in Pigalle

Grace Brophy
(Italy)
The Last Enemy
A Deadly Paradise

Henry Chang
(Chinatown)
Chinatown Beat
Year of the Dog
Red Jade
Death Money

Gary Corby
(Ancient Greece)
The Pericles Commission
The Ionia Sanction
Sacred Games
The Marathon Conspiracy

Colin Cotterill
(Laos)
The Coroner's Lunch
Thirty-Three Teeth
Disco for the Departed
Anarchy and Old Dogs
Curse of the Pogo Stick
The Merry Misogynist
Love Songs from a Shallow Grave
Slash and Burn
The Woman Who Wouldn't Die

Garry Disher
(Australia)
The Dragon Man
Kittyhawk Down
Snapshot
Chain of Evidence
Blood Moon
Wyatt
Whispering Death
Port Vila Blues
Fallout

David Downing
(World War II Germany)
Zoo Station
Silesian Station
Stettin Station
Potsdam Station
Lehrter Station
Masaryk Station

(World War I)
Jack of Spies

Leighton Gage
(Brazil)
Blood of the Wicked
Buried Strangers
Dying Gasp
Every Bitter Thing
A Vine in the Blood
Perfect Hatred
The Ways of Evil Men

Michael Genelin
(Slovakia)
Siren of the Waters
Dark Dreams
The Magician's Accomplice
Requiem for a Gypsy

Timothy Hallinan
(Thailand)
The Fear Artist
For the Dead

(Timothy Hallinan cont.)
(Los Angeles)
Crashed
Little Elvises
The Fame Thief

Mick Herron
(England)
Dead Lions

Adrian Hyland
(Australia)
Moonlight Downs
Gunshot Road

Stan Jones
(Alaska)
White Sky, Black Ice
Shaman Pass
Village of the Ghost Bears

Lene Kaaberbøl & Agnete Friis
(Denmark)
The Boy in the Suitcase
Invisible Murder
Death of a Nightingale

Graeme Kent
(Solomon Islands)
Devil-Devil
One Blood

James Lilliefors
(Global Thrillers)
Viral
The Leviathan Effect

Martin Limón
(South Korea)
Jade Lady Burning
Slicky Boys
Buddha's Money
The Door to Bitterness
The Wandering Ghost
G.I. Bones
Mr. Kill
The Joy Brigade
Nightmare Range
The Man with the Iron Sickle

Peter Lovesey
(Bath, England)
The Last Detective
The Vault
On the Edge
The Reaper

(Peter Lovesey cont.)
Rough Cider
The False Inspector Dew
Diamond Dust
Diamond Solitaire
The House Sitter
The Summons
Bloodhounds
Upon a Dark Night
The Circle
The Secret Hangman
The Headhunters
Skeleton Hill
Stagestruck
Cop to Corpse
The Tooth Tattoo
The Stone Wife

Jassy Mackenzie
(South Africa)
Random Violence
Stolen Lives
The Fallen
Pale Horses

Seichō Matsumoto
(Japan)
Inspector Imanishi Investigates

James McClure
(South Africa)
The Steam Pig
The Caterpillar Cop
The Gooseberry Fool
Snake
The Sunday Hangman
The Blood of an Englishman
The Artful Egg
The Song Dog

Jan Merete Weiss
(Italy)
These Dark Things
A Few Drops of Blood

Magdalen Nabb
(Italy)
Death of an Englishman
Death of a Dutchman
Death in Springtime

(Magdalen Nabb cont.)
Death in Autumn
The Marshal and the Madwoman
The Marshal and the Murderer
The Marshal's Own Case
The Marshal Makes His Report
The Marshal at the Villa Torrini
Property of Blood
Some Bitter Taste
The Innocent
Vita Nuova
The Monster of Florence

Fuminori Nakamura
(Japan)
The Thief
Evil and the Mask

Stuart Neville
(Northern Ireland)
The Ghosts of Belfast
Collusion
Stolen Souls
Ratlines

Eliot Pattison
(Tibet)
Prayer of the Dragon
The Lord of Death

Rebecca Pawel
(1930s Spain)
Death of a Nationalist
Law of Return
The Watcher in the Pine
The Summer Snow

Qiu Xiaolong
(China)
Death of a Red Heroine
A Loyal Character Dancer
When Red is Black

Matt Beynon Rees
(Palestine)
The Collaborator of Bethlehem
A Grave in Gaza
The Samaritan's Secret
The Fourth Assassin

John Straley
(Alaska)
The Woman Who Married a Bear
The Curious Eat Themselves
The Big Both Ways
Cold Storage, Alaska

Akimitsu Takagi
(Japan)
The Tattoo Murder Case
Honeymoon to Nowhere
The Informer

Helene Tursten
(Sweden)
Detective Inspector Huss
The Torso
The Glass Devil
Night Rounds
The Golden Calf
The Fire Dance

Janwillem van de Wetering
(Holland)
Outsider in Amsterdam
Tumbleweed
The Corpse on the Dike
Death of a Hawker
The Japanese Corpse
The Blond Baboon
The Maine Massacre
The Mind-Murders
The Streetbird
The Rattle-Rat
Hard Rain
Just a Corpse at Twilight
Hollow-Eyed Angel
The Perfidious Parrot
Amsterdam Cops: Collected Stories

Timothy Williams
(Guadeloup)
Another Sun
Return from Nowhere